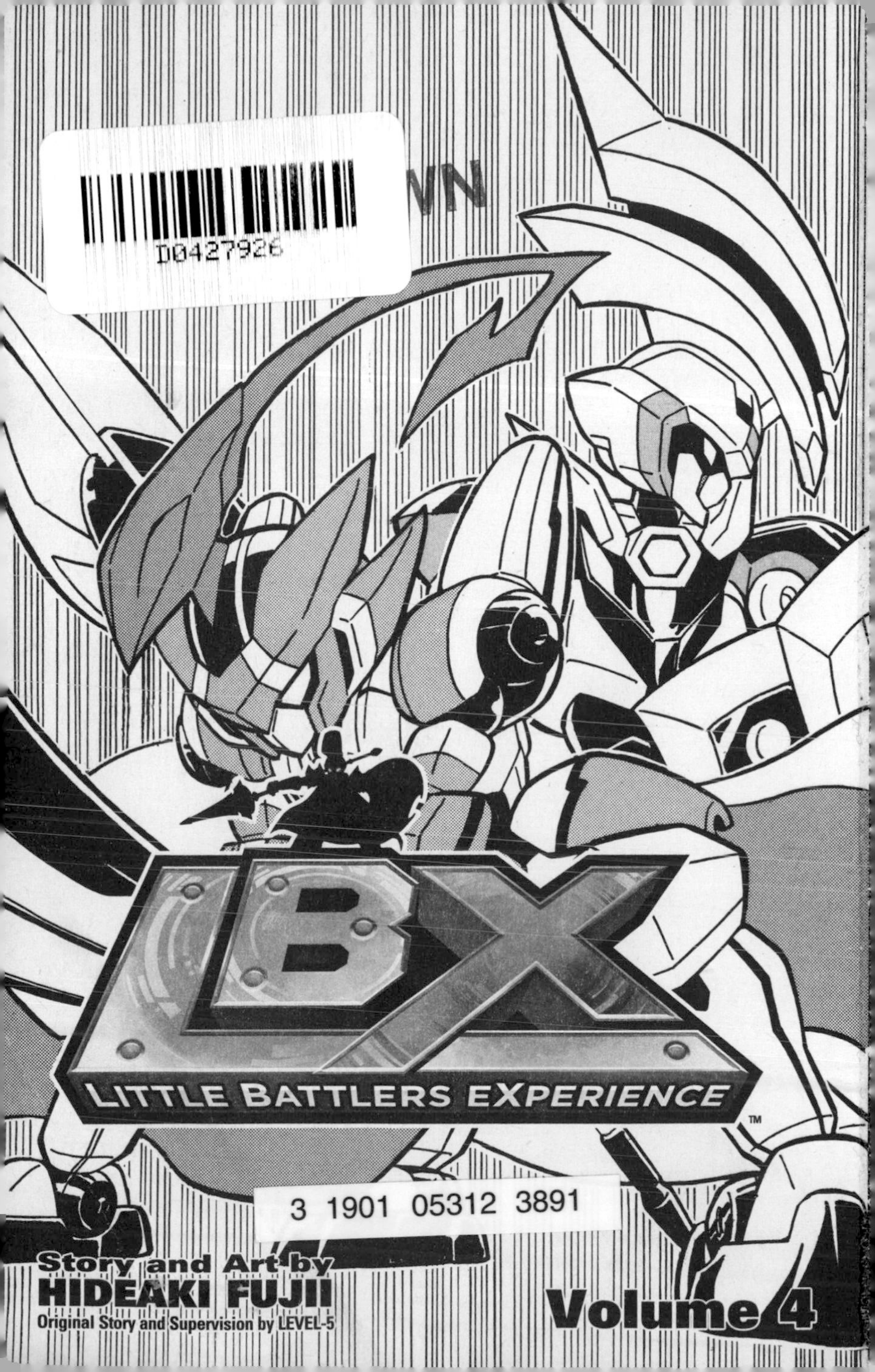

LBX
LITTLE BATTLERS EXPERIENCE™

Story and Art by
HIDEAKI FUJII
Original Story and Supervision by LEVEL-5

Volume 4

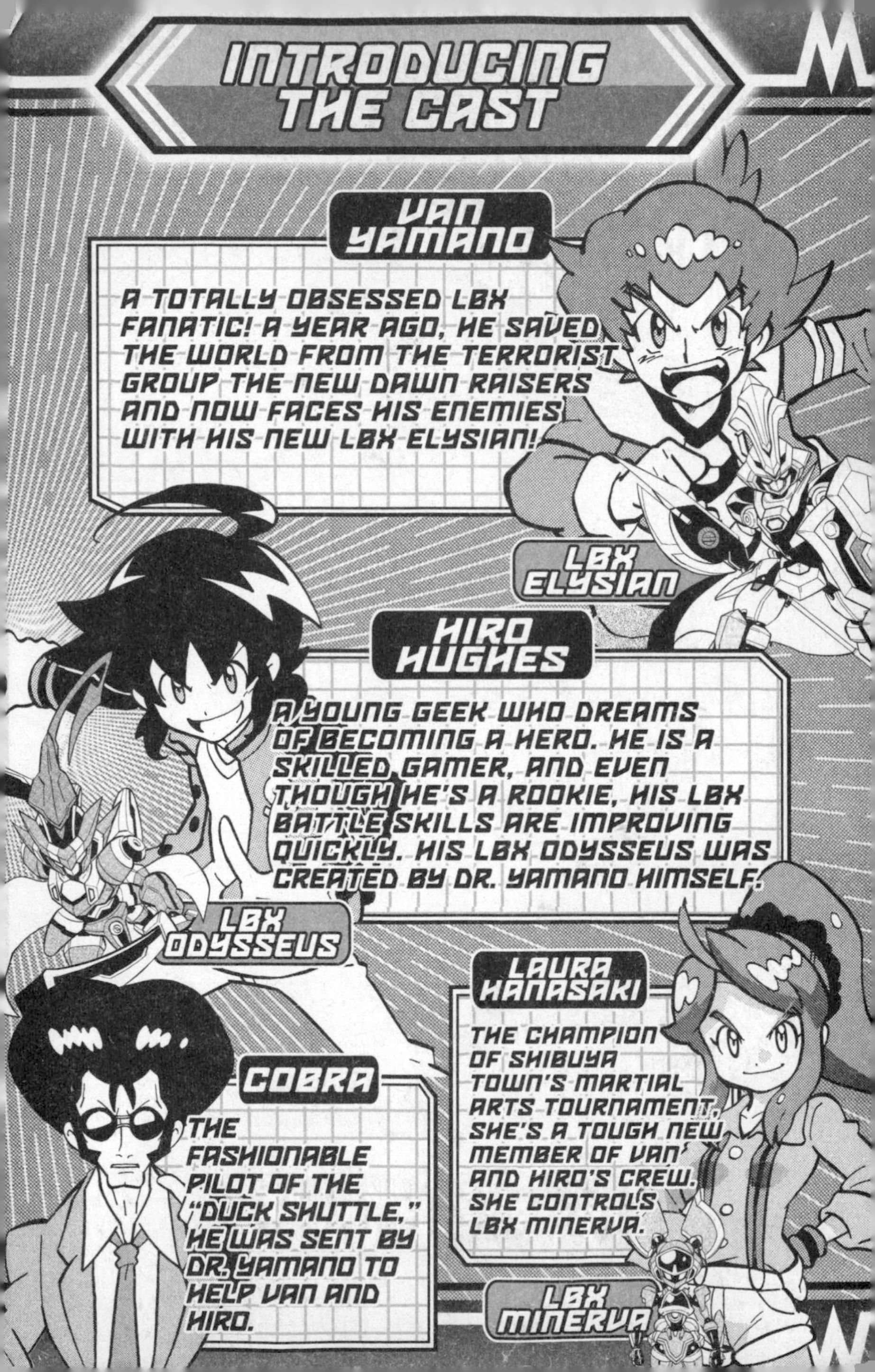
INTRODUCING THE CAST
VAN YAMANO
A TOTALLY OBSESSED LBX FANATIC! A YEAR AGO, HE SAVED THE WORLD FROM THE TERRORIST GROUP THE NEW DAWN RAISERS AND NOW FACES HIS ENEMIES WITH HIS NEW LBX ELYSIAN!
LBX ELYSIAN
HIRO HUGHES
A YOUNG GEEK WHO DREAMS OF BECOMING A HERO. HE IS A SKILLED GAMER, AND EVEN THOUGH HE'S A ROOKIE, HIS LBX BATTLE SKILLS ARE IMPROVING QUICKLY. HIS LBX ODYSSEUS WAS CREATED BY DR. YAMANO HIMSELF.
LBX ODYSSEUS
LAURA HANASAKI
THE CHAMPION OF SHIBUYA TOWN'S MARTIAL ARTS TOURNAMENT, SHE'S A TOUGH NEW MEMBER OF VAN AND HIRO'S CREW. SHE CONTROLS LBX MINERVA.
LBX MINERVA
COBRA
THE FASHIONABLE PILOT OF THE "DUCK SHUTTLE," HE WAS SENT BY DR. YAMANO TO HELP VAN AND HIRO.

MASKED MAN

TYLER OSGOOD

DR. YAMANO

KURT BRYANT

AMY COHEN

TABLE OF CONTENTS

STORY SO FAR...

A LIFELONG FAN OF LBXs, VAN YAMANO WAS REUNITED WITH HIS FATHER TO BATTLE THE TERRORIST THREAT OF THE NEW DAWN RAISERS. AFTER VALIANTLY FIGHTING HIS WAY THROUGH THE ENEMY LBXs, HE WAS CONFRONTED BY LEX, HIS FRIEND AND COMRADE. SHOCKED BY LEX'S BETRAYAL, VAN WAS FORCED TO FIGHT AND DEFEAT HIM. A YEAR HAS NOW PASSED, BUT A NEW ENEMY IS CLOSING IN...

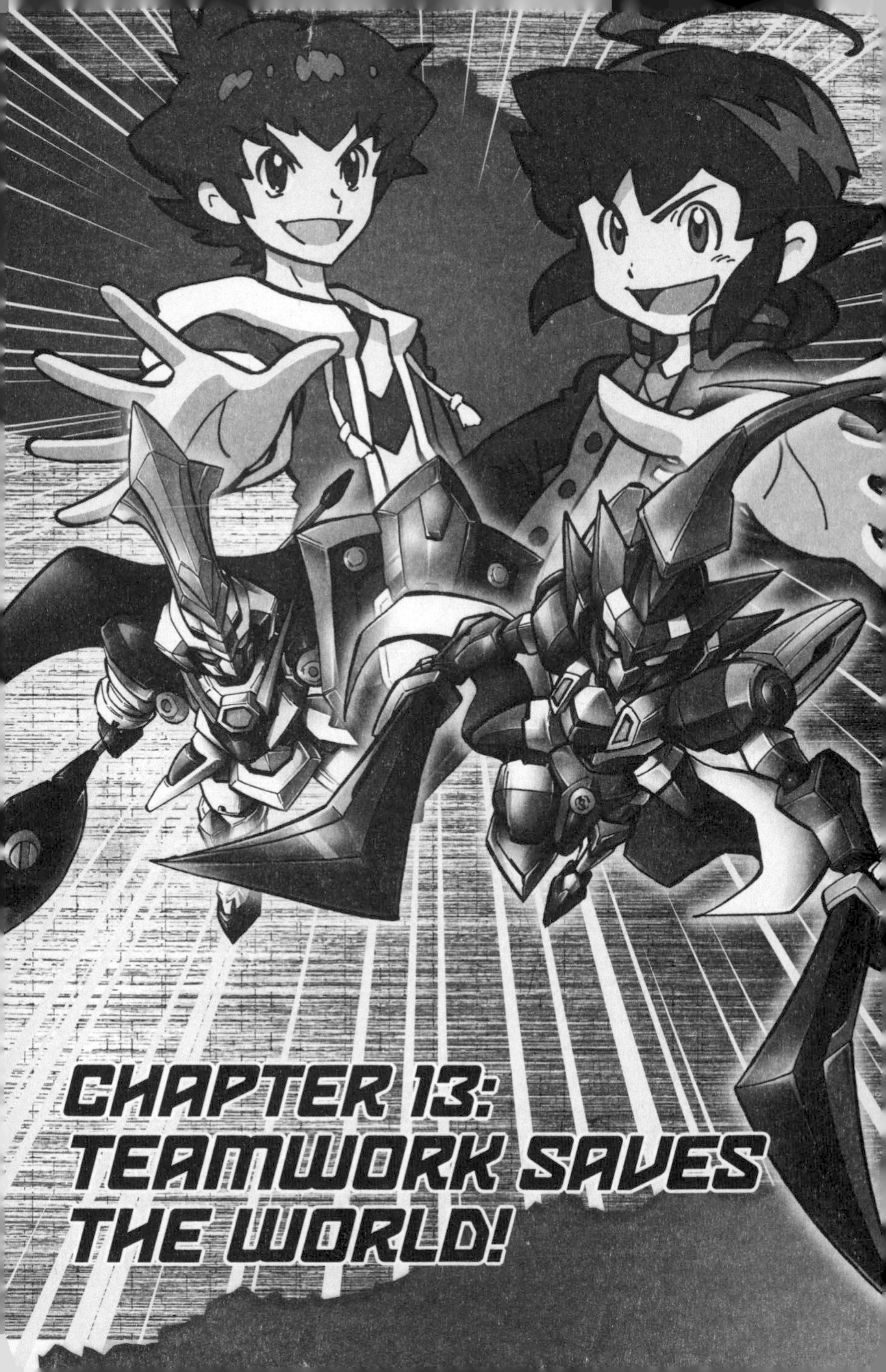
CHAPTER 13:
TEAMWORK SAVES
THE WORLD!

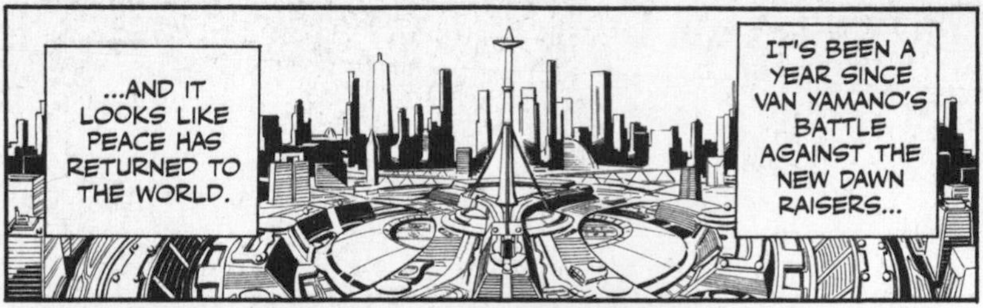
IT'S BEEN A YEAR SINCE VAN YAMANO'S BATTLE AGAINST THE NEW DAWN RAISERS...
...AND IT LOOKS LIKE PEACE HAS RETURNED TO THE WORLD.

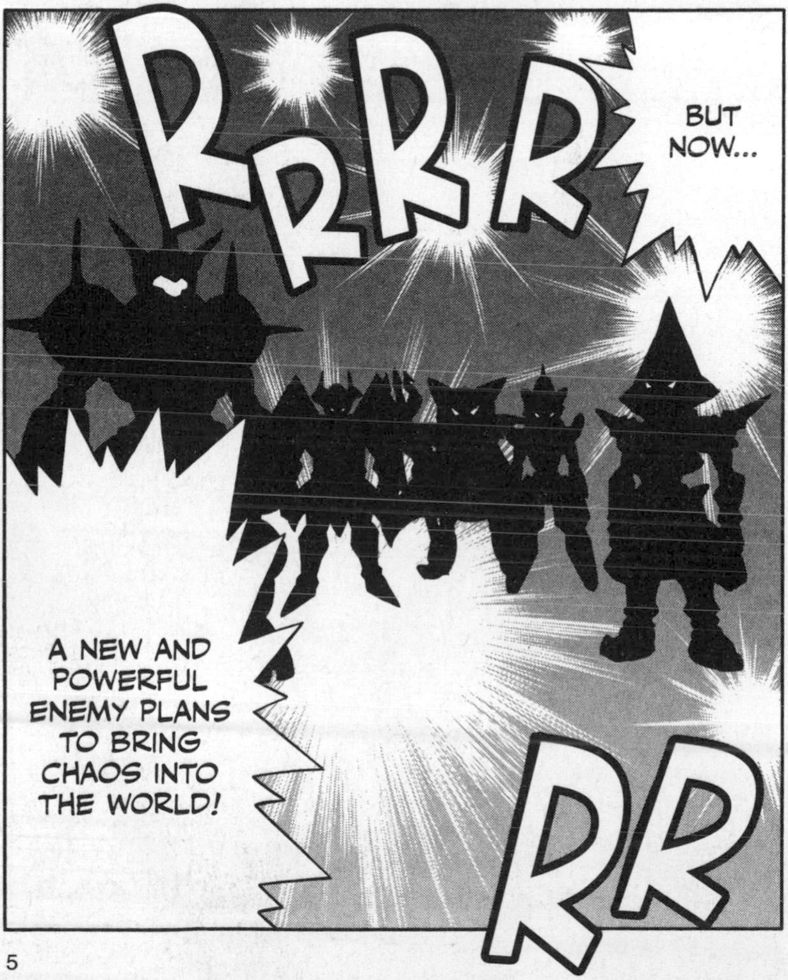
RRRR
BUT NOW...
A NEW AND POWERFUL ENEMY PLANS TO BRING CHAOS INTO THE WORLD!
RR

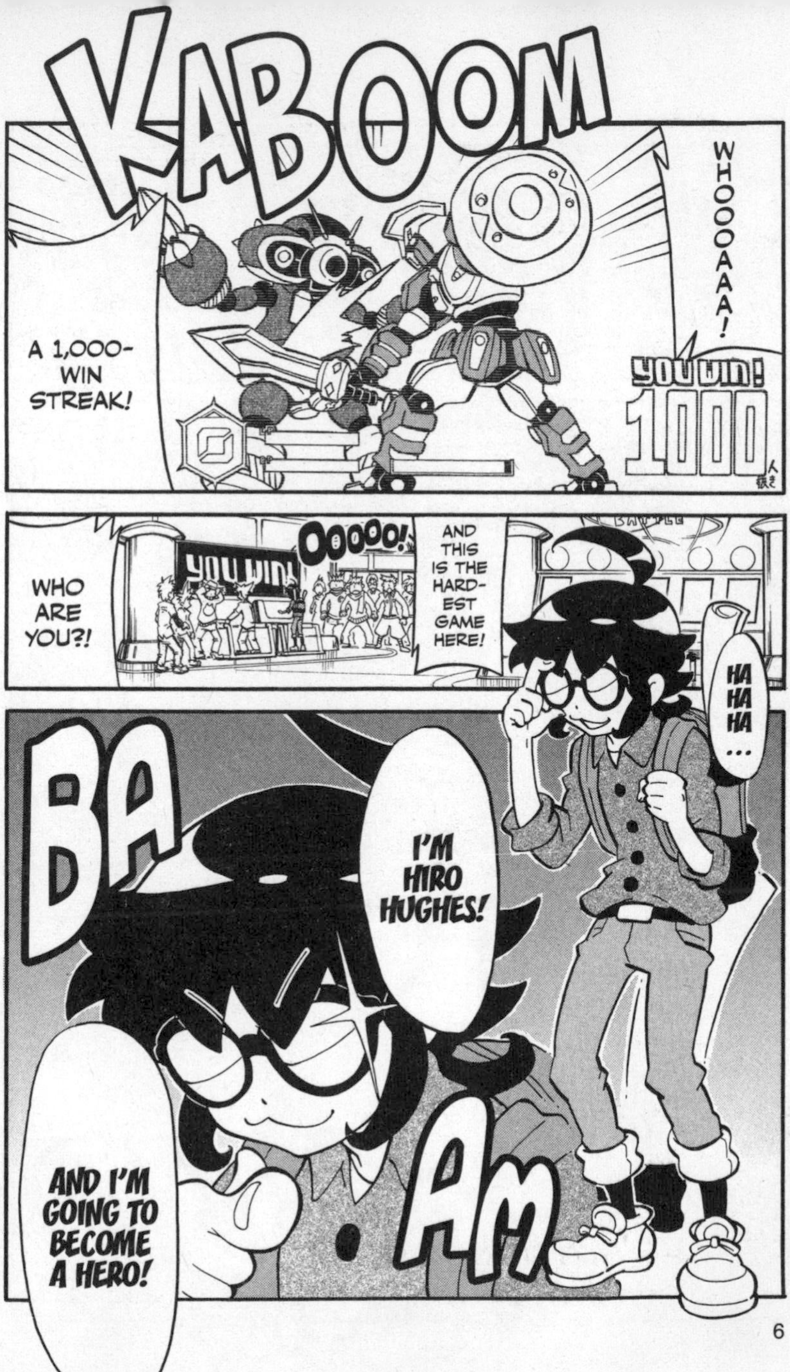
KABOOM
WHOOOAAA!
YOU WIN!
1000
A 1,000-WIN STREAK!
AND THIS IS THE HARDEST GAME HERE!
OOOOO!
YOU WIN!
WHO ARE YOU?!
HA HA HA...
I'M HIRO HUGHES!
BAAM
AND I'M GOING TO BECOME A HERO!

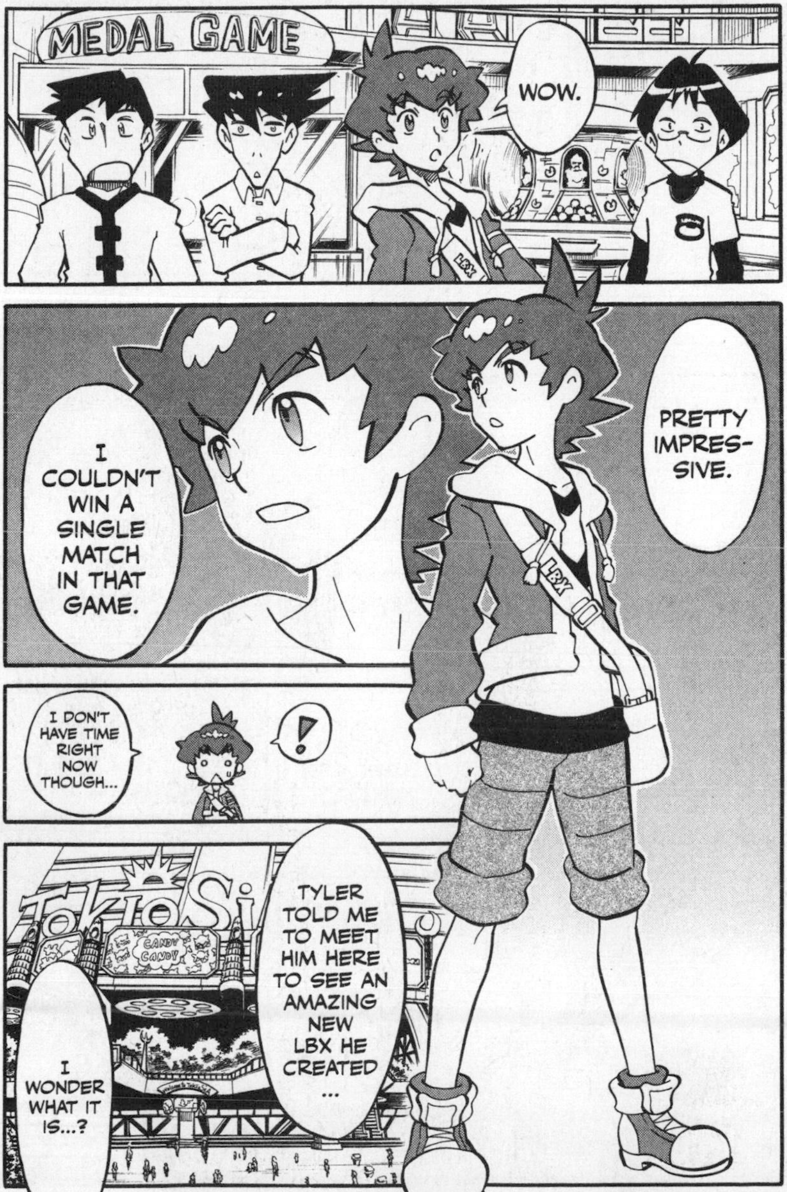
MEDAL GAME
WOW.
PRETTY IMPRES-SIVE.
I COULDN'T WIN A SINGLE MATCH IN THAT GAME.
!
I DON'T HAVE TIME RIGHT NOW THOUGH...
CANDY CANDY
TYLER TOLD ME TO MEET HIM HERE TO SEE AN AMAZING NEW LBX HE CREATED ...
I WONDER WHAT IT IS...?

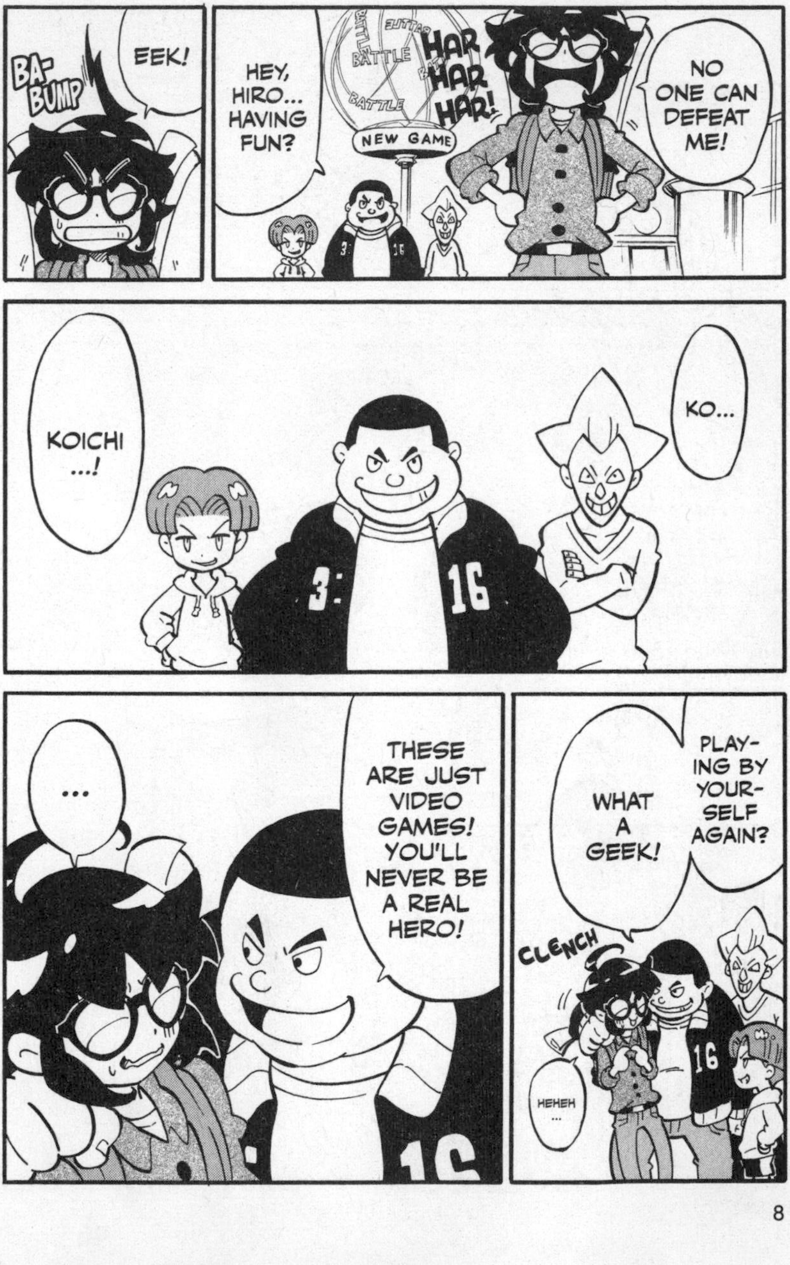
NO ONE CAN DEFEAT ME!
HAR HAR HAR!
BATTLE
NEW GAME
HEY, HIRO... HAVING FUN?
EEK!
BA-BUMP
KO...
KOICHI ...!
PLAYING BY YOURSELF AGAIN?
WHAT A GEEK!
CLENCH
HEHEH ...
THESE ARE JUST VIDEO GAMES! YOU'LL NEVER BE A REAL HERO!
...

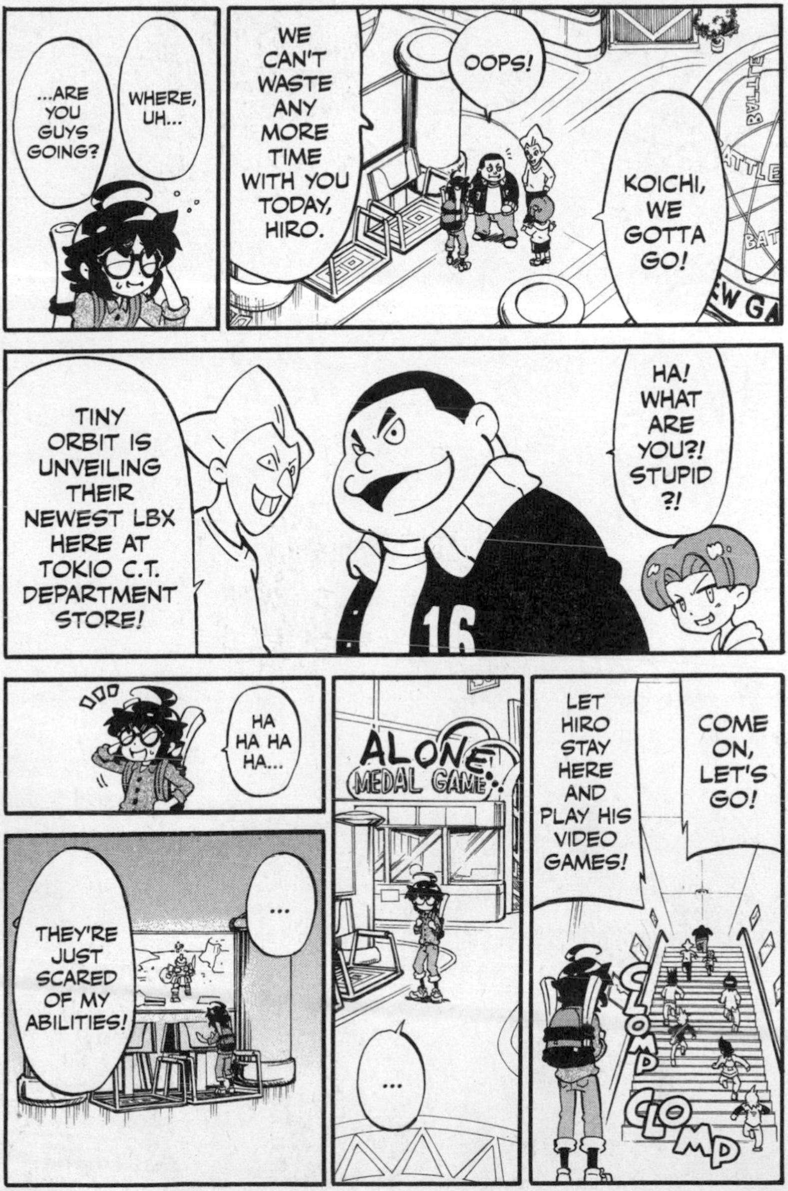
KOICHI, WE GOTTA GO!
OOPS!
WE CAN'T WASTE ANY MORE TIME WITH YOU TODAY, HIRO.
BATTLE
WHERE, UH...
...ARE YOU GUYS GOING?
HA! WHAT ARE YOU?! STUPID?!
TINY ORBIT IS UNVEILING THEIR NEWEST LBX HERE AT TOKIO C.T. DEPARTMENT STORE!
16
COME ON, LET'S GO!
LET HIRO STAY HERE AND PLAY HIS VIDEO GAMES!
CLOMP
CLOMP
CLOMP
ALONE
MEDAL GAME
...
HA HA HA HA...
...
THEY'RE JUST SCARED OF MY ABILITIES!

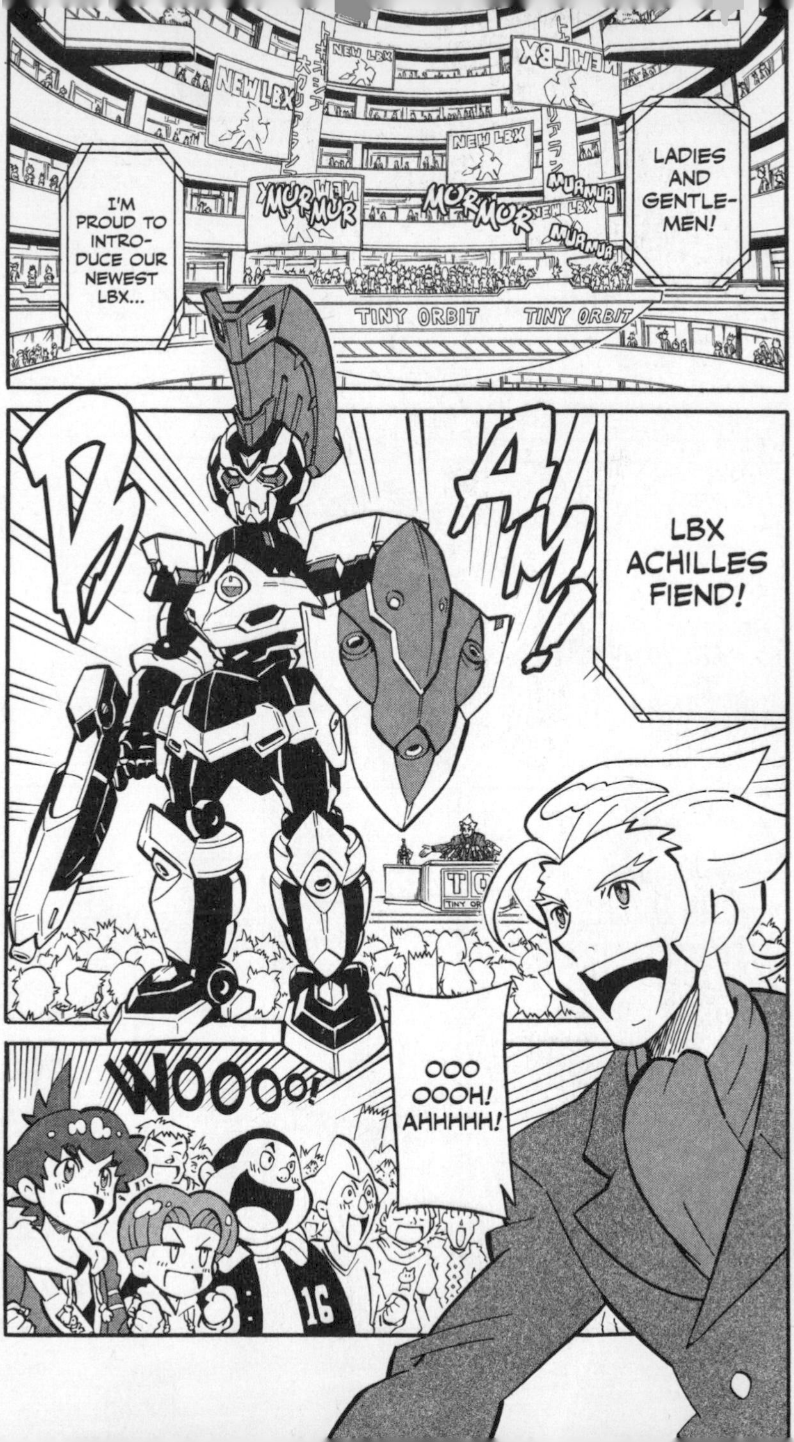
LADIES AND GENTLEMEN!
NEW LBX
MURMUR
TINY ORBIT
I'M PROUD TO INTRODUCE OUR NEWEST LBX...
LBX ACHILLES FIEND!
BAM!
OOO OOOH! AHHHHH!
WOOOO!

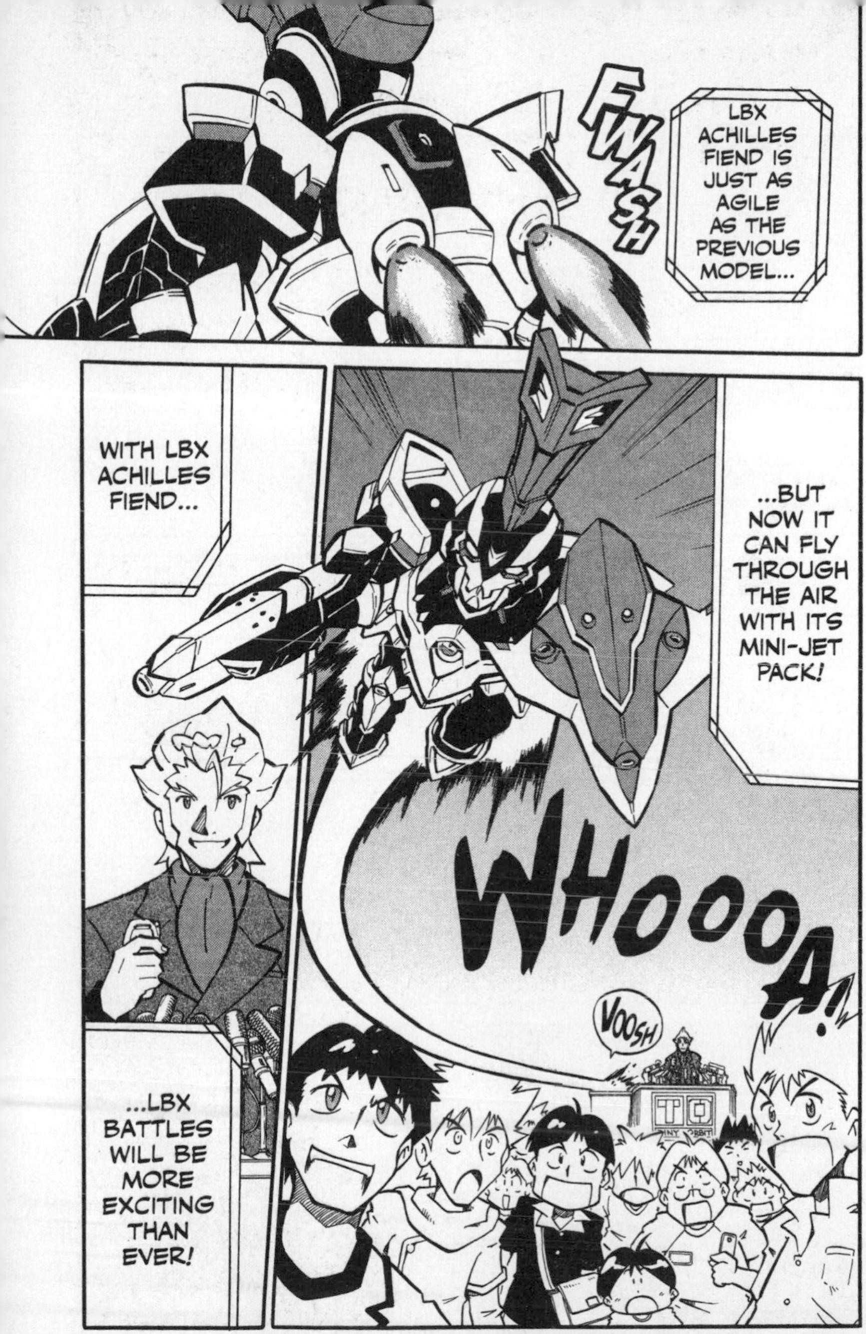
FWASH
LBX ACHILLES FIEND IS JUST AS AGILE AS THE PREVIOUS MODEL...
...BUT NOW IT CAN FLY THROUGH THE AIR WITH ITS MINI-JET PACK!
WHOOOA!
VOOSH
WITH LBX ACHILLES FIEND...
...LBX BATTLES WILL BE MORE EXCITING THAN EVER!

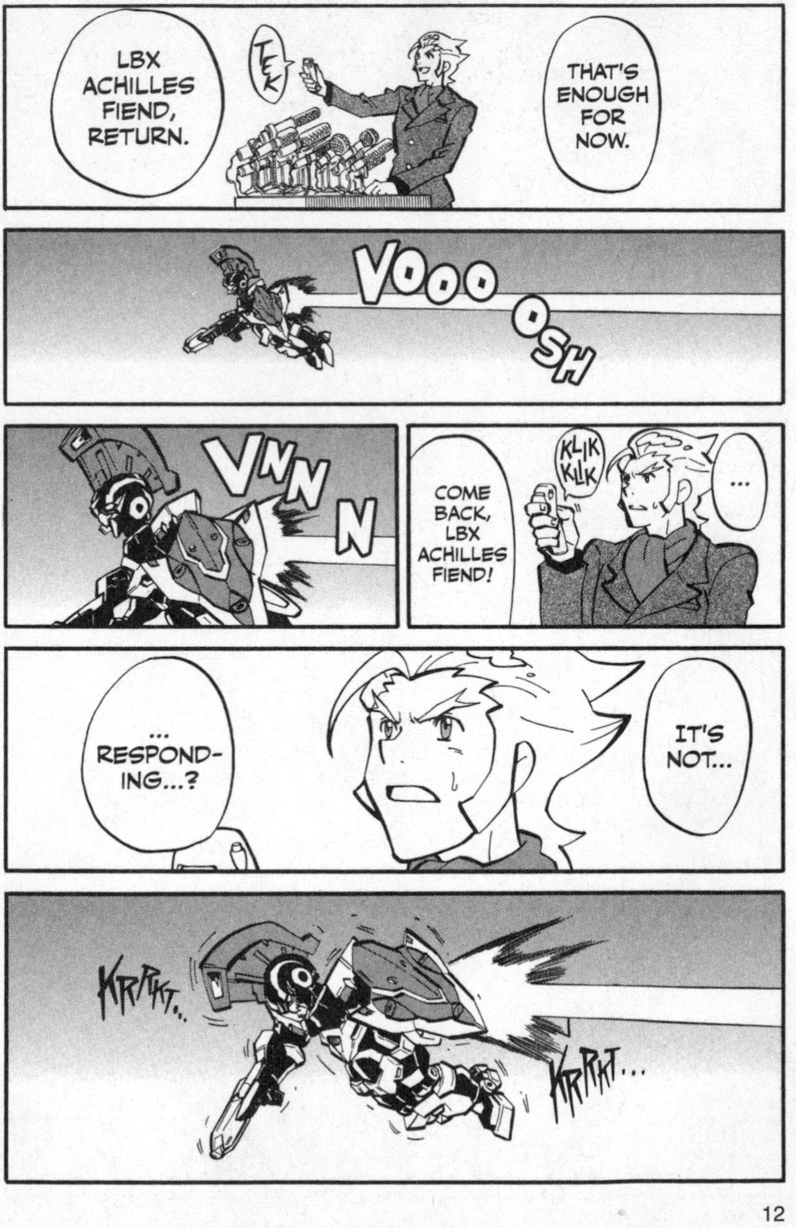
THAT'S ENOUGH FOR NOW.
TEK
LBX ACHILLES FIEND, RETURN.
VOOOOSH
...
KLIK KLIK
COME BACK, LBX ACHILLES FIEND!
VNNN
IT'S NOT...
... RESPOND-ING...?
KRRKT...
KRRKT..

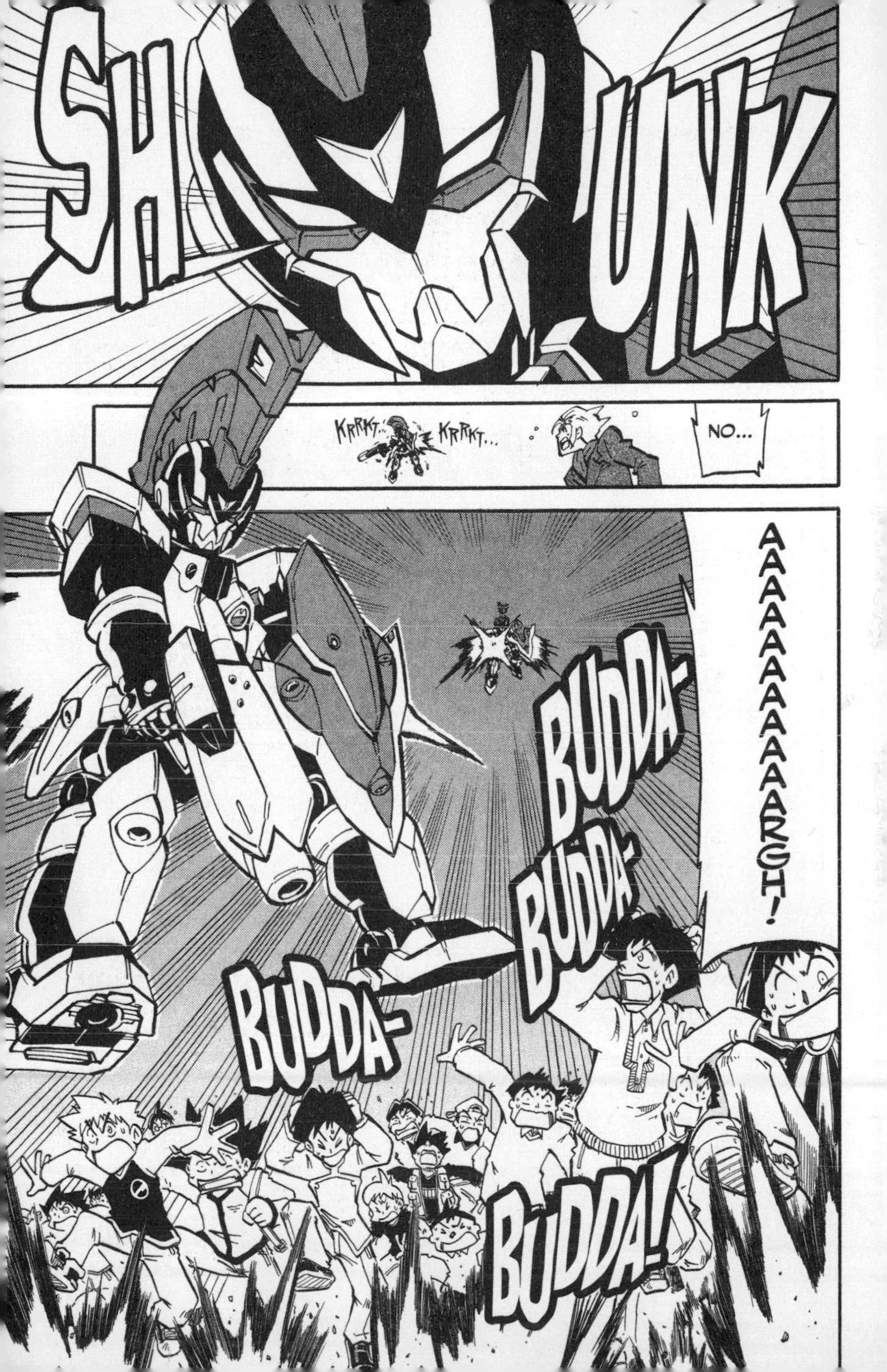
SH
UNK
NO...
KRRKT... KRRKT...
AAAAAAAAAAARGH!
BUDDA-
BUDDA-
BUDDA-
BUDDA!

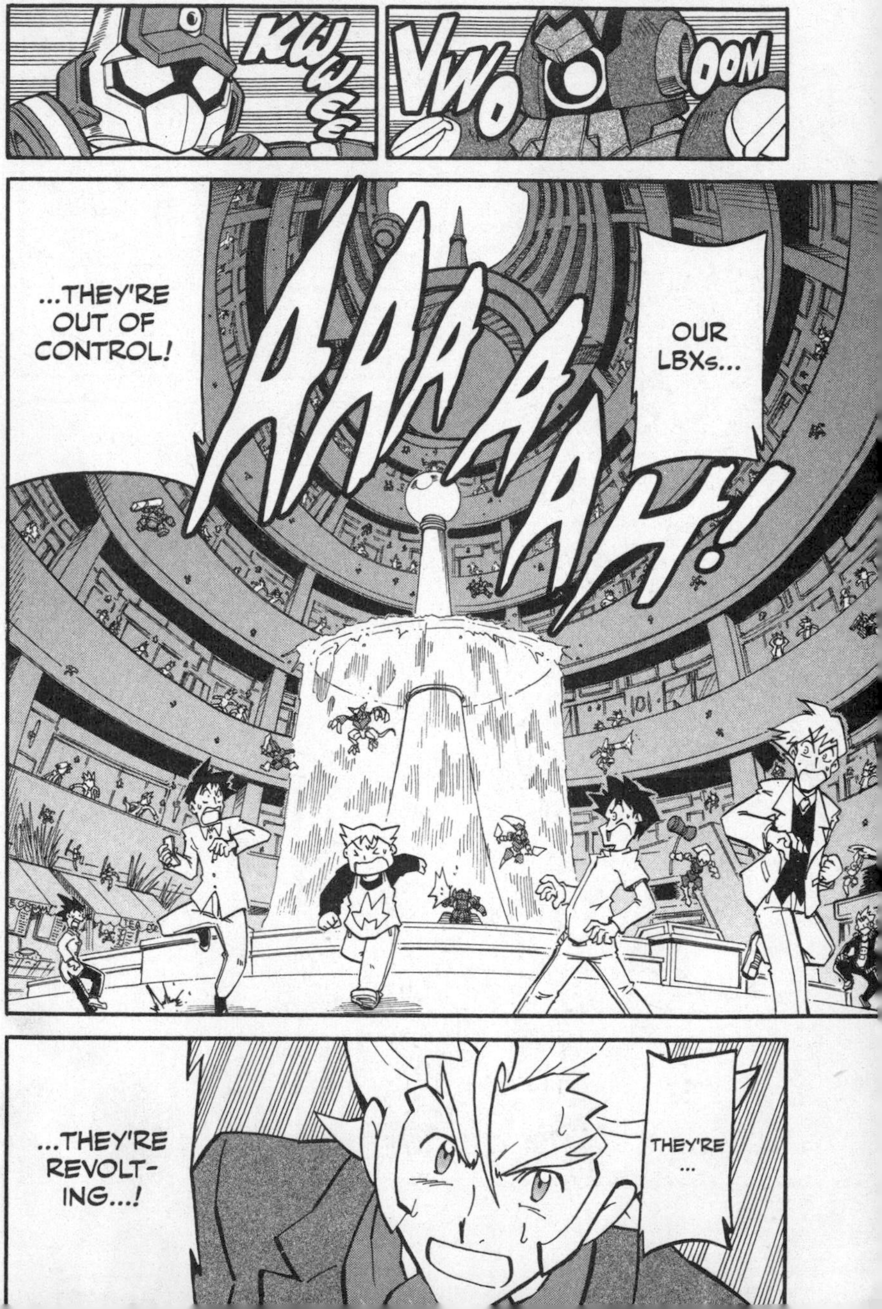
VWO
OOM
KWWEE
OUR LBXs...
...THEY'RE OUT OF CONTROL!
AAAAAH!
THEY'RE ...
...THEY'RE REVOLT-ING...!

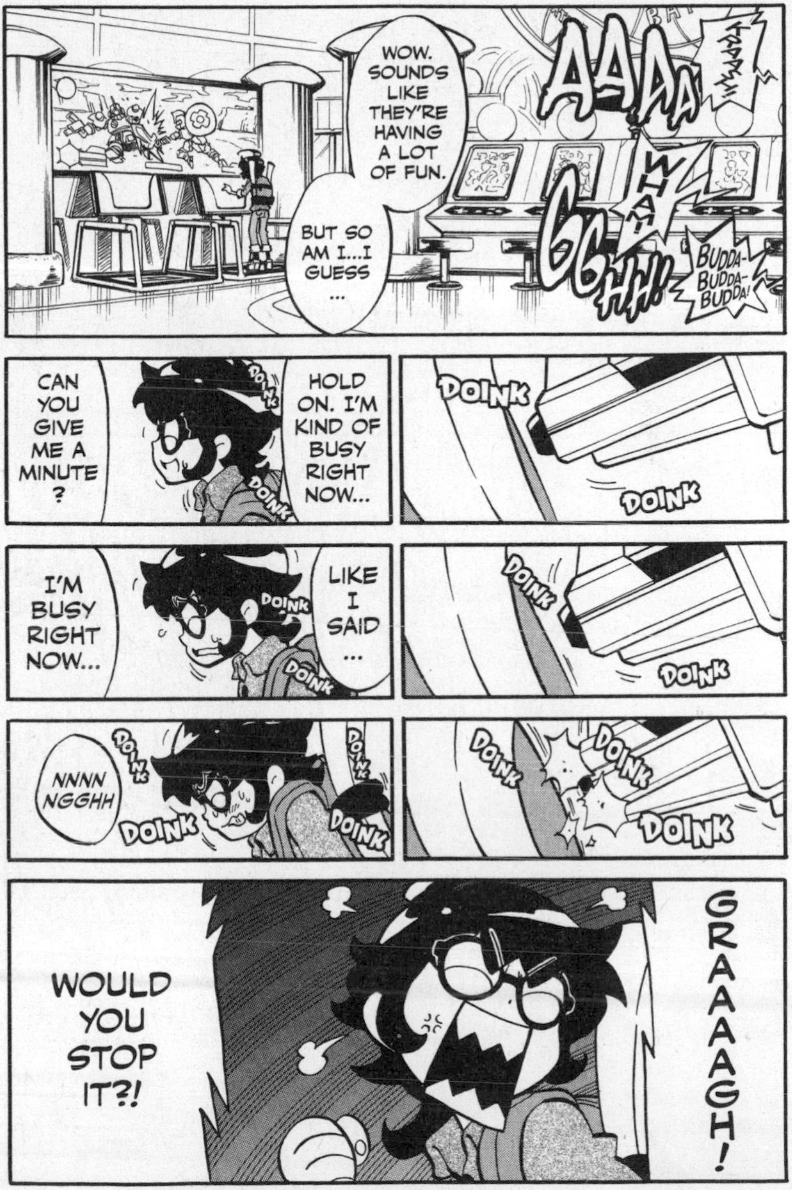
KRAAASH!!
AAAAGGHH!
WHAT!
BUDDA-BUDDA-BUDDA!
WOW. SOUNDS LIKE THEY'RE HAVING A LOT OF FUN.
BUT SO AM I...I GUESS...
DOINK
DOINK
HOLD ON. I'M KIND OF BUSY RIGHT NOW...
CAN YOU GIVE ME A MINUTE?
DOINK
DOINK
DOINK
DOINK
LIKE I SAID...
I'M BUSY RIGHT NOW...
DOINK
DOINK
DOINK
DOINK
DOINK
DOINK
DOINK
NNNNNGGHH
DOINK
GRAAAAGH!
WOULD YOU STOP IT?!

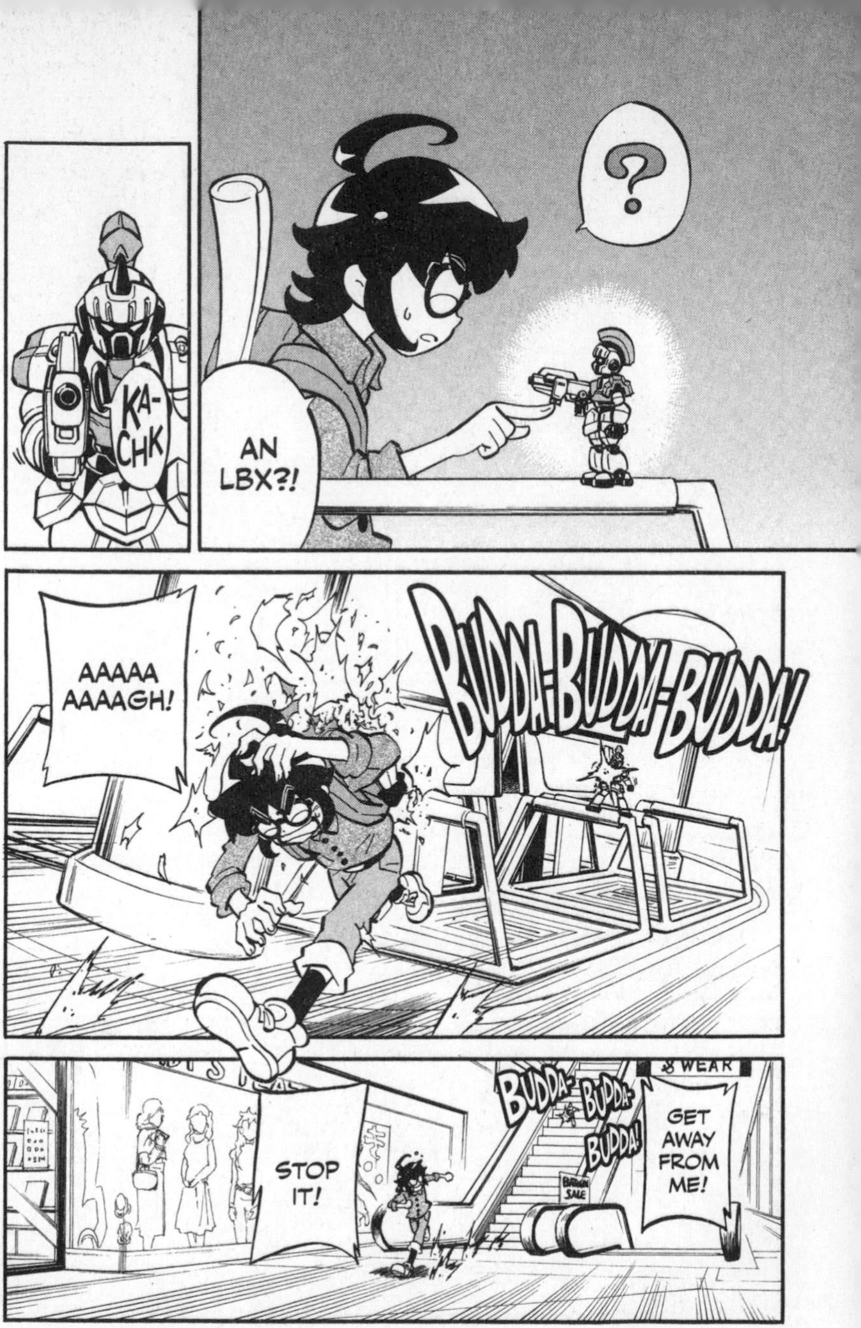
?
AN LBX?!
KA-CHK
BUDDA-BUDDA-BUDDA!
AAAAA AAAAGH!
GET AWAY FROM ME!
BUDDA-BUDDA-BUDDA!
STOP IT!

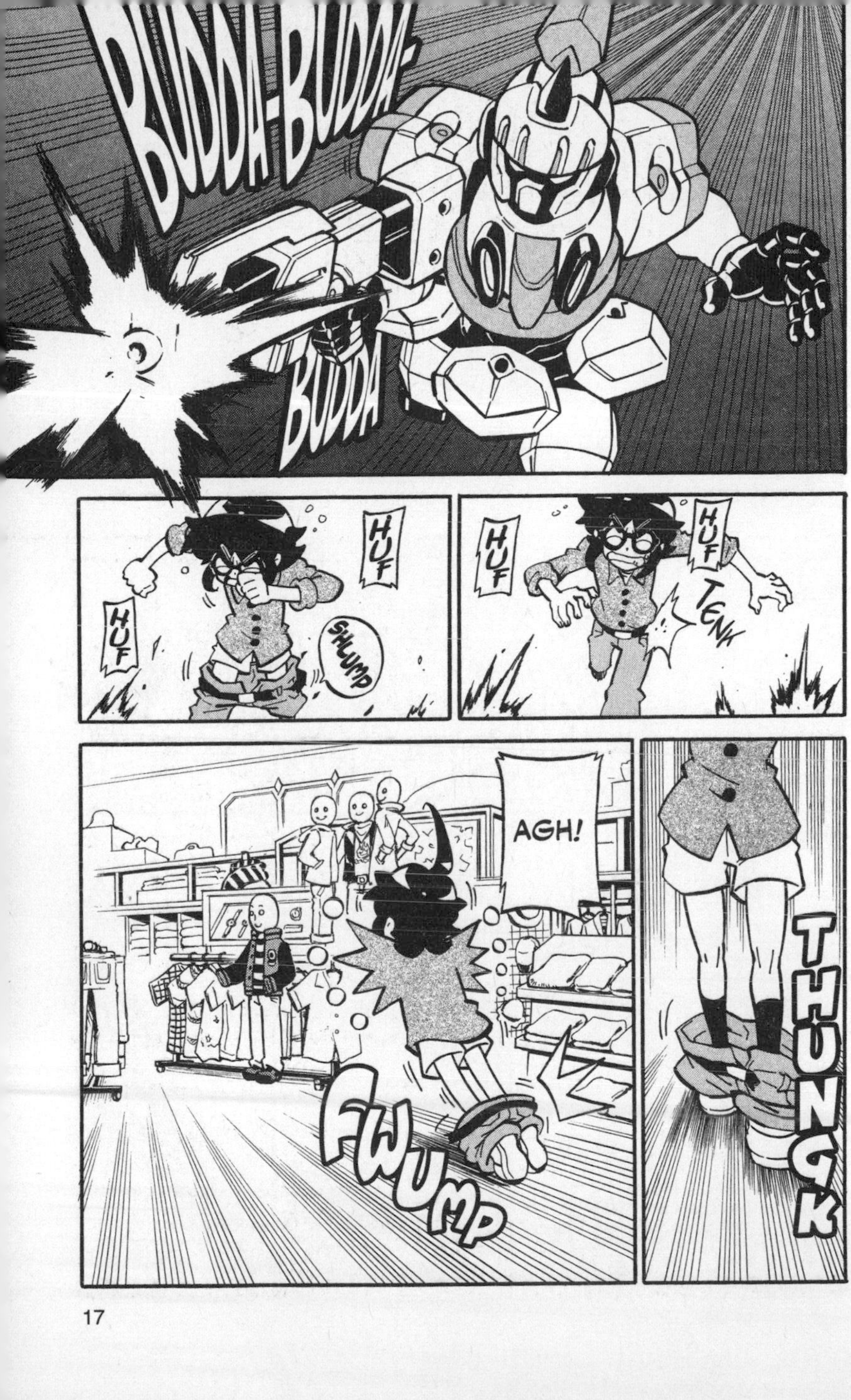
BUDDA-BUDDA-
BUDDA
HUF
HUF
TENK
HUF
SHLUMP
HUF
THUNGK
AGH!
FWUMP

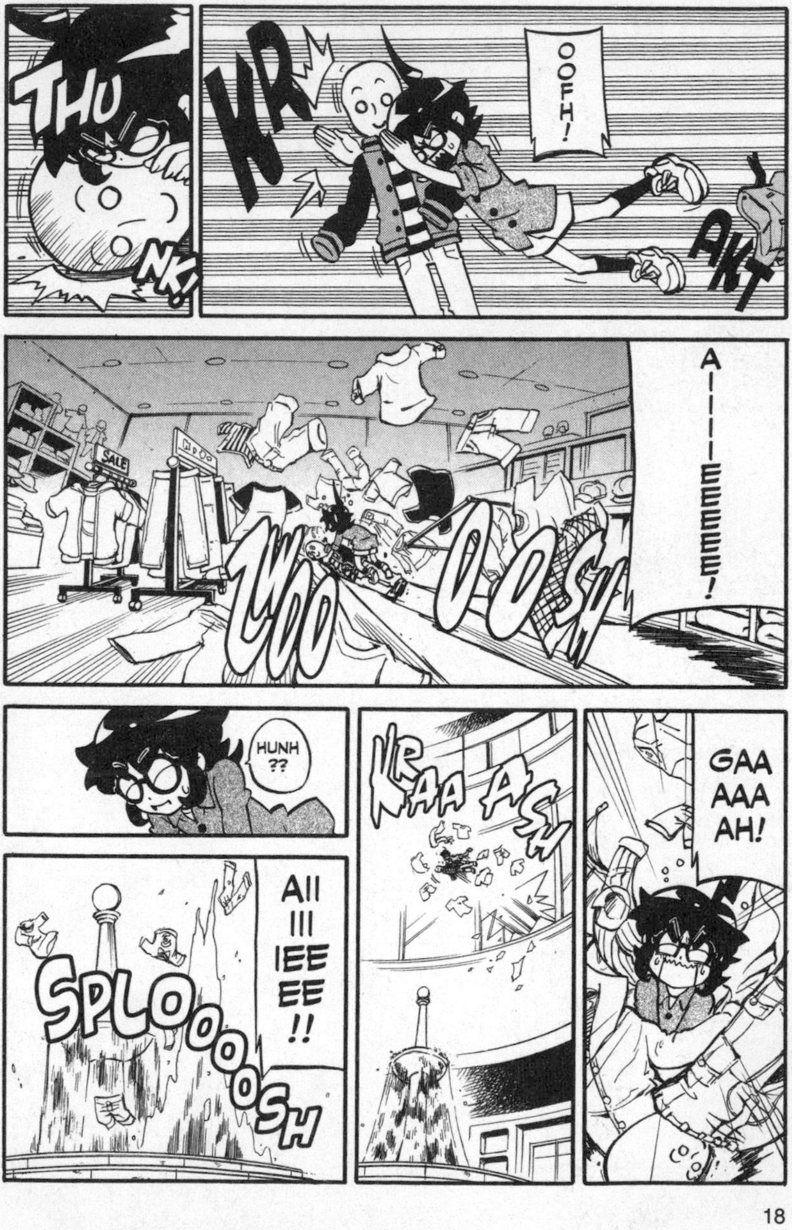

HR
OOFH!
AKT
THU
NK!
A-IIIIEEEEEE!
WHOOOOSH
SALE
GAA AAA AH!
KRAAASH
HUNH ??
AII III IEE EE !!
SPLOOOOOSH

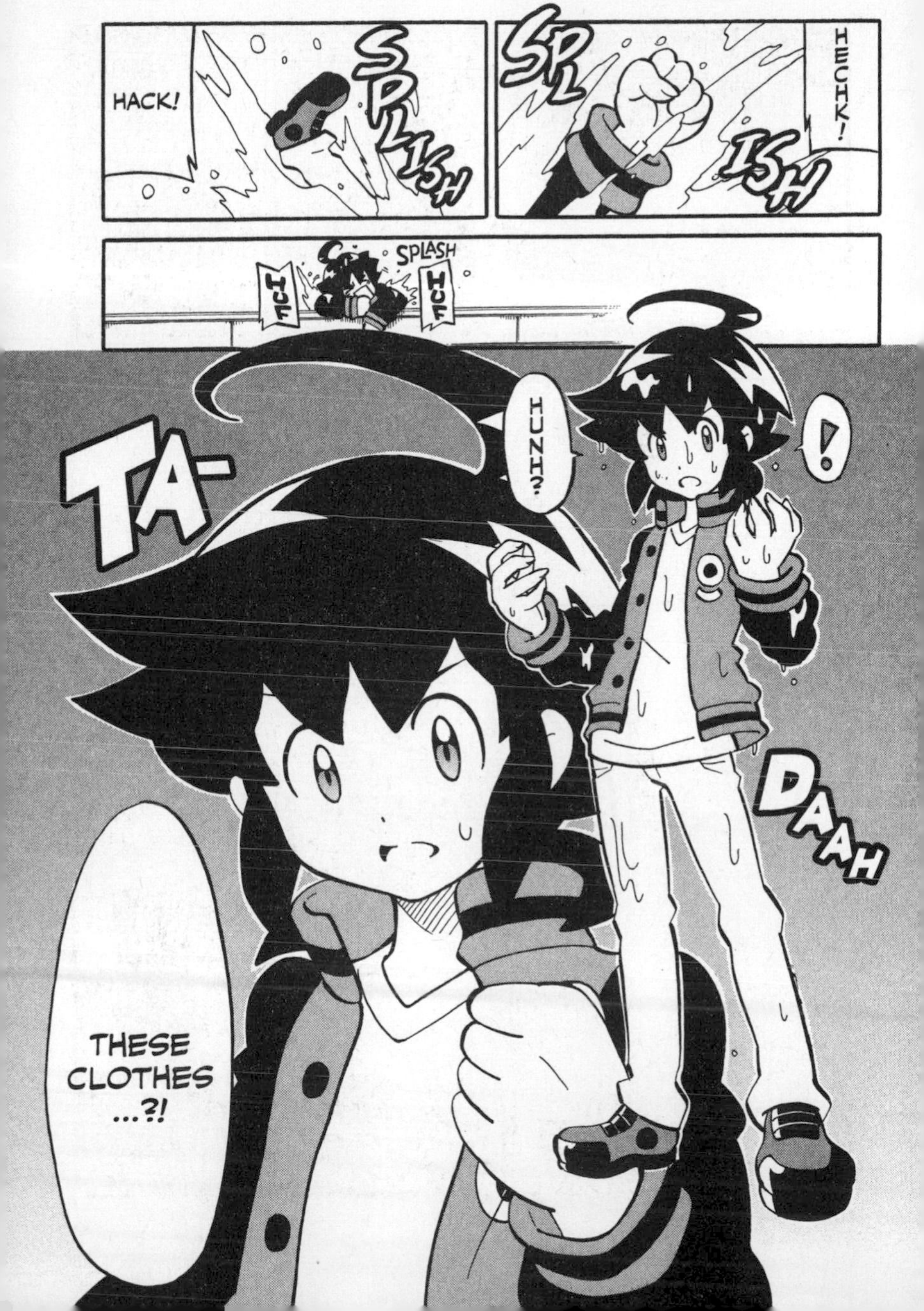
HECHK!
SPL ISH
HACK!
SPLISH
SPLASH
HUF
HUF
!
HUNH?
TA-
DAAH
THESE CLOTHES ...?!

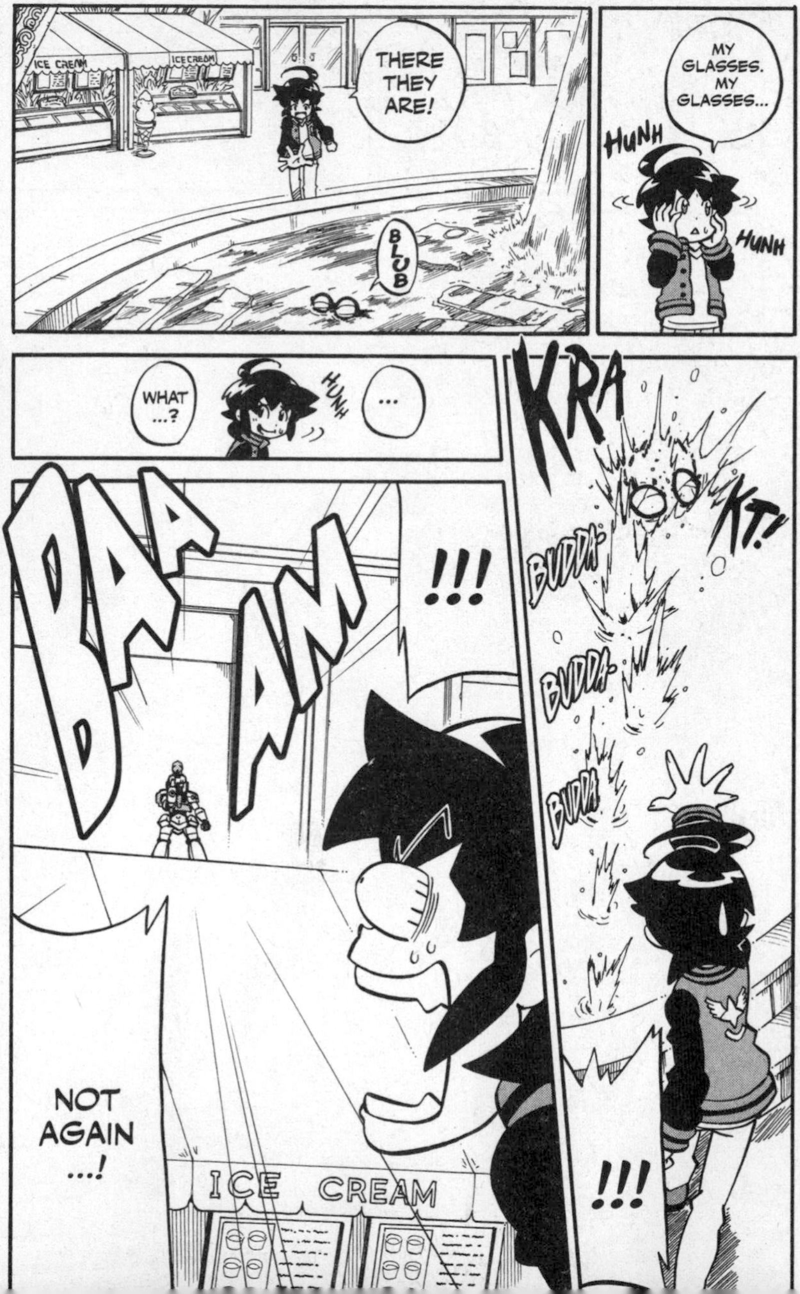
MY GLASSES. MY GLASSES...
HUNH
HUNH
THERE THEY ARE!
BLUB
KRA
KT!
BUDDA
BUDDA
BUDDA
!!!
...
HUNH
WHAT ...?
BAAM
!!!
NOT AGAIN ...!
ICE CREAM

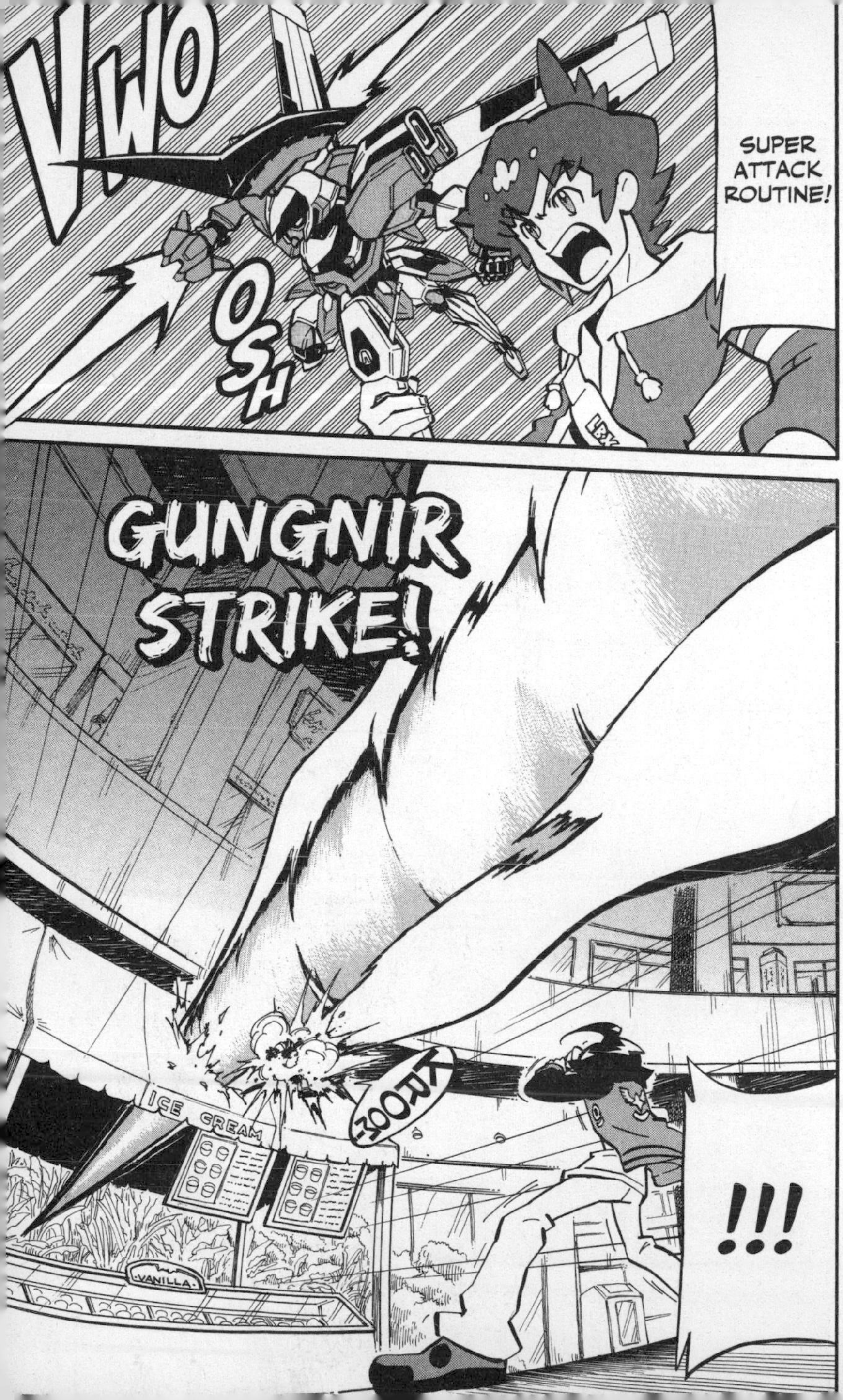
SUPER ATTACK ROUTINE!
VWOOSH
GUNGNIR STRIKE!
KROOK-
ICE CREAM
VANILLA
!!!

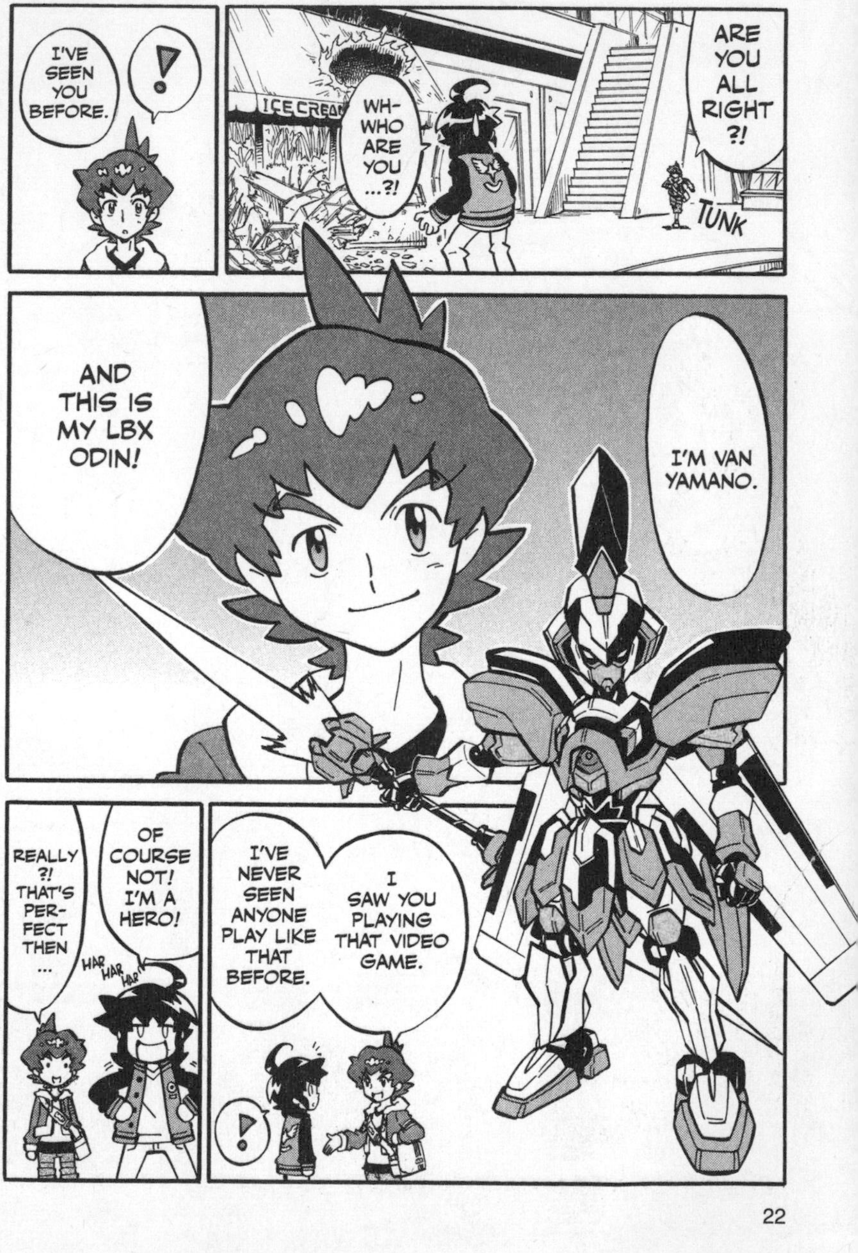
ARE YOU ALL RIGHT?!
TUNK
WH- WHO ARE YOU ...?!
!
I'VE SEEN YOU BEFORE.
I'M VAN YAMANO.
AND THIS IS MY LBX ODIN!
I SAW YOU PLAYING THAT VIDEO GAME.
I'VE NEVER SEEN ANYONE PLAY LIKE THAT BEFORE.
!
OF COURSE NOT! I'M A HERO!
HAR HAR HAR
REALLY?! THAT'S PER-FECT THEN ...

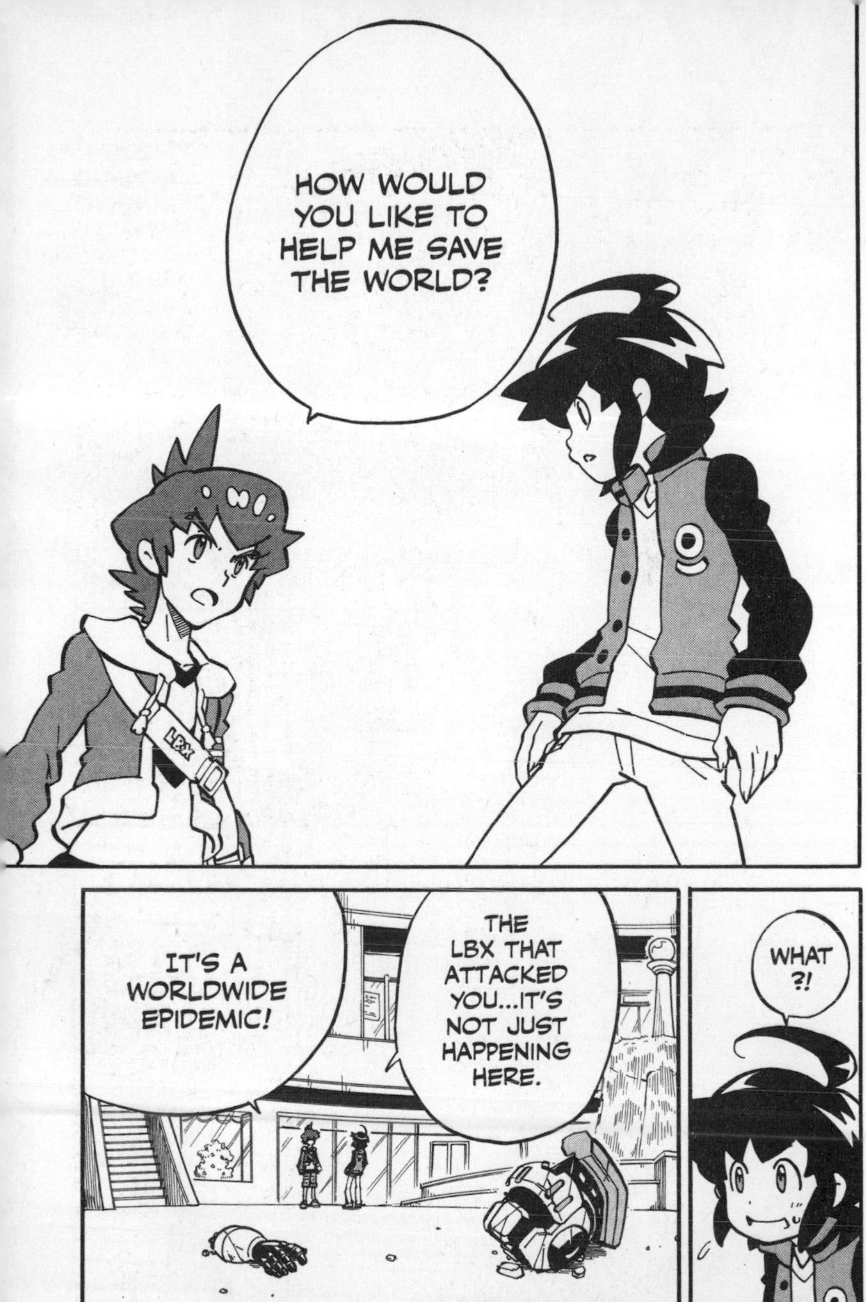
HOW WOULD YOU LIKE TO HELP ME SAVE THE WORLD?
WHAT ?!
THE LBX THAT ATTACKED YOU...IT'S NOT JUST HAPPENING HERE.
IT'S A WORLDWIDE EPIDEMIC!
LBX

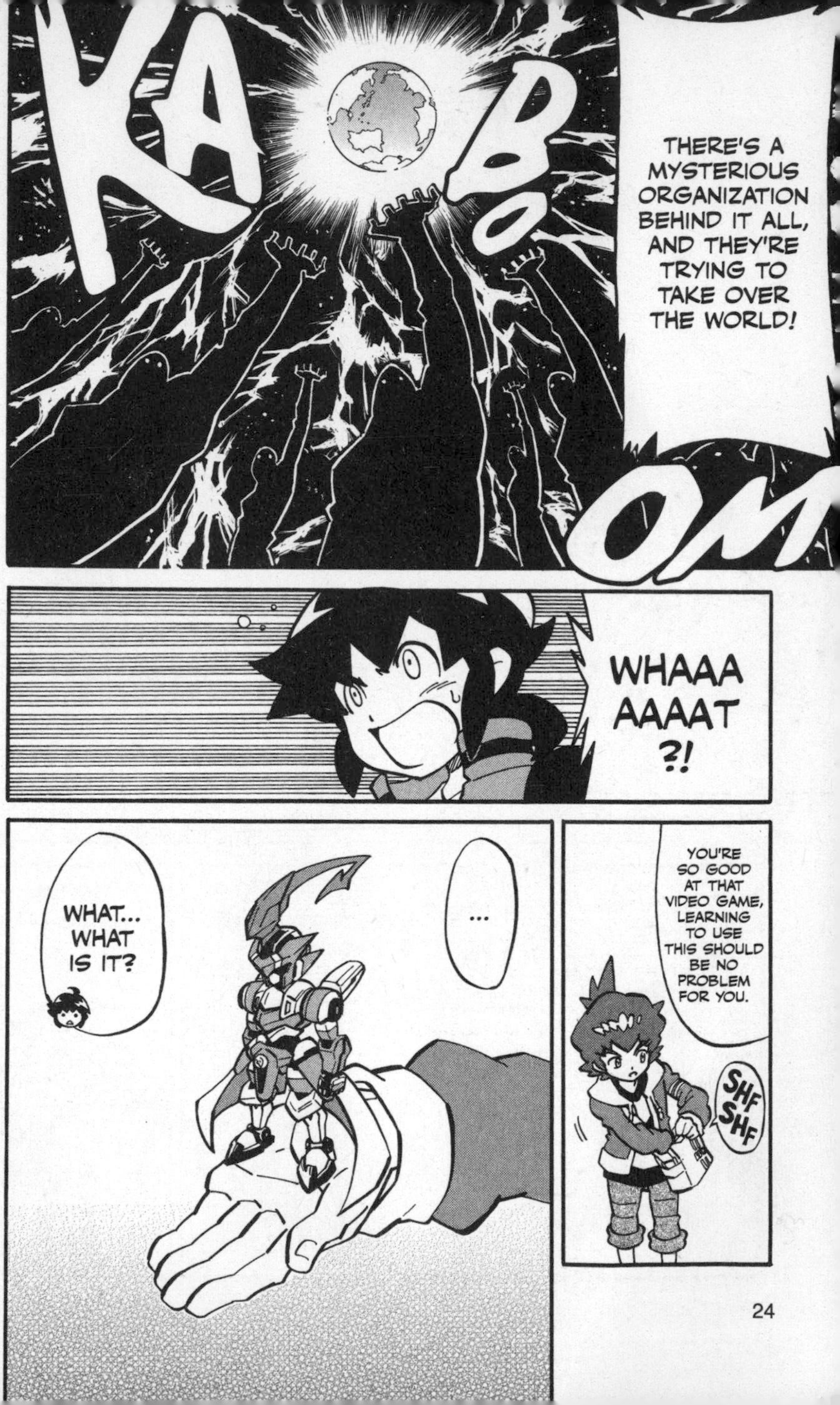
THERE'S A MYSTERIOUS ORGANIZATION BEHIND IT ALL, AND THEY'RE TRYING TO TAKE OVER THE WORLD!
KABOOM
WHAAAAAAAT?!
YOU'RE SO GOOD AT THAT VIDEO GAME, LEARNING TO USE THIS SHOULD BE NO PROBLEM FOR YOU.
SHF SHF
...
WHAT... WHAT IS IT?

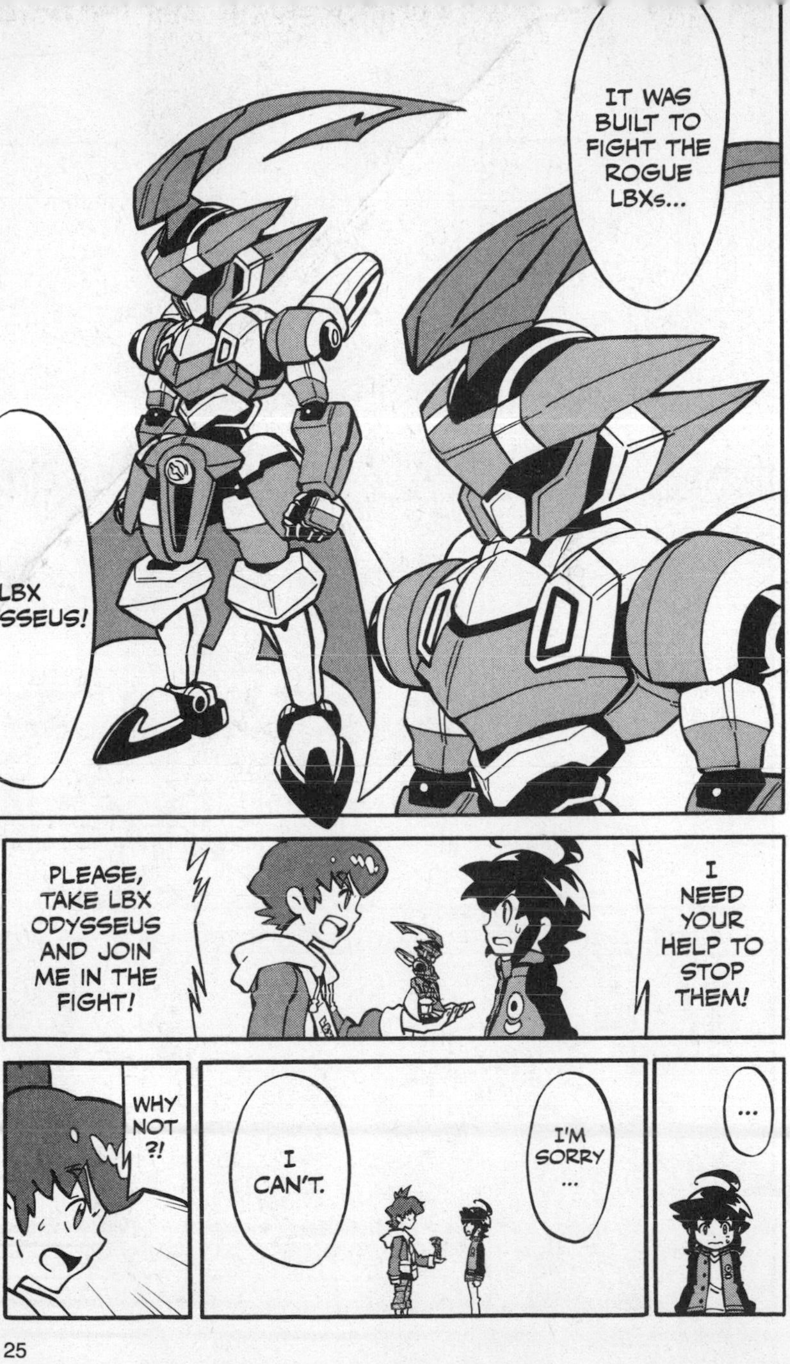
IT WAS BUILT TO FIGHT THE ROGUE LBXs...
LBX ODYSSEUS!
I NEED YOUR HELP TO STOP THEM!
PLEASE, TAKE LBX ODYSSEUS AND JOIN ME IN THE FIGHT!
...
I'M SORRY ...
I CAN'T.
WHY NOT ?!

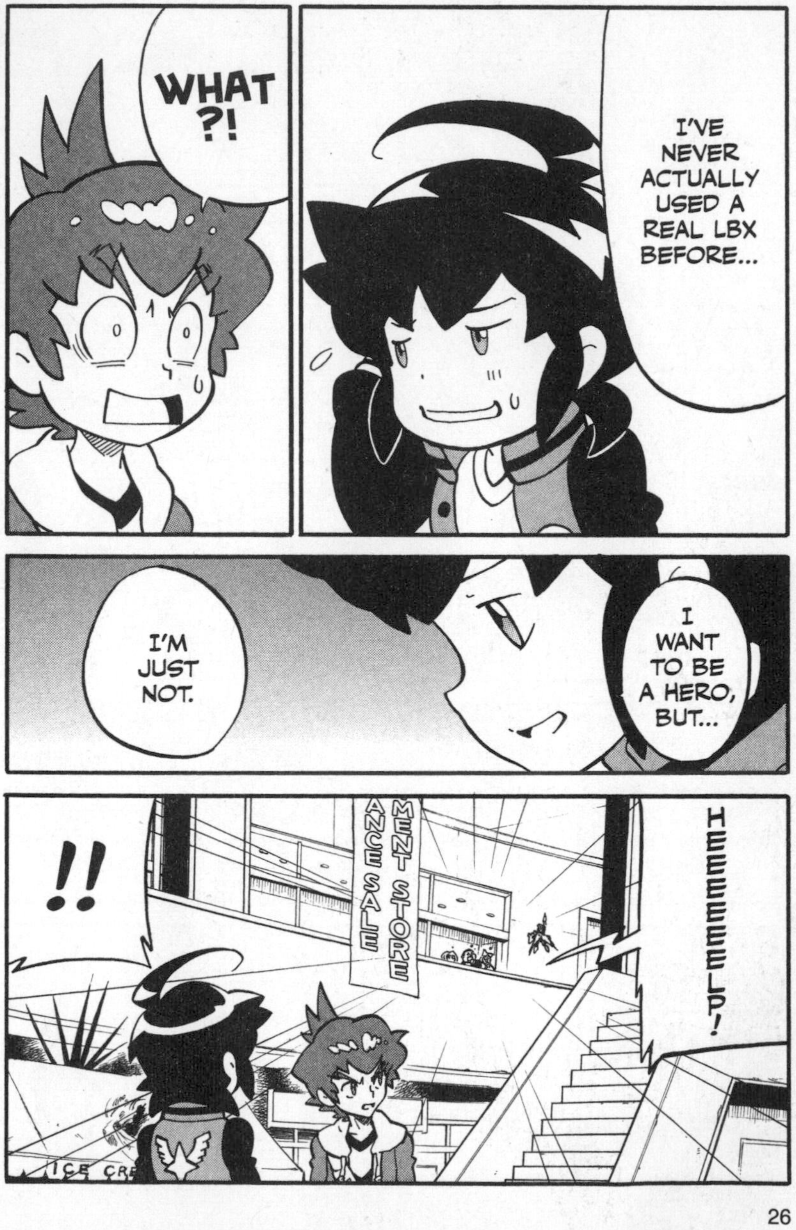
I'VE NEVER ACTUALLY USED A REAL LBX BEFORE...
WHAT ?!
I WANT TO BE A HERO, BUT...
I'M JUST NOT.
HEEEEEELP!
!!
MENT STORE
ANCE SALE
ICE CRE

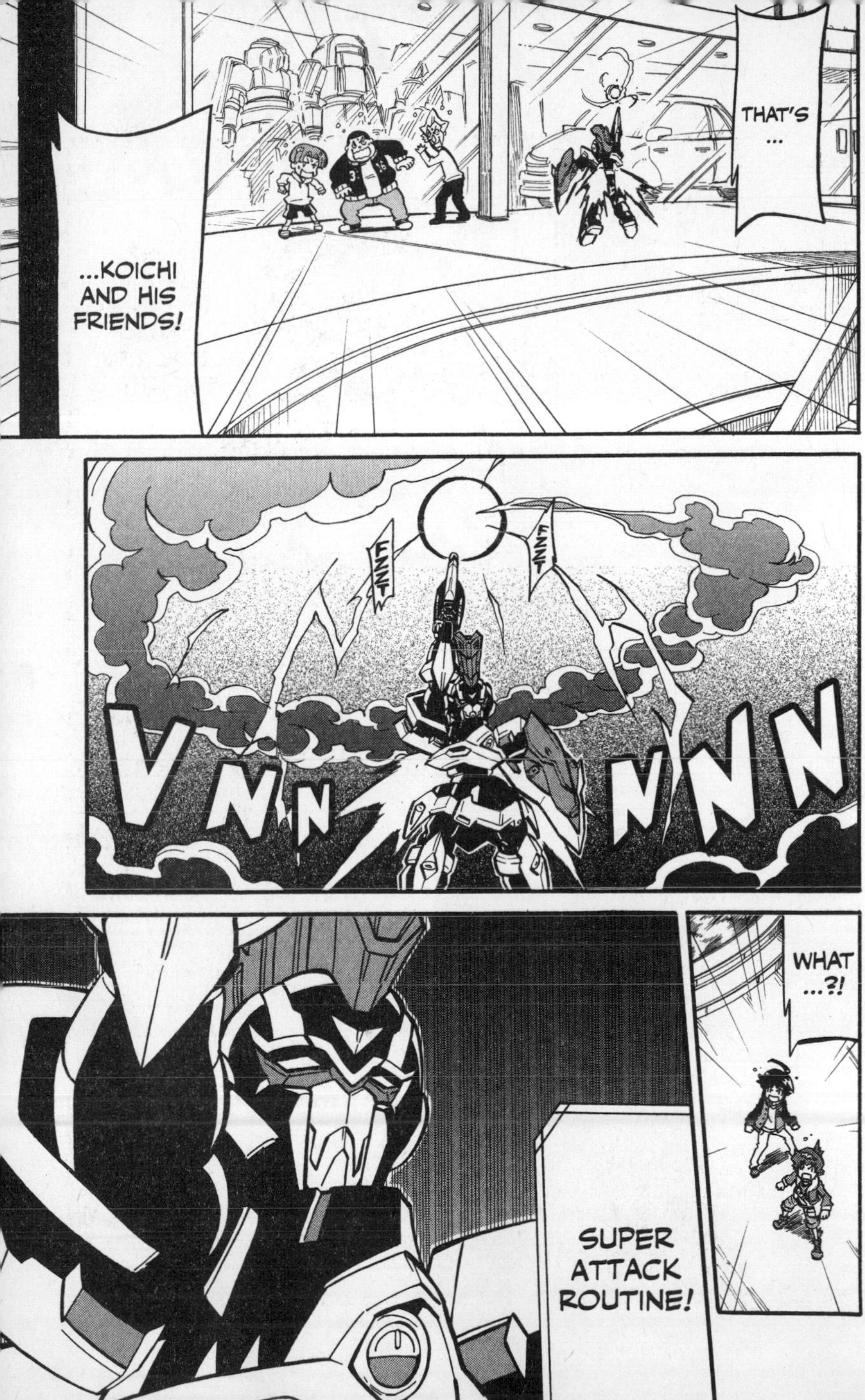
THAT'S ...
...KOICHI AND HIS FRIENDS!
FZZT
FZZT
VNNNNNNN
WHAT ...?!
SUPER ATTACK ROUTINE!

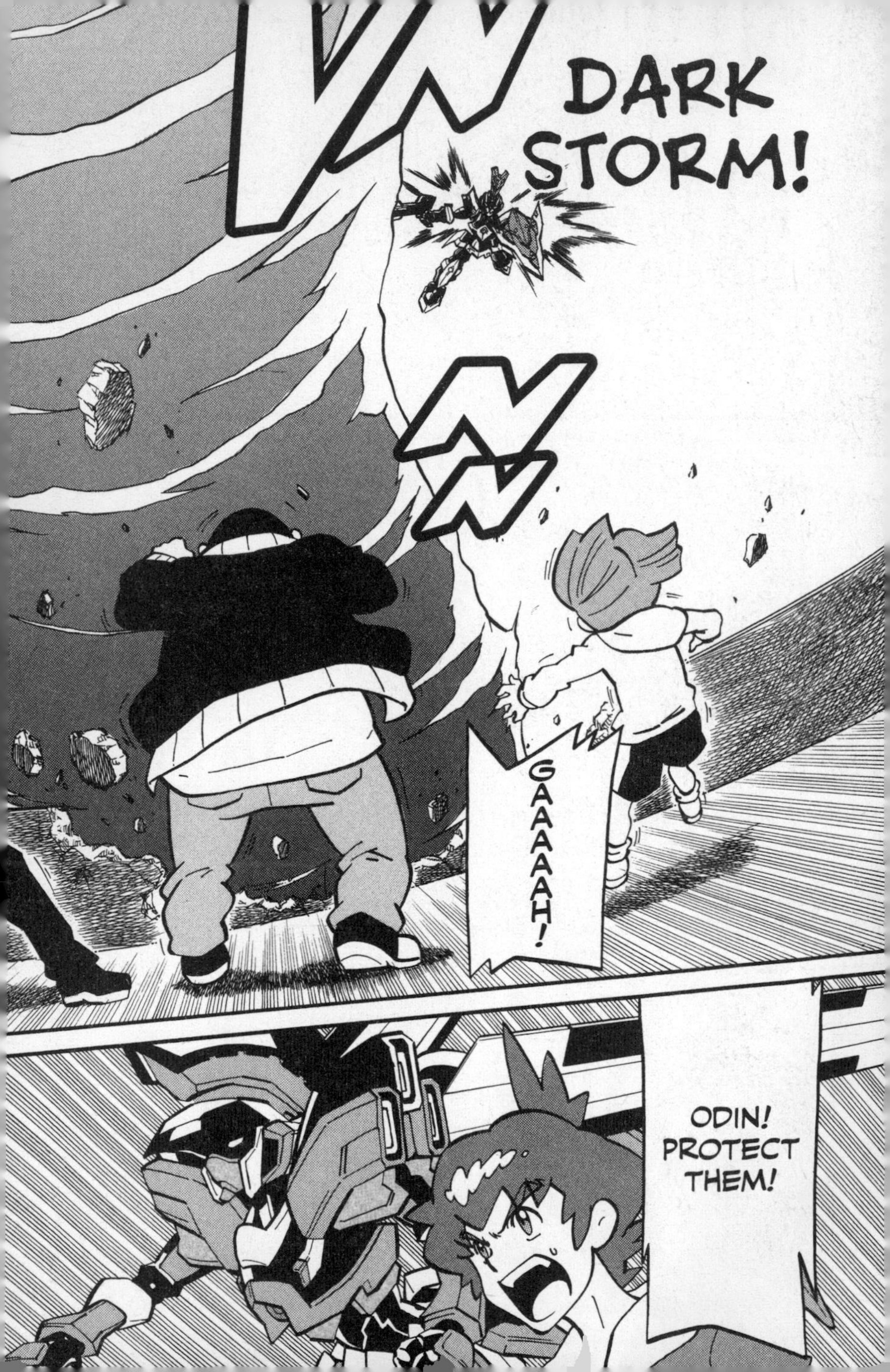
DARK STORM!
GAAAAAAH!
ODIN! PROTECT THEM!

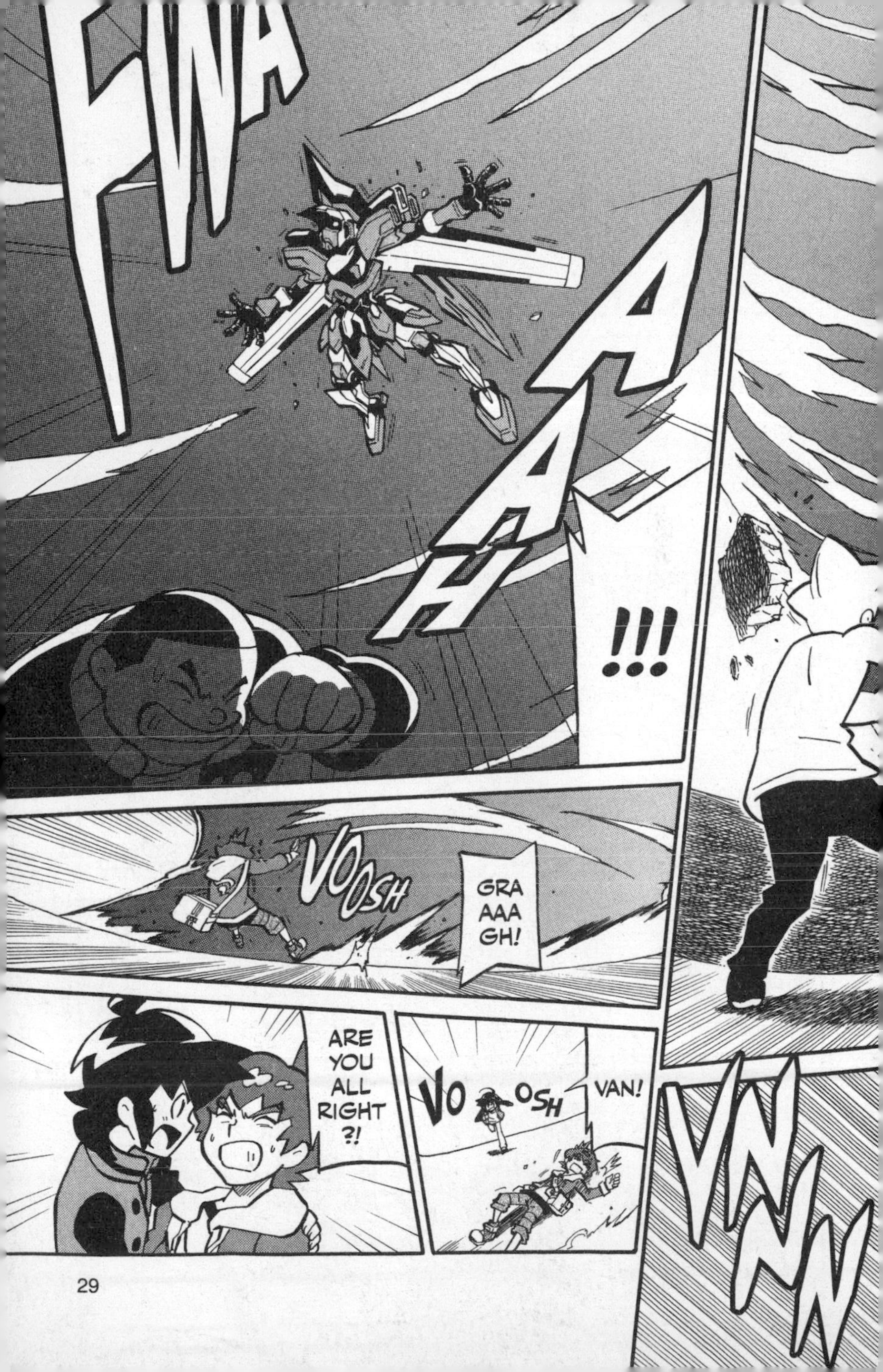

VNNN
FWAAAH
!!!
GRAAAAGH!
VOOSH
VAN!
VOOSH
ARE YOU ALL RIGHT?!

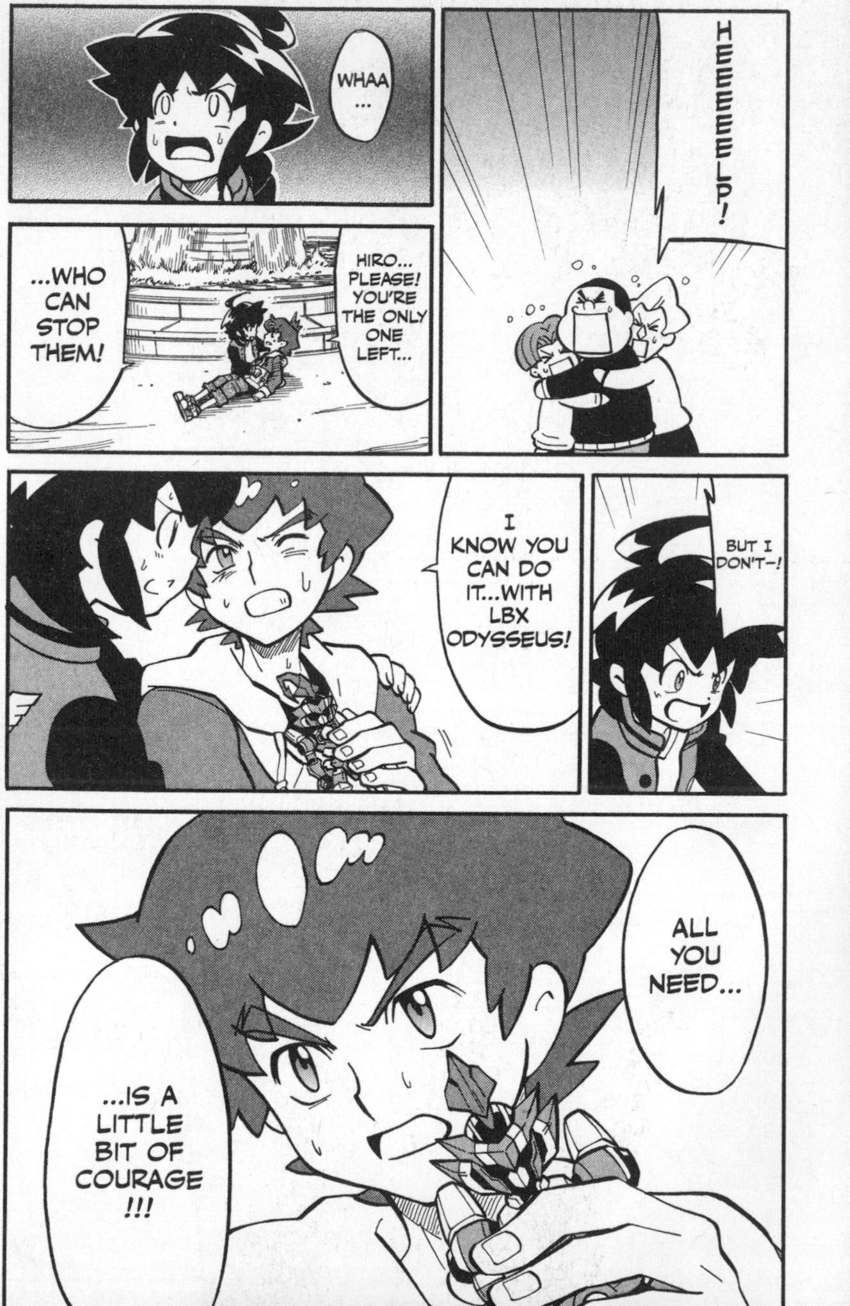
HEEEEELP!
WHAA...
HIRO... PLEASE! YOU'RE THE ONLY ONE LEFT...
...WHO CAN STOP THEM!
BUT I DON'T-!
I KNOW YOU CAN DO IT...WITH LBX ODYSSEUS!
ALL YOU NEED...
...IS A LITTLE BIT OF COURAGE!!!

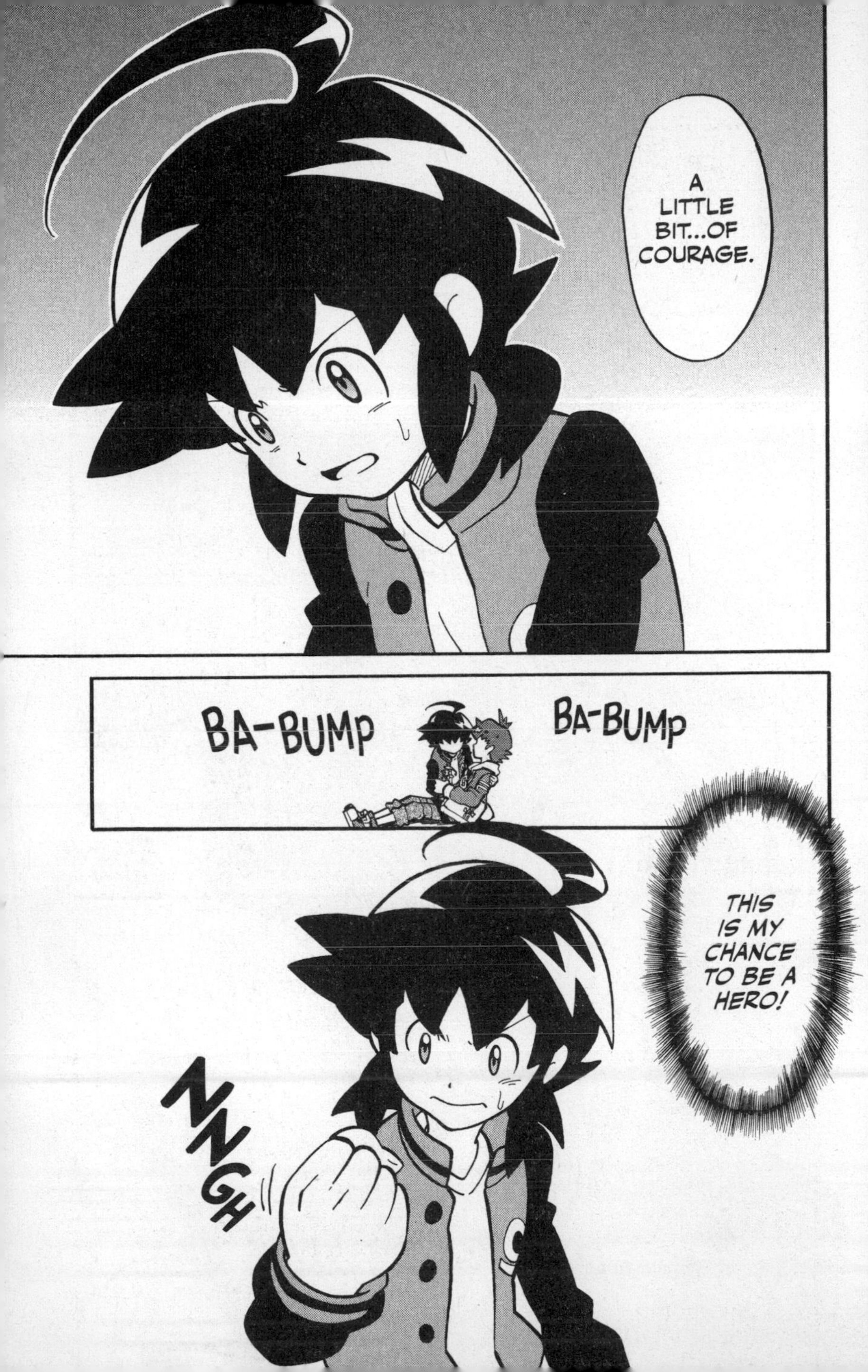
A LITTLE BIT...OF COURAGE.
BA-BUMP
BA-BUMP
THIS IS MY CHANCE TO BE A HERO!
NNGH

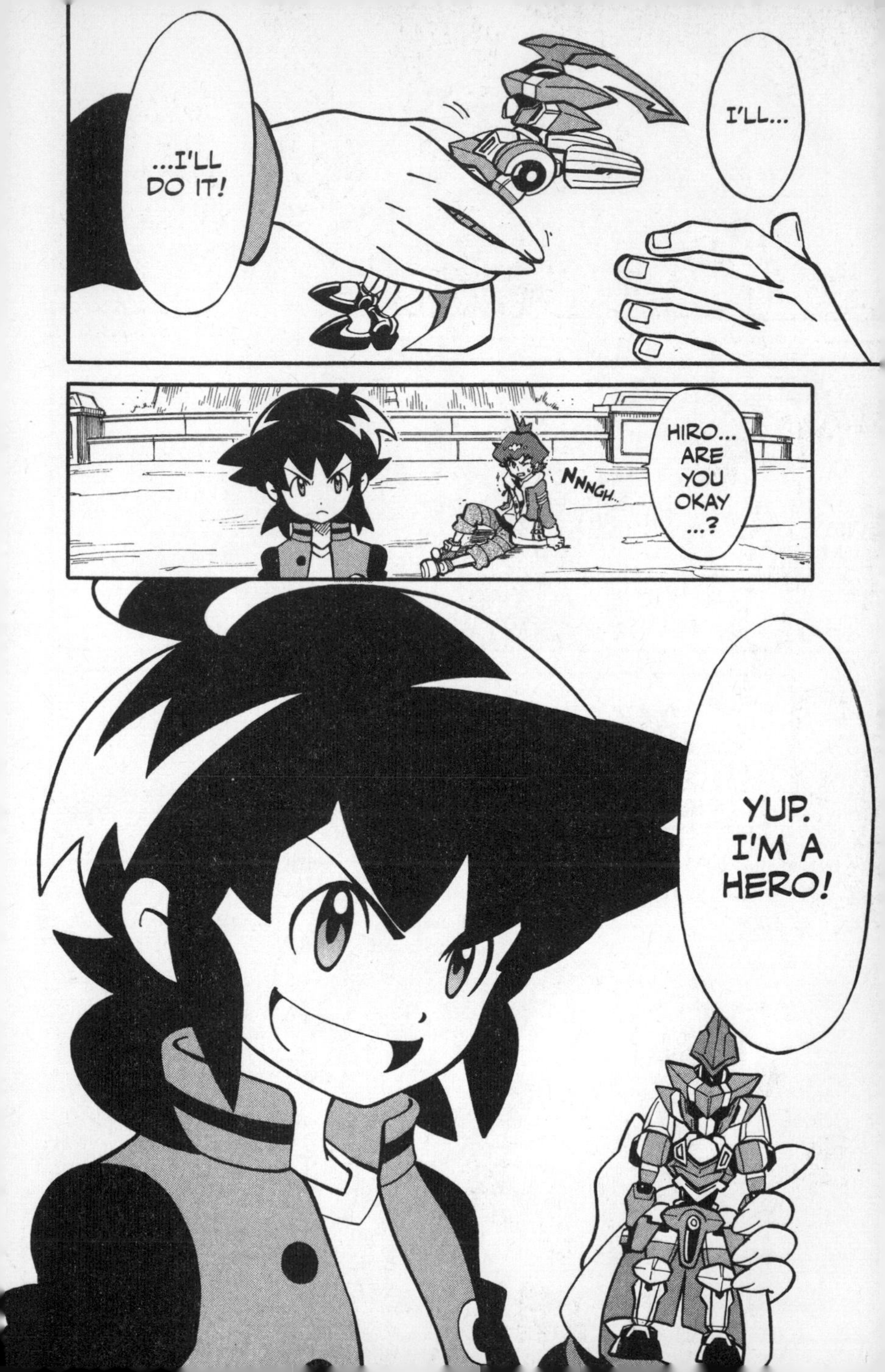
I'LL...
...I'LL DO IT!
HIRO... ARE YOU OKAY ...?
NNNGH...
YUP. I'M A HERO!

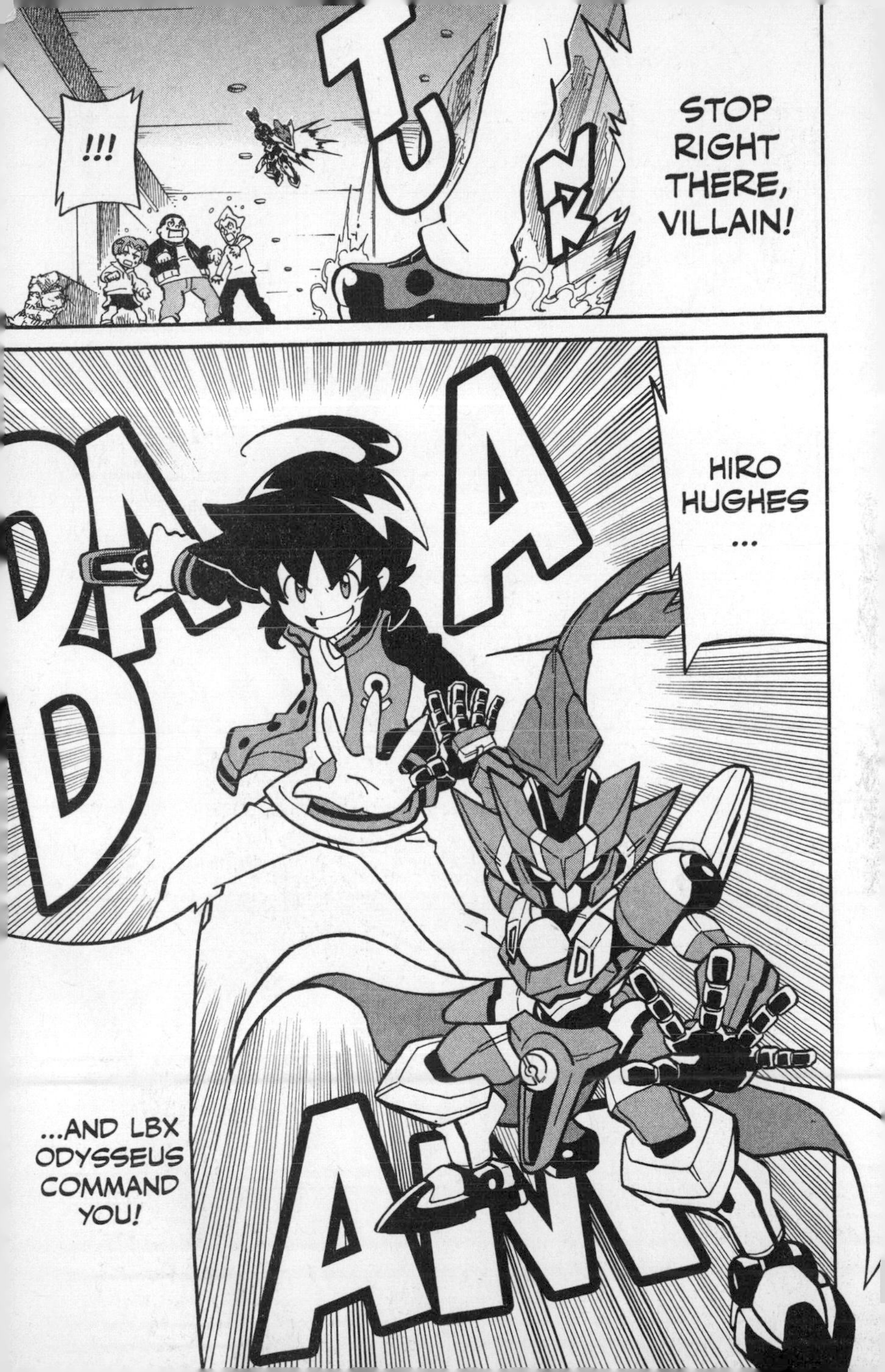
STOP RIGHT THERE, VILLAIN!
!!!
HIRO HUGHES ...
...AND LBX ODYSSEUS COMMAND YOU!

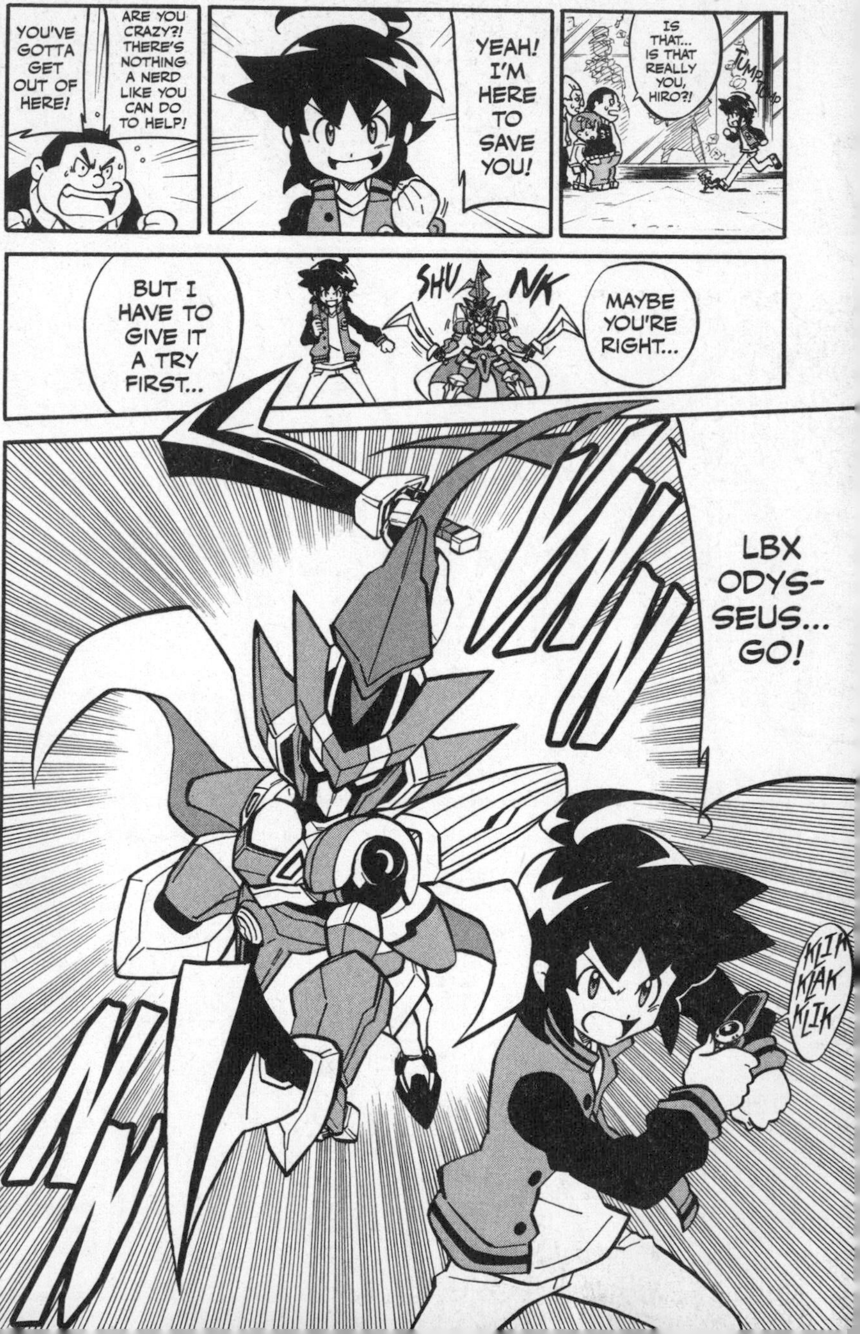
IS THAT... IS THAT REALLY YOU, HIRO?!
TUMP TUMP
YEAH! I'M HERE TO SAVE YOU!
ARE YOU CRAZY?! THERE'S NOTHING A NERD LIKE YOU CAN DO TO HELP!
YOU'VE GOTTA GET OUT OF HERE!
MAYBE YOU'RE RIGHT...
SHUNK
BUT I HAVE TO GIVE IT A TRY FIRST...
LBX ODYS-SEUS... GO!
KLIK KLAK KLIK

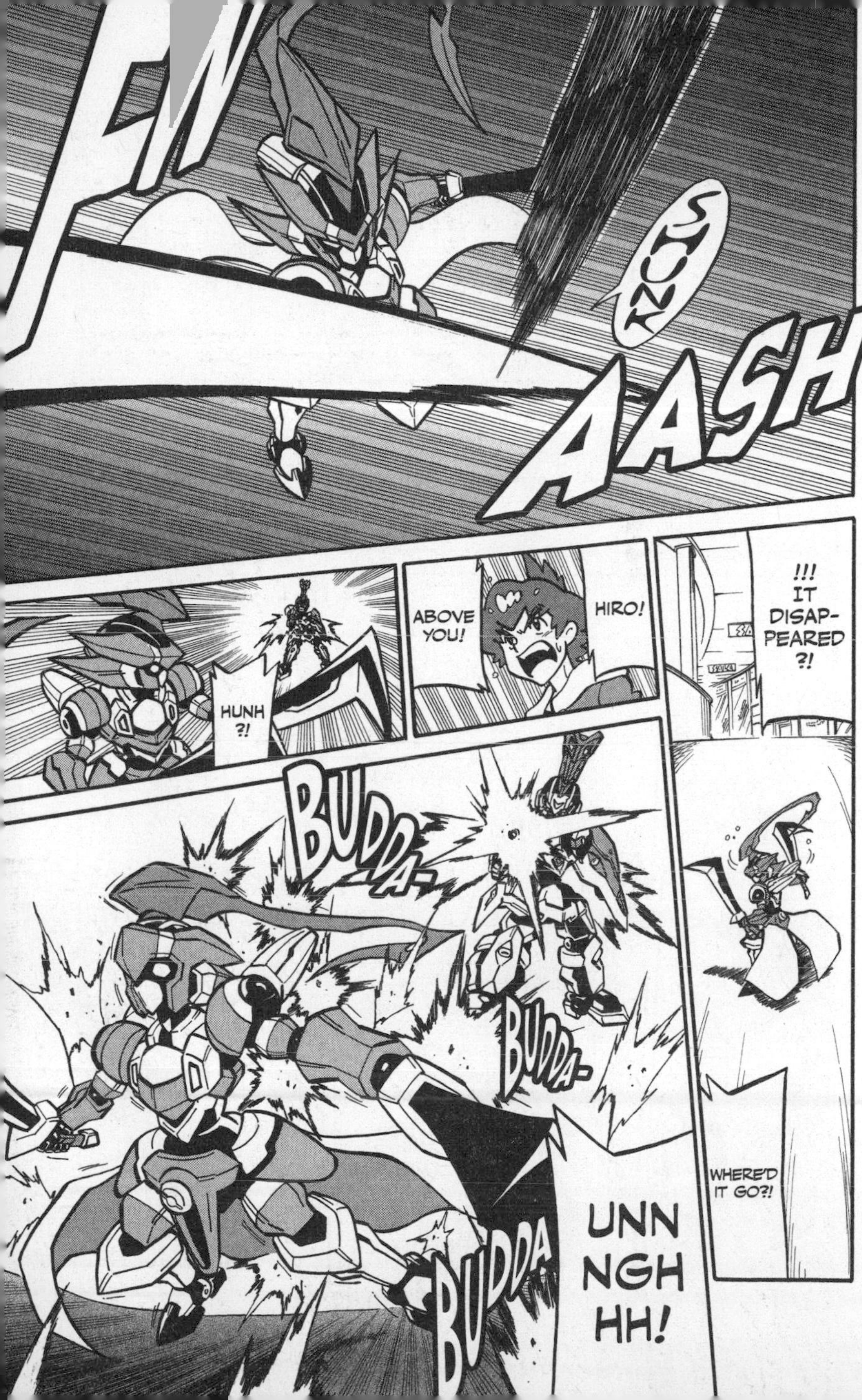
SHUNK
AASH
!!! IT DISAPPEARED?!
HIRO!
ABOVE YOU!
HUNH ?!
WHERE'D IT GO?!
BUDDA-
BUDDA-
UNN NGH HH!
BUDDA

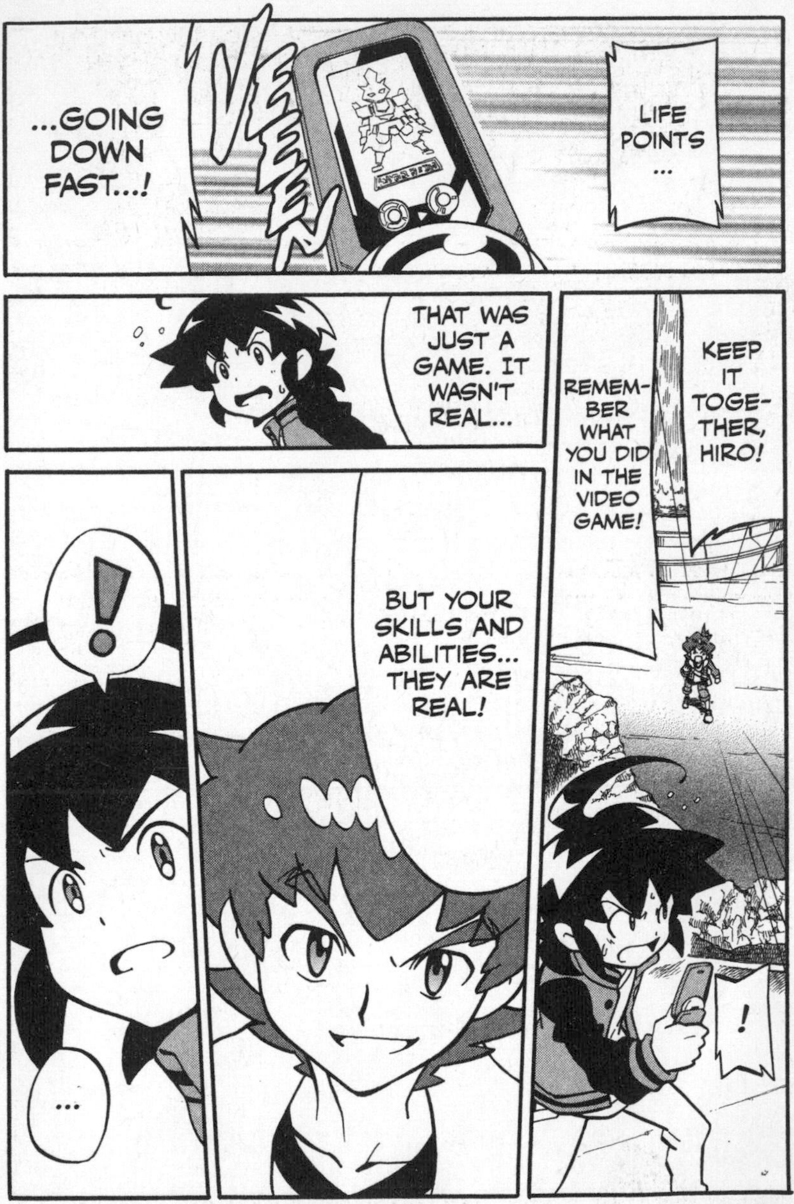
LIFE POINTS ...
...GOING DOWN FAST...!
KEEP IT TOGE-THER, HIRO!
REMEM-BER WHAT YOU DID IN THE VIDEO GAME!
!
THAT WAS JUST A GAME. IT WASN'T REAL...
BUT YOUR SKILLS AND ABILITIES... THEY ARE REAL!
!
...

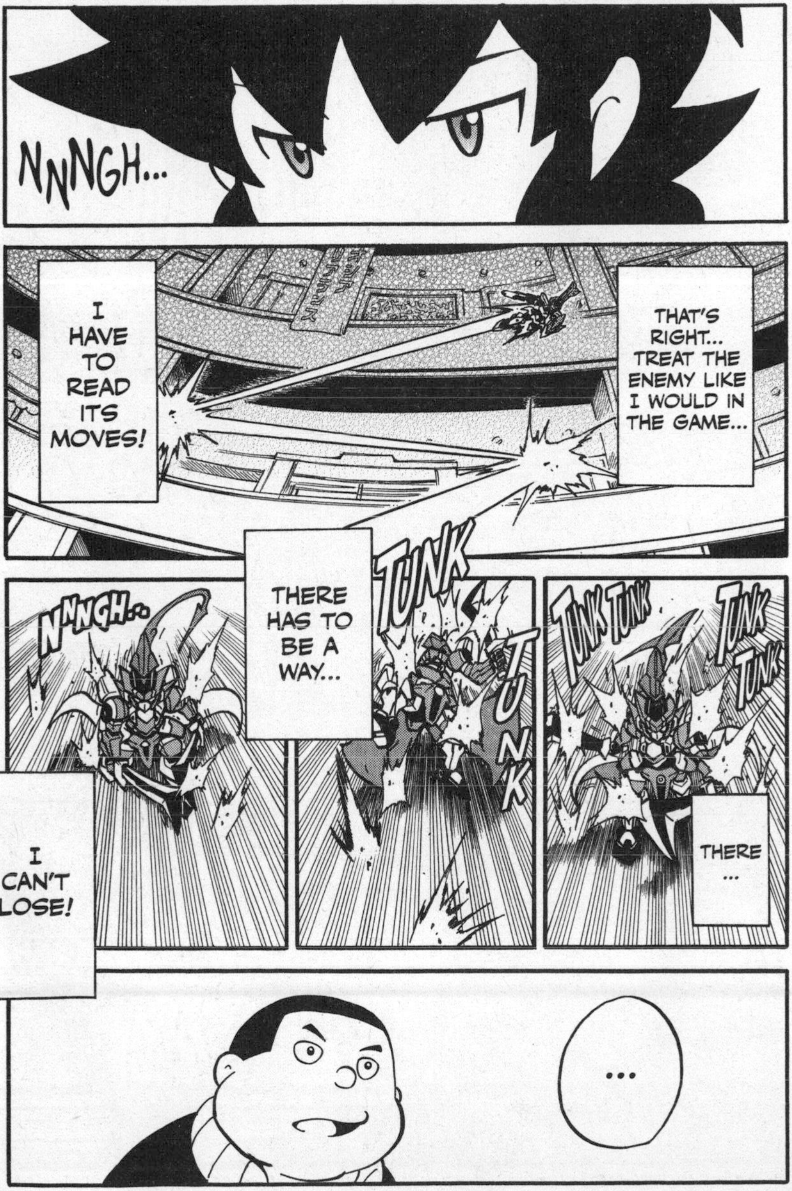
NNNGH...
THAT'S RIGHT... TREAT THE ENEMY LIKE I WOULD IN THE GAME...
I HAVE TO READ ITS MOVES!
TUNK TUNK
TUNK TUNK
THERE...
TUNK
TUNK
THERE HAS TO BE A WAY...
NNNGH..
I CAN'T LOSE!
...

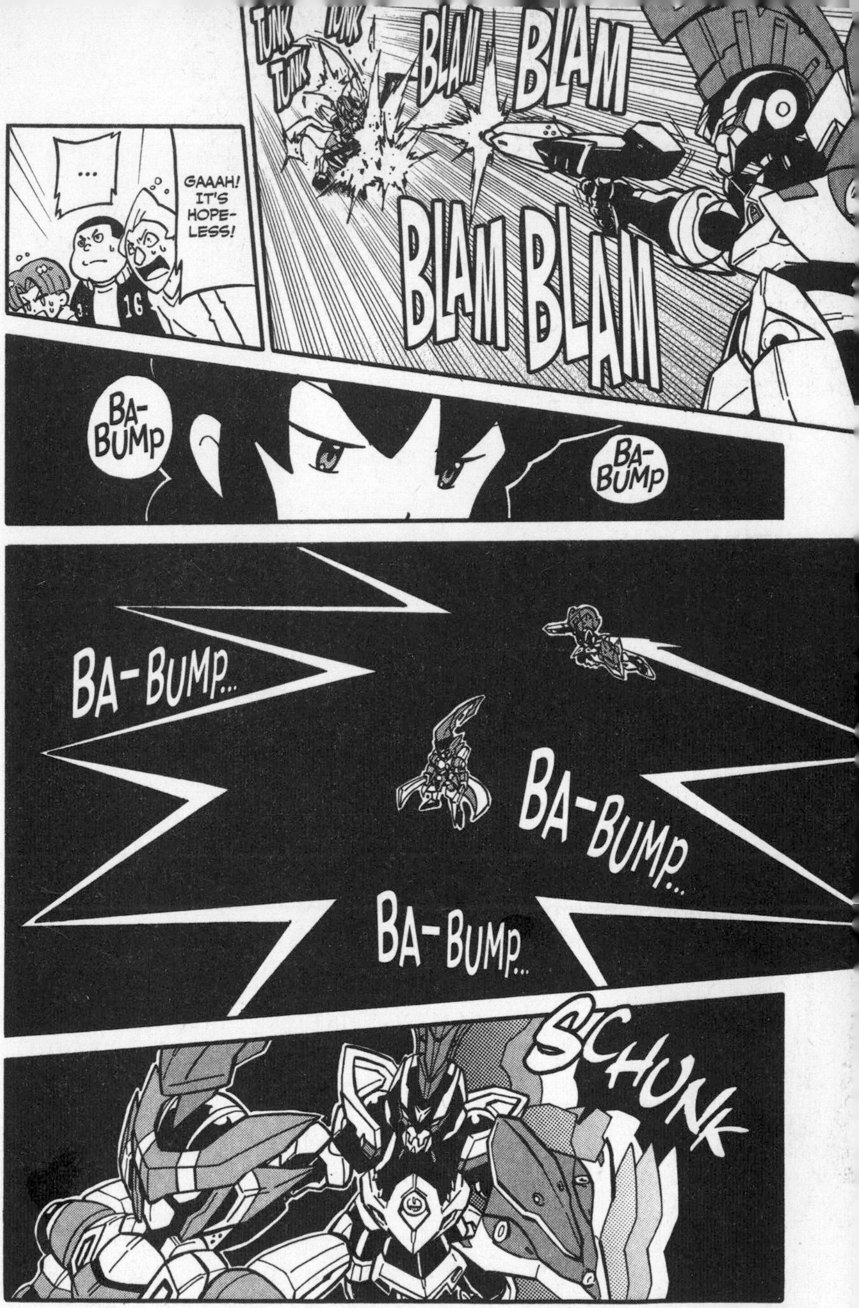
BLAM BLAM
TUNK TUNK TUNK
BLAM BLAM
...
GAAAH! IT'S HOPELESS!
BA-BUMP
BA-BUMP
BA-BUMP...
BA-BUMP...
BA-BUMP...
SCHUNK

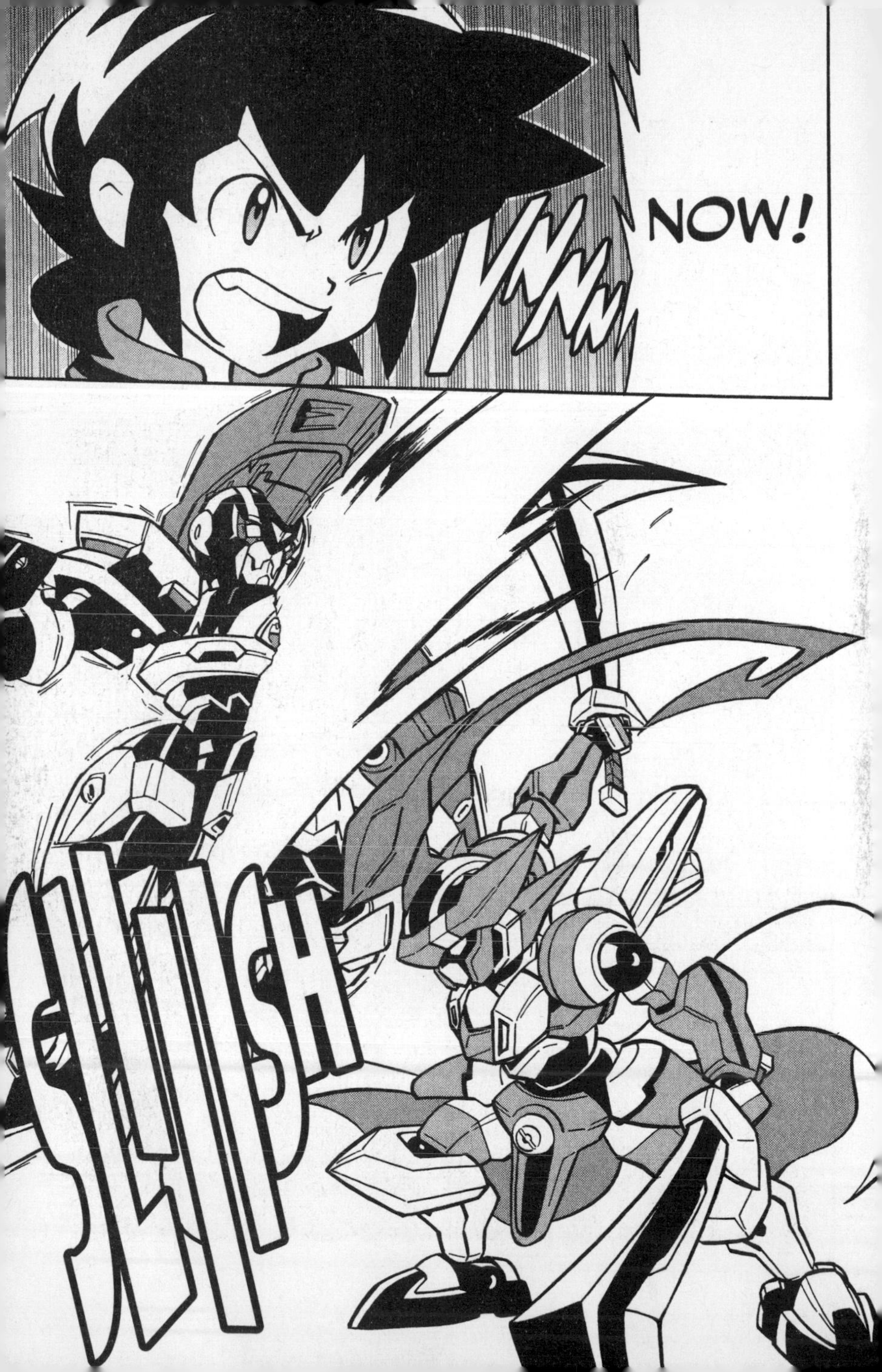
NOW!
SWISH

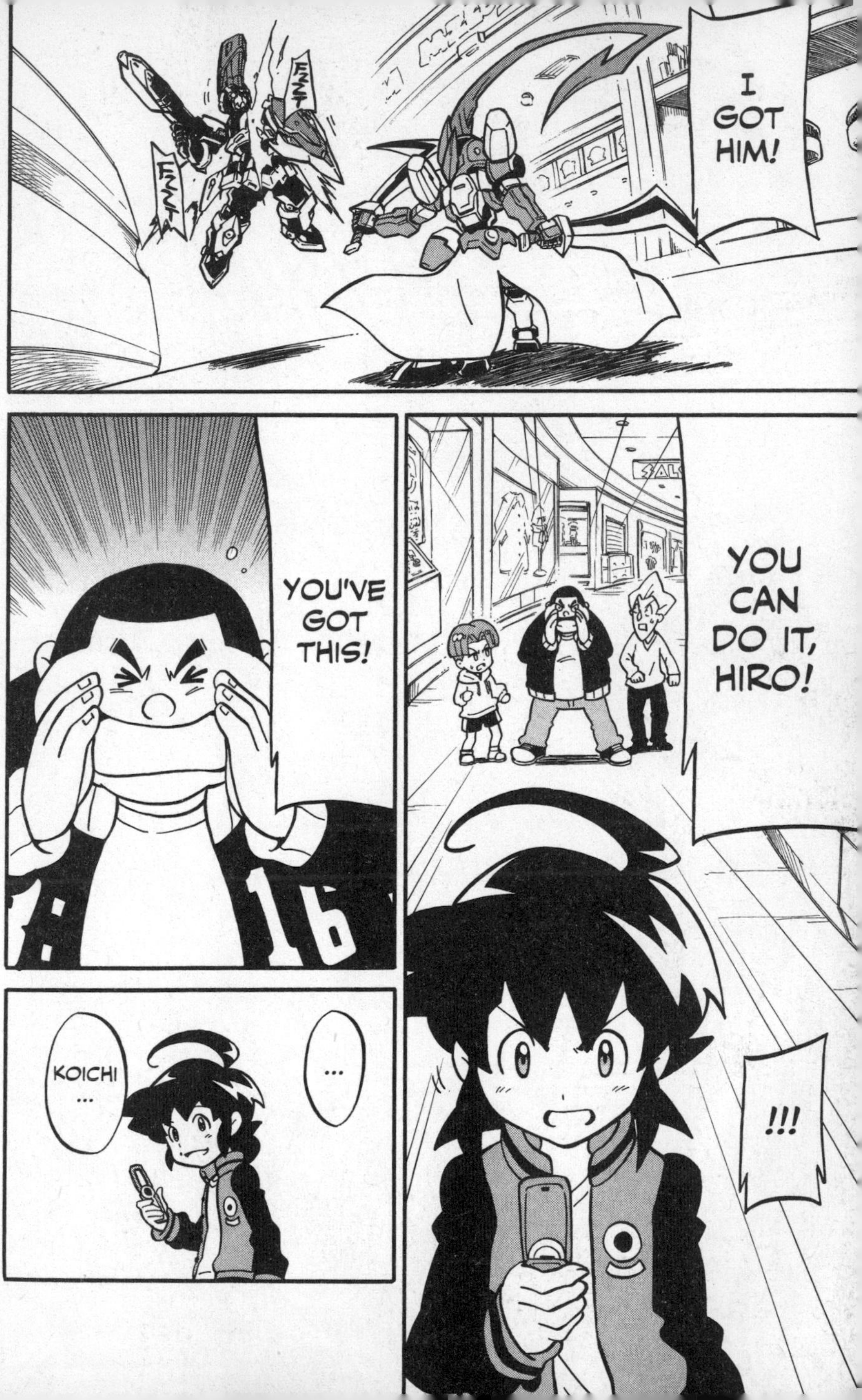
FZZT
FZZT
I GOT HIM!
YOU CAN DO IT, HIRO!
YOU'VE GOT THIS!
!!!
...
KOICHI ...

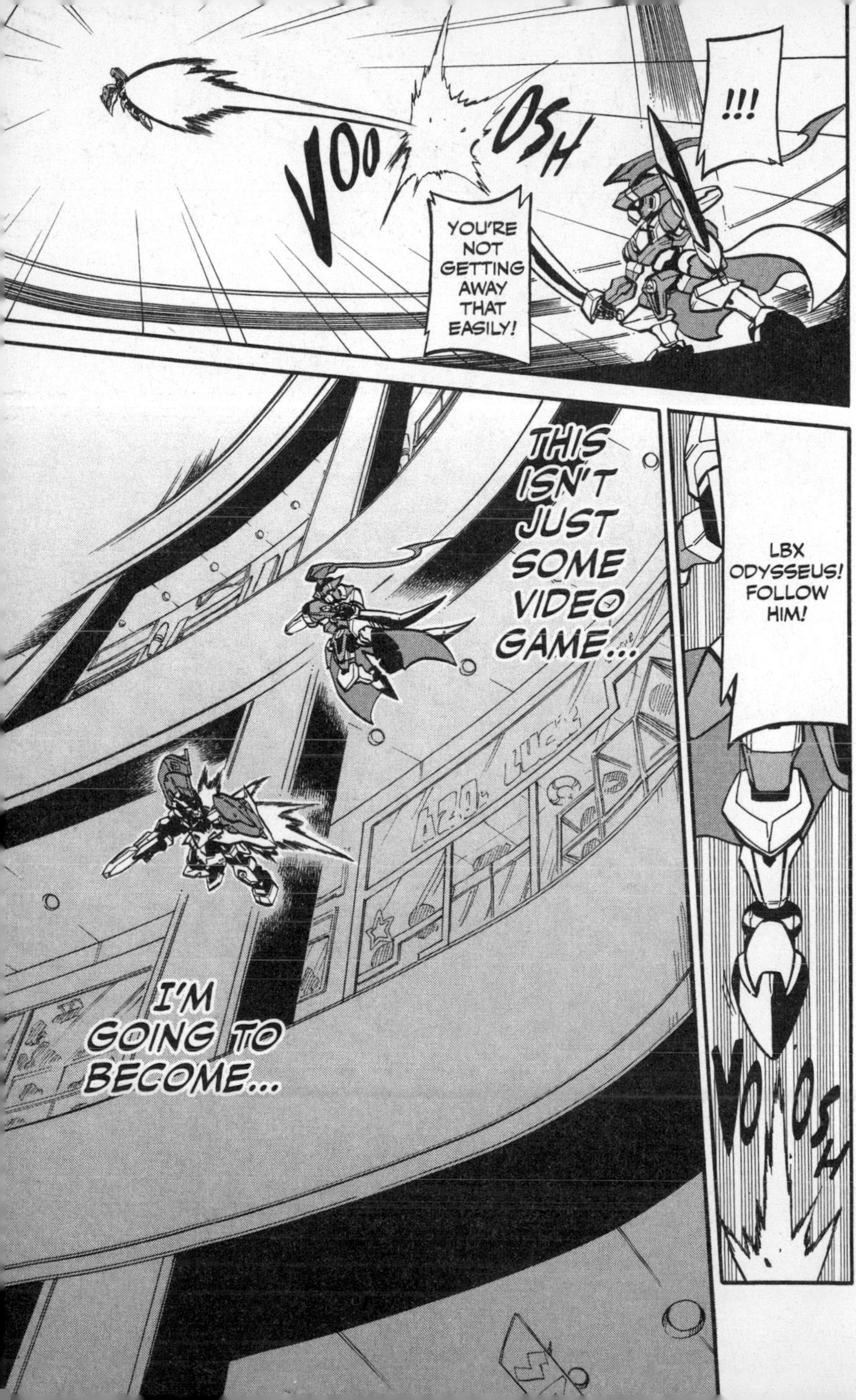
!!!
VOO OSH
YOU'RE NOT GETTING AWAY THAT EASILY!
LBX ODYSSEUS! FOLLOW HIM!
VOOOSH
THIS ISN'T JUST SOME VIDEO GAME...
I'M GOING TO BECOME...

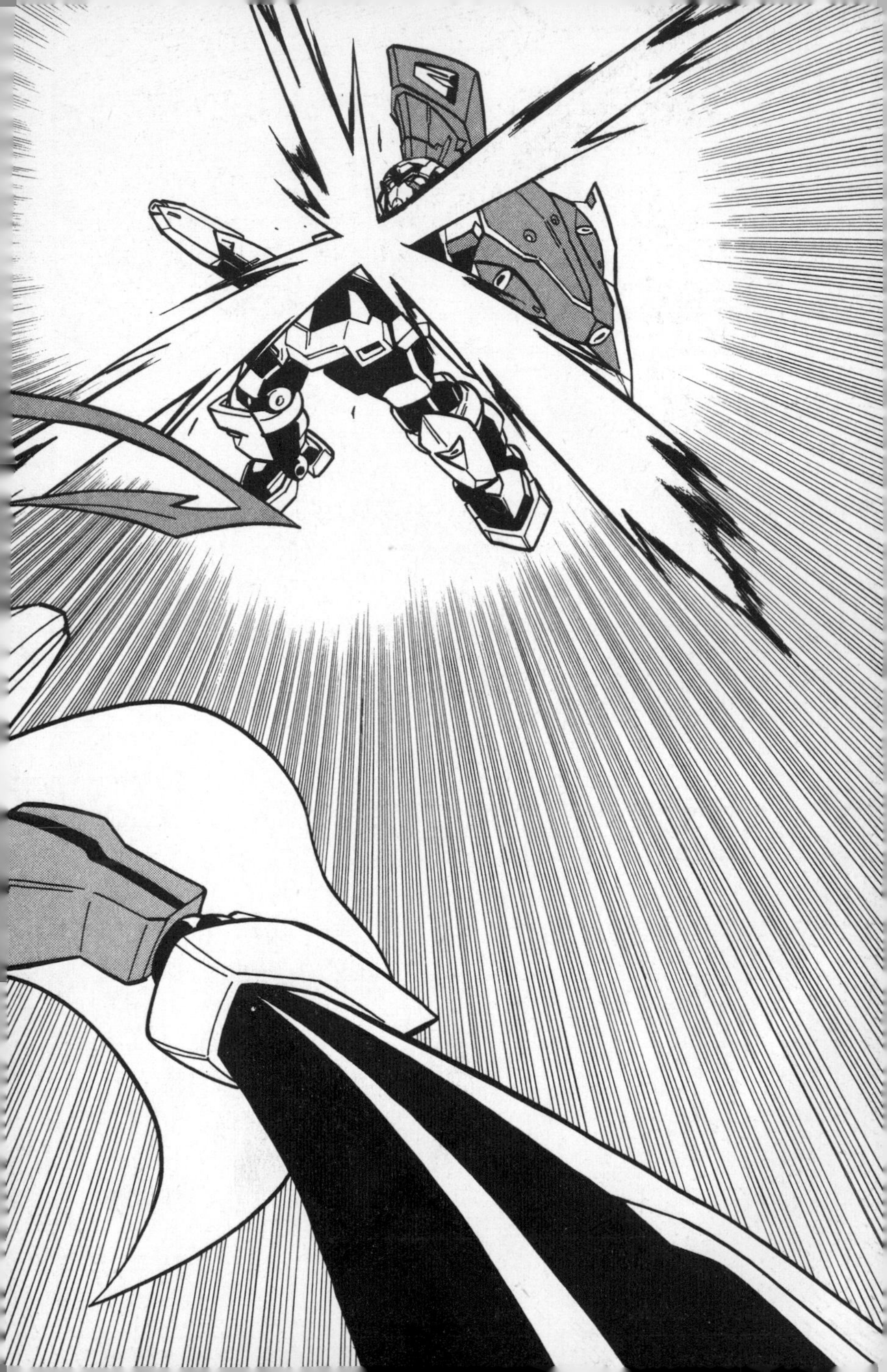

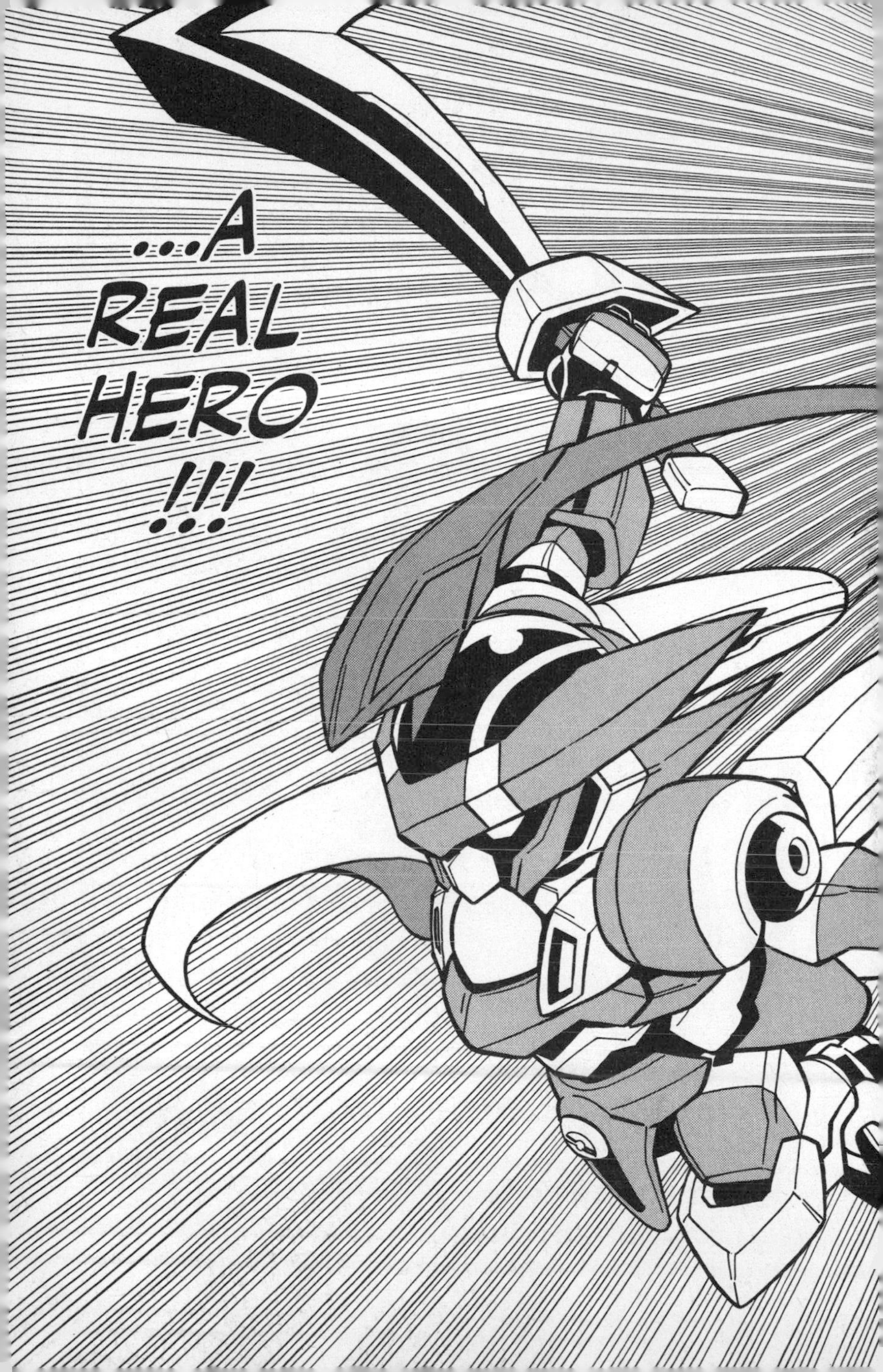
...A REAL HERO !!!

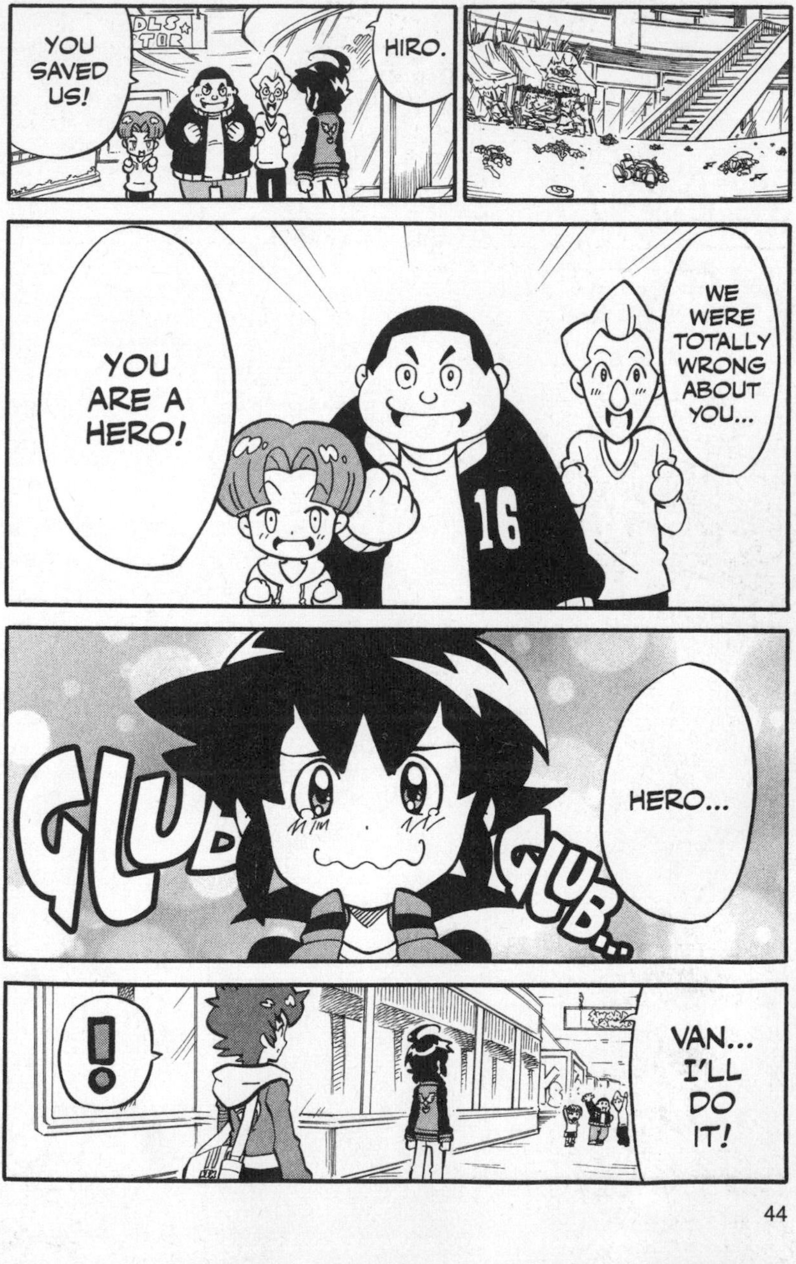
HIRO.
YOU SAVED US!
WE WERE TOTALLY WRONG ABOUT YOU...
YOU ARE A HERO!
HERO...
GLUB...
GLUB
VAN... I'LL DO IT!
!

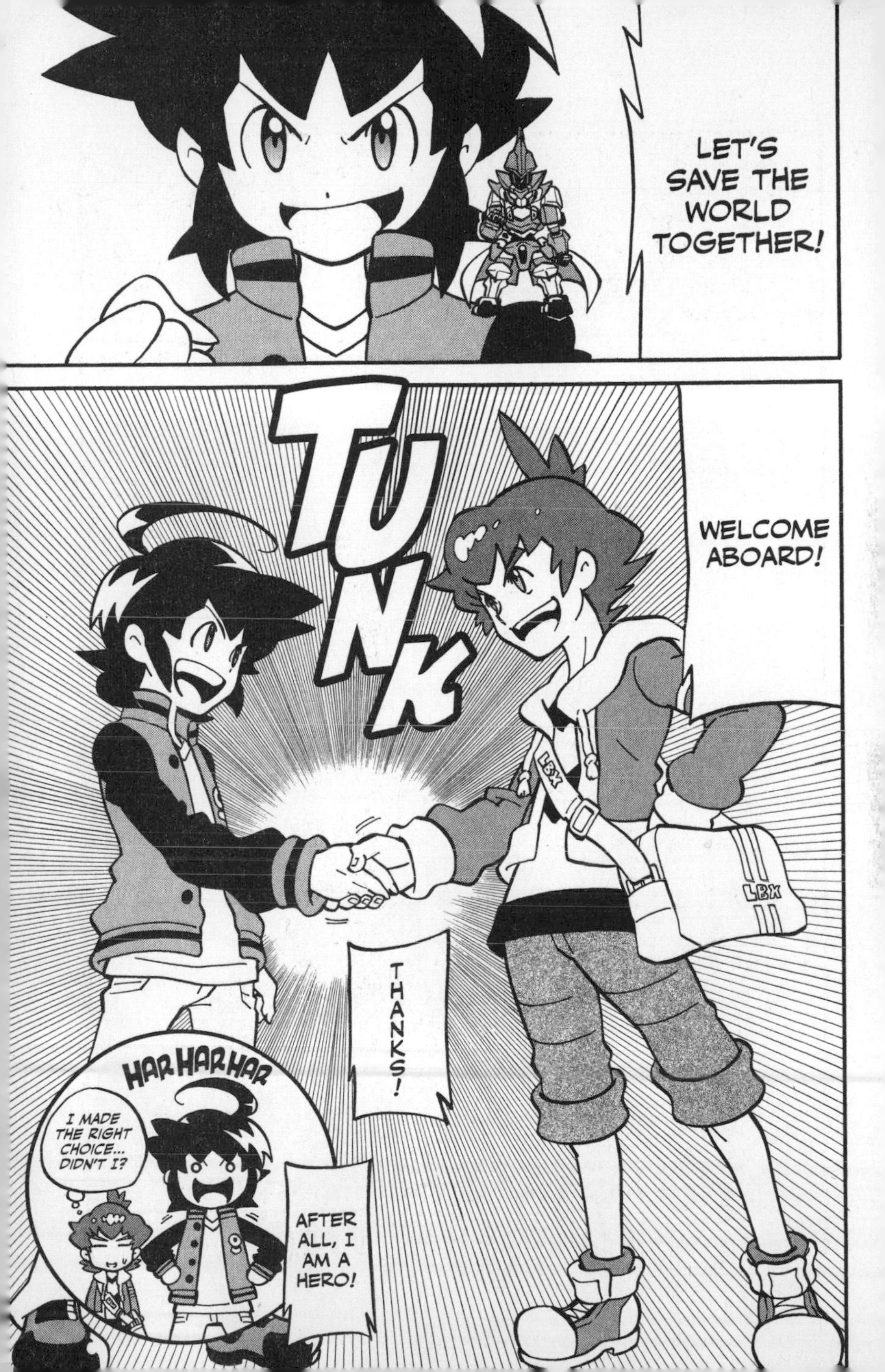
LET'S SAVE THE WORLD TOGETHER!
TUNK
WELCOME ABOARD!
THANKS!
AFTER ALL, I AM A HERO!
HAR HAR HAR
I MADE THE RIGHT CHOICE... DIDN'T I?
LBX
LBX

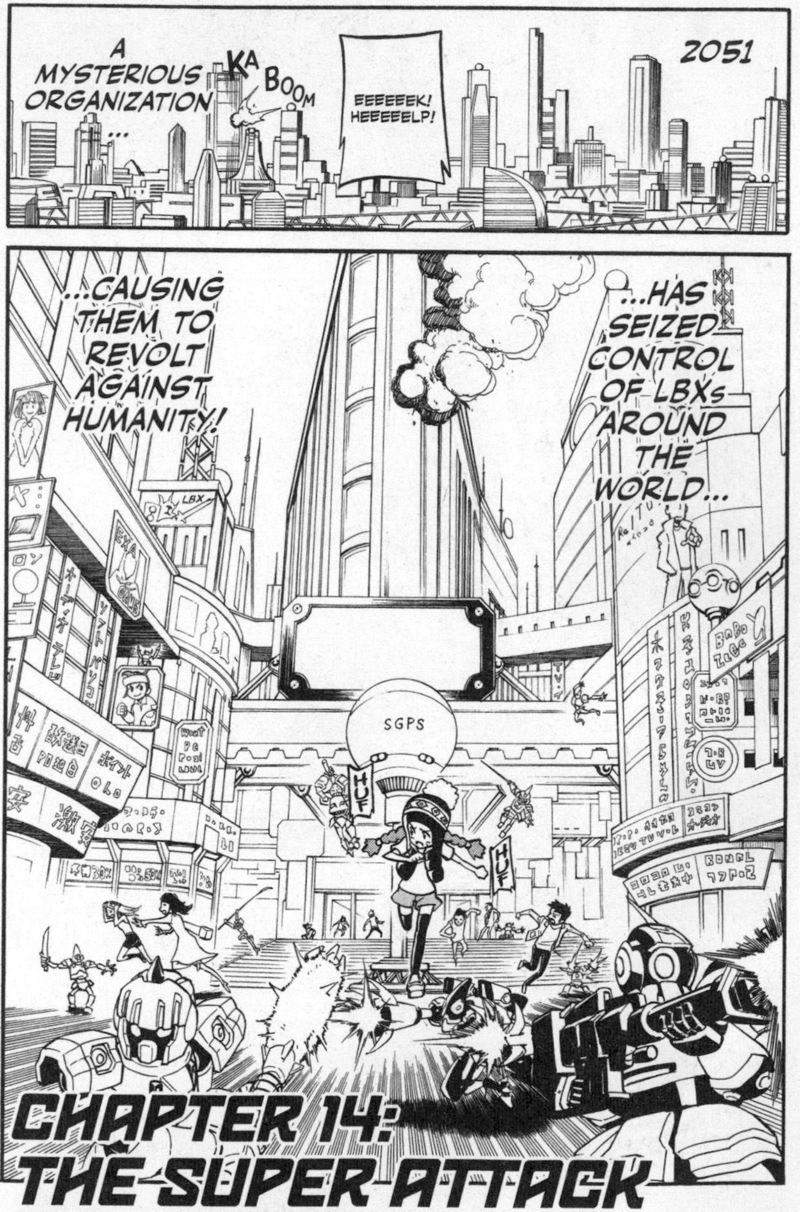
2051
EEEEEEK! HEEEEELP!
KA BOOM
A MYSTERIOUS ORGANIZATION ...
...HAS SEIZED CONTROL OF LBXs AROUND THE WORLD...
...CAUSING THEM TO REVOLT AGAINST HUMANITY!
SGPS
HUF
HUF
LBX

CHAPTER 14: THE SUPER ATTACK ROUTINE!

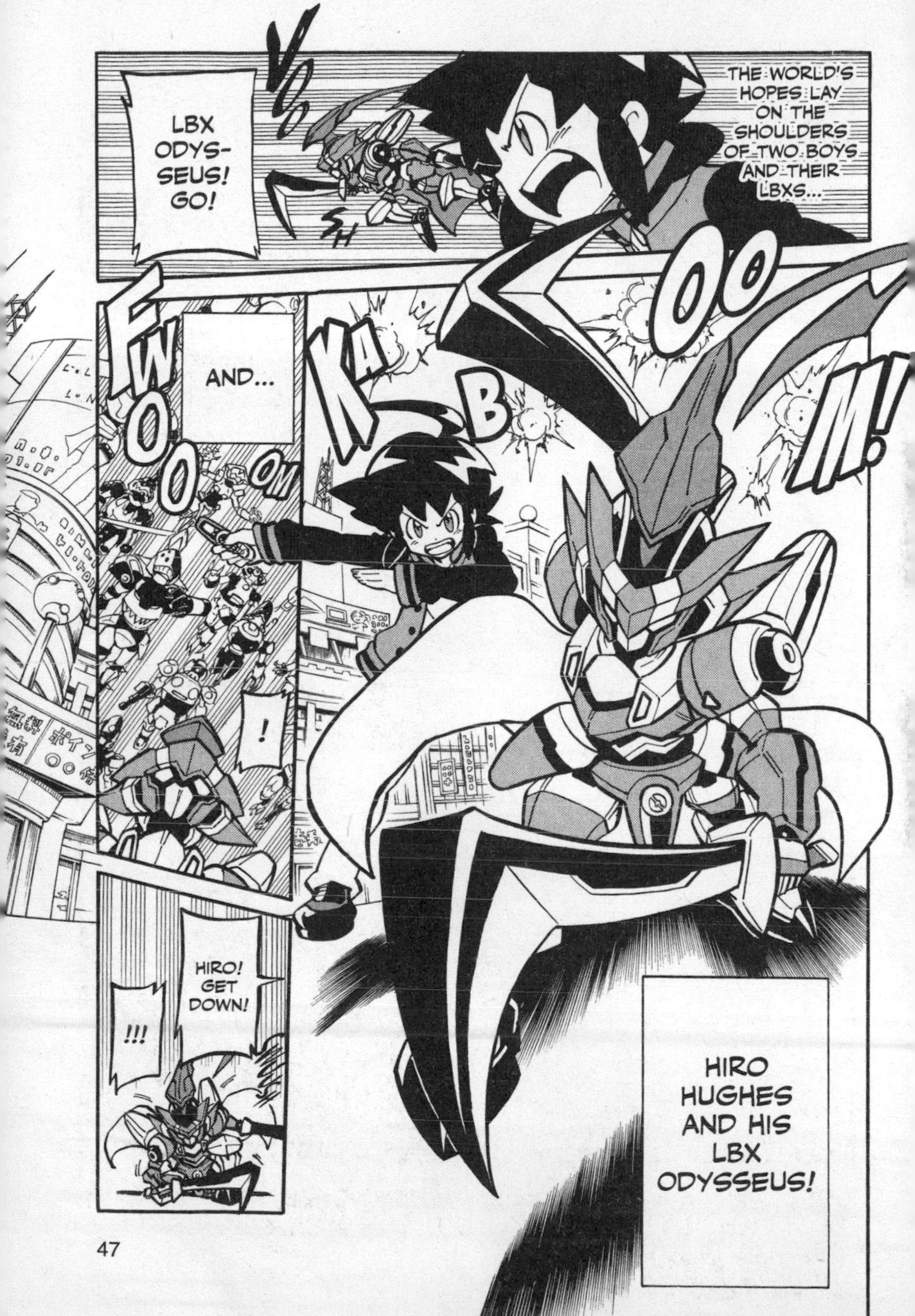
THE WORLD'S HOPES LAY ON THE SHOULDERS OF TWO BOYS AND THEIR LBXS...
VOOO
LBX ODYS-SEUS! GO!
SH
KA-BOOOM!
HIRO HUGHES AND HIS LBX ODYSSEUS!
FWOOOOM
AND...
!
HIRO! GET DOWN!
!!!

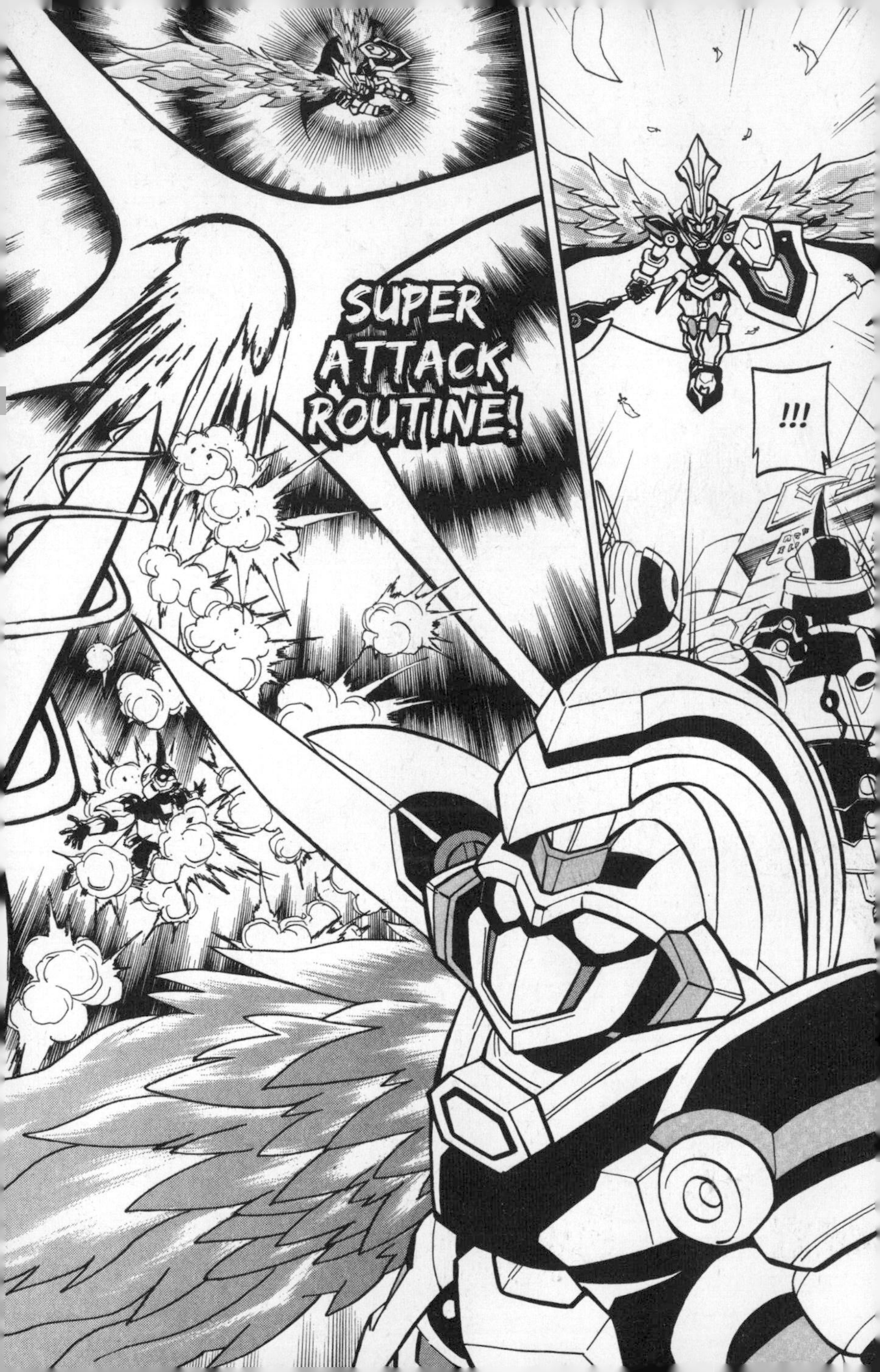
!!!
SUPER ATTACK ROUTINE!

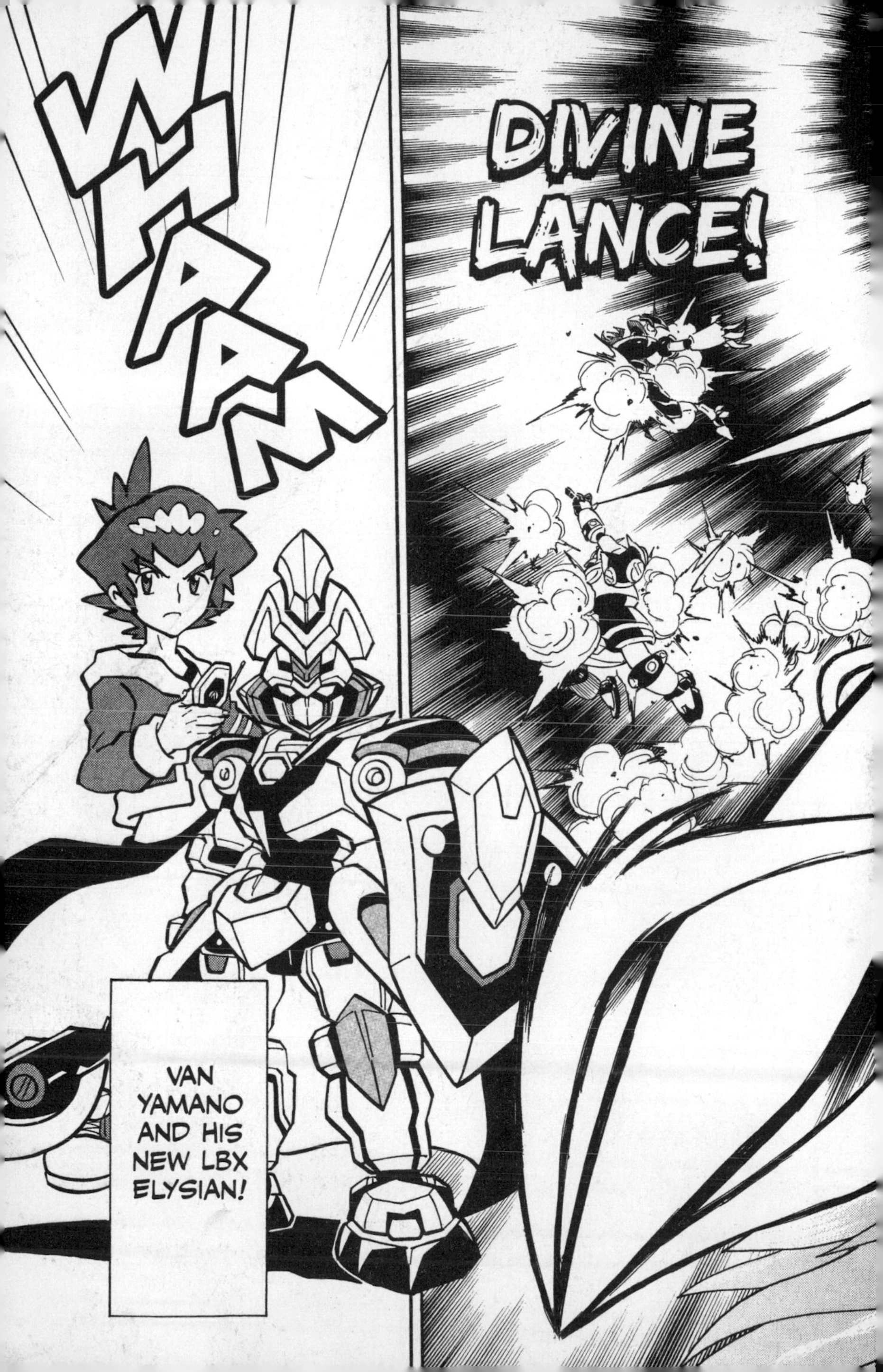
DIVINE LANCE!
WHAM
VAN YAMANO AND HIS NEW LBX ELYSIAN!

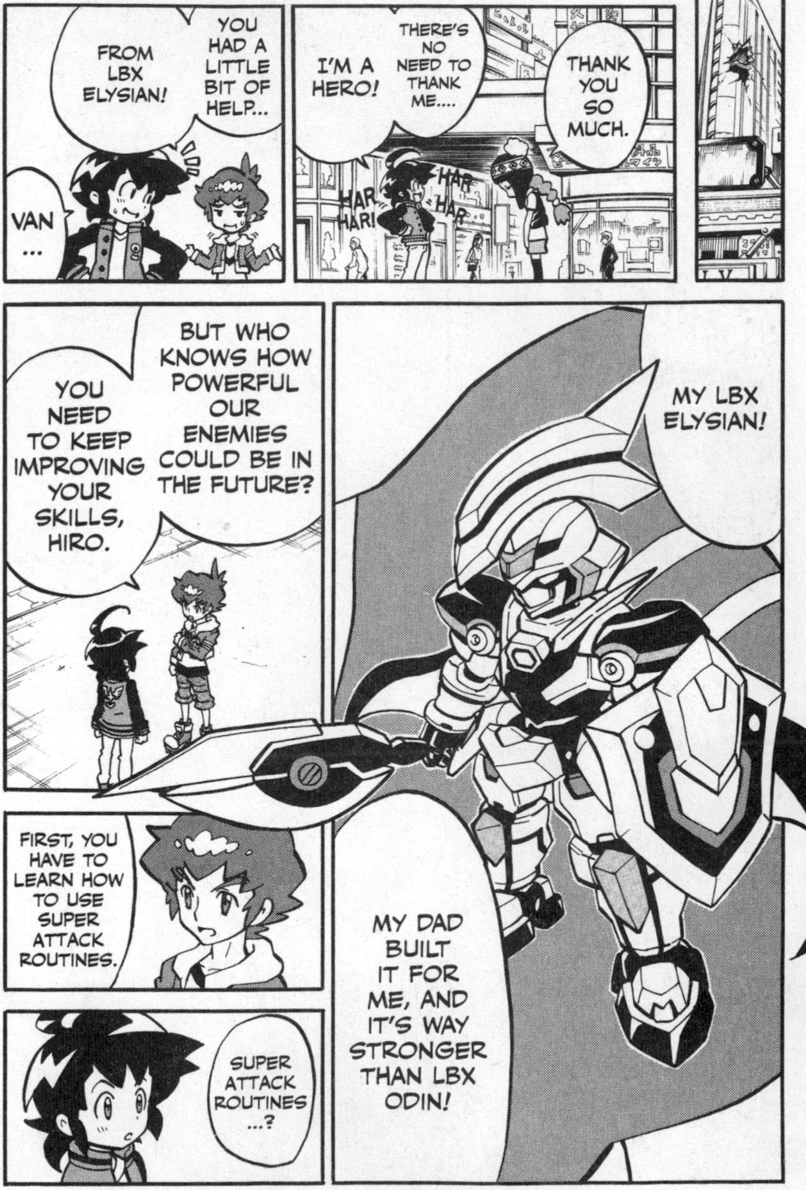
THANK YOU SO MUCH.
THERE'S NO NEED TO THANK ME....
I'M A HERO!
HAR HAR!
HAR HAR
YOU HAD A LITTLE BIT OF HELP...
FROM LBX ELYSIAN!
VAN ...
MY LBX ELYSIAN!
MY DAD BUILT IT FOR ME, AND IT'S WAY STRONGER THAN LBX ODIN!
BUT WHO KNOWS HOW POWERFUL OUR ENEMIES COULD BE IN THE FUTURE?
YOU NEED TO KEEP IMPROVING YOUR SKILLS, HIRO.
FIRST, YOU HAVE TO LEARN HOW TO USE SUPER ATTACK ROUTINES.
SUPER ATTACK ROUTINES ...?

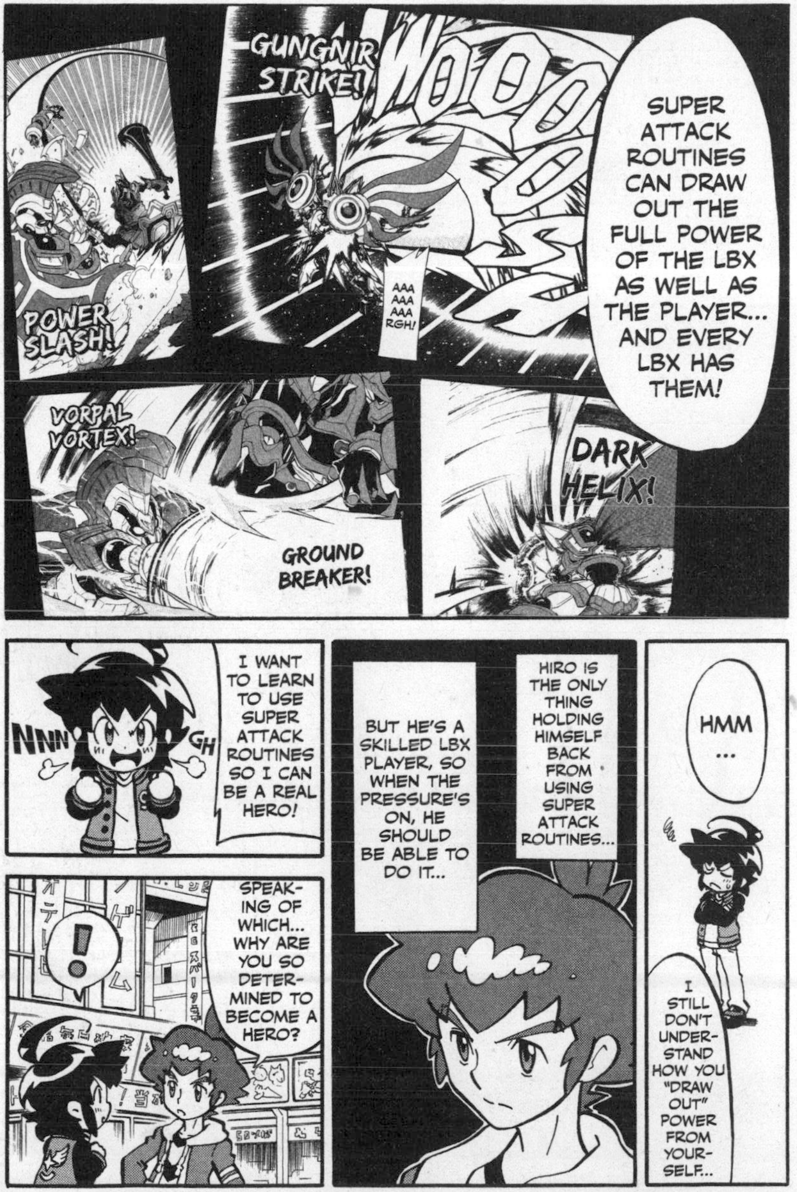
SUPER ATTACK ROUTINES CAN DRAW OUT THE FULL POWER OF THE LBX AS WELL AS THE PLAYER... AND EVERY LBX HAS THEM!
GUNGNIR STRIKE!
AAA AAA AAA RGH!
POWER SLASH!
DARK HELIX!
VORPAL VORTEX!
GROUND BREAKER!
HMM ...
I STILL DON'T UNDER-STAND HOW YOU "DRAW OUT" POWER FROM YOUR-SELF...
HIRO IS THE ONLY THING HOLDING HIMSELF BACK FROM USING SUPER ATTACK ROUTINES...
BUT HE'S A SKILLED LBX PLAYER, SO WHEN THE PRESSURE'S ON, HE SHOULD BE ABLE TO DO IT...
I WANT TO LEARN TO USE SUPER ATTACK ROUTINES SO I CAN BE A REAL HERO!
NNN GH
!
SPEAK-ING OF WHICH... WHY ARE YOU SO DETER-MINED TO BECOME A HERO?

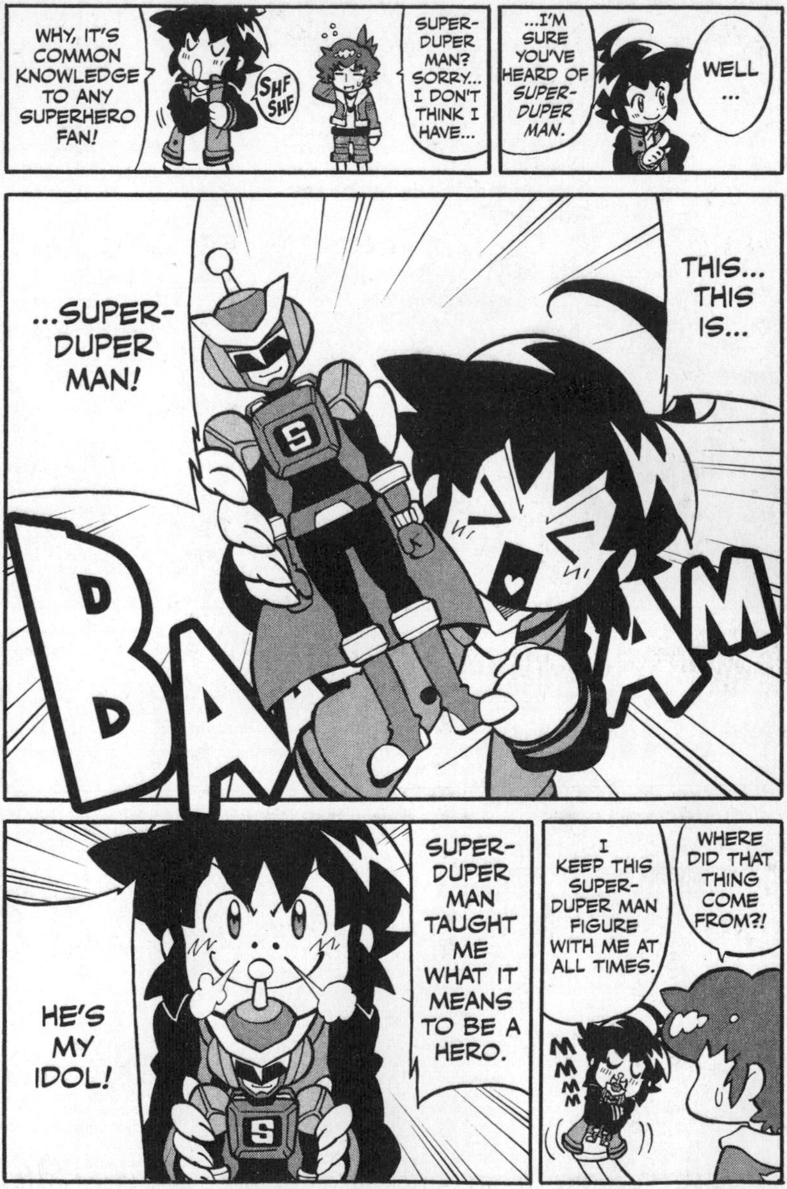
WELL ...
...I'M SURE YOU'VE HEARD OF SUPER-DUPER MAN.
SUPER-DUPER MAN? SORRY... I DON'T THINK I HAVE...
SHF SHF
WHY, IT'S COMMON KNOWLEDGE TO ANY SUPERHERO FAN!
THIS... THIS IS...
...SUPER-DUPER MAN!
BAM
WHERE DID THAT THING COME FROM?!
I KEEP THIS SUPER-DUPER MAN FIGURE WITH ME AT ALL TIMES.
MMMM
SUPER-DUPER MAN TAUGHT ME WHAT IT MEANS TO BE A HERO.
HE'S MY IDOL!

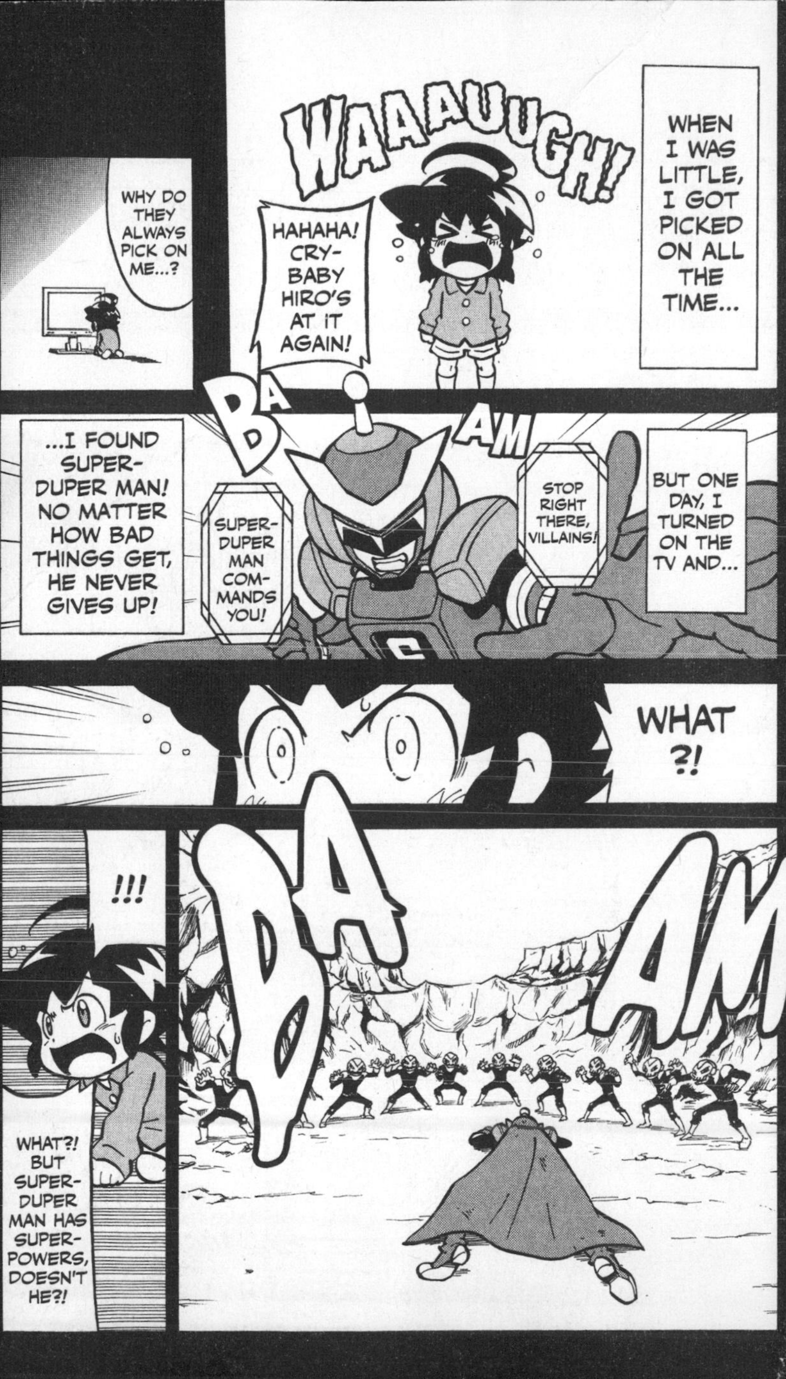
WHEN I WAS LITTLE, I GOT PICKED ON ALL THE TIME...
WAAAUUGH!
HAHAHA! CRY-BABY HIRO'S AT IT AGAIN!
WHY DO THEY ALWAYS PICK ON ME...?
BUT ONE DAY, I TURNED ON THE TV AND...
BAAM
STOP RIGHT THERE, VILLAINS!
SUPER-DUPER MAN COMMANDS YOU!
...I FOUND SUPER-DUPER MAN! NO MATTER HOW BAD THINGS GET, HE NEVER GIVES UP!
WHAT ?!
BAAM
!!!
WHAT?! BUT SUPER-DUPER MAN HAS SUPER-POWERS, DOESN'T HE?!

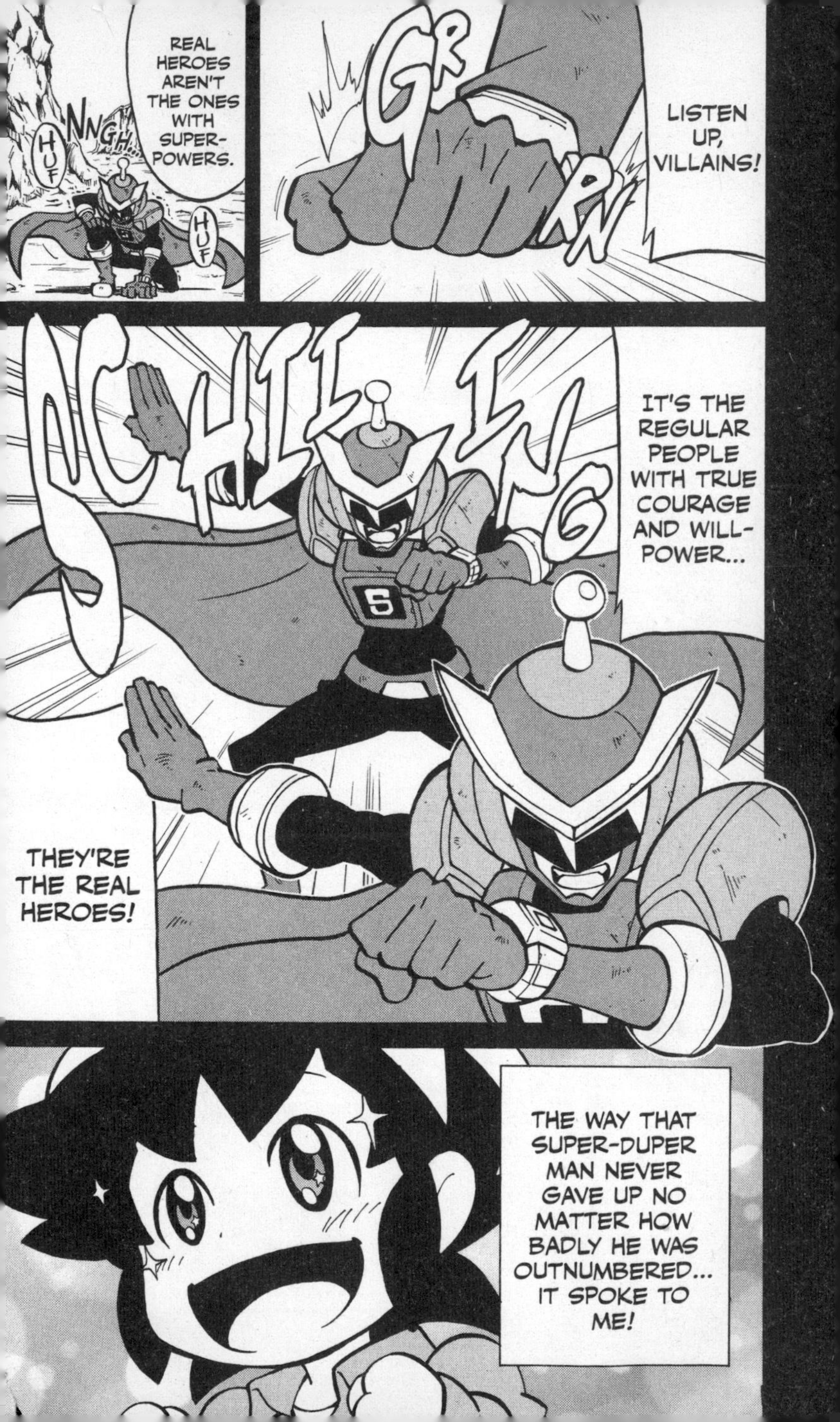

LISTEN UP, VILLAINS!
GRRN
REAL HEROES AREN'T THE ONES WITH SUPER-POWERS.
NNGH...
HUF
HUF
SCHIIING
IT'S THE REGULAR PEOPLE WITH TRUE COURAGE AND WILL-POWER...
THEY'RE THE REAL HEROES!
THE WAY THAT SUPER-DUPER MAN NEVER GAVE UP NO MATTER HOW BADLY HE WAS OUTNUMBERED... IT SPOKE TO ME!

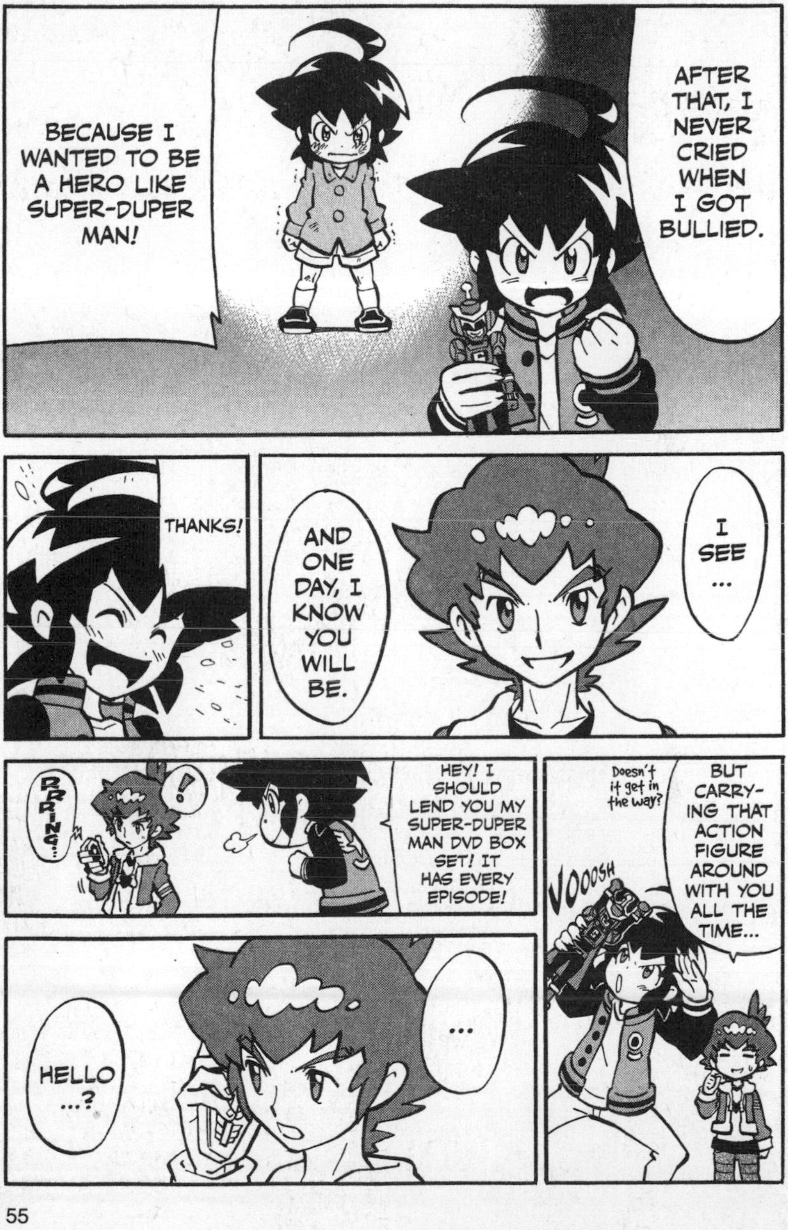
AFTER THAT, I NEVER CRIED WHEN I GOT BULLIED.
BECAUSE I WANTED TO BE A HERO LIKE SUPER-DUPER MAN!
I SEE ...
AND ONE DAY, I KNOW YOU WILL BE.
THANKS!
BUT CARRYING THAT ACTION FIGURE AROUND WITH YOU ALL THE TIME...
Doesn't it get in the way?
VOOOSH
HEY! I SHOULD LEND YOU MY SUPER-DUPER MAN DVD BOX SET! IT HAS EVERY EPISODE!
!
RRRING...
...
HELLO ...?

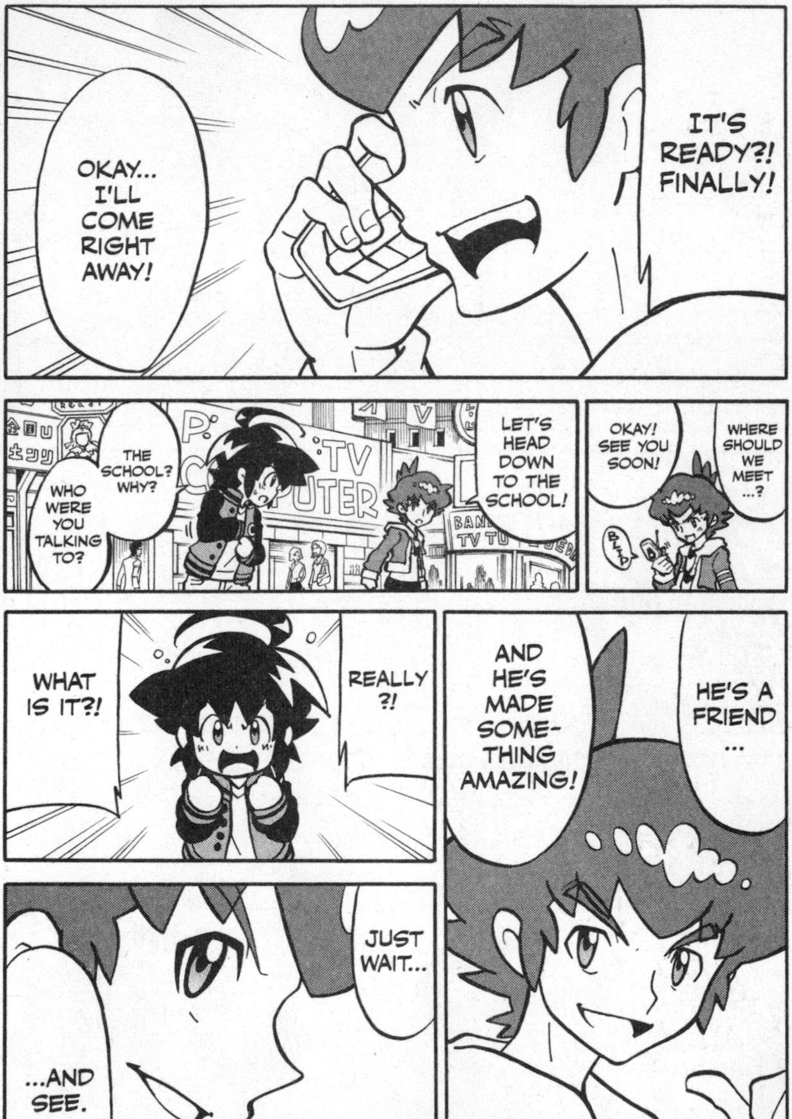
IT'S READY?! FINALLY!
OKAY... I'LL COME RIGHT AWAY!
WHERE SHOULD WE MEET ...?
OKAY! SEE YOU SOON!
LET'S HEAD DOWN TO THE SCHOOL!
THE SCHOOL? WHY?
WHO WERE YOU TALKING TO?
HE'S A FRIEND ...
AND HE'S MADE SOME-THING AMAZING!
REALLY ?!
WHAT IS IT?!
JUST WAIT...
...AND SEE.

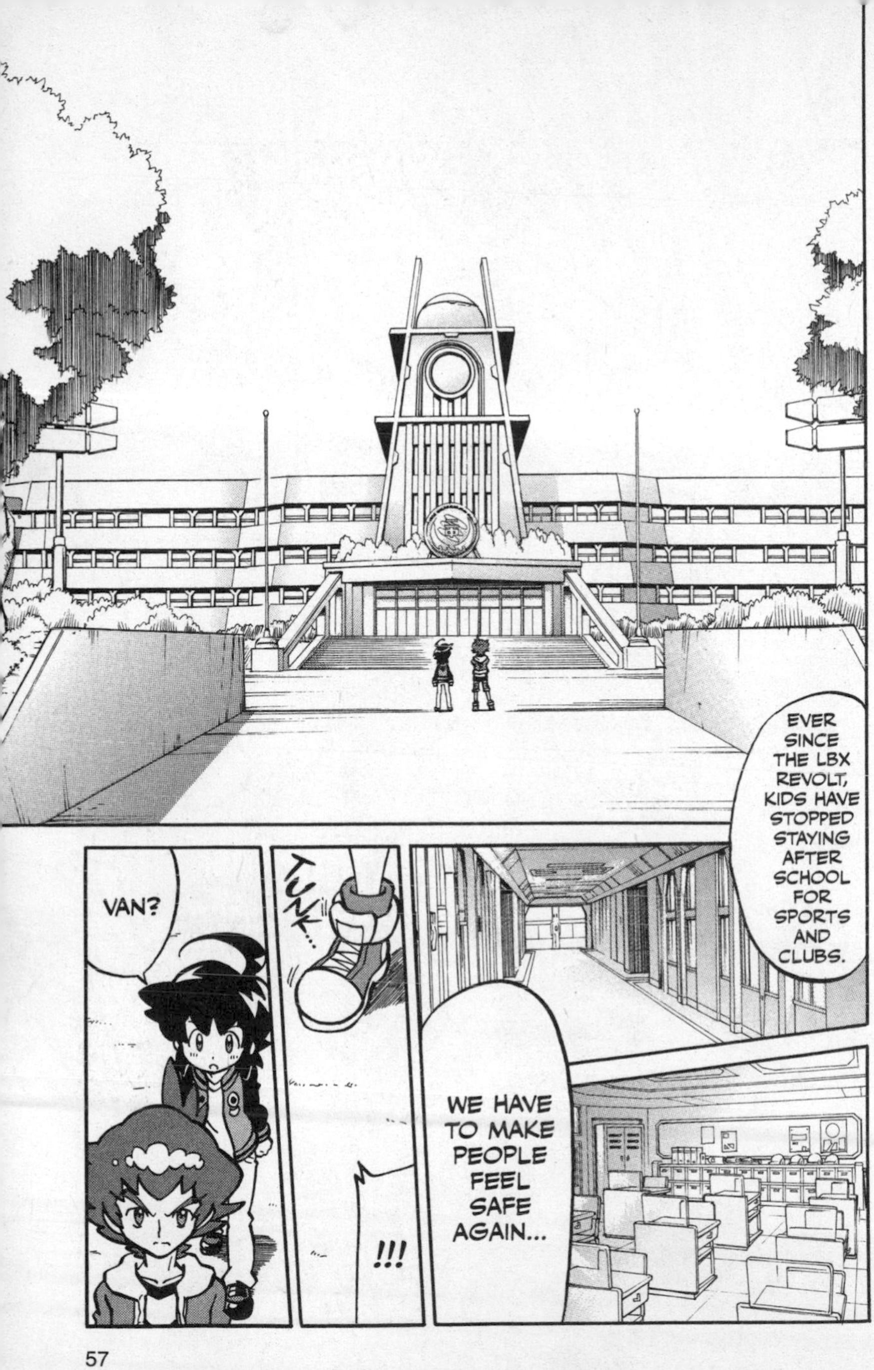
EVER SINCE THE LBX REVOLT, KIDS HAVE STOPPED STAYING AFTER SCHOOL FOR SPORTS AND CLUBS.
WE HAVE TO MAKE PEOPLE FEEL SAFE AGAIN...
TUNK...
!!!
VAN?

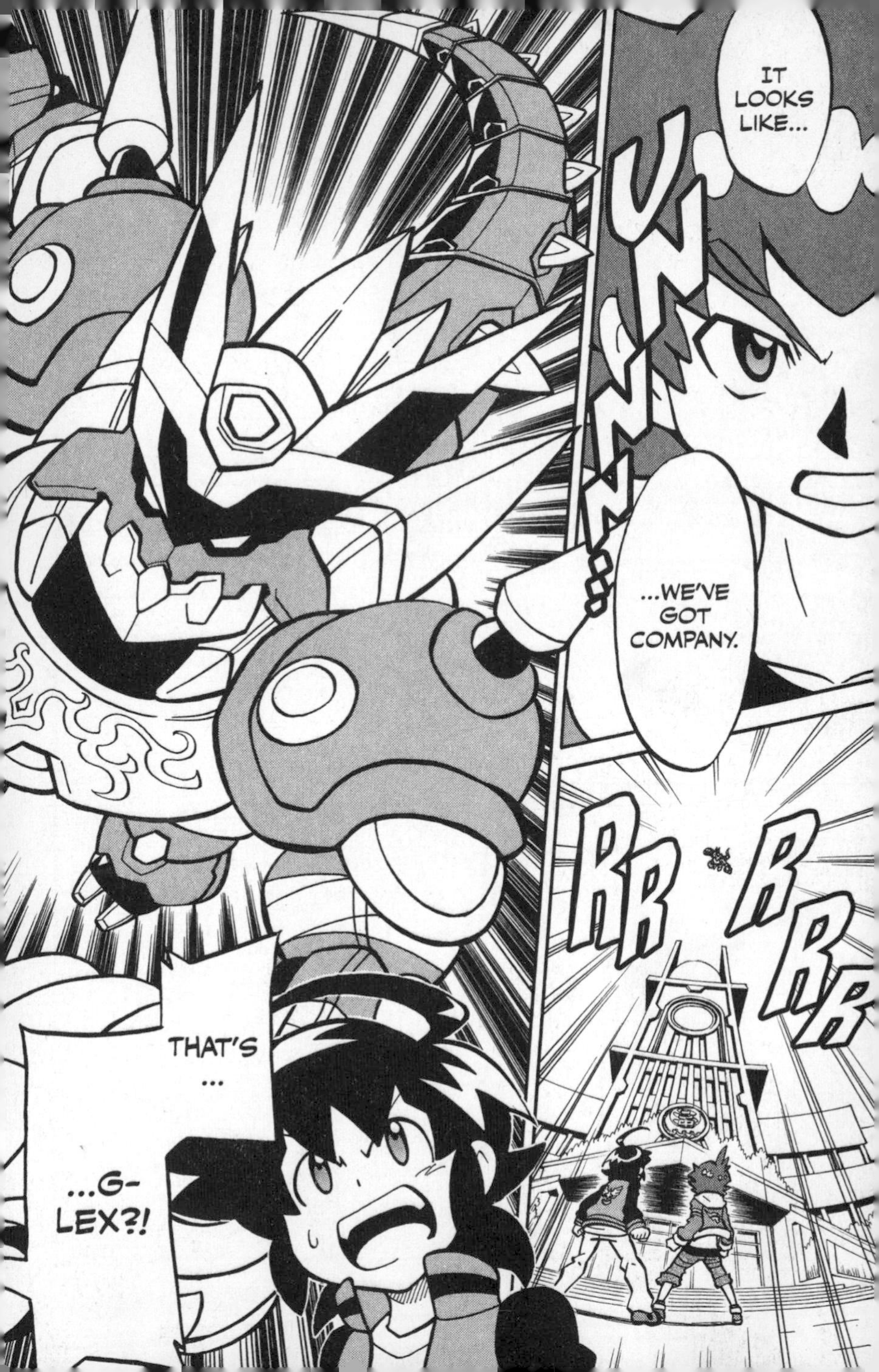
IT LOOKS LIKE...
...WE'VE GOT COMPANY.
RR RRRR
THAT'S ...
...G-LEX?!

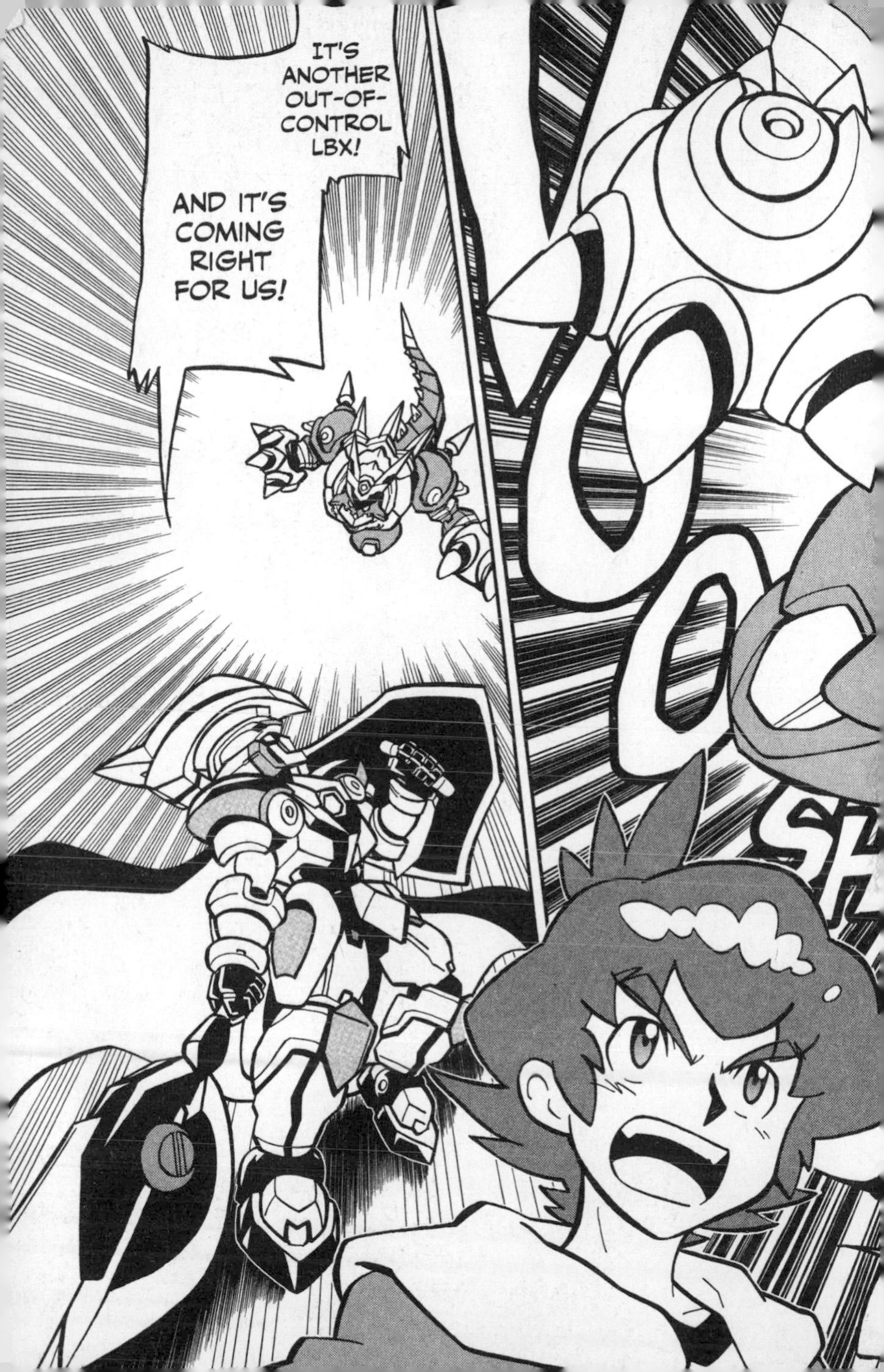
IT'S ANOTHER OUT-OF-CONTROL LBX!
AND IT'S COMING RIGHT FOR US!

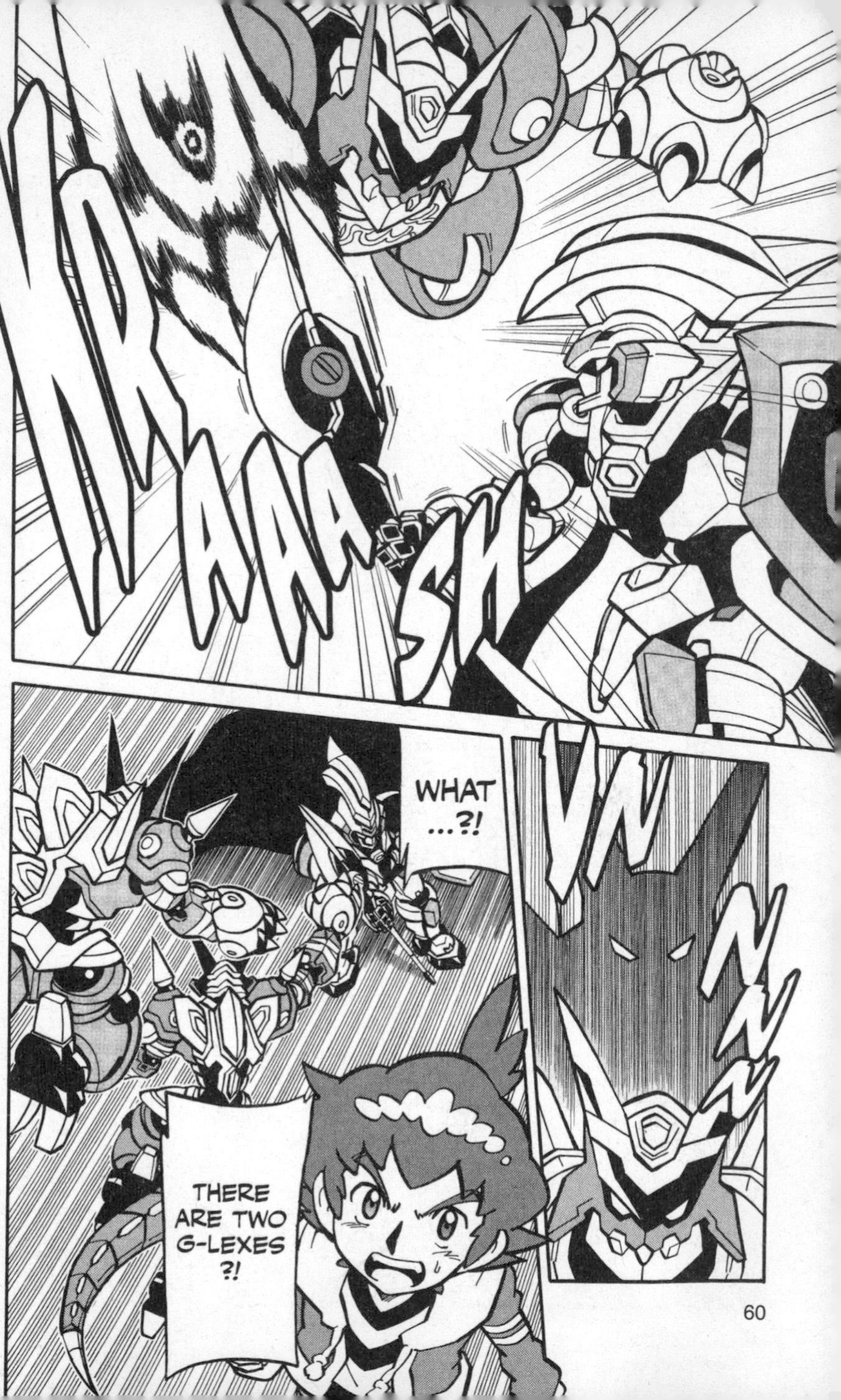
KRAAASH
WHAT ...?!
THERE ARE TWO G-LEXES ?!

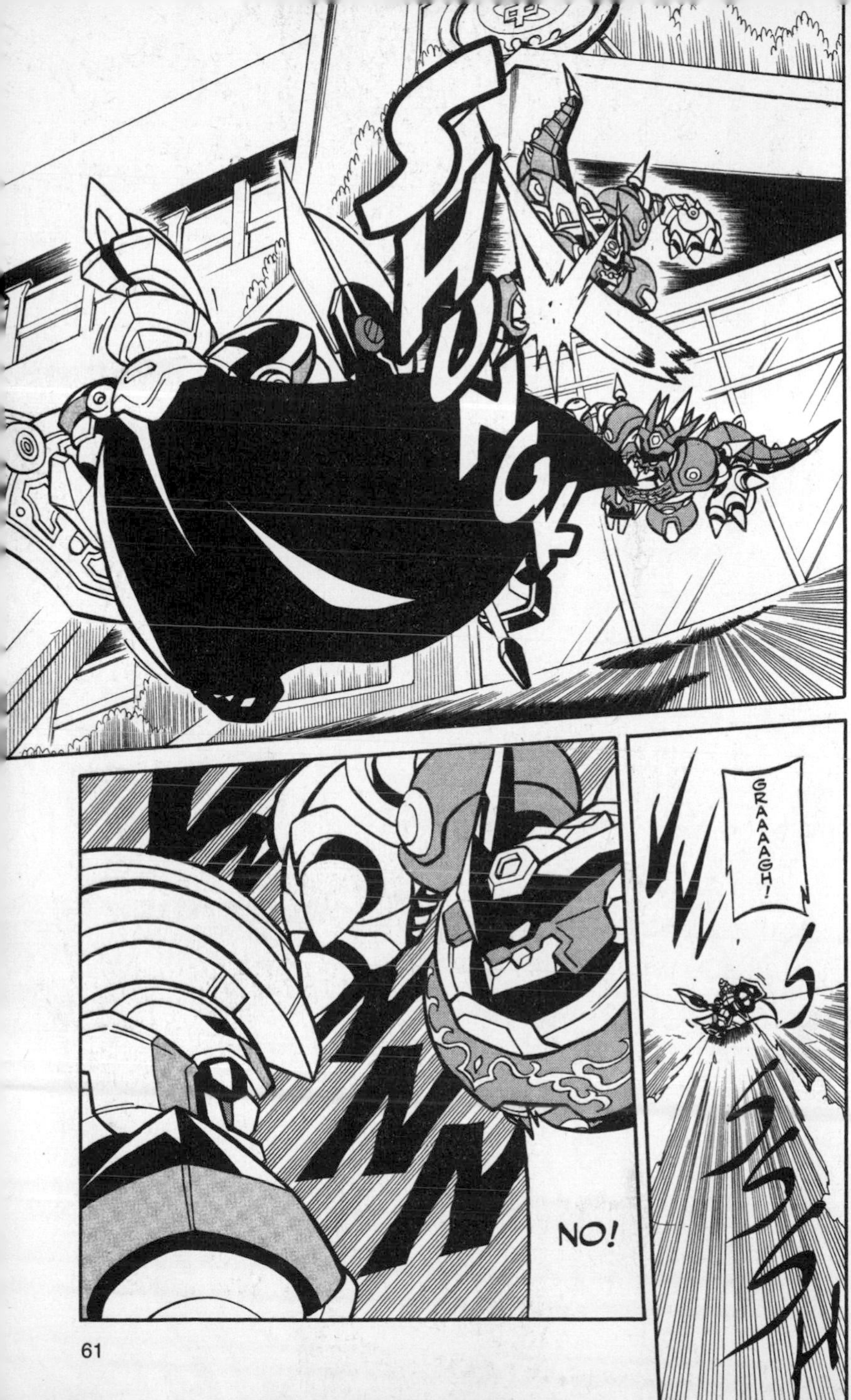
SHOCK
GRAAAAGH!
NO!

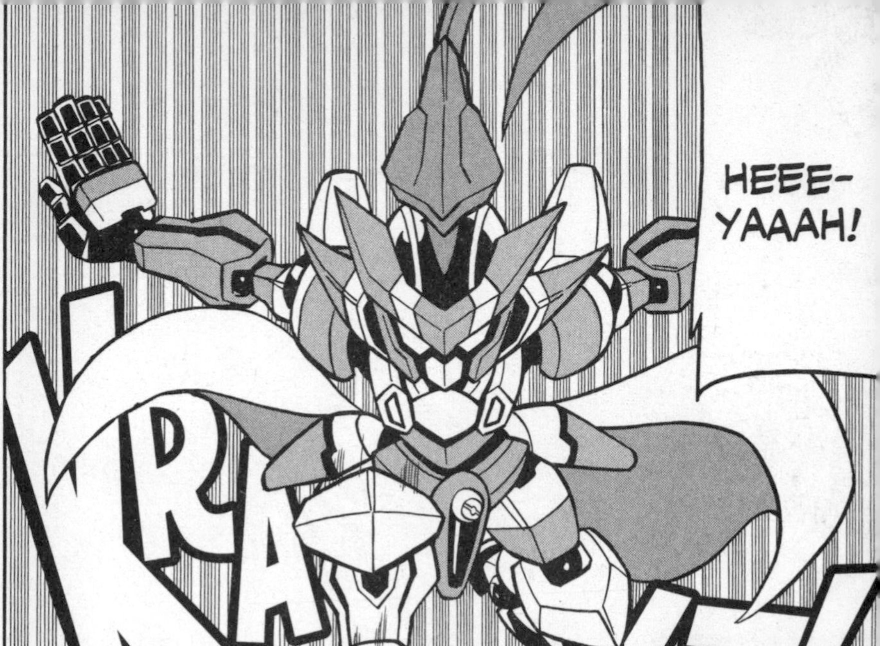
HEEEE-YAAAH!
KRAKT!
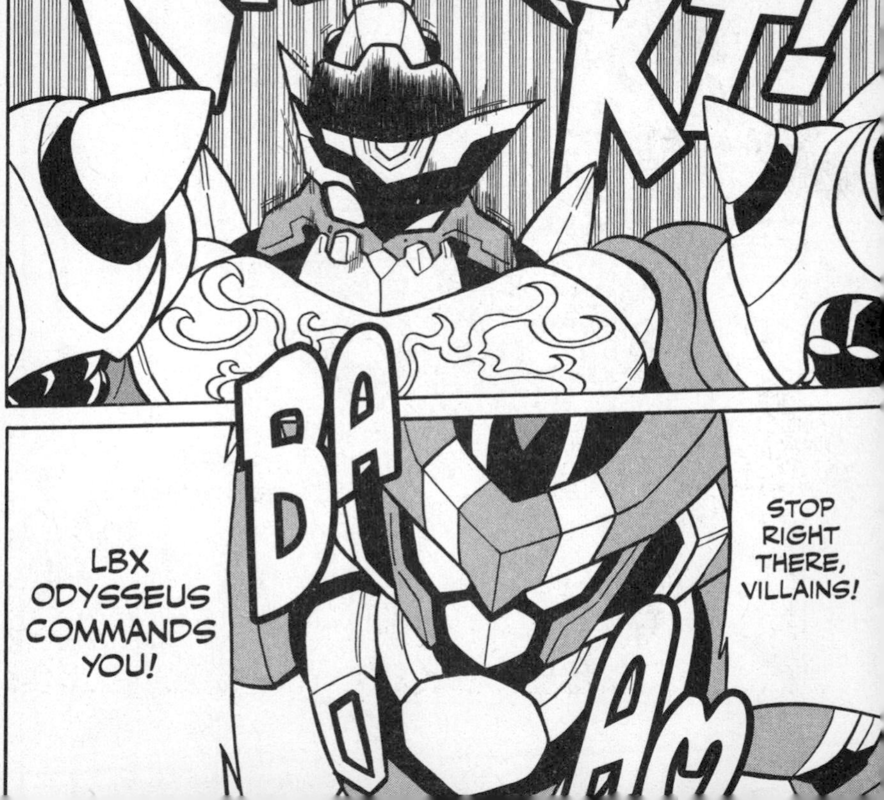
STOP RIGHT THERE, VILLAINS!
LBX ODYSSEUS COMMANDS YOU!

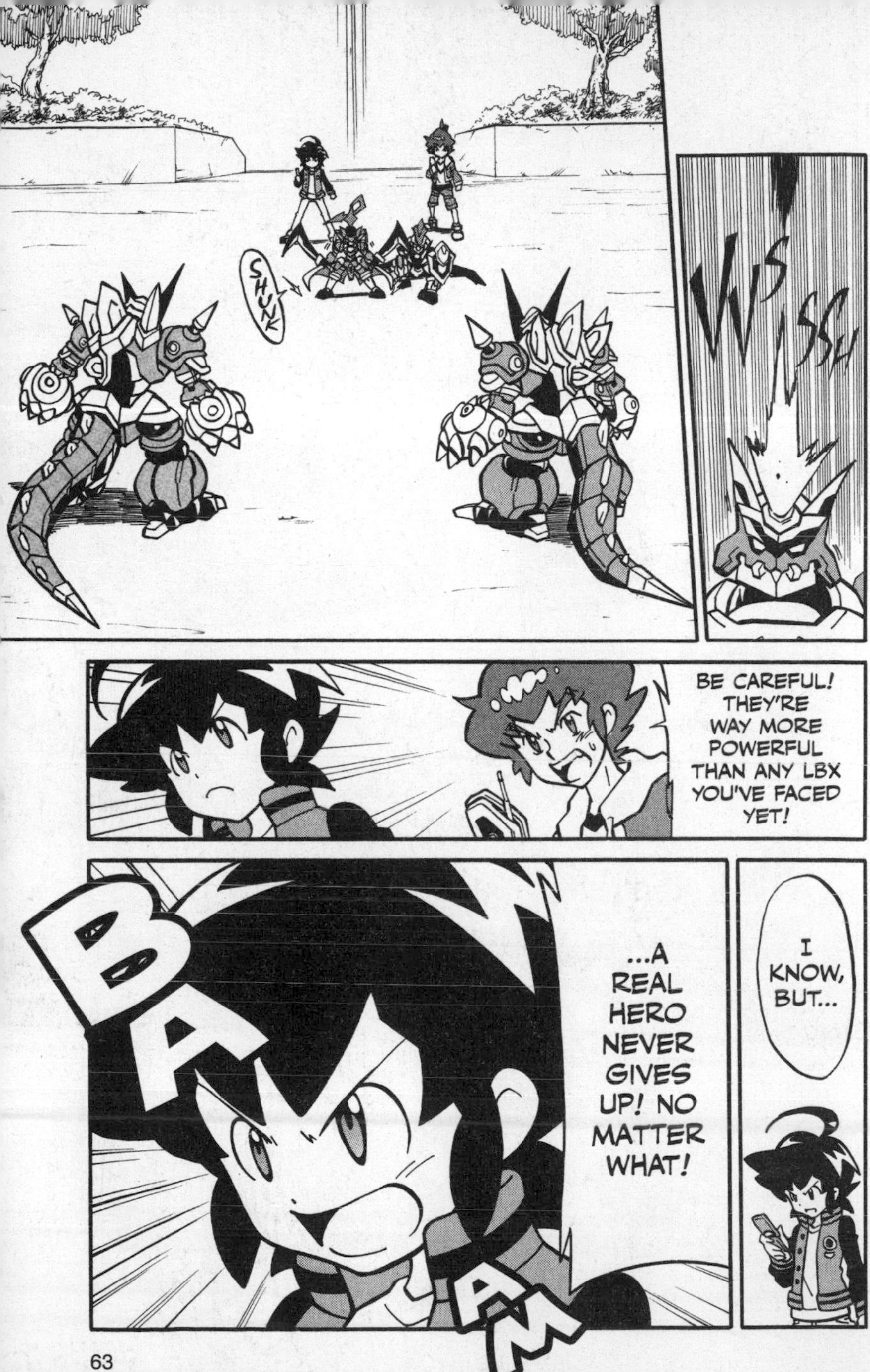
WISSSH
SHUNK
BE CAREFUL! THEY'RE WAY MORE POWERFUL THAN ANY LBX YOU'VE FACED YET!
I KNOW, BUT...
...A REAL HERO NEVER GIVES UP! NO MATTER WHAT!
BAAM

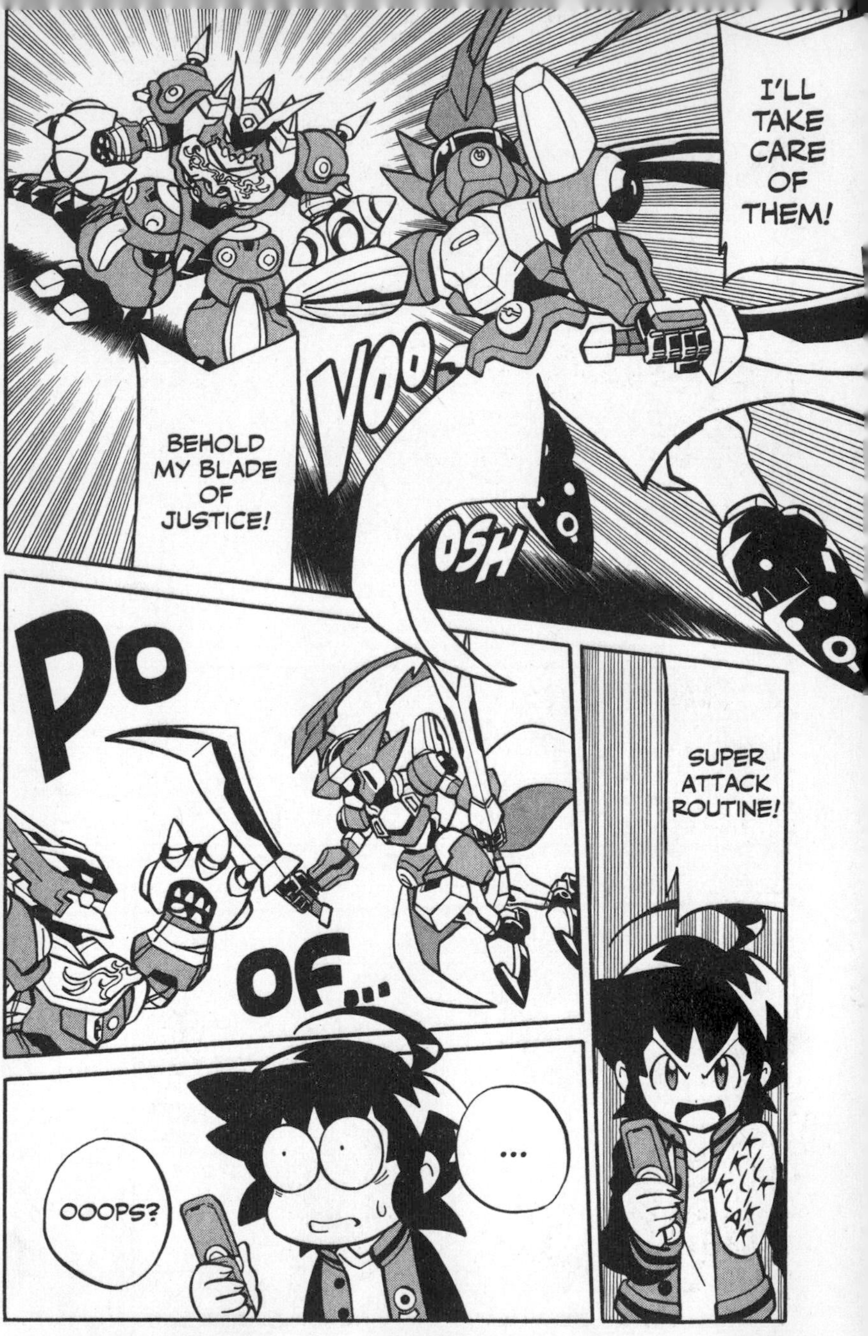
I'LL TAKE CARE OF THEM!
BEHOLD MY BLADE OF JUSTICE!
VOO-OSH
SUPER ATTACK ROUTINE!
KLIK KLIK KLAK
PO OF...
...
OOOPS?

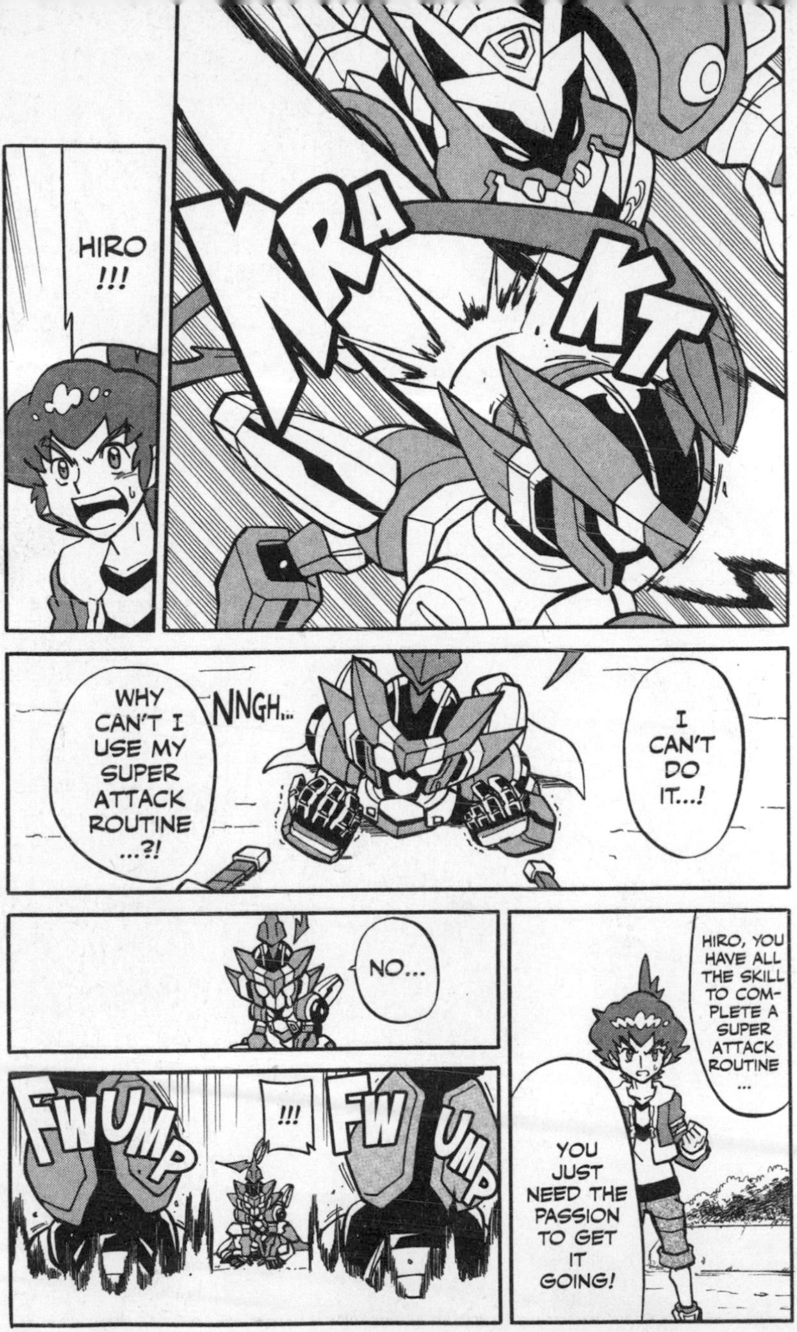
KRAKT
HIRO !!!
I CAN'T DO IT...!
NNGH...
WHY CAN'T I USE MY SUPER ATTACK ROUTINE ...?!
HIRO, YOU HAVE ALL THE SKILL TO COMPLETE A SUPER ATTACK ROUTINE ...
YOU JUST NEED THE PASSION TO GET IT GOING!
NO...
FWUMP
!!!
FWUMP

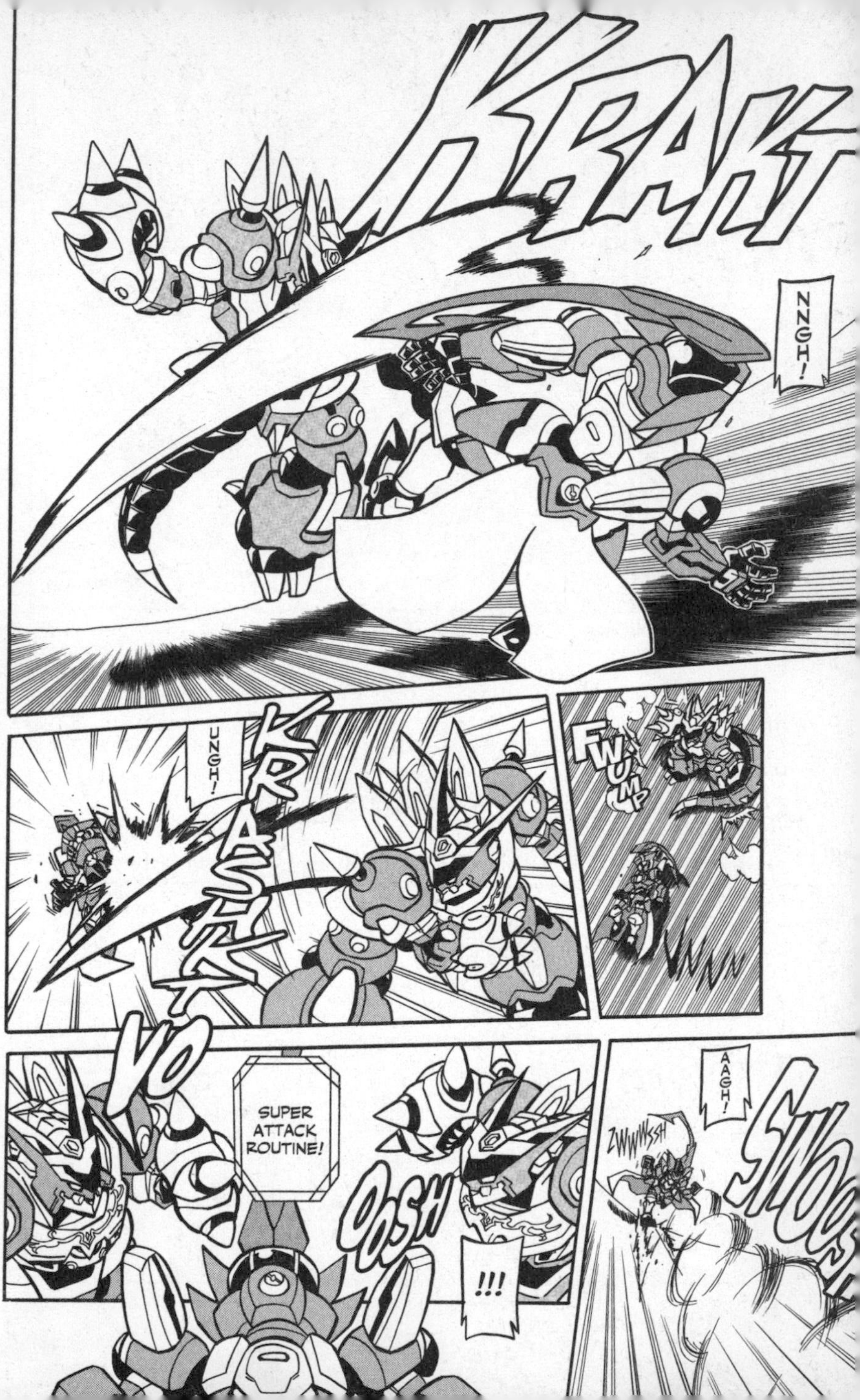
KRAKT
NNGH!
FWUMP
UNGH!
KRASHKT
AAGH!
ZWWWSSH
SHOOSH
VOOSH
SUPER ATTACK ROUTINE!
!!!

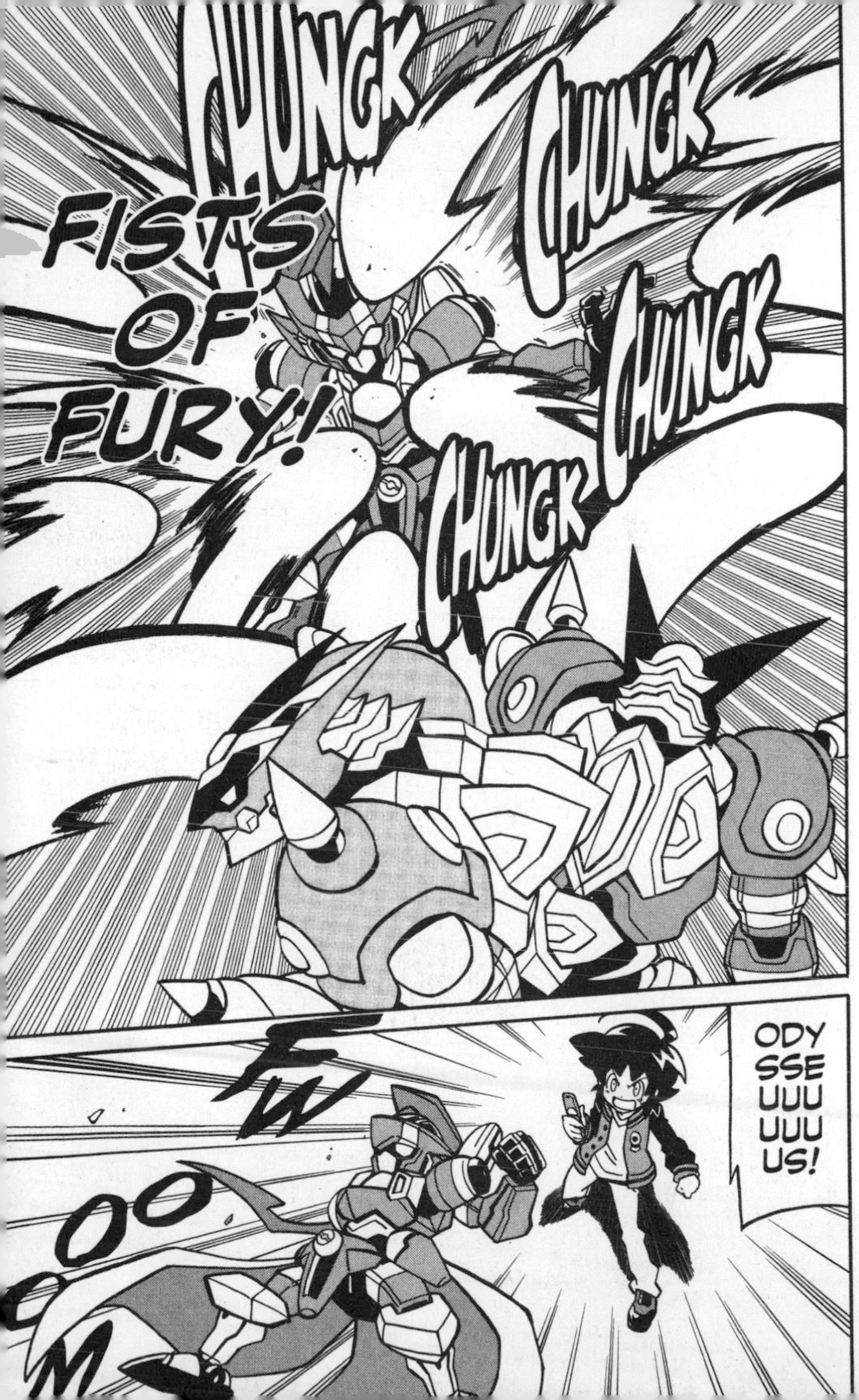
CHUNCK
CHUNCK
CHUNCK
CHUNCK
FISTS OF FURY!
ODYSSEUUUUUUUS!

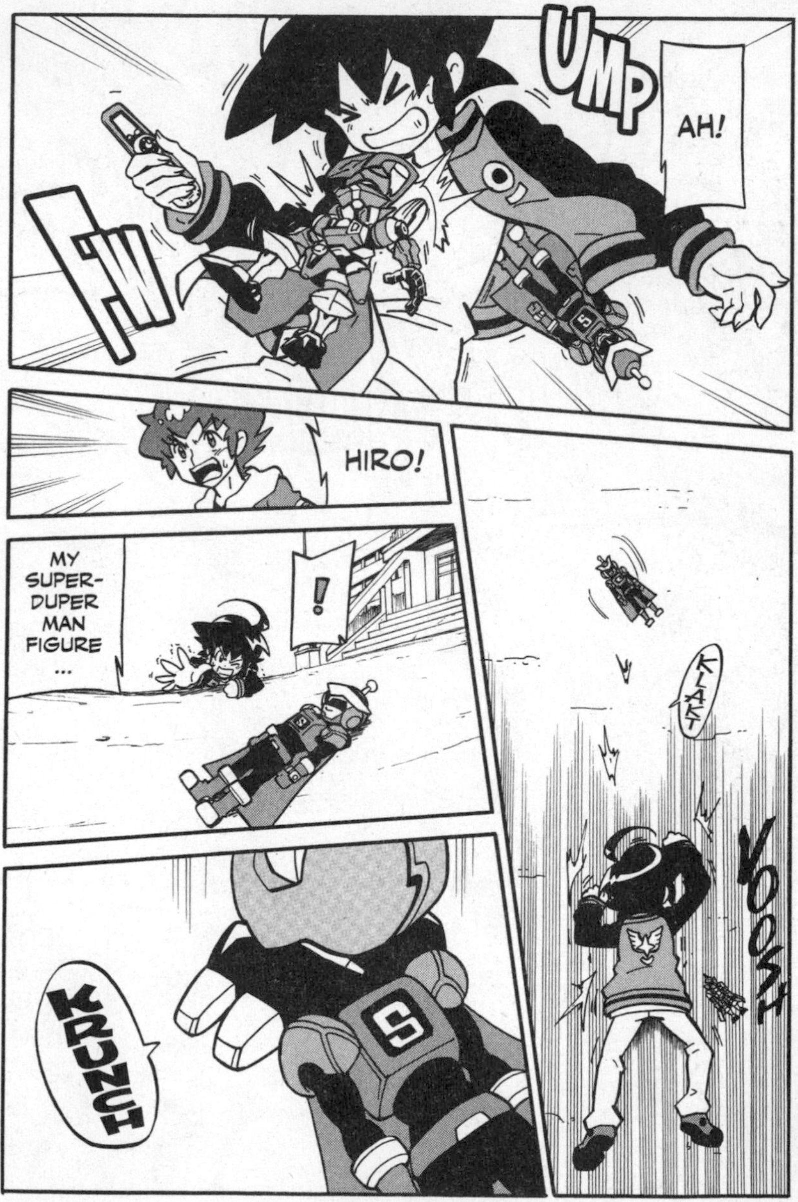
AH!
UMP
KLAKT
VOOSH
HIRO!
!
MY SUPER-DUPER MAN FIGURE ...
KRUNCH

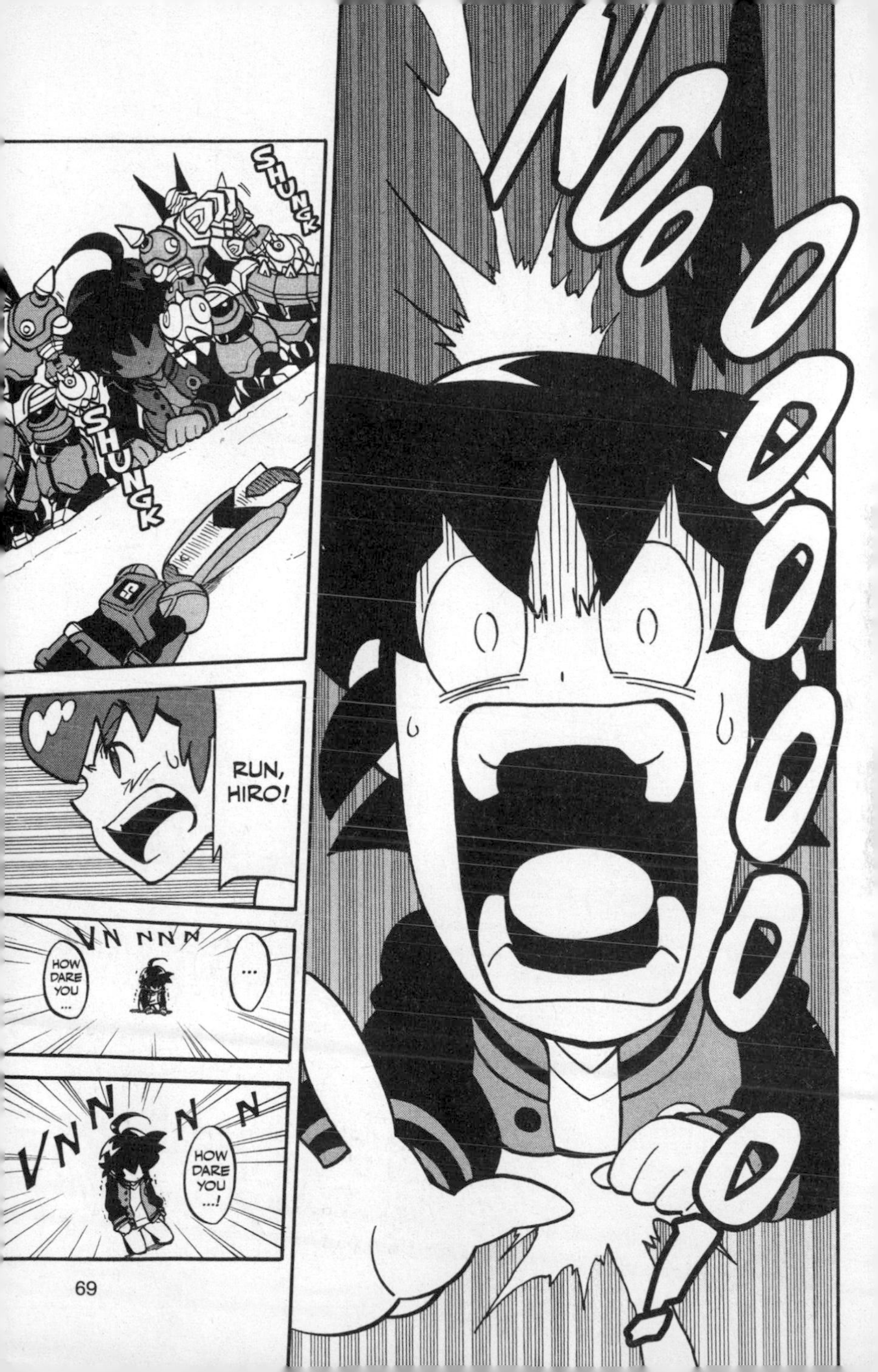
NOOOOOOOOOOOOO!
SHUNGK
SHUNGK
RUN, HIRO!
VN NNN
...
HOW DARE YOU...
VNNNNN
HOW DARE YOU...!

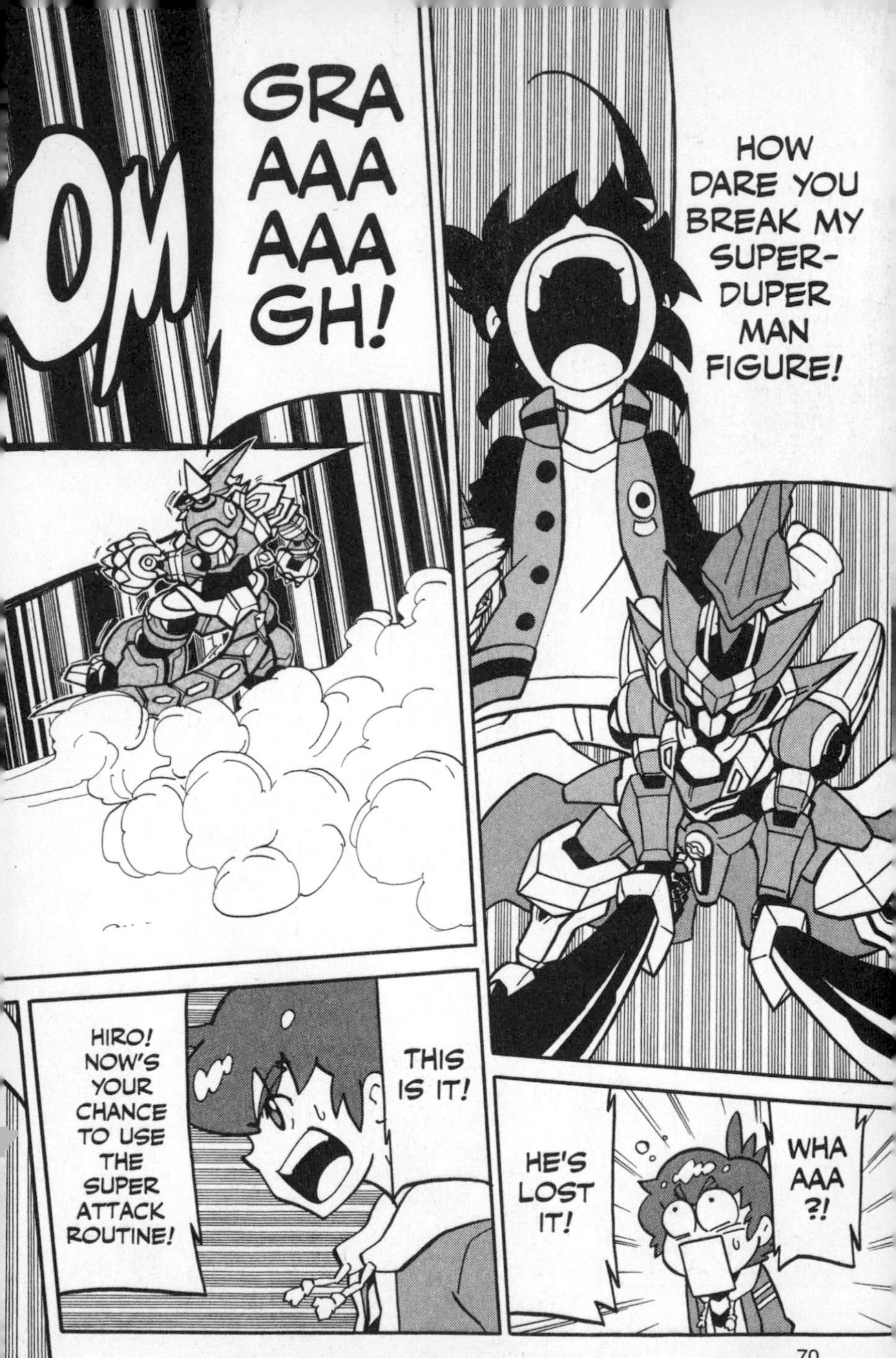
HOW DARE YOU BREAK MY SUPER-DUPER MAN FIGURE!
OM
GRAAAAAAAAGH!
WHAAAA?!
HE'S LOST IT!
THIS IS IT!
HIRO! NOW'S YOUR CHANCE TO USE THE SUPER ATTACK ROUTINE!

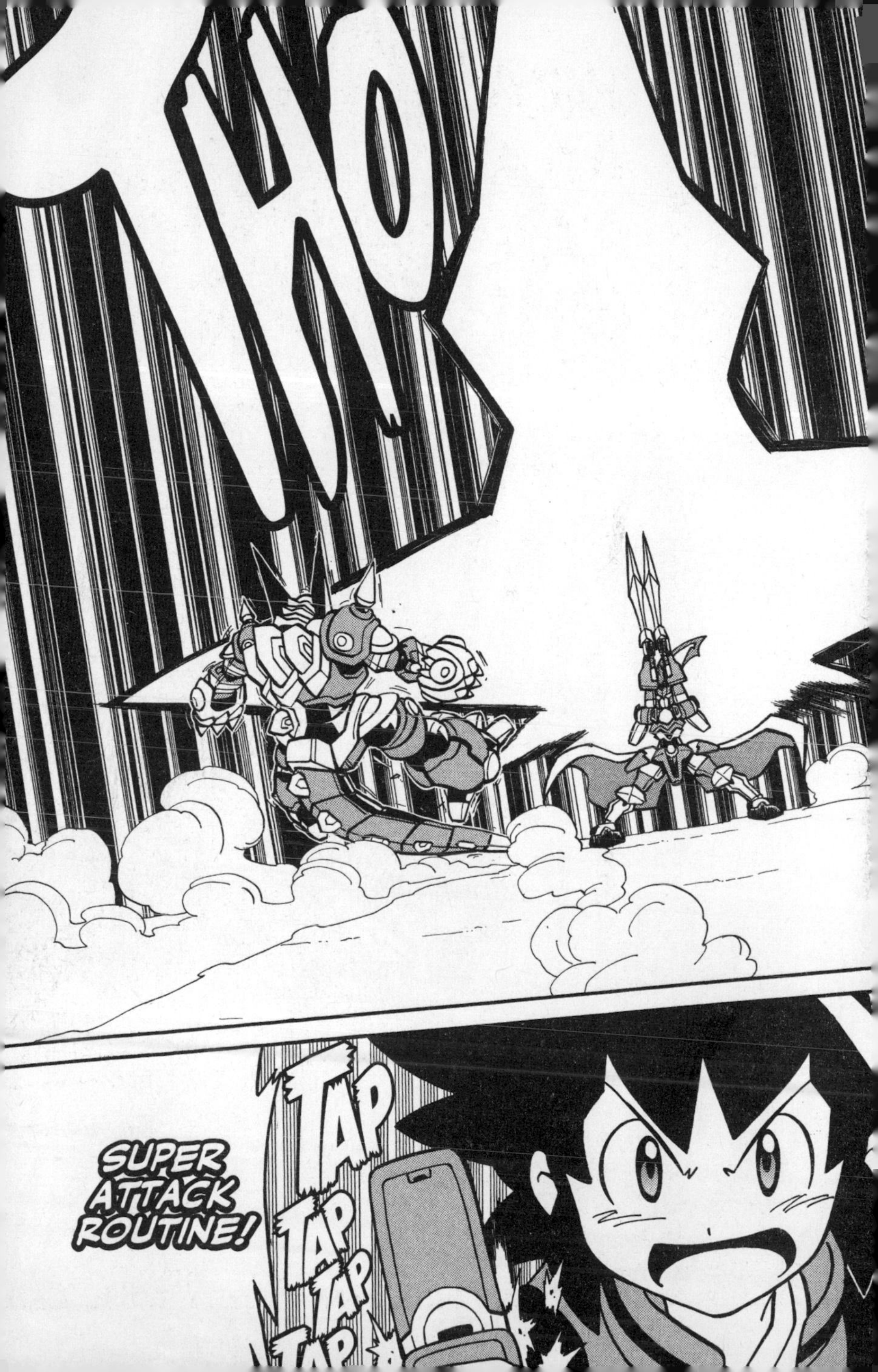
TAP
TAP
TAP
TAP
SUPER ATTACK ROUTINE!

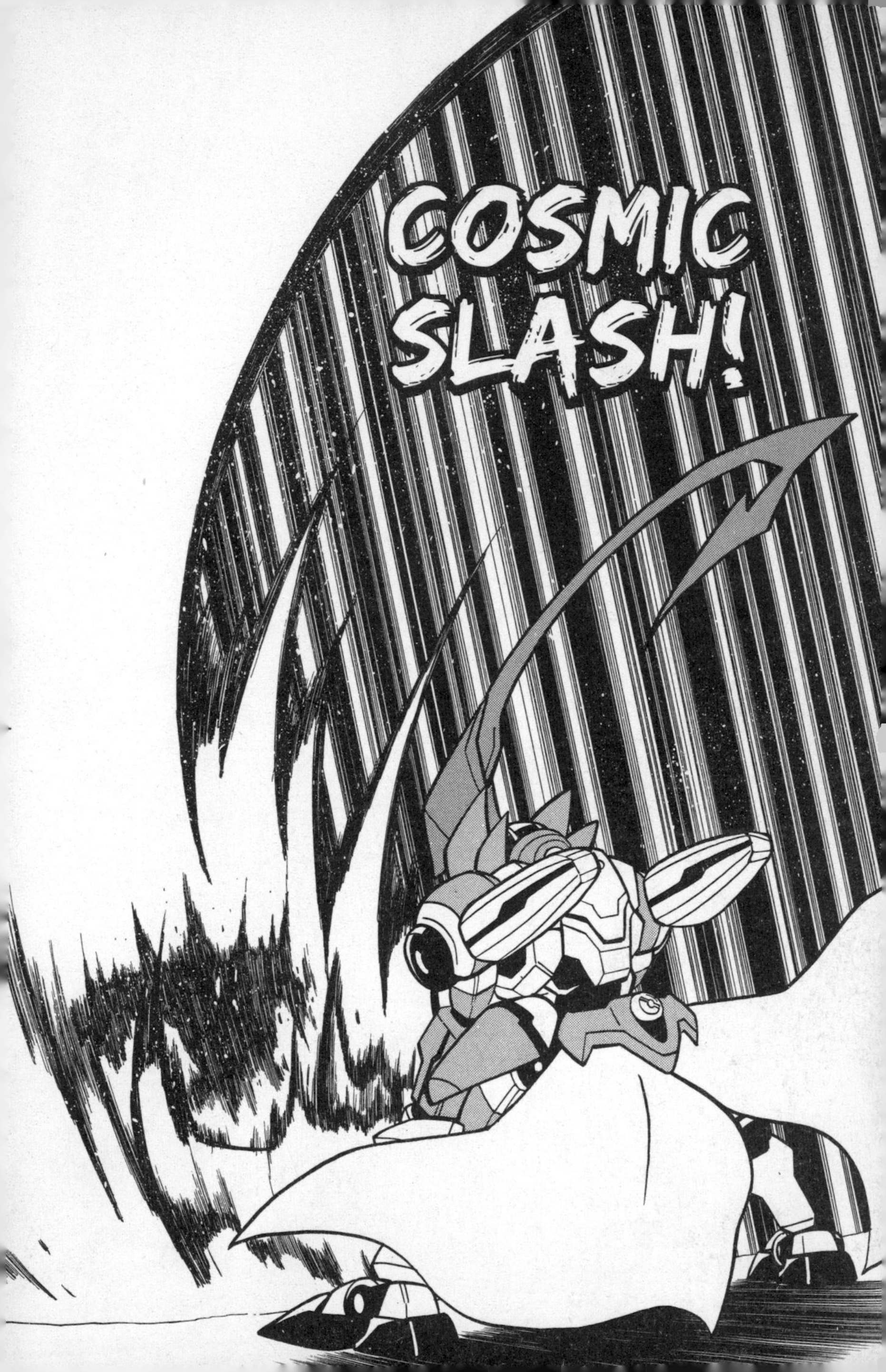
COSMIC SLASH!

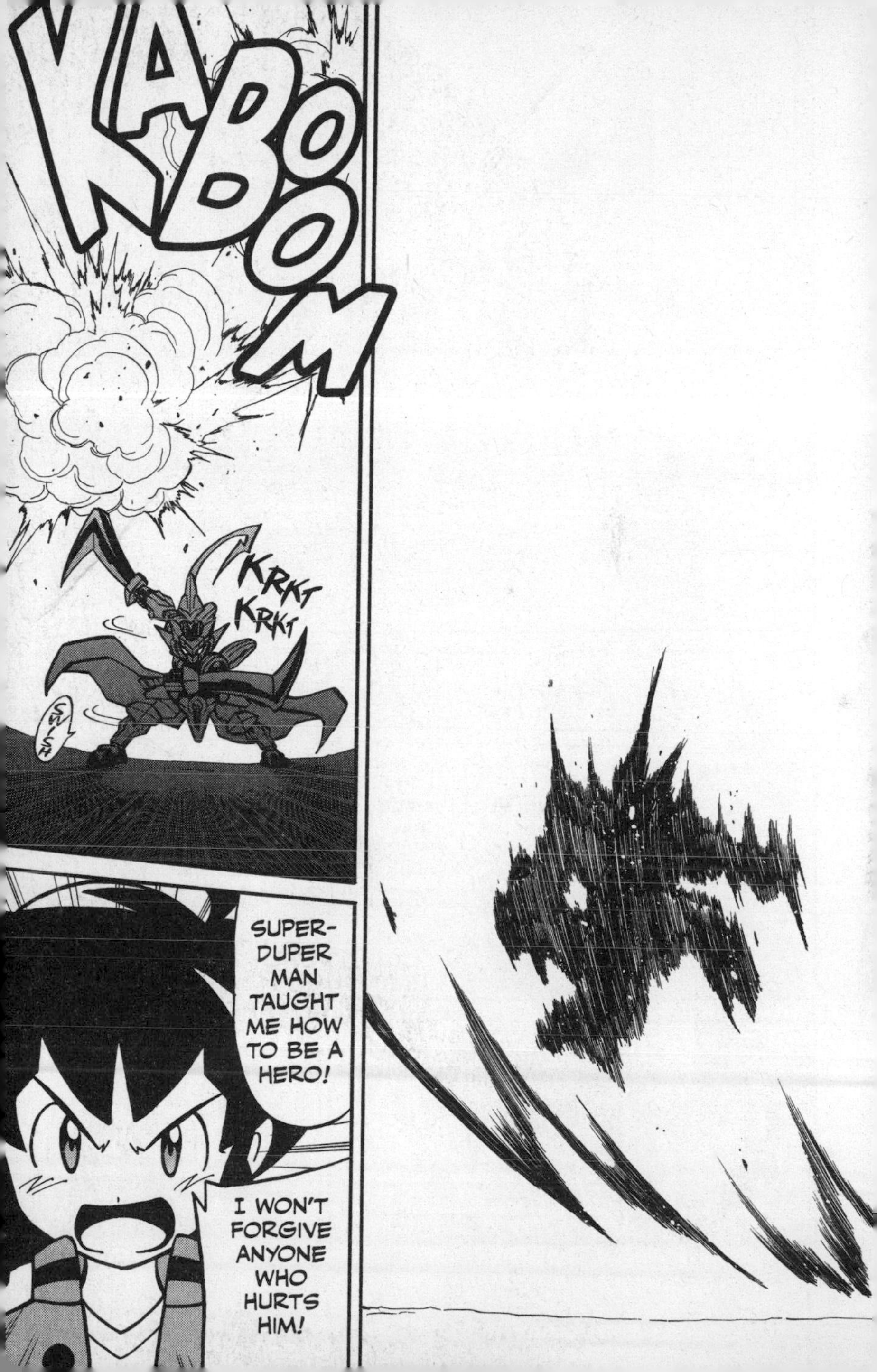
KABOOM
KRKT KRKT
SWISH
SUPER-DUPER MAN TAUGHT ME HOW TO BE A HERO!
I WON'T FORGIVE ANYONE WHO HURTS HIM!

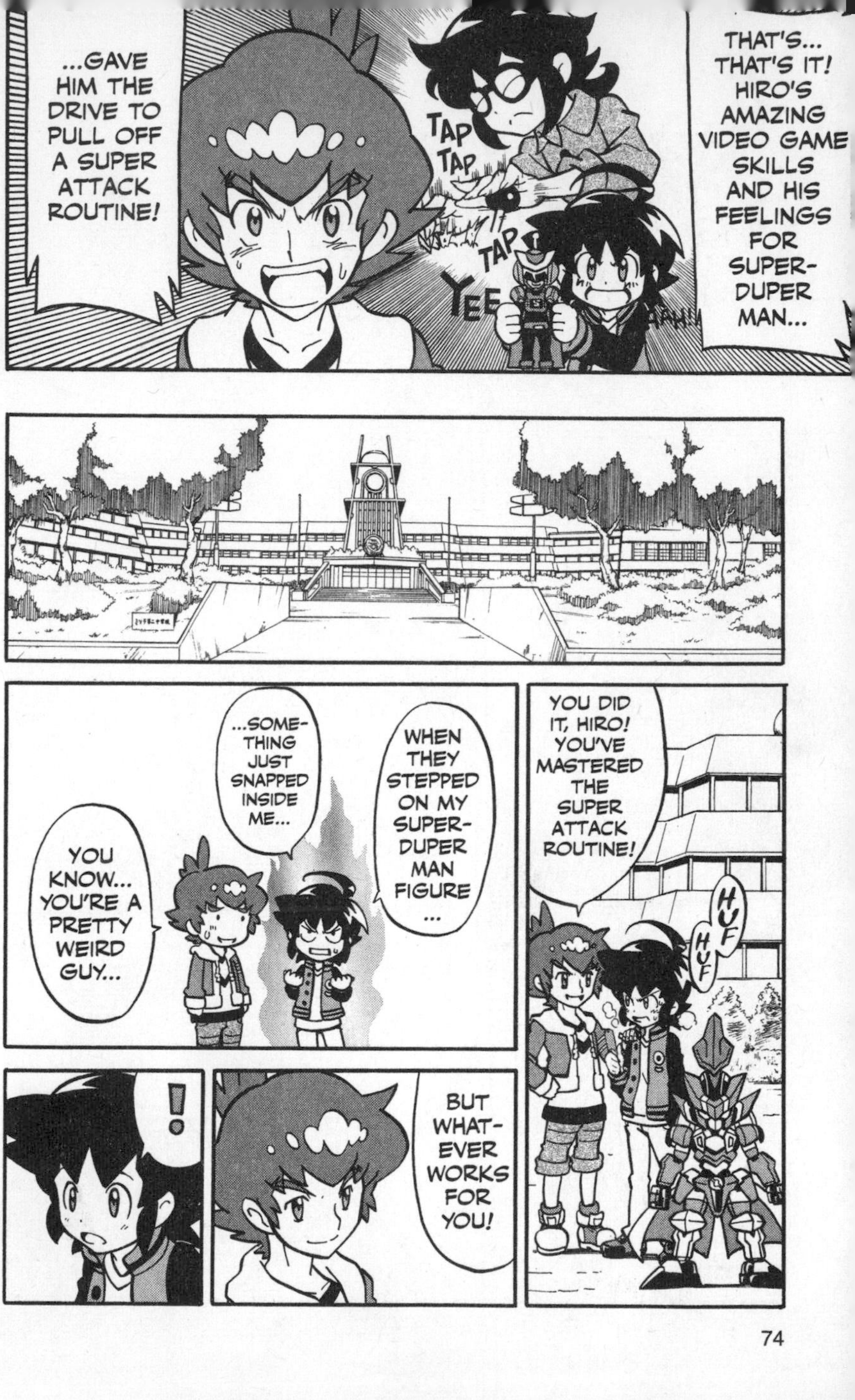
THAT'S... THAT'S IT! HIRO'S AMAZING VIDEO GAME SKILLS AND HIS FEELINGS FOR SUPER-DUPER MAN...
TAP TAP
TAP
YEE
AAH!!
...GAVE HIM THE DRIVE TO PULL OFF A SUPER ATTACK ROUTINE!
YOU DID IT, HIRO! YOU'VE MASTERED THE SUPER ATTACK ROUTINE!
HUF
HUF
WHEN THEY STEPPED ON MY SUPER-DUPER MAN FIGURE ...
...SOME-THING JUST SNAPPED INSIDE ME...
YOU KNOW... YOU'RE A PRETTY WEIRD GUY...
BUT WHAT-EVER WORKS FOR YOU!
!

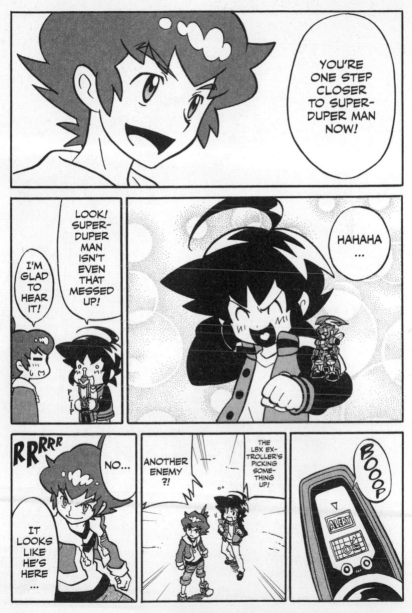

YOU'RE ONE STEP CLOSER TO SUPER-DUPER MAN NOW!
HAHAHA ...
LOOK! SUPER-DUPER MAN ISN'T EVEN THAT MESSED UP!
I'M GLAD TO HEAR IT!
PLIP
BOOOP
ALERT
THE LBX EX-TROLLER'S PICKING SOME-THING UP!
ANOTHER ENEMY ?!
RRRRR
NO...
IT LOOKS LIKE HE'S HERE ...

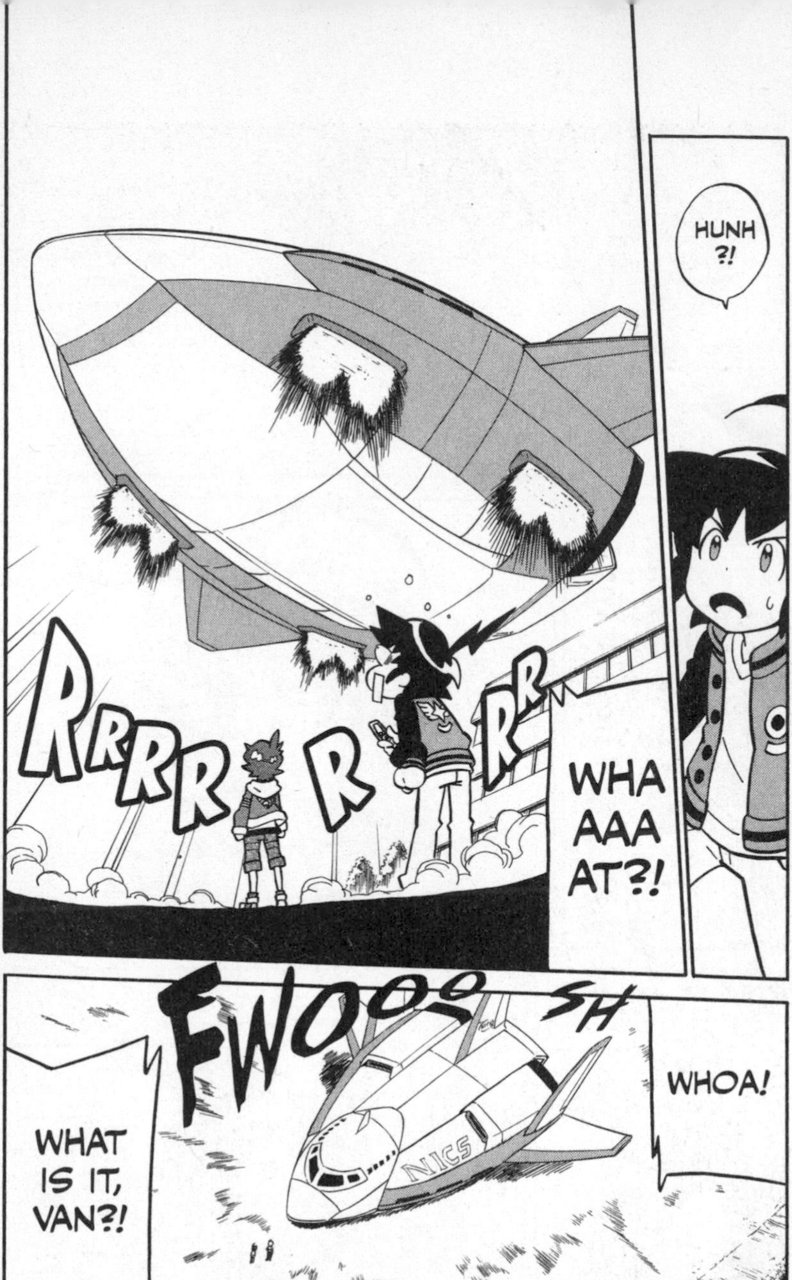
HUNH ?!
WHA AAA AT?!
RRRRRRR
WHOA!
FWOOOSH
NICS
WHAT IS IT, VAN?!

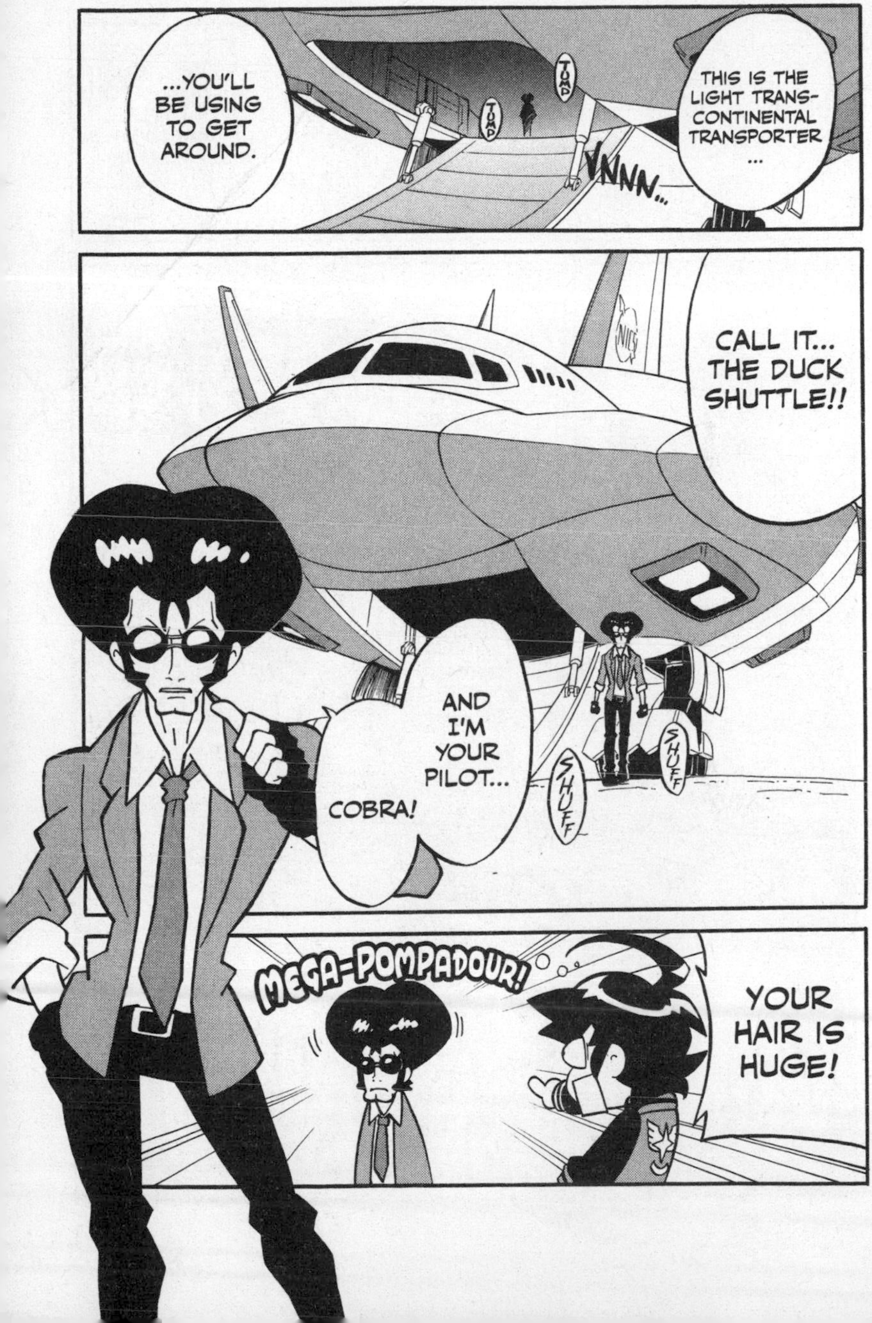
THIS IS THE LIGHT TRANS-CONTINENTAL TRANSPORTER ...
VNNN...
TUMP
TUMP
...YOU'LL BE USING TO GET AROUND.
CALL IT... THE DUCK SHUTTLE!!
SHUFF
SHUFF
AND I'M YOUR PILOT...
COBRA!
YOUR HAIR IS HUGE!
MEGA-POMPADOUR!

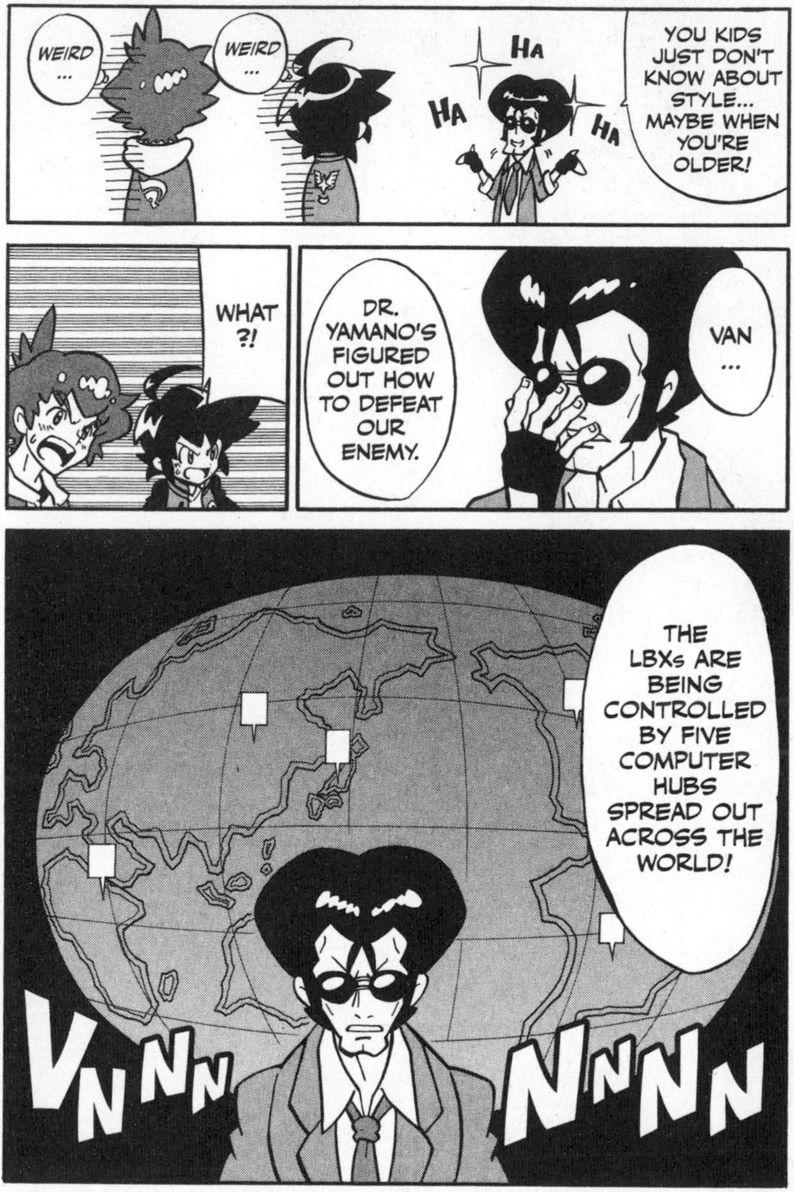

YOU KIDS JUST DON'T KNOW ABOUT STYLE... MAYBE WHEN YOU'RE OLDER!
HA HA HA
WEIRD ...
WEIRD ...
VAN ...
DR. YAMANO'S FIGURED OUT HOW TO DEFEAT OUR ENEMY.
WHAT ?!
THE LBXs ARE BEING CONTROLLED BY FIVE COMPUTER HUBS SPREAD OUT ACROSS THE WORLD!
VNNN NNNNN

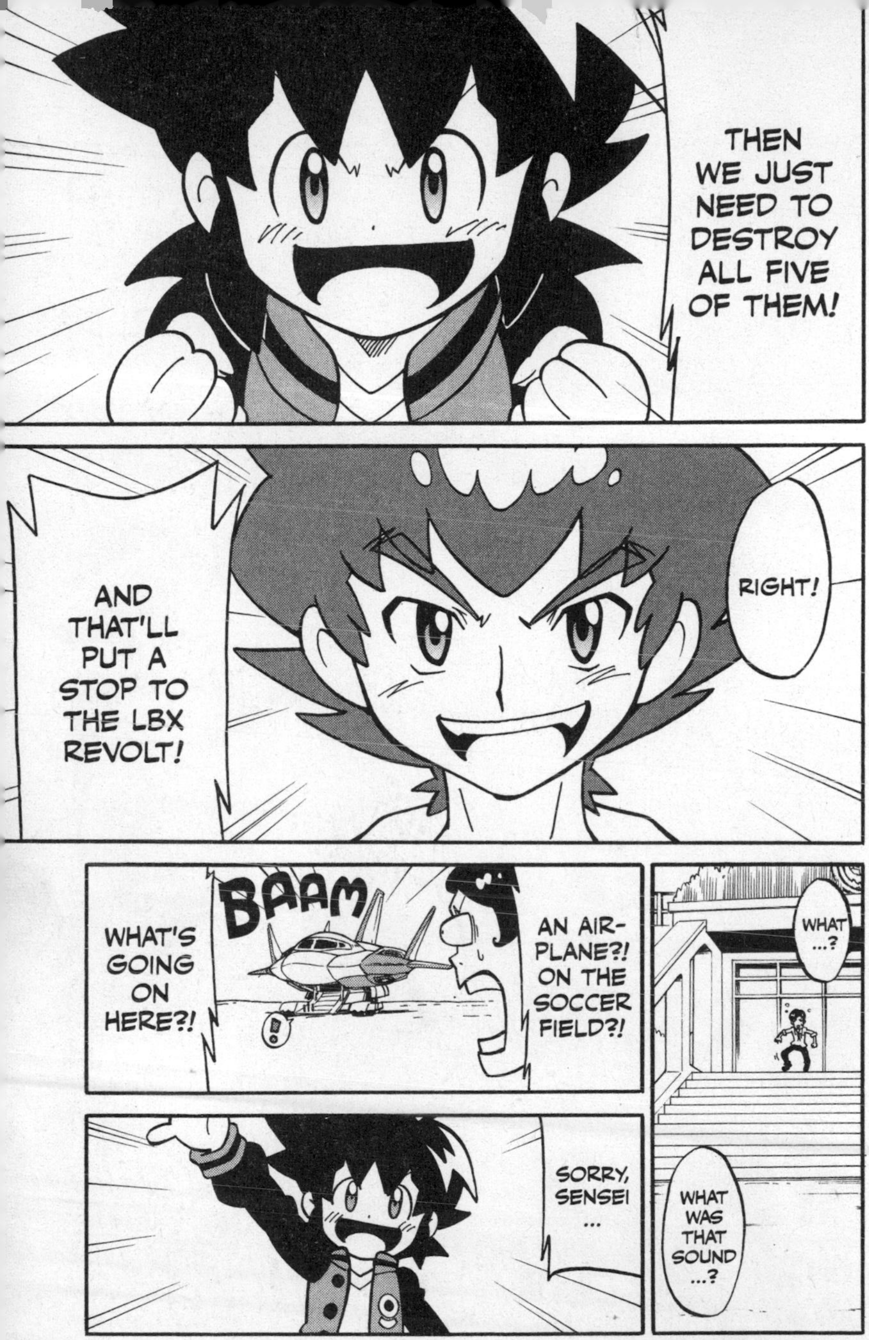
THEN WE JUST NEED TO DESTROY ALL FIVE OF THEM!
RIGHT!
AND THAT'LL PUT A STOP TO THE LBX REVOLT!
WHAT ...?
WHAT WAS THAT SOUND ...?
AN AIR-PLANE?! ON THE SOCCER FIELD?!
BAAM
WHAT'S GOING ON HERE?!
SORRY, SENSEI ...

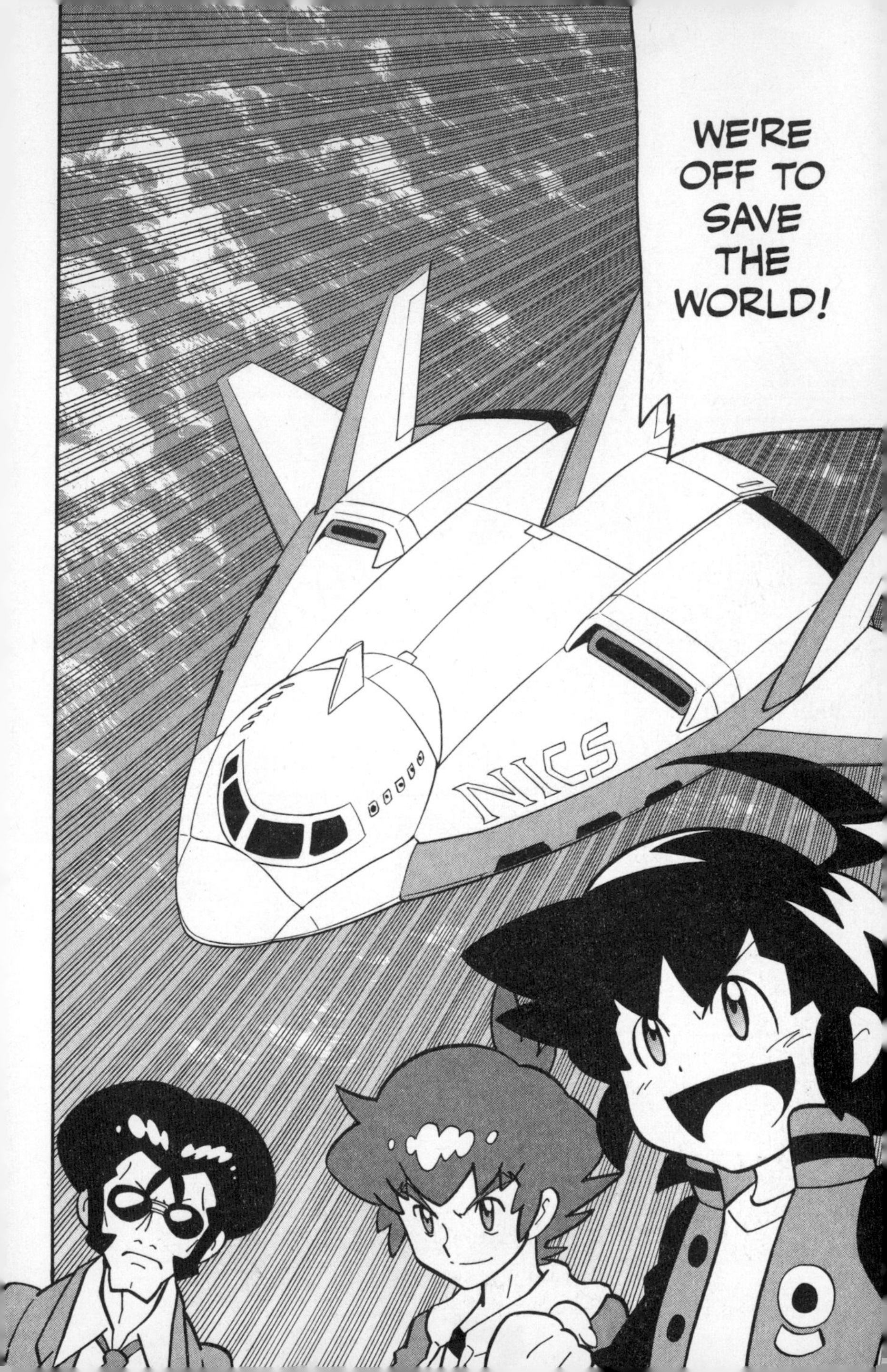
WE'RE OFF TO SAVE THE WORLD!
NICS

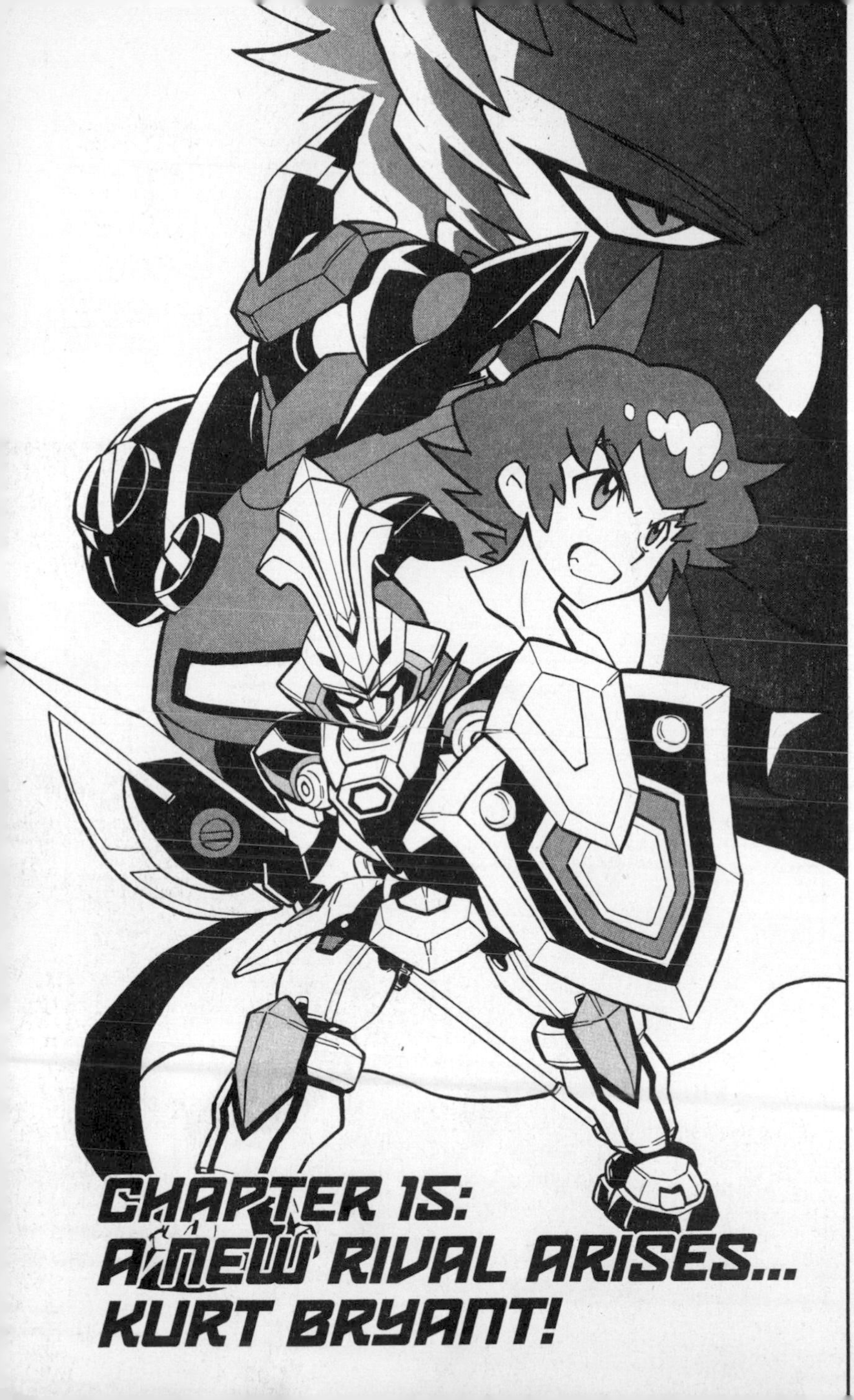
CHAPTER 15:
A NEW RIVAL ARISES...
KURT BRYANT!

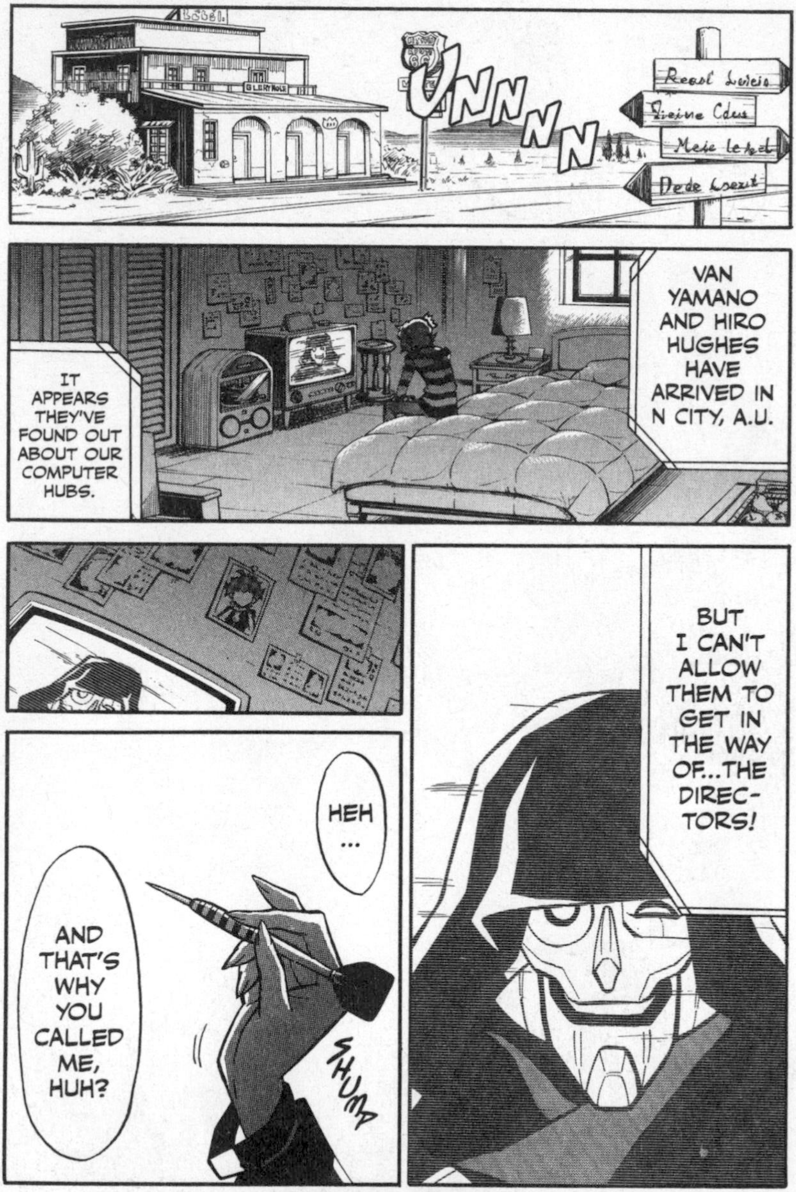
UNNNNN
VAN YAMANO AND HIRO HUGHES HAVE ARRIVED IN N CITY, A.U.
IT APPEARS THEY'VE FOUND OUT ABOUT OUR COMPUTER HUBS.
BUT I CAN'T ALLOW THEM TO GET IN THE WAY OF...THE DIRECTORS!
HEH...
AND THAT'S WHY YOU CALLED ME, HUH?

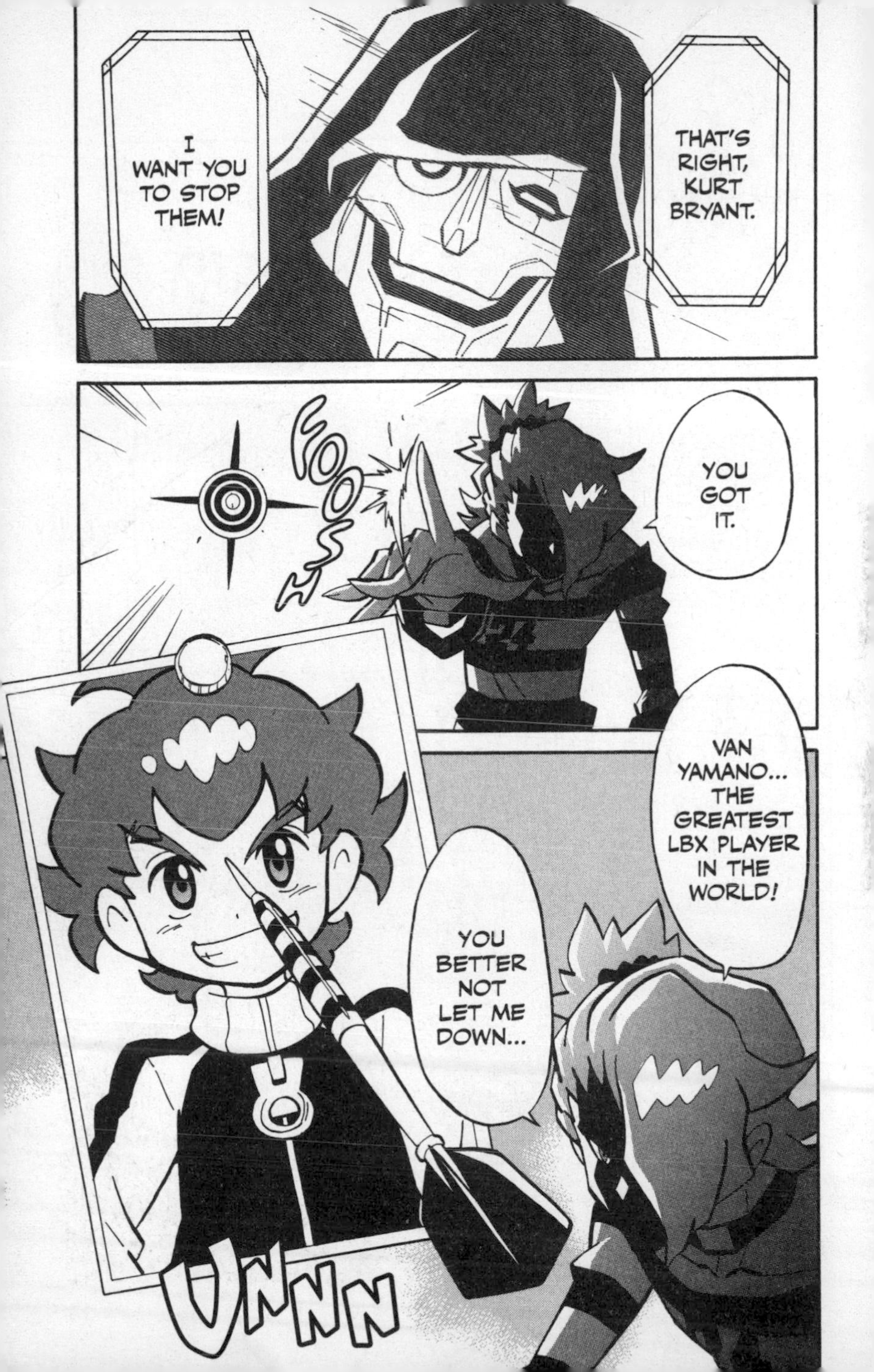
THAT'S RIGHT, KURT BRYANT.
I WANT YOU TO STOP THEM!
YOU GOT IT.
FOOSH
VAN YAMANO... THE GREATEST LBX PLAYER IN THE WORLD!
YOU BETTER NOT LET ME DOWN...
UNNN

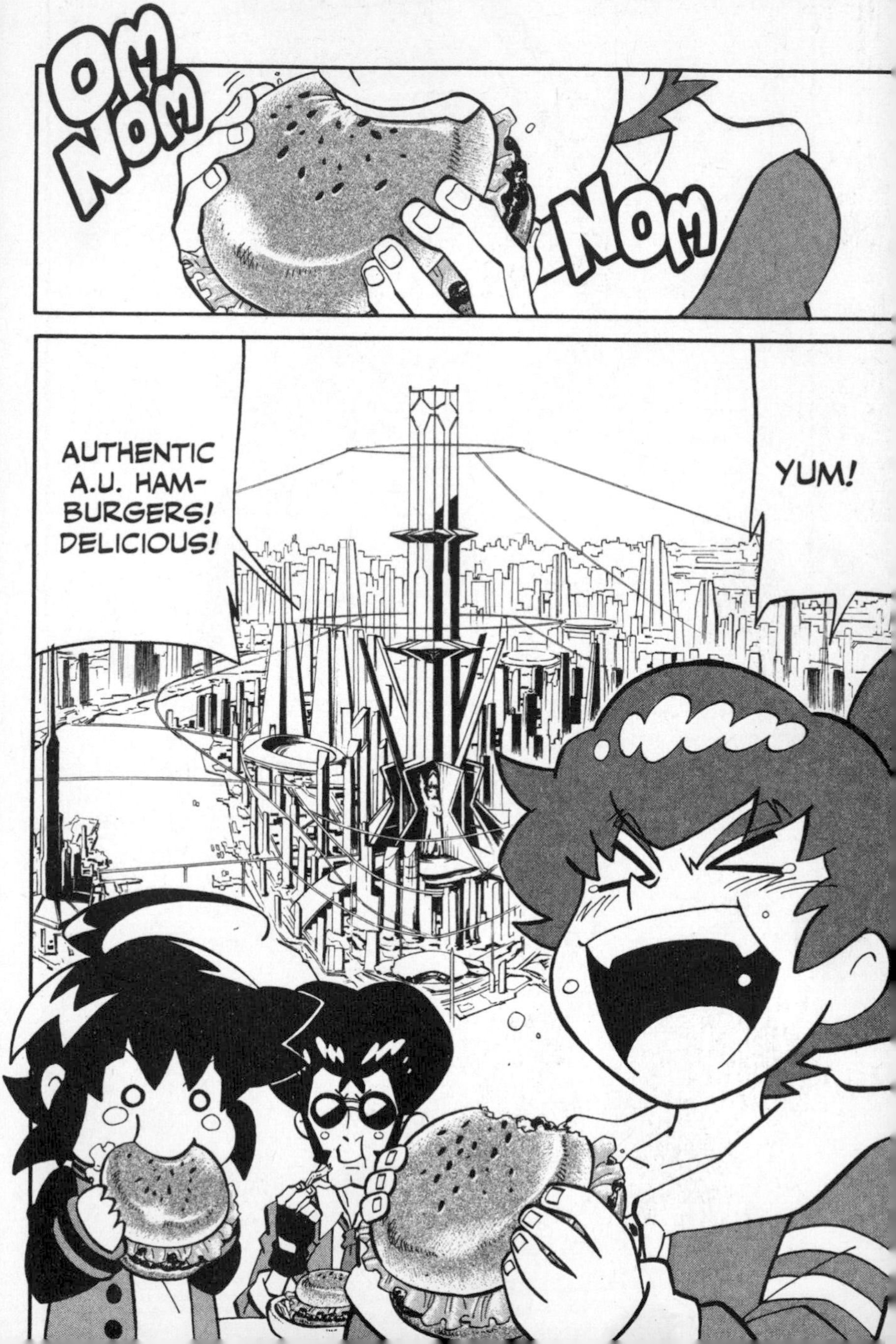
OM NOM
NOM
YUM!
AUTHENTIC A.U. HAM-BURGERS! DELICIOUS!

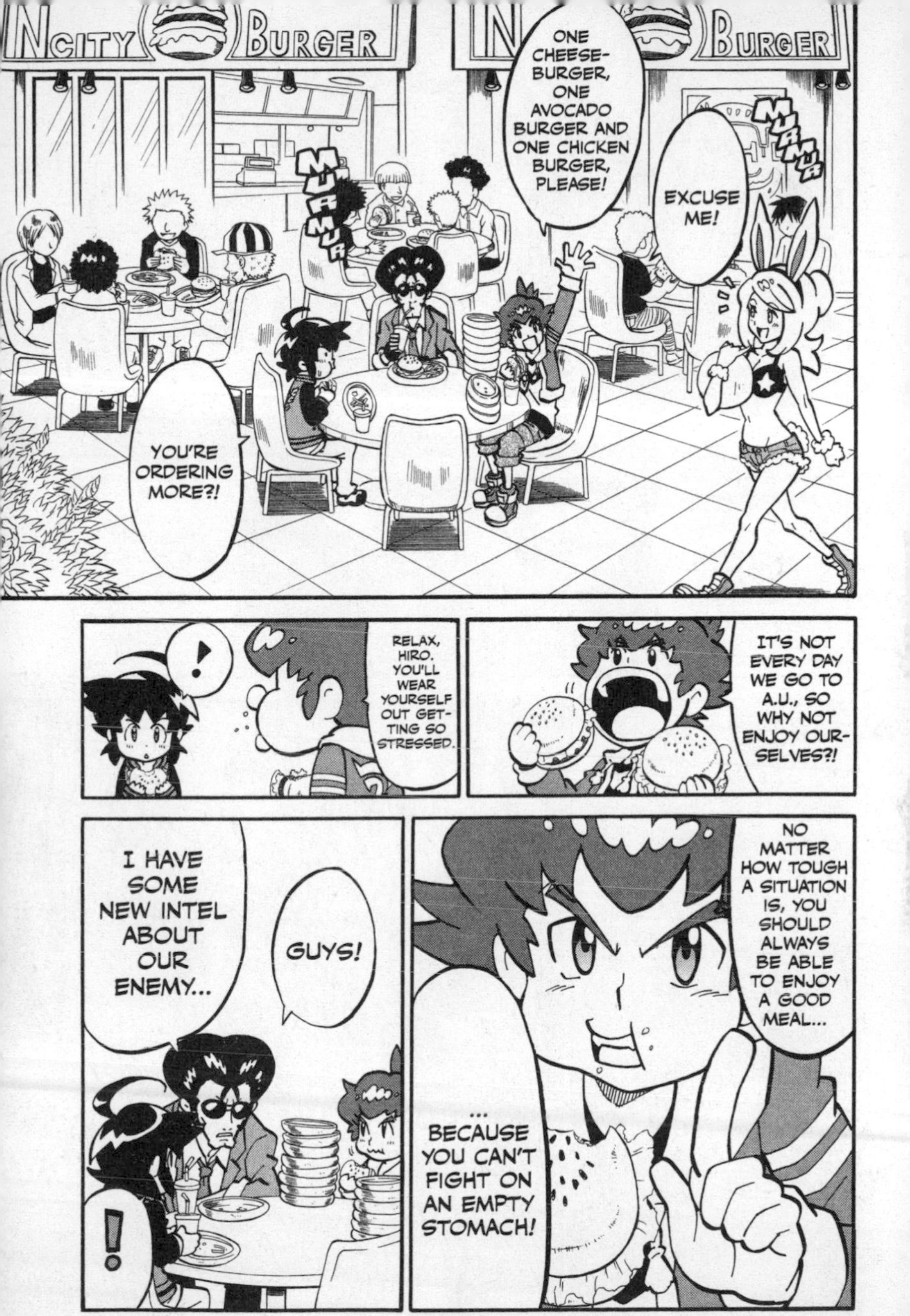
MURMUR
EXCUSE ME!
ONE CHEESE-BURGER, ONE AVOCADO BURGER AND ONE CHICKEN BURGER, PLEASE!
MURMUR
YOU'RE ORDERING MORE?!
IT'S NOT EVERY DAY WE GO TO A.U., SO WHY NOT ENJOY OURSELVES?!
RELAX, HIRO. YOU'LL WEAR YOURSELF OUT GETTING SO STRESSED.
!
NO MATTER HOW TOUGH A SITUATION IS, YOU SHOULD ALWAYS BE ABLE TO ENJOY A GOOD MEAL...
...BECAUSE YOU CAN'T FIGHT ON AN EMPTY STOMACH!
GUYS!
I HAVE SOME NEW INTEL ABOUT OUR ENEMY...
!

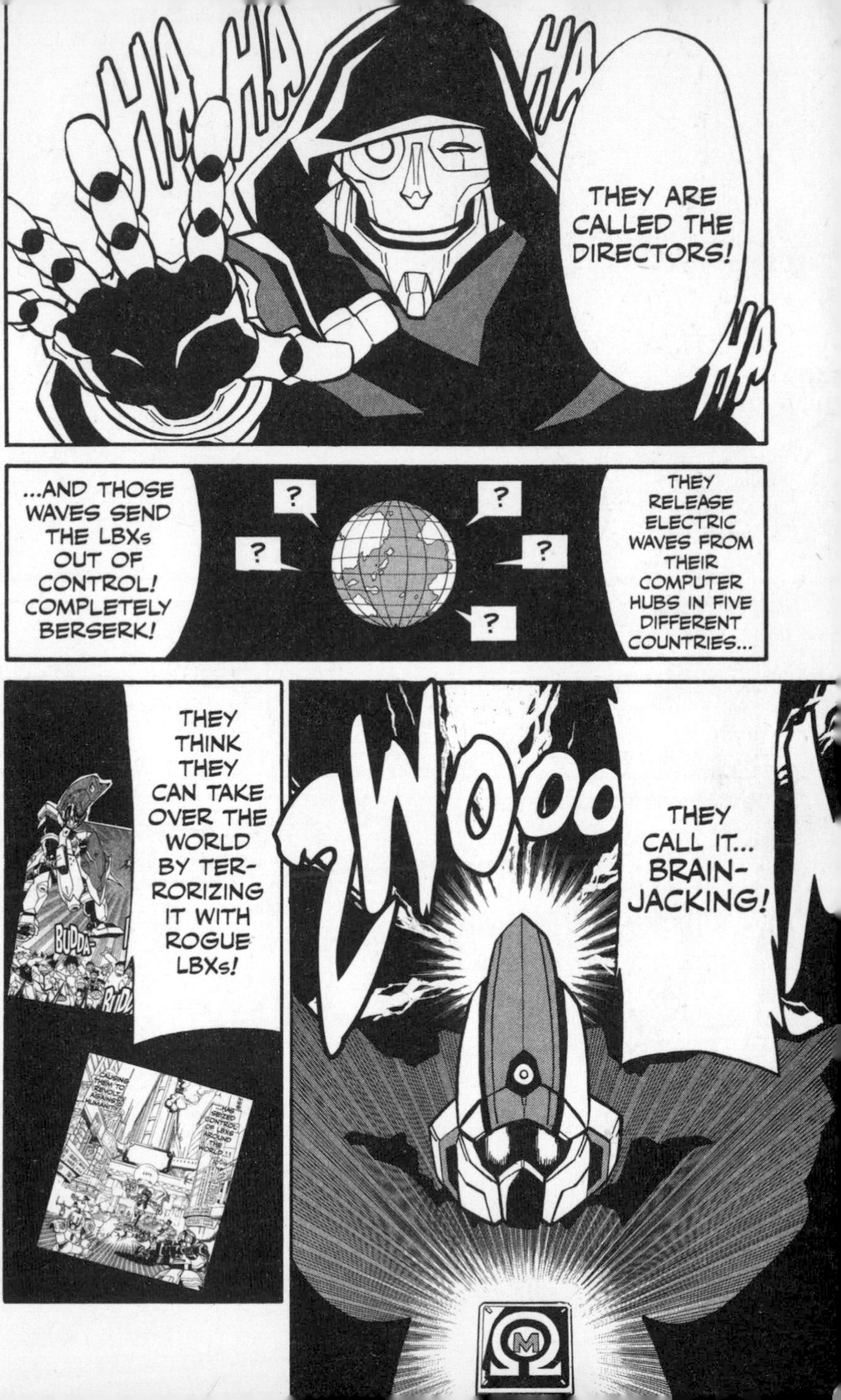
HA HA HA
THEY ARE CALLED THE DIRECTORS!
HA HA
THEY RELEASE ELECTRIC WAVES FROM THEIR COMPUTER HUBS IN FIVE DIFFERENT COUNTRIES...
?
?
?
?
?
...AND THOSE WAVES SEND THE LBXs OUT OF CONTROL! COMPLETELY BERSERK!
WOOOM
THEY CALL IT... BRAIN-JACKING!
THEY THINK THEY CAN TAKE OVER THE WORLD BY TER-RORIZING IT WITH ROGUE LBXs!

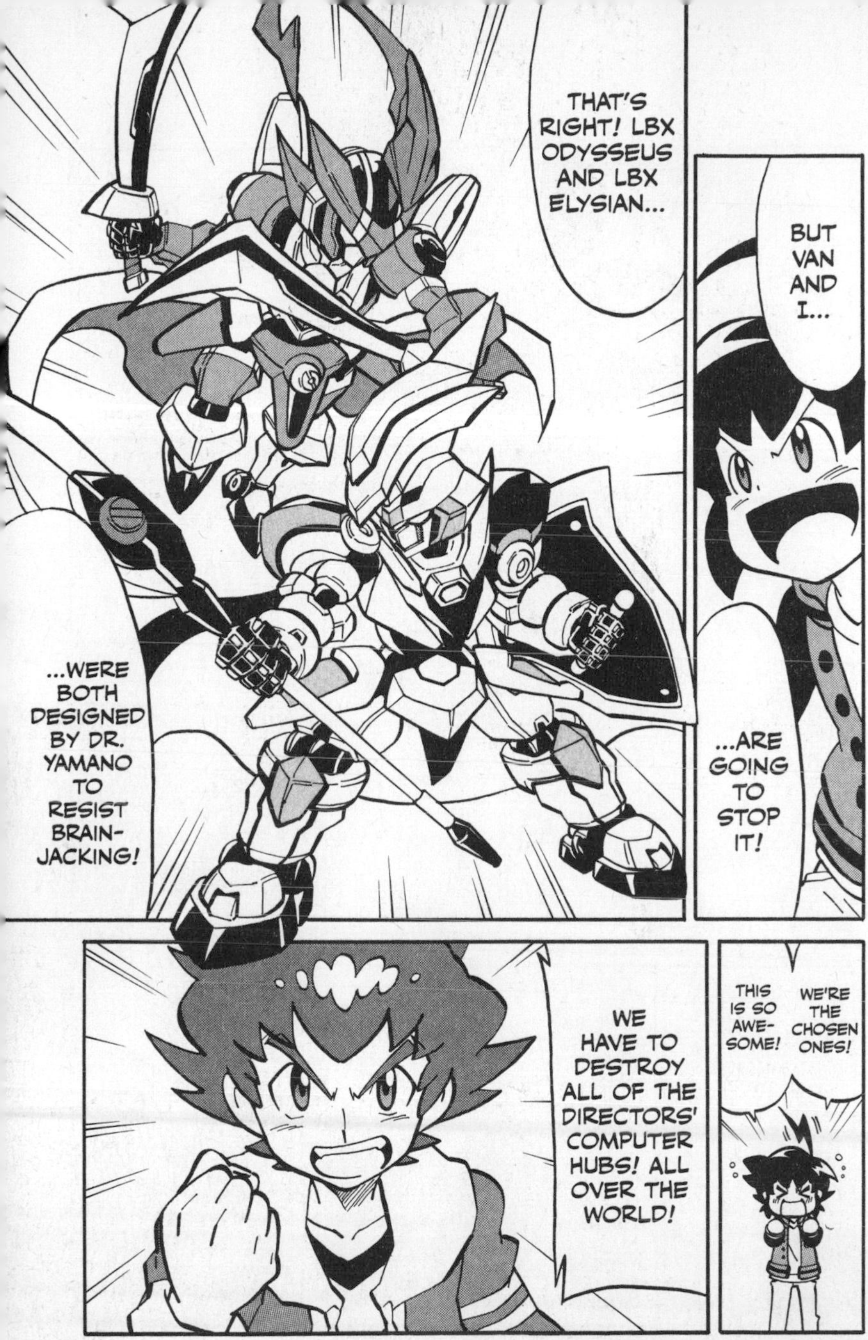
BUT VAN AND I...
...ARE GOING TO STOP IT!
THAT'S RIGHT! LBX ODYSSEUS AND LBX ELYSIAN...
...WERE BOTH DESIGNED BY DR. YAMANO TO RESIST BRAIN-JACKING!
WE'RE THE CHOSEN ONES!
THIS IS SO AWE-SOME!
WE HAVE TO DESTROY ALL OF THE DIRECTORS' COMPUTER HUBS! ALL OVER THE WORLD!

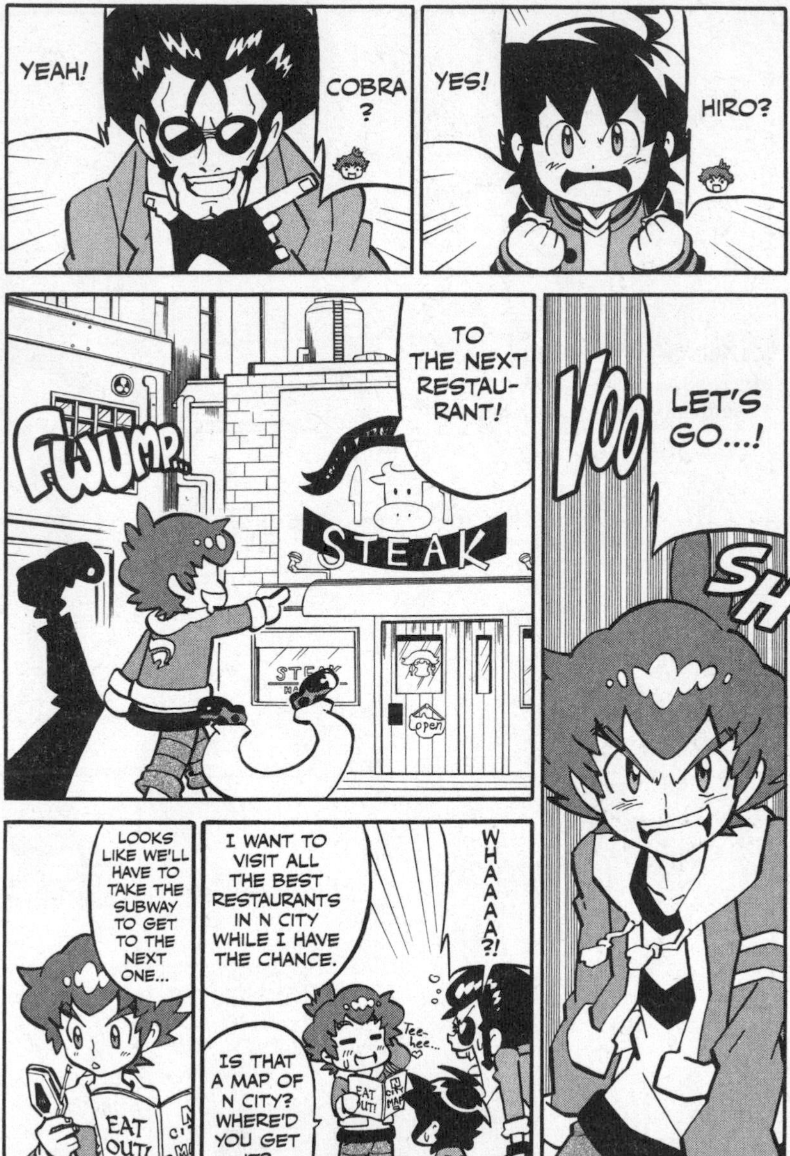
HIRO?
YES!
COBRA ?
YEAH!
LET'S GO...!
VOO
SH
TO THE NEXT RESTAURANT!
FWUMP...
STEAK
STEAK
open
WHAAAA?!
I WANT TO VISIT ALL THE BEST RESTAURANTS IN N CITY WHILE I HAVE THE CHANCE.
Tee-hee...
IS THAT A MAP OF N CITY? WHERE'D YOU GET IT?
EAT OUT!
LOOKS LIKE WE'LL HAVE TO TAKE THE SUBWAY TO GET TO THE NEXT ONE...
EAT OUT!

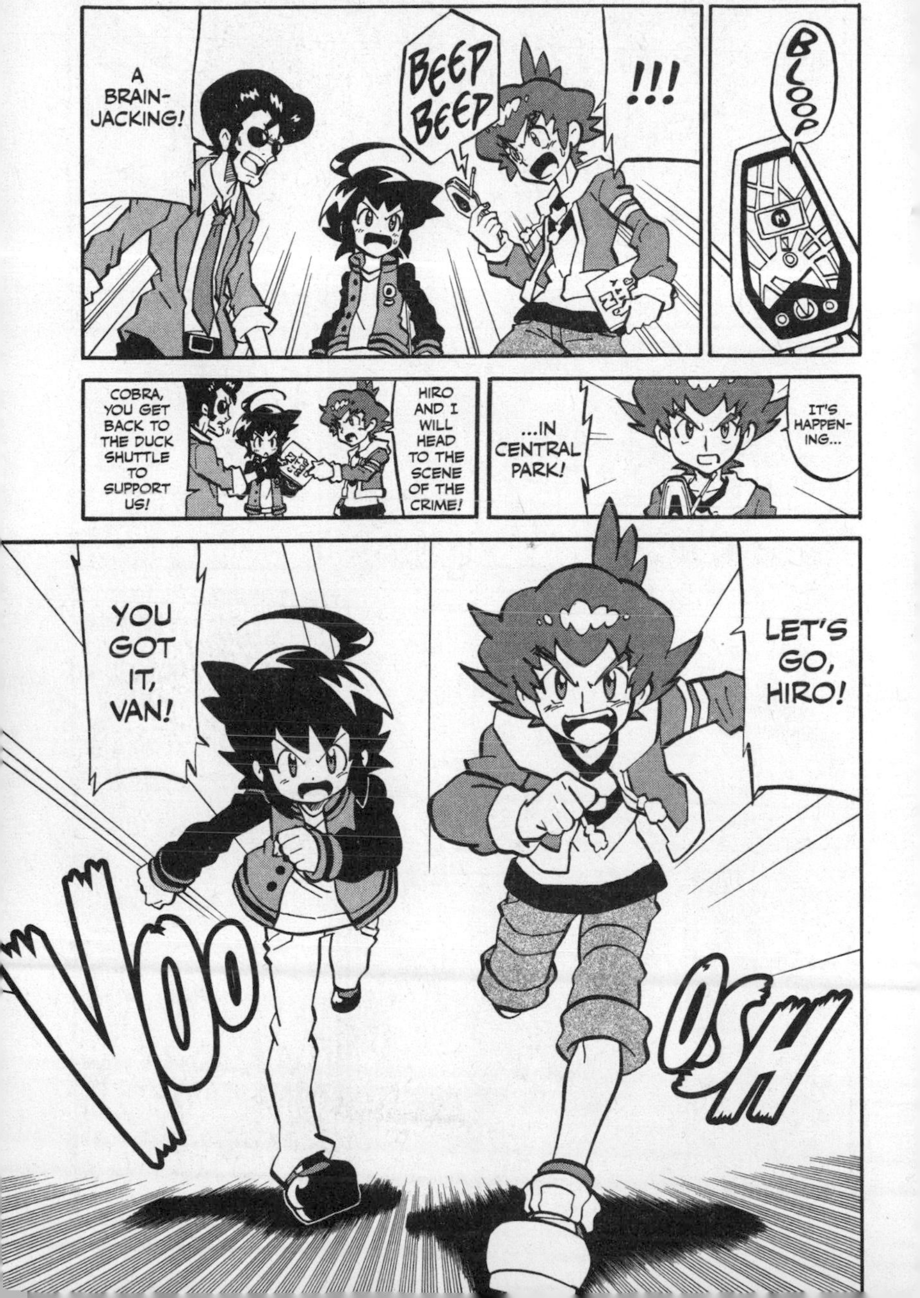
BLOOP
!!!
BEEP BEEP
A BRAIN-JACKING!
IT'S HAPPENING...
...IN CENTRAL PARK!
HIRO AND I WILL HEAD TO THE SCENE OF THE CRIME!
COBRA, YOU GET BACK TO THE DUCK SHUTTLE TO SUPPORT US!
LET'S GO, HIRO!
YOU GOT IT, VAN!
VOOOSH

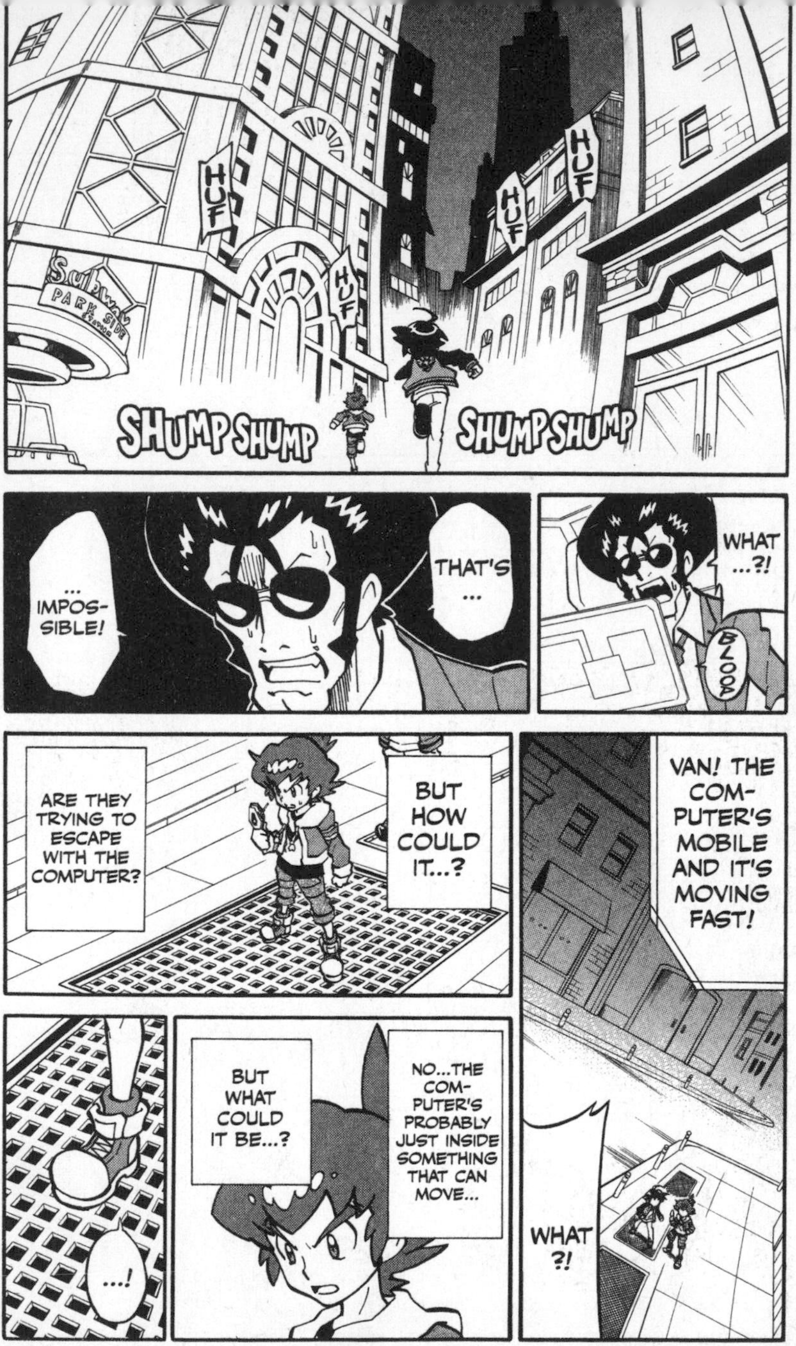
HUF
HUF
HUF
HUF
Subway
PARK SIDE
SHUMP SHUMP
SHUMP SHUMP
WHAT ...?!
BLOOP
THAT'S ...
... IMPOSSIBLE!
VAN! THE COMPUTER'S MOBILE AND IT'S MOVING FAST!
WHAT ?!
BUT HOW COULD IT...?
ARE THEY TRYING TO ESCAPE WITH THE COMPUTER?
NO...THE COMPUTER'S PROBABLY JUST INSIDE SOMETHING THAT CAN MOVE...
BUT WHAT COULD IT BE...?
...!

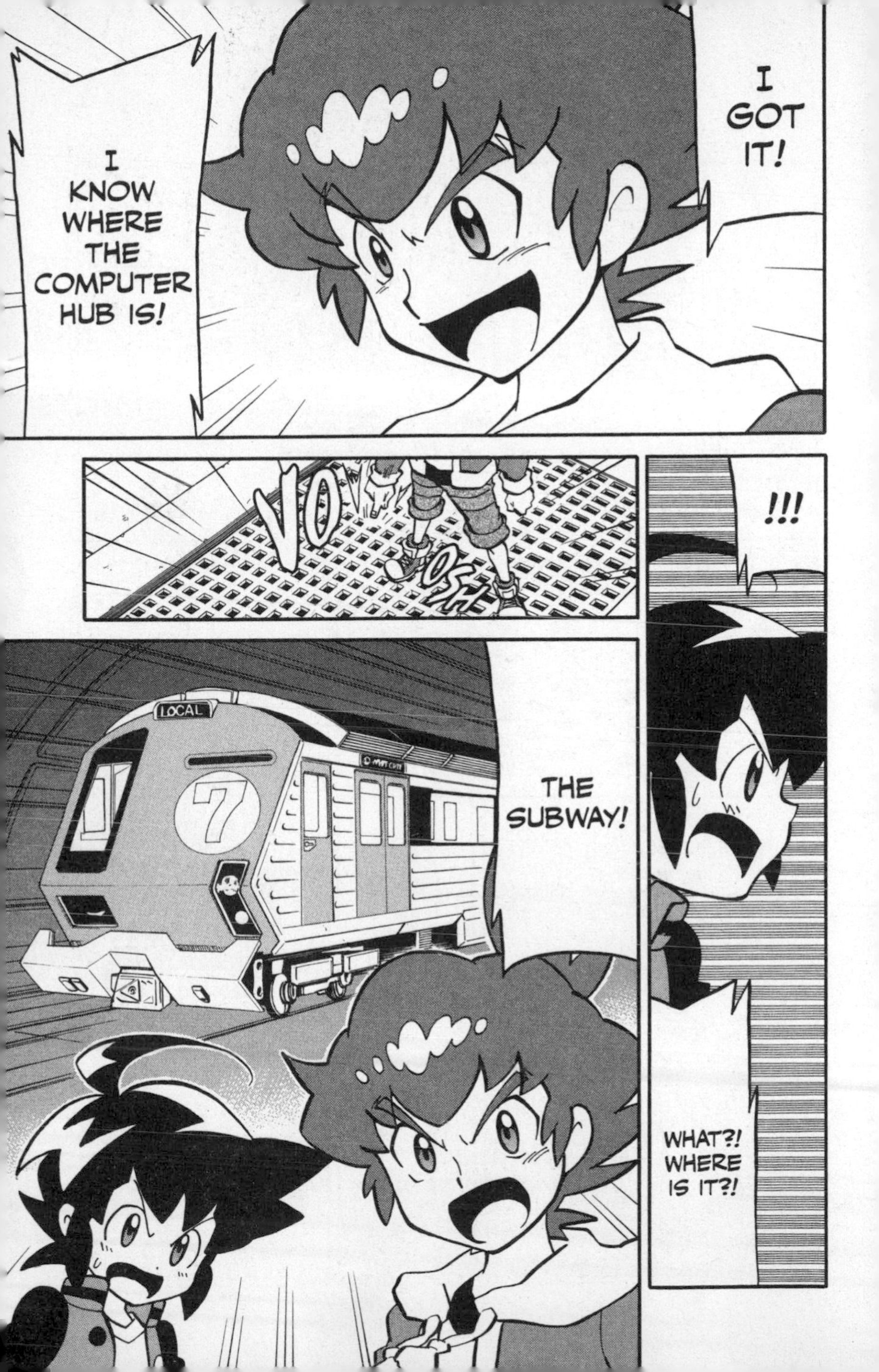
I GOT IT!
I KNOW WHERE THE COMPUTER HUB IS!
!!!
WHAT?! WHERE IS IT?!
VOOSH
THE SUBWAY!
LOCAL
7

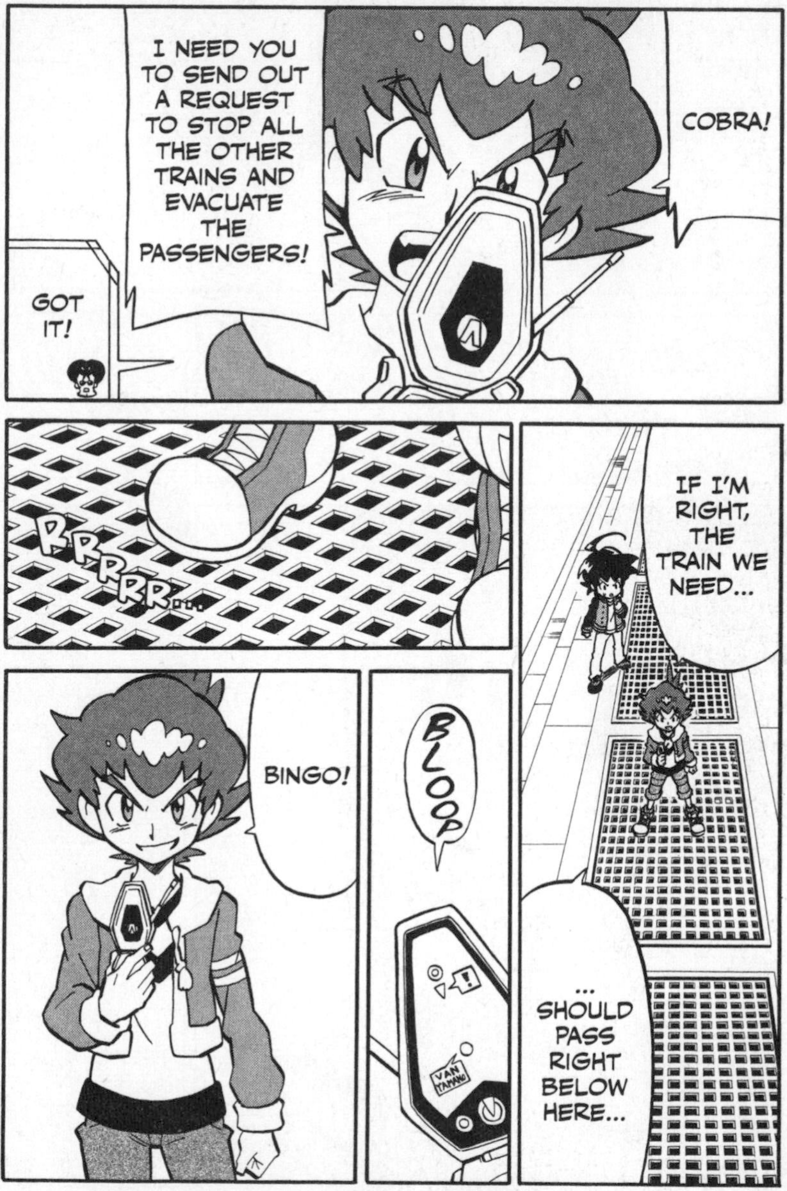
COBRA!
I NEED YOU TO SEND OUT A REQUEST TO STOP ALL THE OTHER TRAINS AND EVACUATE THE PASSENGERS!
GOT IT!
IF I'M RIGHT, THE TRAIN WE NEED...
... SHOULD PASS RIGHT BELOW HERE...
RRRRR...
BLOOP
VAN YAMANO
BINGO!

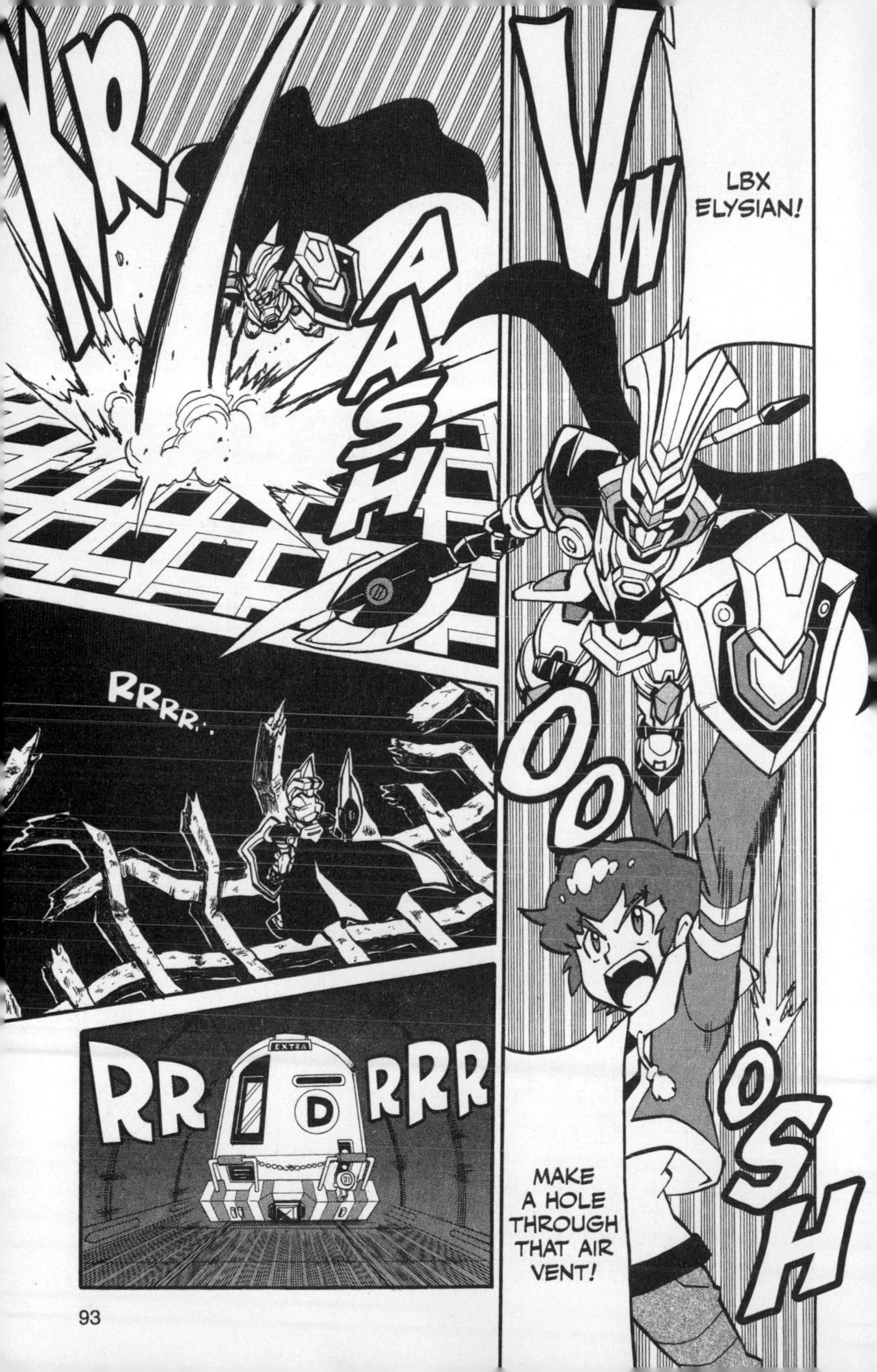
VWOOOSH
LBX ELYSIAN!
MAKE A HOLE THROUGH THAT AIR VENT!
KRAASH
RRRR...
RRRRR
EXTRA
D

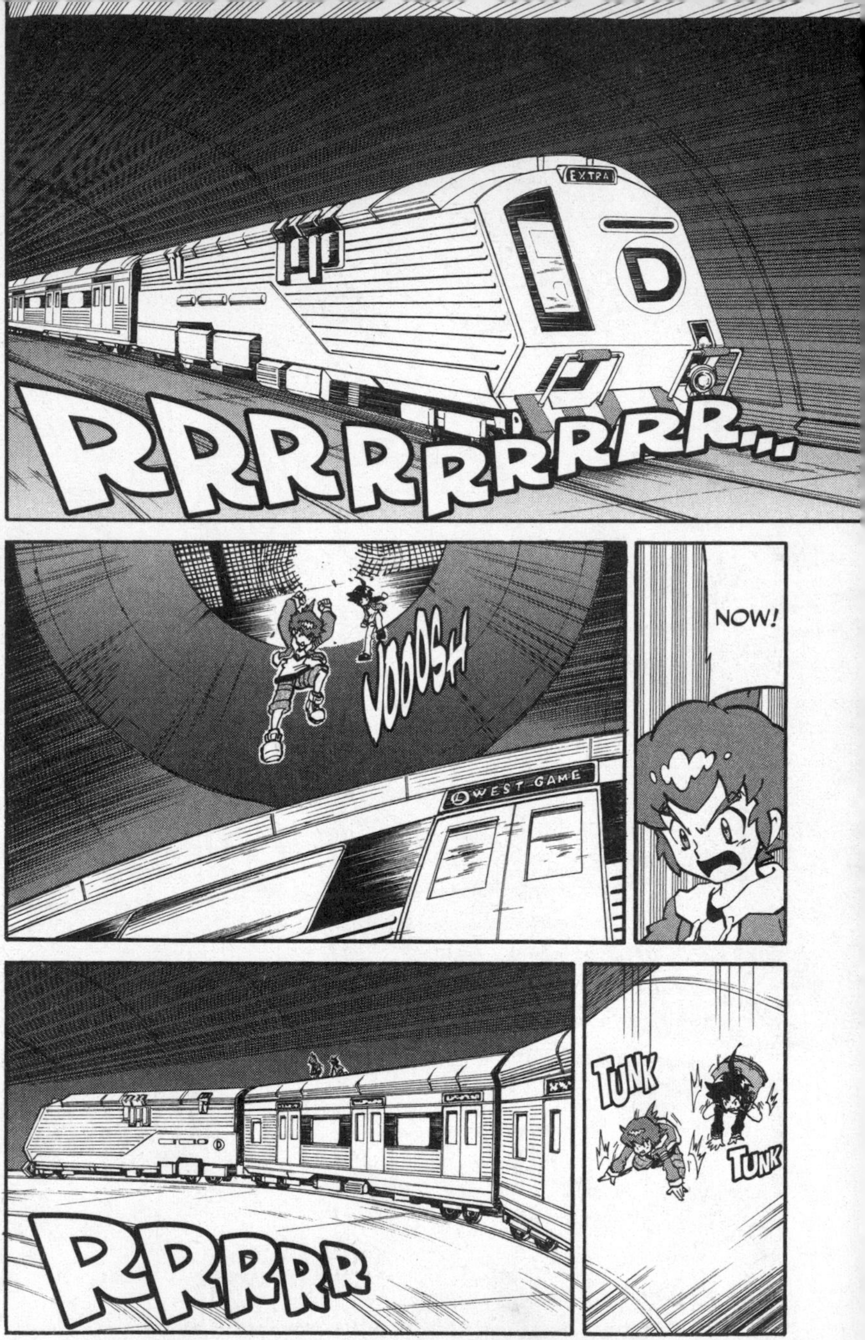
EXTRA
D
RRRRRRRRR...
NOW!
JOOOSH
WEST GAME
TUNK
TUNK
RRRRR

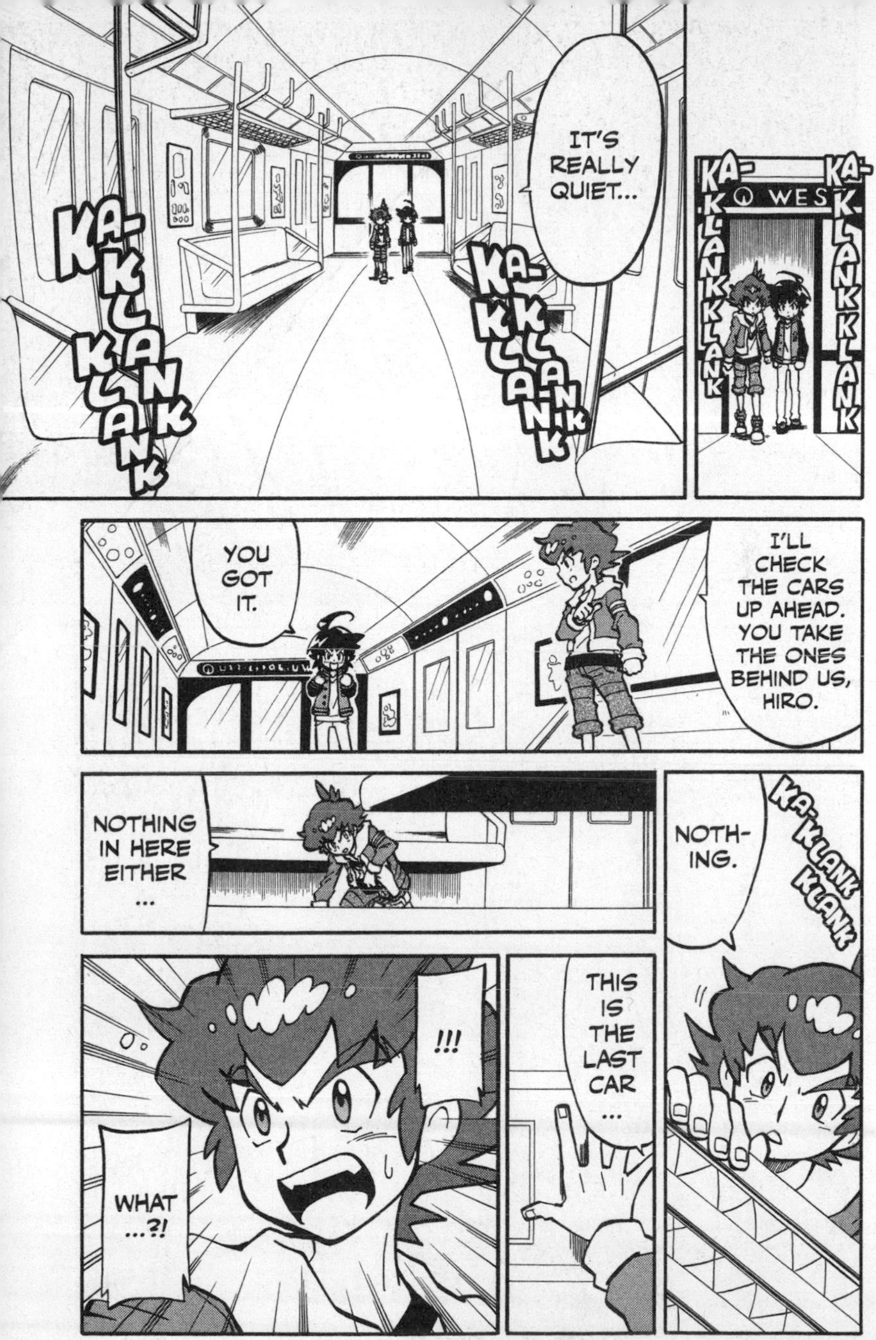
KA-KLANKKLANK
KA-KLANKKLANK
IT'S REALLY QUIET...
KA-KLANK KLANK
KA-KLANK KLANK
I'LL CHECK THE CARS UP AHEAD. YOU TAKE THE ONES BEHIND US, HIRO.
YOU GOT IT.
NOTH-ING.
KA-KLANK KLANK
NOTHING IN HERE EITHER ...
THIS IS THE LAST CAR ...
!!!
WHAT ...?!

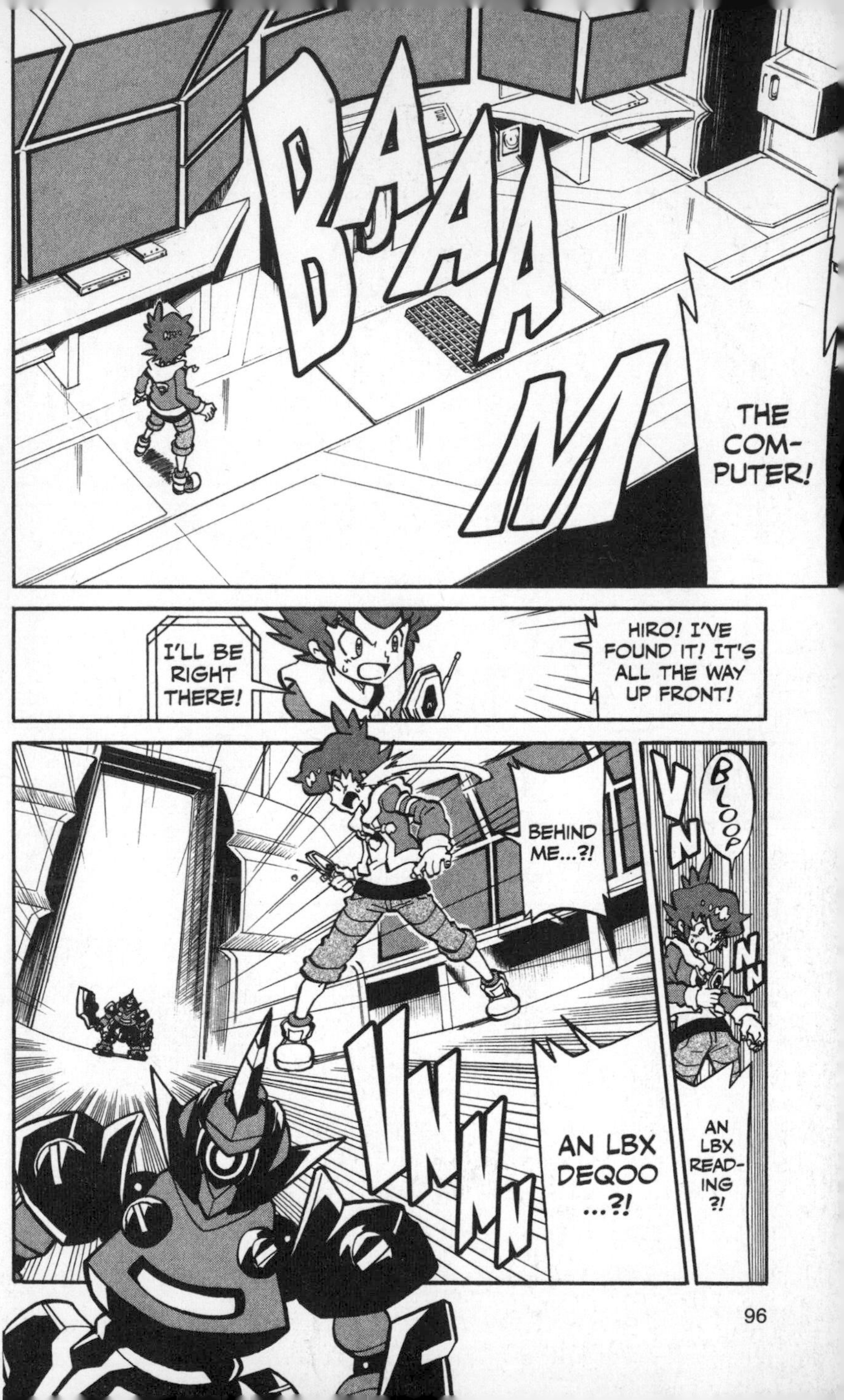
BAAAM
THE COM-PUTER!
HIRO! I'VE FOUND IT! IT'S ALL THE WAY UP FRONT!
I'LL BE RIGHT THERE!
BLOOP
VNN
AN LBX READ-ING?!
BEHIND ME...?!
UNNNN
AN LBX DEQOO ...?!

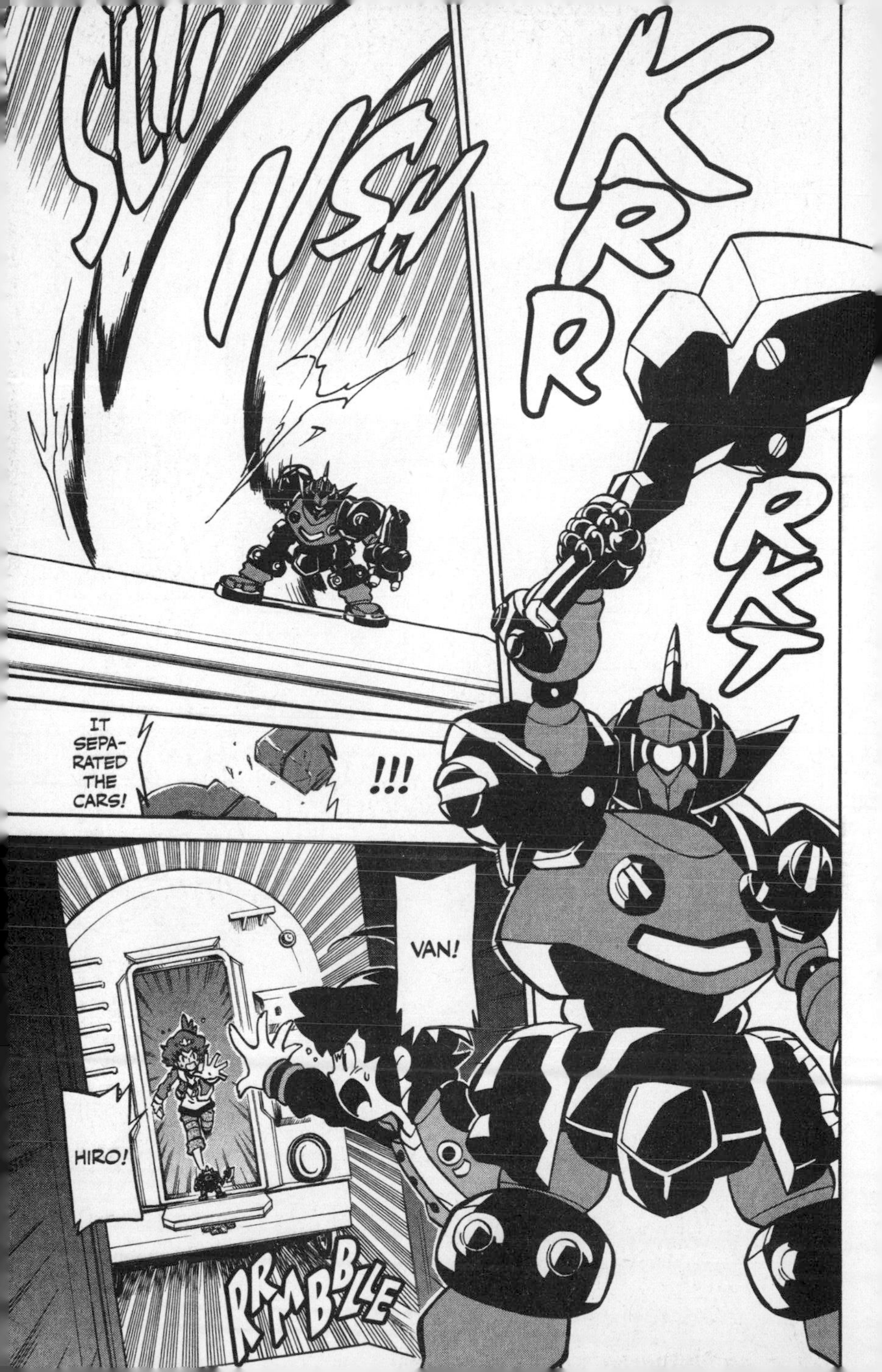

KRRR
RRT
SLUISH
!!!
IT SEPA-RATED THE CARS!
VAN!
HIRO!
RRMBBLLE

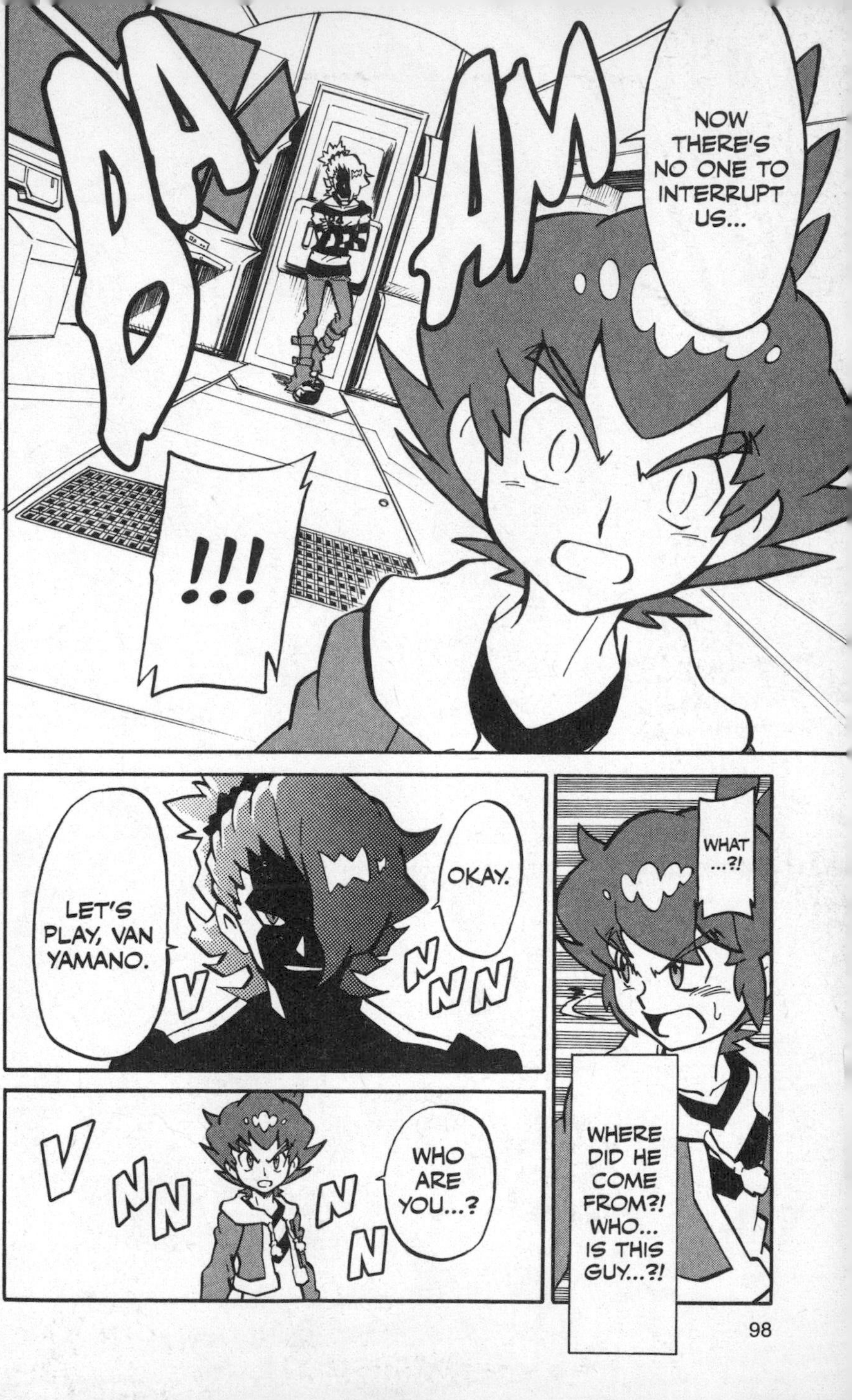
NOW THERE'S NO ONE TO INTERRUPT US...
BAAM
!!!
WHAT ...?!
WHERE DID HE COME FROM?! WHO... IS THIS GUY...?!
OKAY.
LET'S PLAY, VAN YAMANO.
VNNNN
WHO ARE YOU...?
VNNNNN

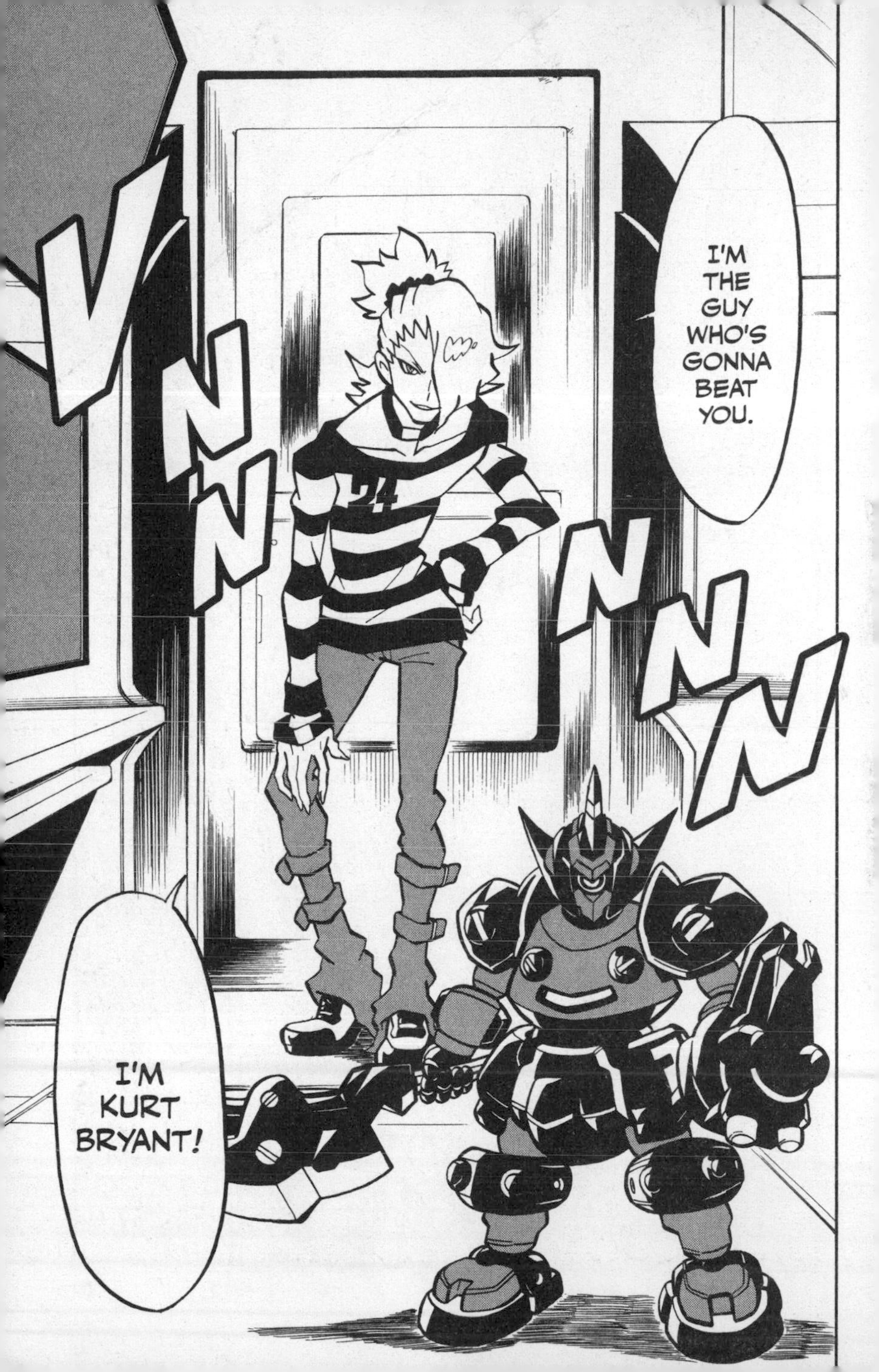
I'M THE GUY WHO'S GONNA BEAT YOU.
VNNNNN
I'M KURT BRYANT!

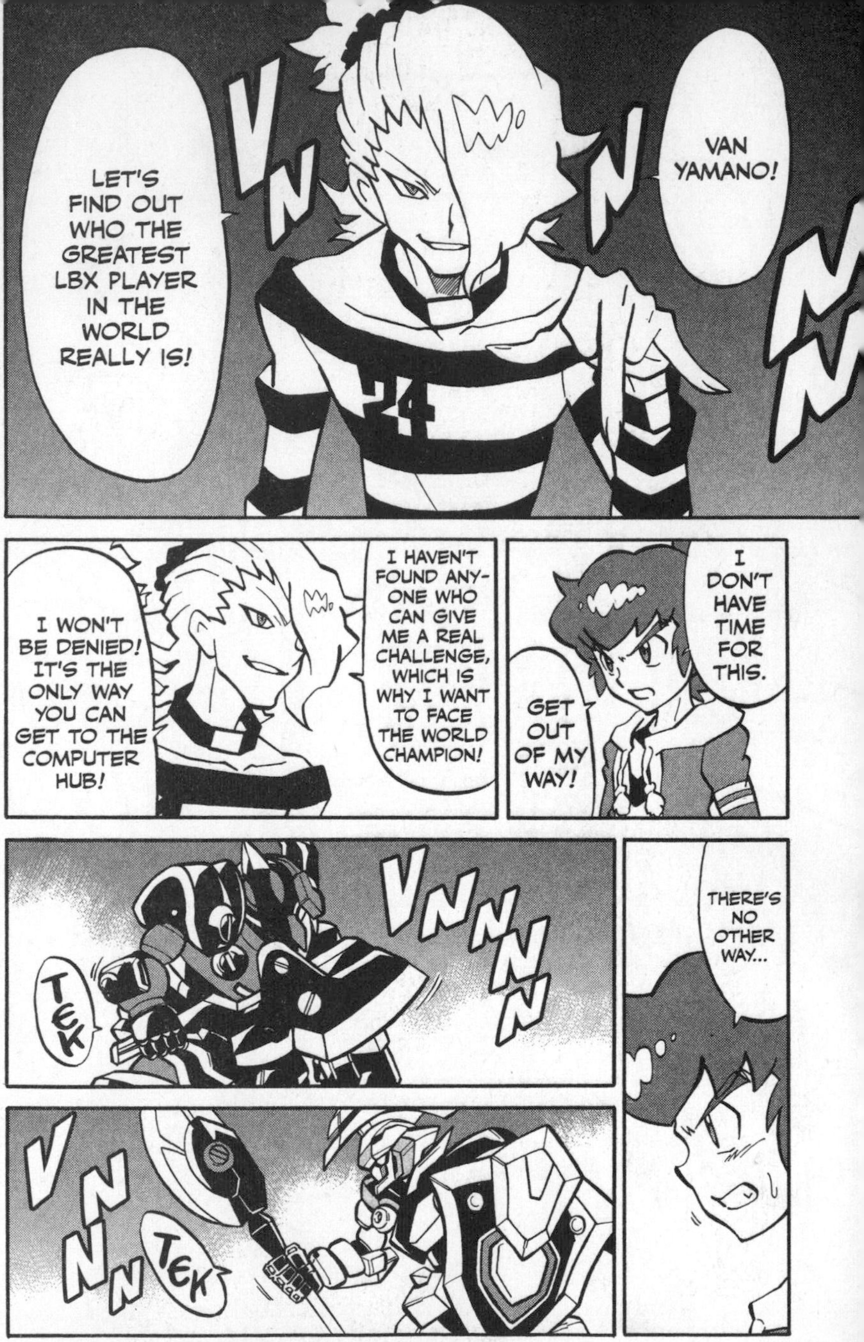
VAN YAMANO!
VNN
NNN
LET'S FIND OUT WHO THE GREATEST LBX PLAYER IN THE WORLD REALLY IS!
I DON'T HAVE TIME FOR THIS.
GET OUT OF MY WAY!
I HAVEN'T FOUND ANYONE WHO CAN GIVE ME A REAL CHALLENGE, WHICH IS WHY I WANT TO FACE THE WORLD CHAMPION!
I WON'T BE DENIED! IT'S THE ONLY WAY YOU CAN GET TO THE COMPUTER HUB!
THERE'S NO OTHER WAY...
VNNNNN
TEK
VNNN
TEK

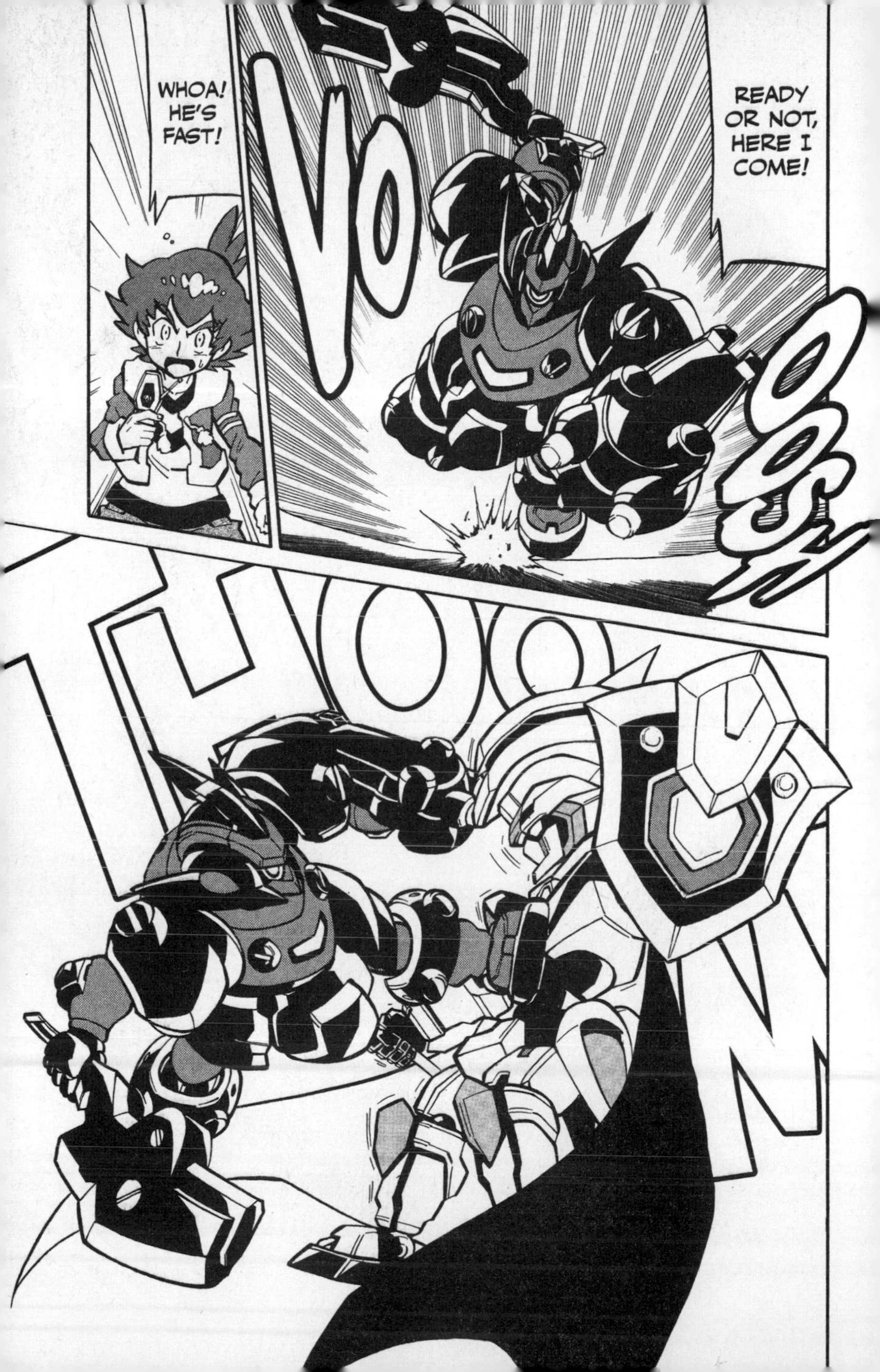
READY OR NOT, HERE I COME!
VOOOSH!
WHOA! HE'S FAST!

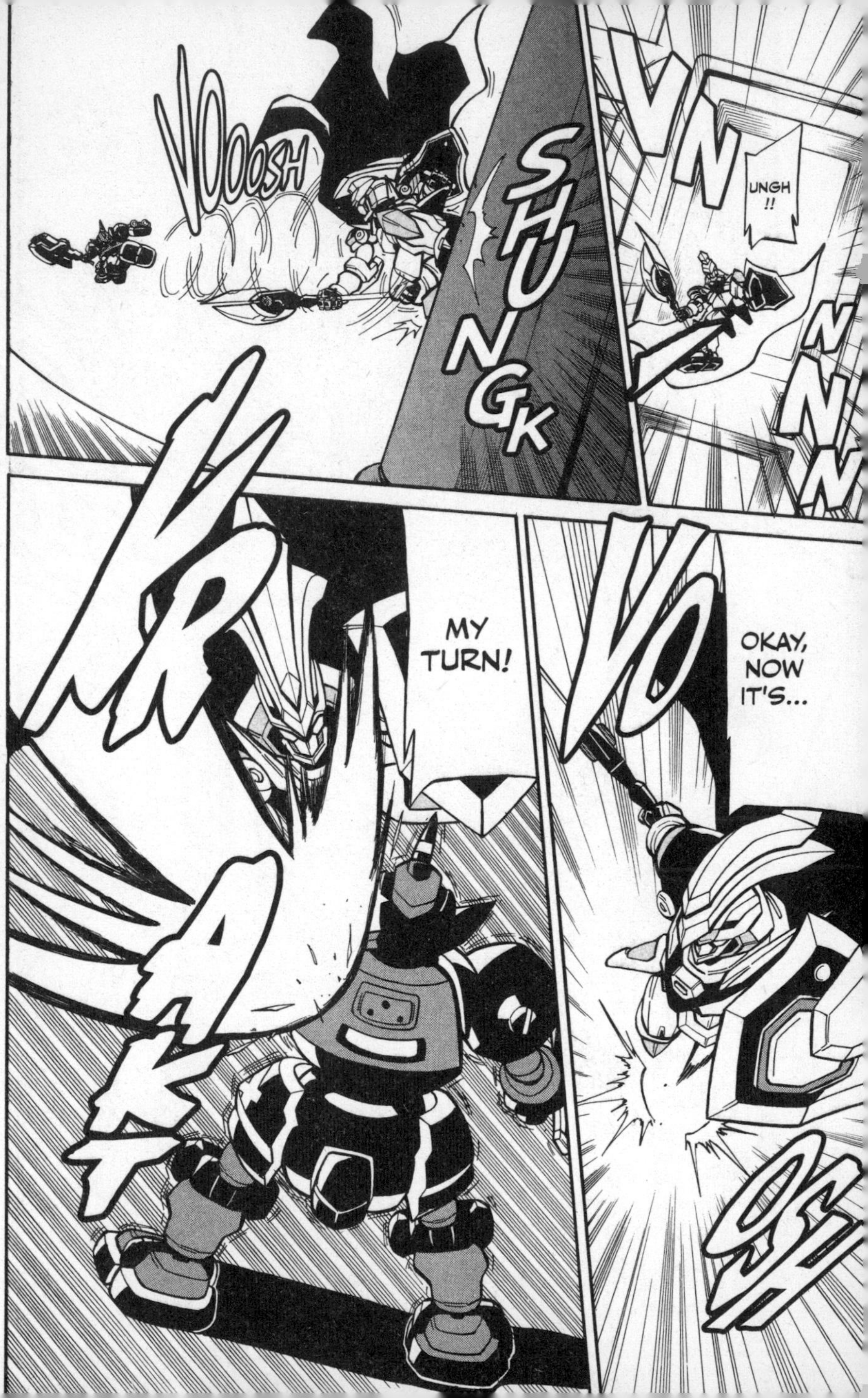
VN
UNGH !!
NNNN
VOOOSH
SHUNGK
VO
OKAY, NOW IT'S...
MY TURN!

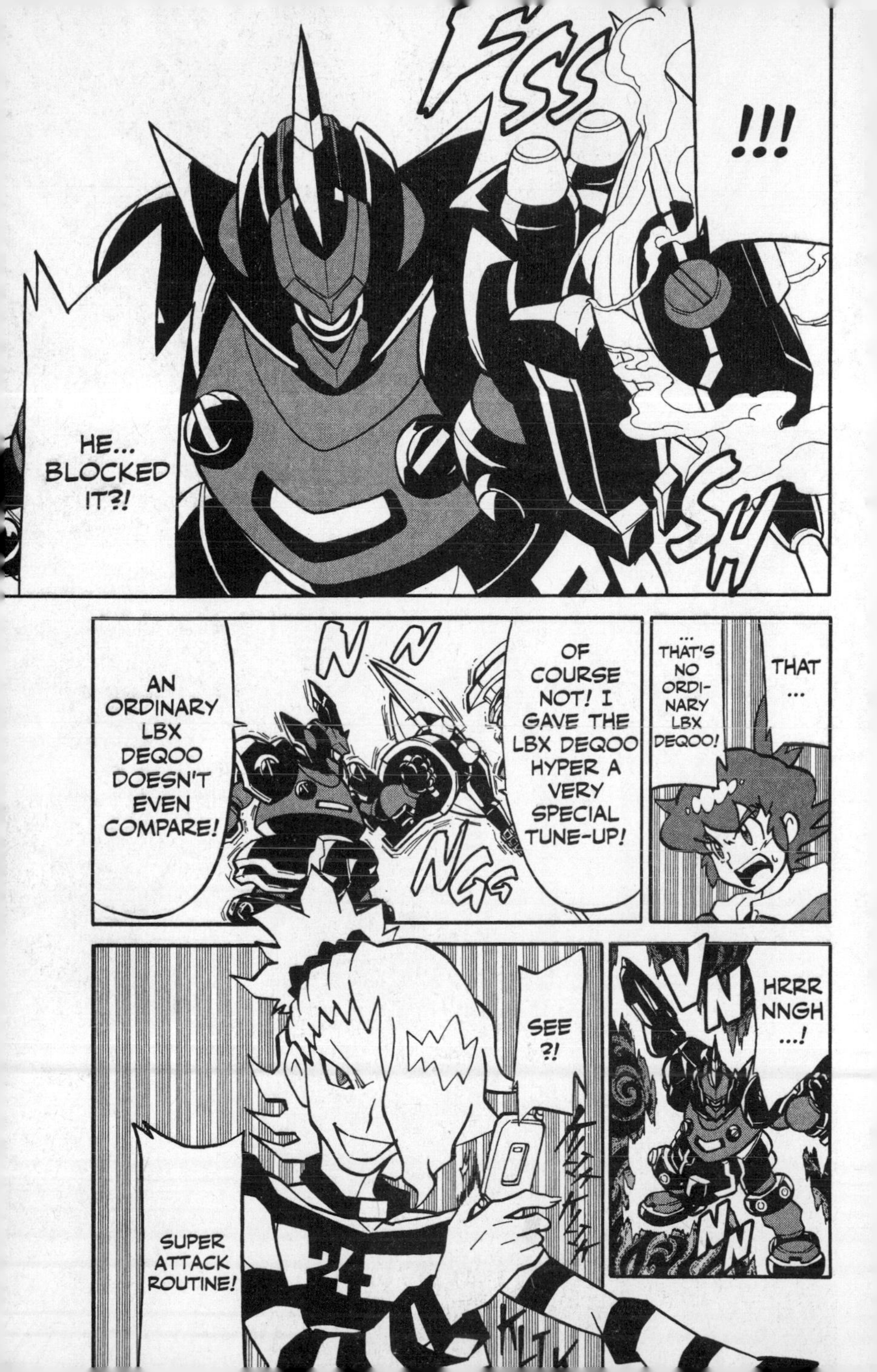
!!!
FSSS
HE... BLOCKED IT?!
THAT...
...THAT'S NO ORDINARY LBX DEQOO!
OF COURSE NOT! I GAVE THE LBX DEQOO HYPER A VERY SPECIAL TUNE-UP!
N N
NGG
AN ORDINARY LBX DEQOO DOESN'T EVEN COMPARE!
HRRRNNGH...!
VN
NN
SEE?!
SUPER ATTACK ROUTINE!

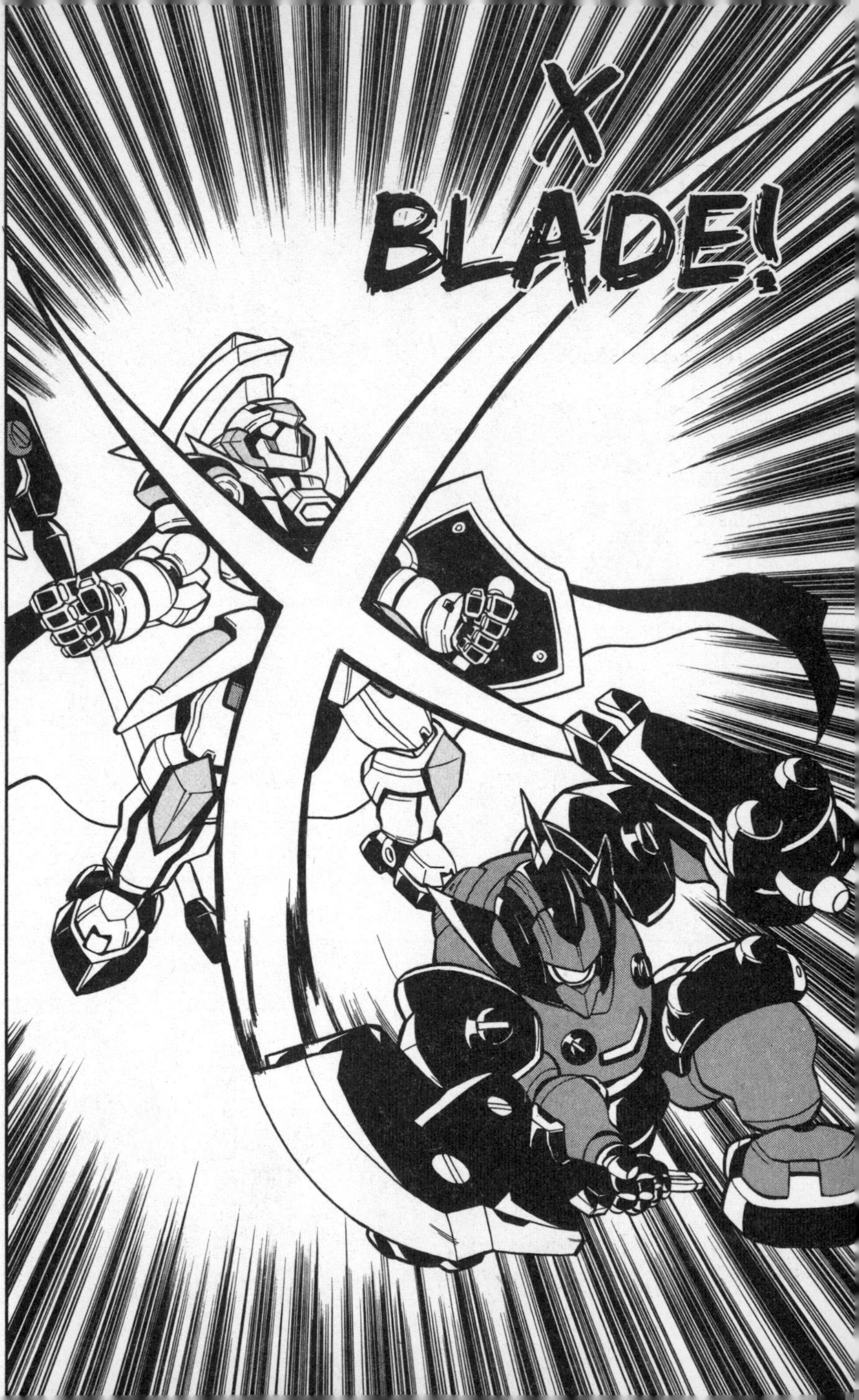
X
BLADE!

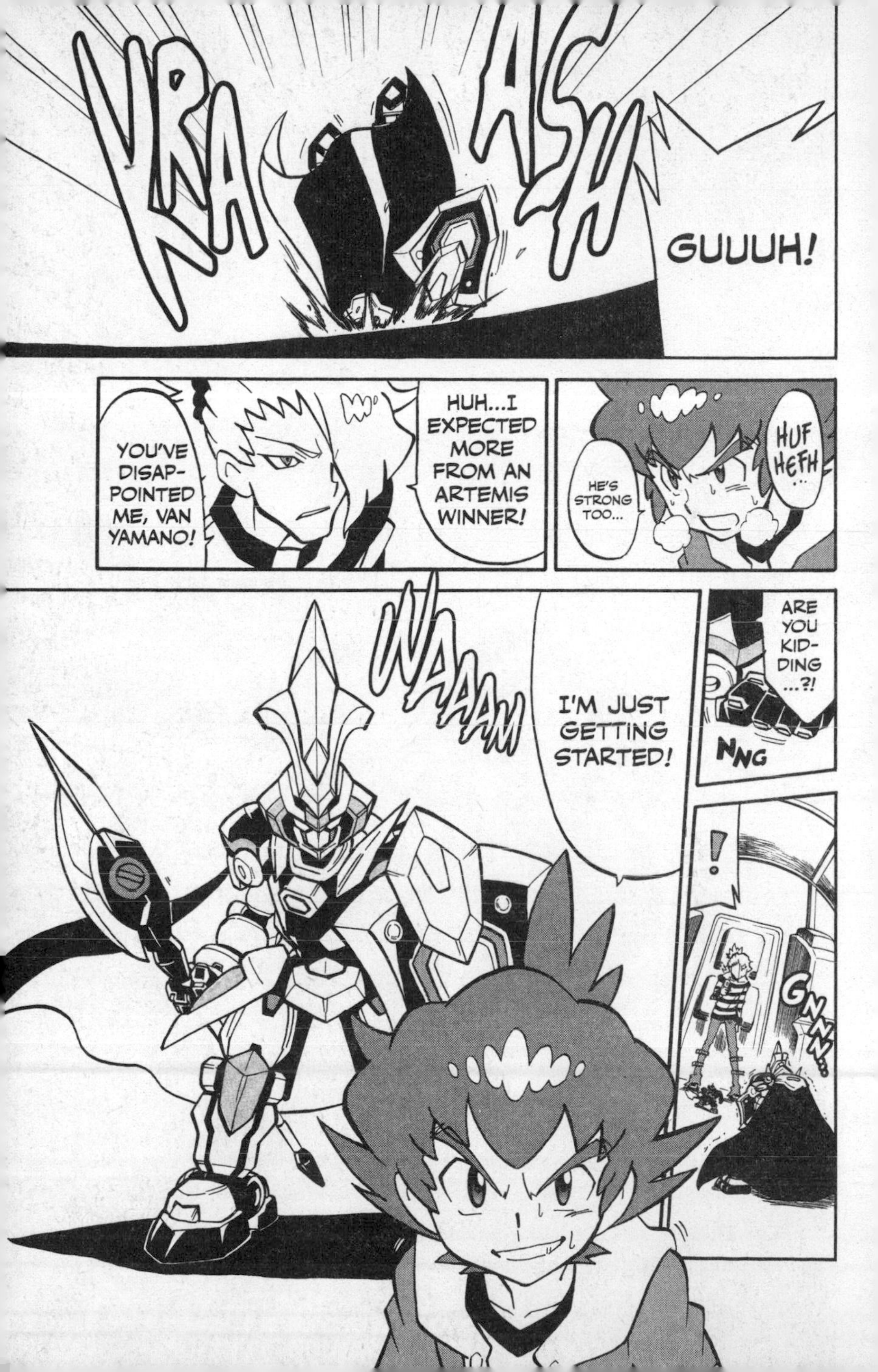
VRAASH
GUUUH!
HUF HEFH...
HE'S STRONG TOO...
HUH...I EXPECTED MORE FROM AN ARTEMIS WINNER!
YOU'VE DISAP-POINTED ME, VAN YAMANO!
ARE YOU KID-DING...?!
NNG
!
GNNN...
WAAAM
I'M JUST GETTING STARTED!

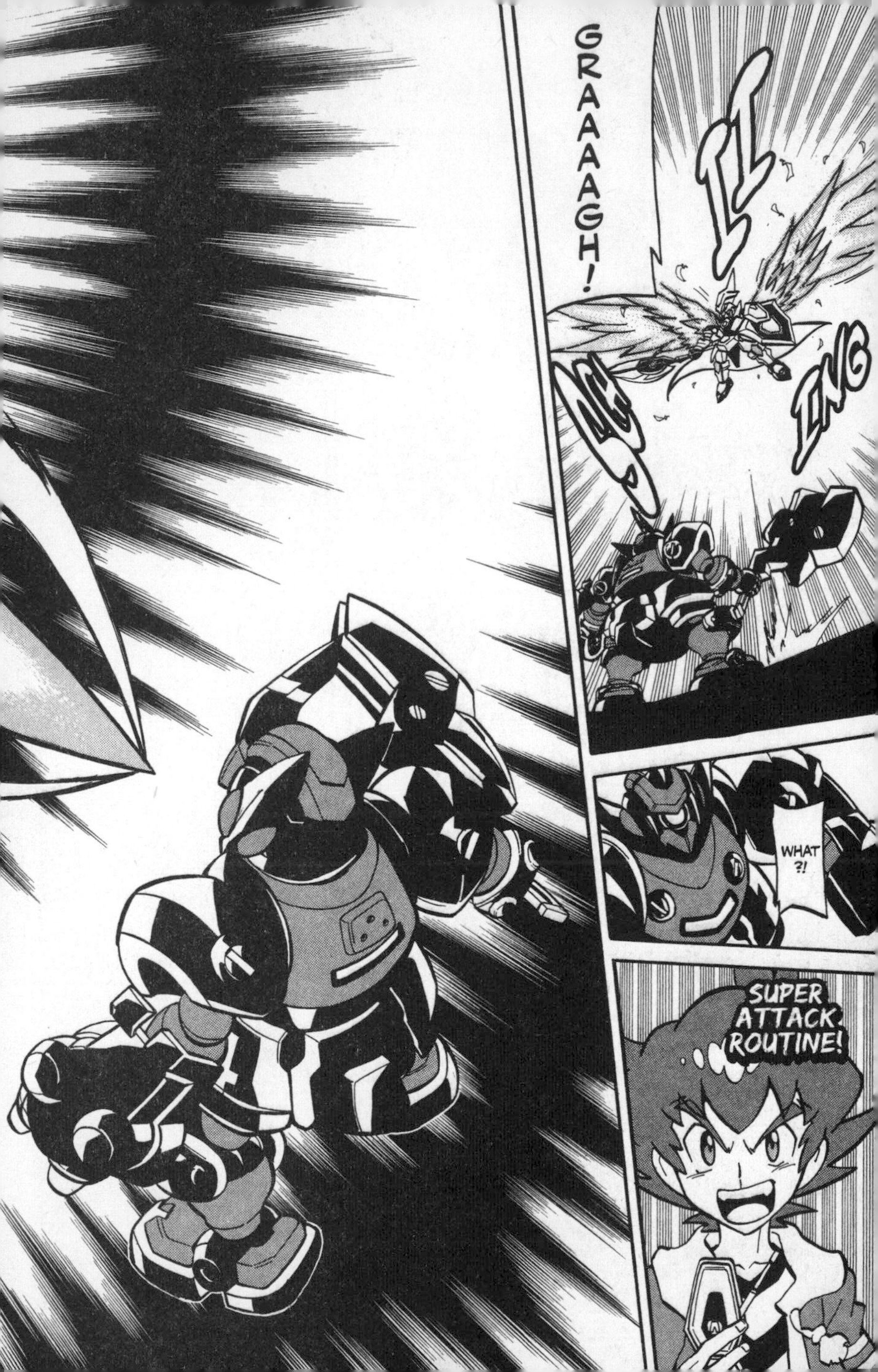
GRAAAAGH!
WHAT ?!
SUPER ATTACK ROUTINE!

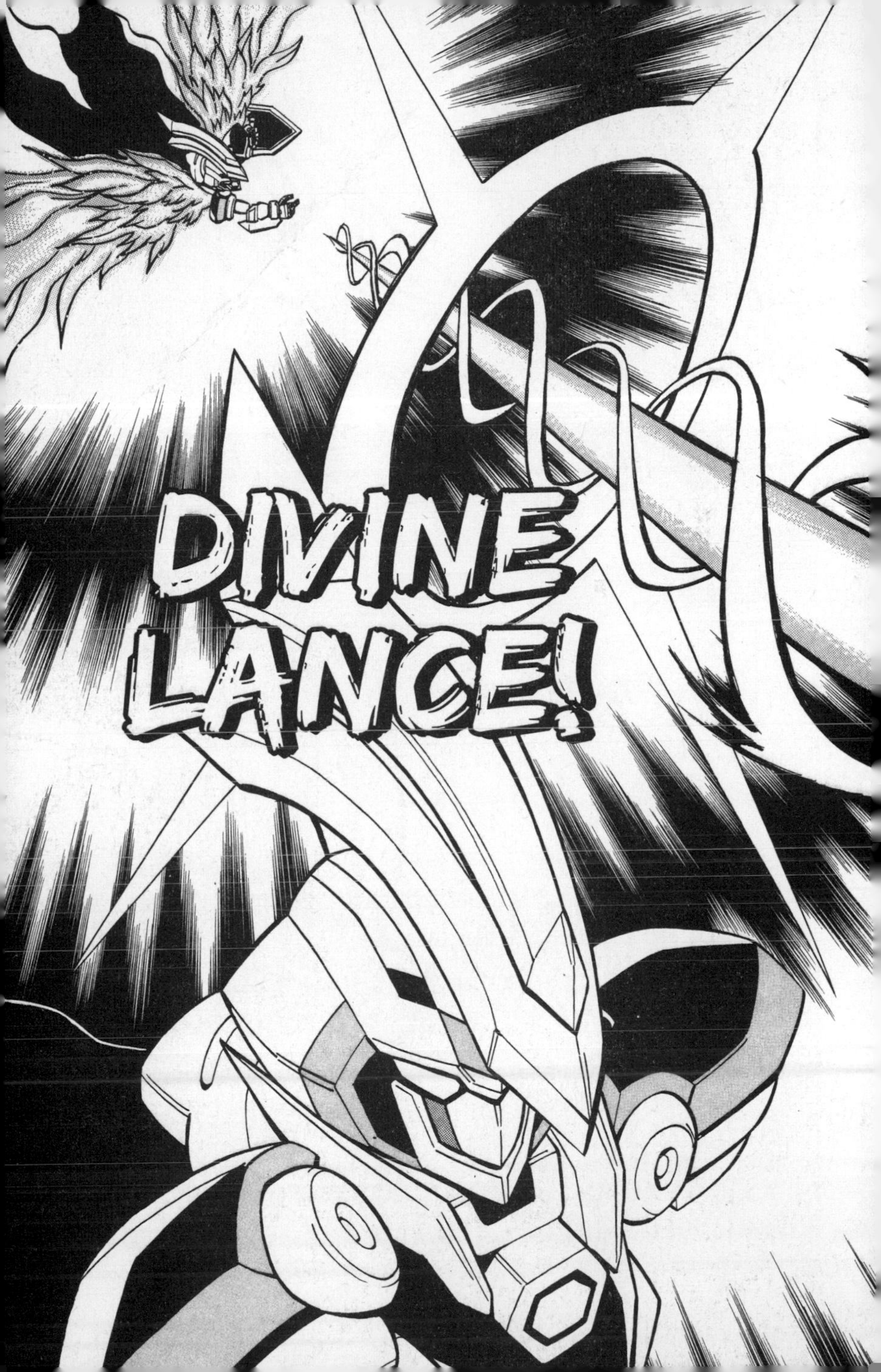
DIVINE LANCE!

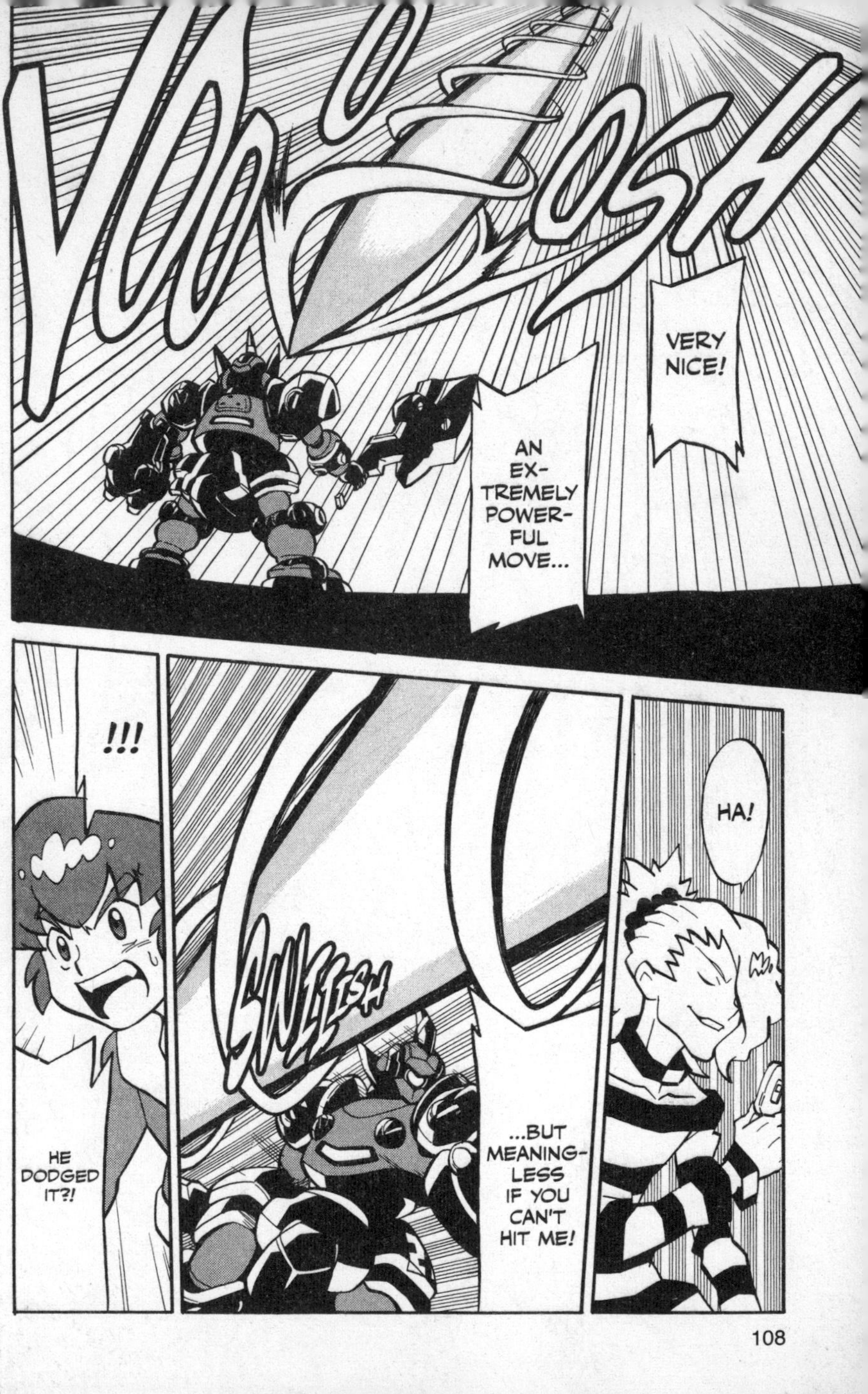
VERY NICE!
AN EX-TREMELY POWER-FUL MOVE...
HA!
...BUT MEANING-LESS IF YOU CAN'T HIT ME!
SWIIISH
!!!
HE DODGED IT?!

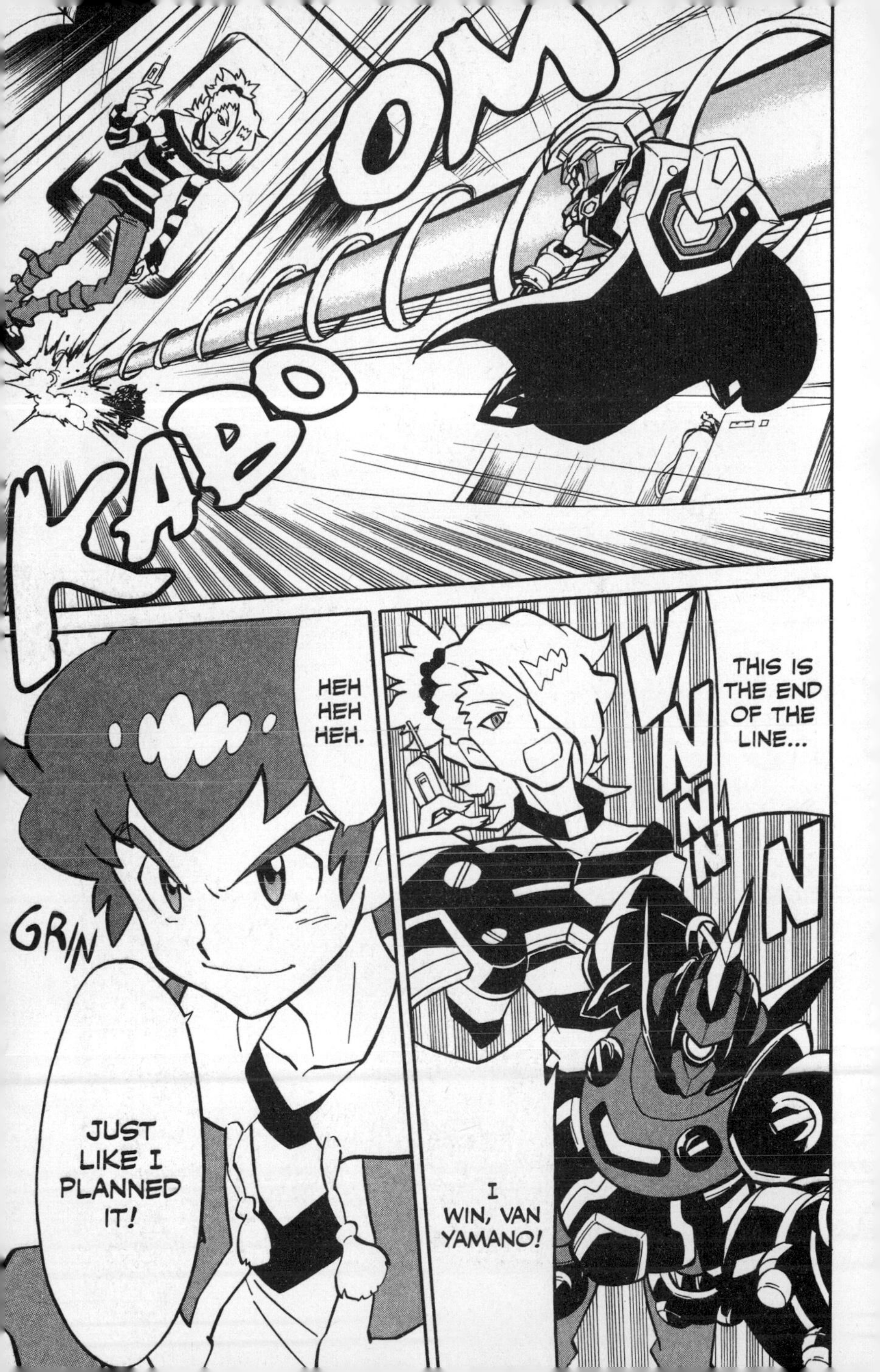
KABOOM
THIS IS THE END OF THE LINE...
VNNNNN
I WIN, VAN YAMANO!
HEH HEH HEH.
GRIN
JUST LIKE I PLANNED IT!

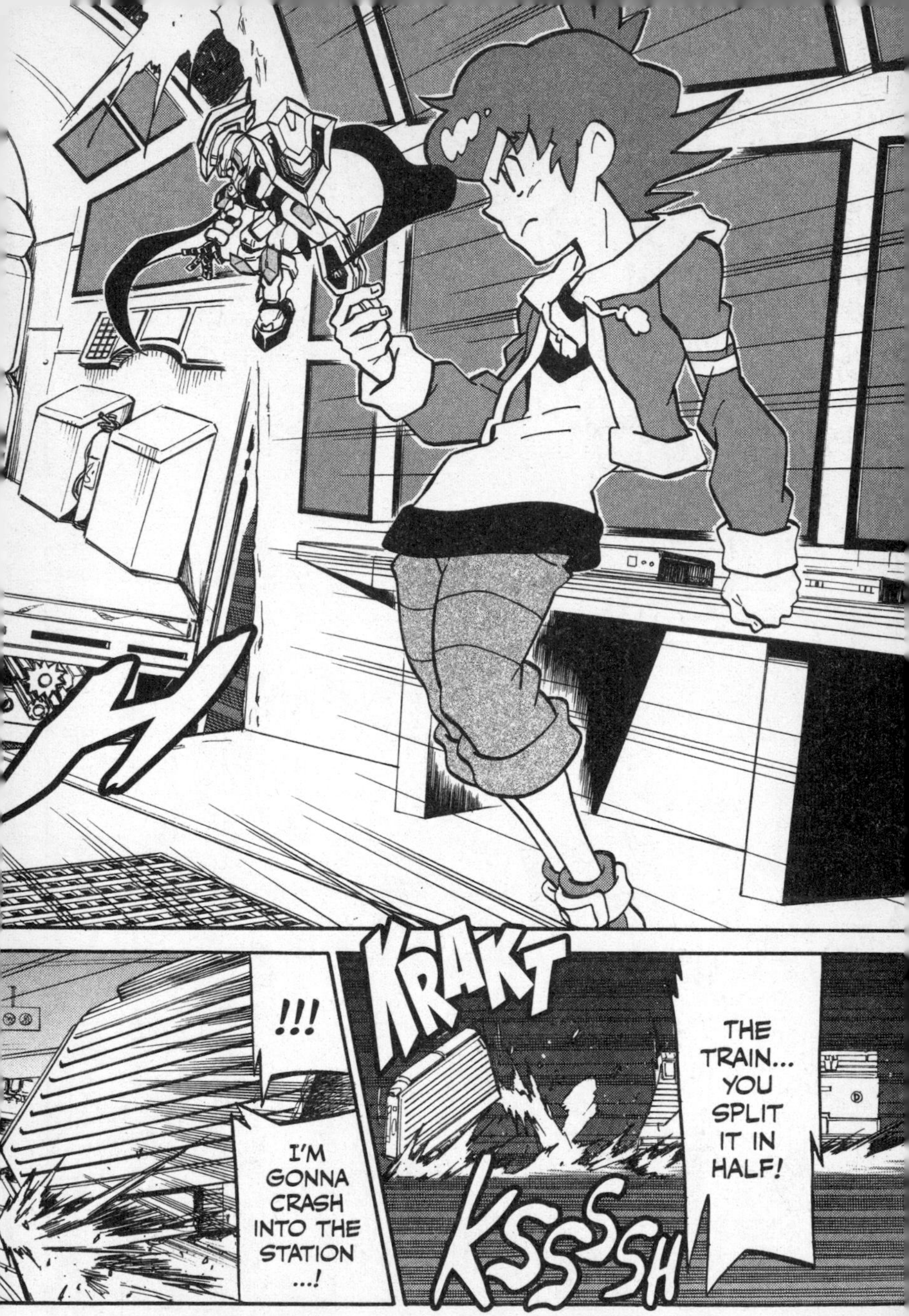
KRAKT
THE TRAIN... YOU SPLIT IT IN HALF!
KSSSSH
!!!
I'M GONNA CRASH INTO THE STATION ...!

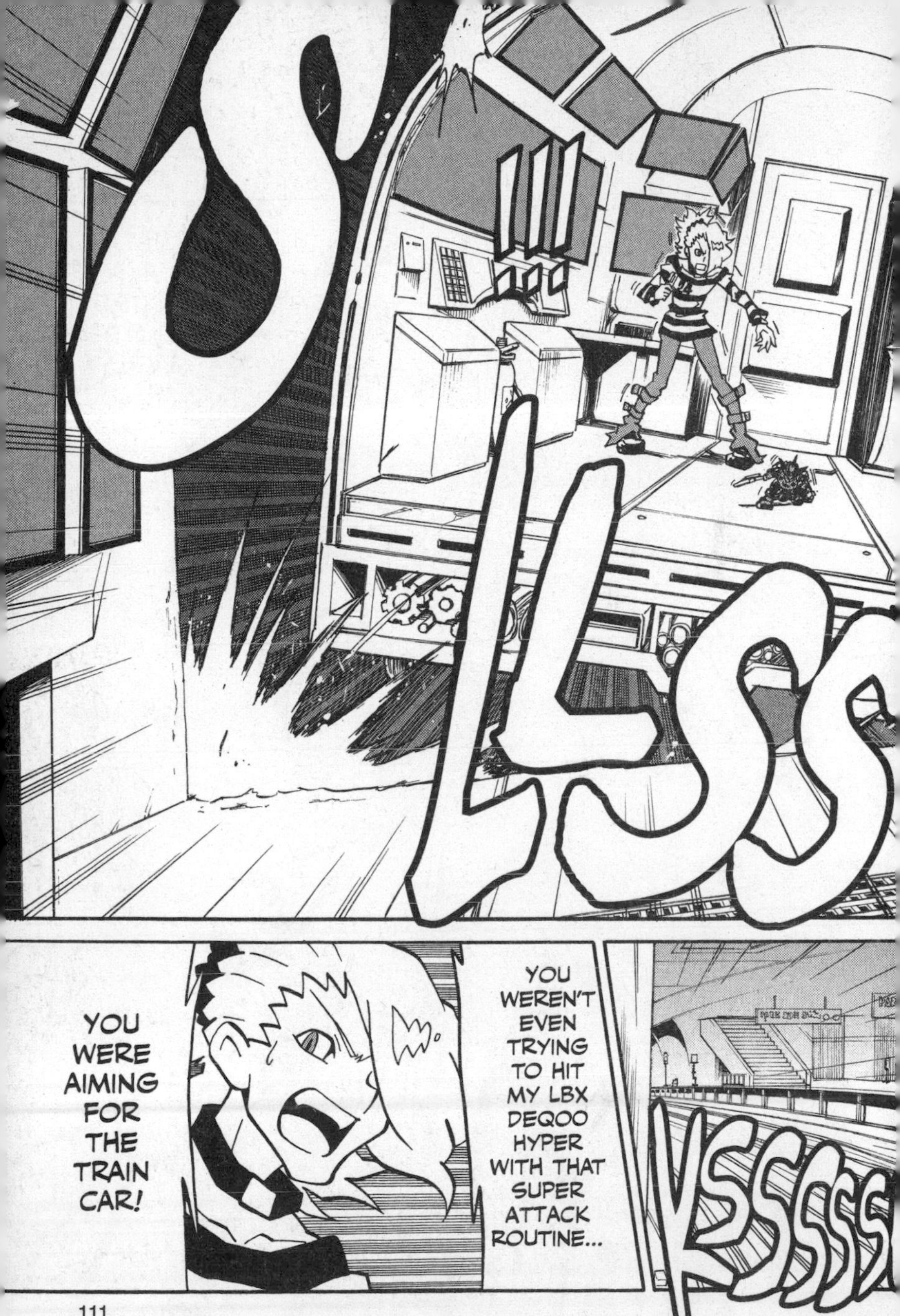
YOU WEREN'T EVEN TRYING TO HIT MY LBX DEQOO HYPER WITH THAT SUPER ATTACK ROUTINE...
YOU WERE AIMING FOR THE TRAIN CAR!

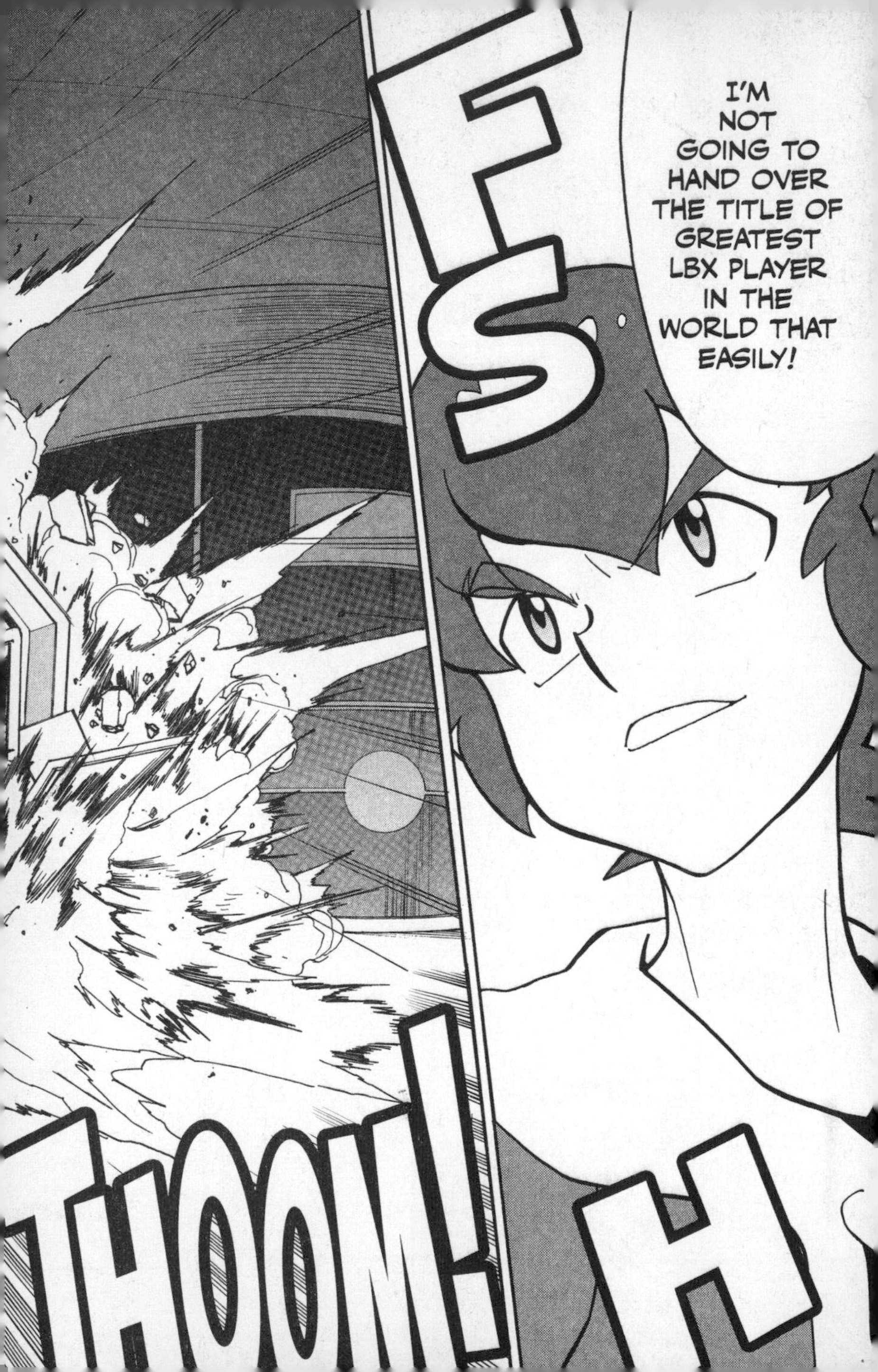
I'M NOT GOING TO HAND OVER THE TITLE OF GREATEST LBX PLAYER IN THE WORLD THAT EASILY!
THOOM!

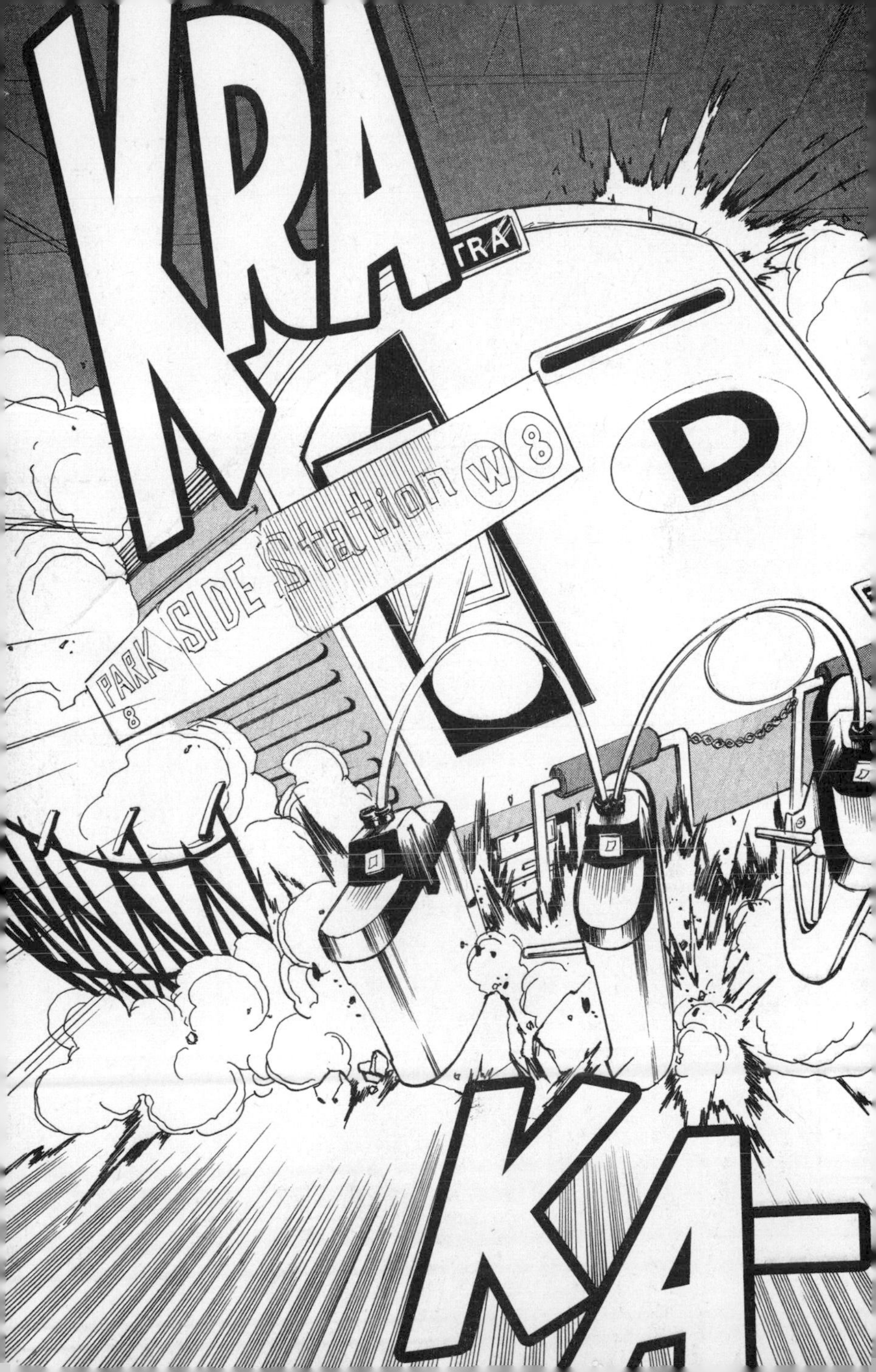

VRA
TRA
PARK SIDE Station W 8
PARK 8
KA-

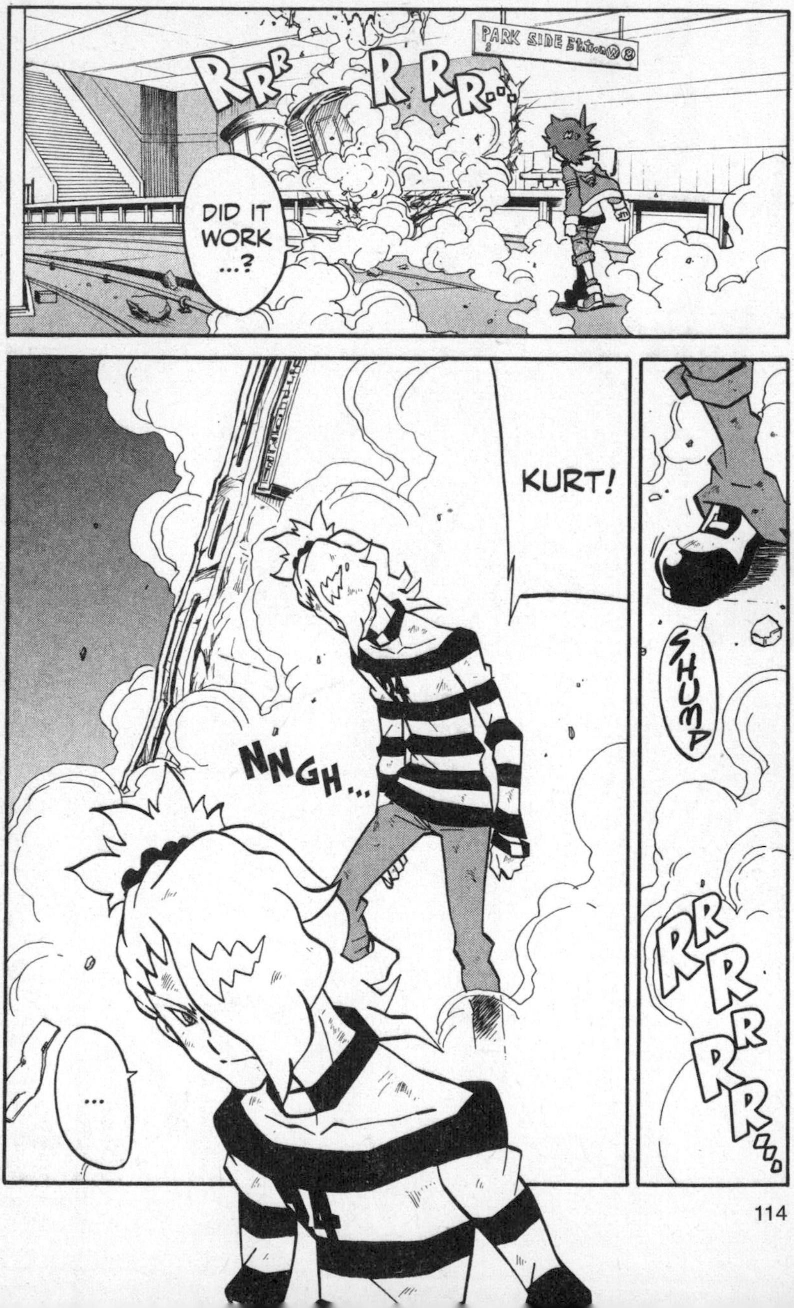
PARK SIDE Station
RRR R R R...
DID IT WORK ...?
SHUMP
RRRRRR...
KURT!
NNGH...
...

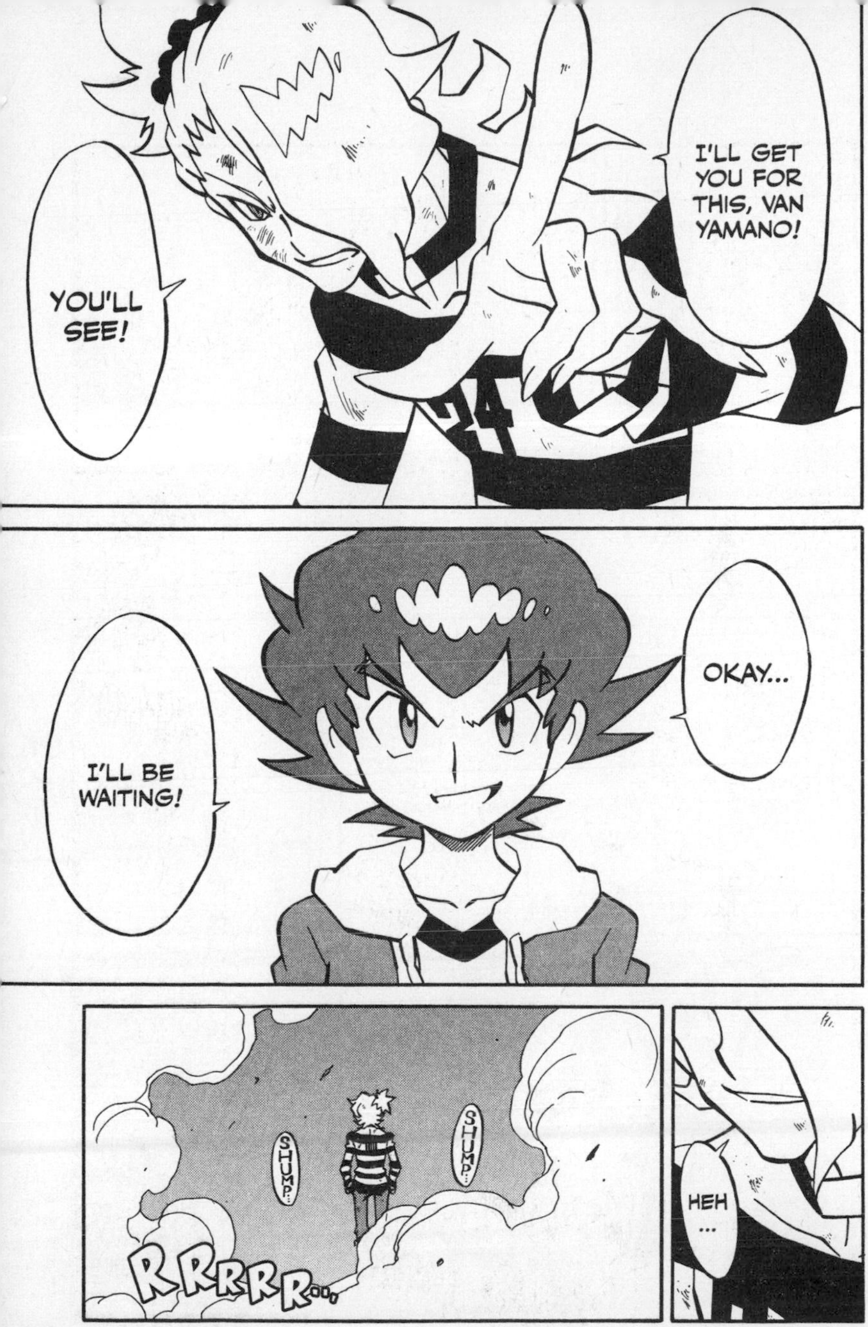
I'LL GET YOU FOR THIS, VAN YAMANO!
YOU'LL SEE!
OKAY...
I'LL BE WAITING!
HEH ...
SHUMP...
SHUMP...
RRRRR...

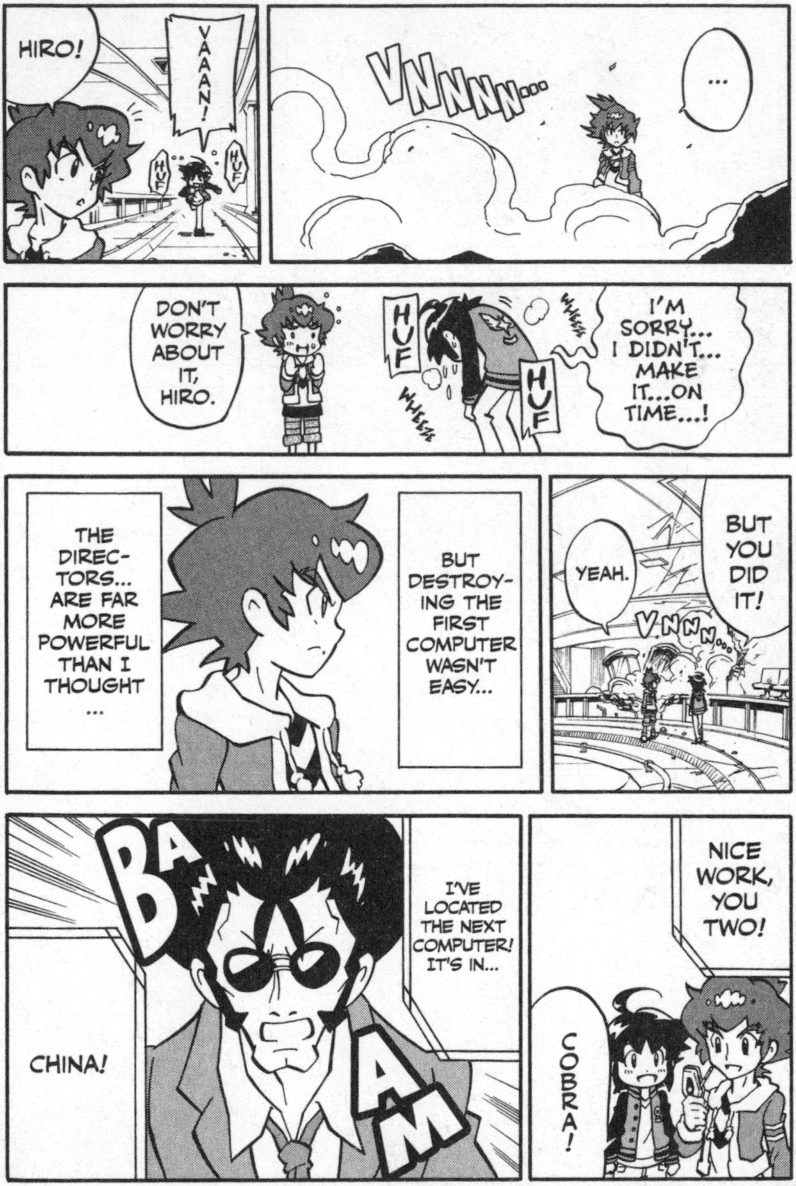
...
VNNNN...
VAAAAN!
HIRO!
HUF
HUF
I'M SORRY... I DIDN'T... MAKE IT...ON TIME...!
WHEESS
HUF
HUF
WHEESS
DON'T WORRY ABOUT IT, HIRO.
BUT YOU DID IT!
YEAH.
V.NNN...
BUT DESTROYING THE FIRST COMPUTER WASN'T EASY...
THE DIRECTORS... ARE FAR MORE POWERFUL THAN I THOUGHT...
NICE WORK, YOU TWO!
COBRA!
I'VE LOCATED THE NEXT COMPUTER! IT'S IN...
BAAM
CHINA!

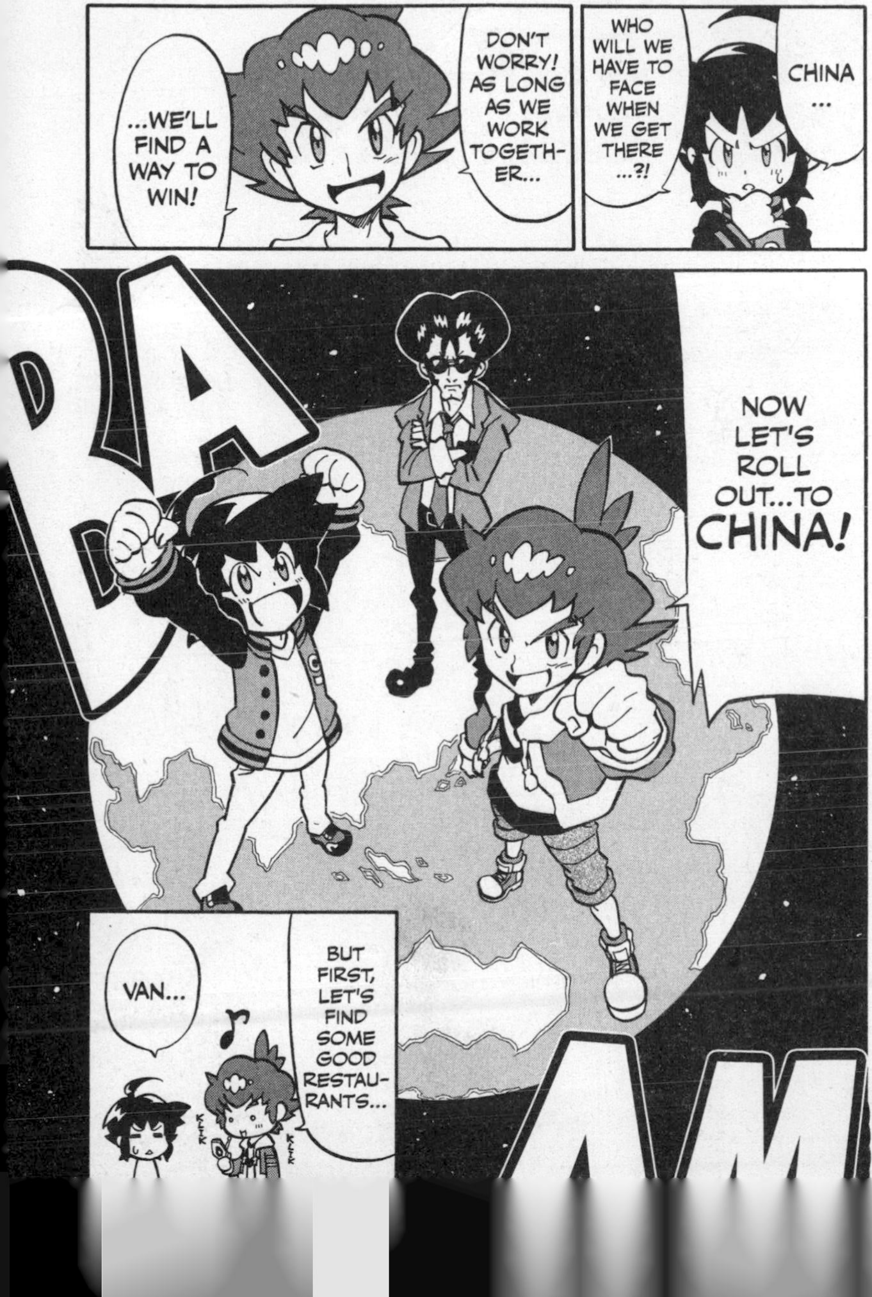
CHINA ...
WHO WILL WE HAVE TO FACE WHEN WE GET THERE ...?!
DON'T WORRY! AS LONG AS WE WORK TOGETH-ER...
...WE'LL FIND A WAY TO WIN!
NOW LET'S ROLL OUT...TO CHINA!
BUT FIRST, LET'S FIND SOME GOOD RESTAU-RANTS...
KLIK
KLIK
VAN...

CHAPTER 16: THE TOTAL CONTROL FREAK

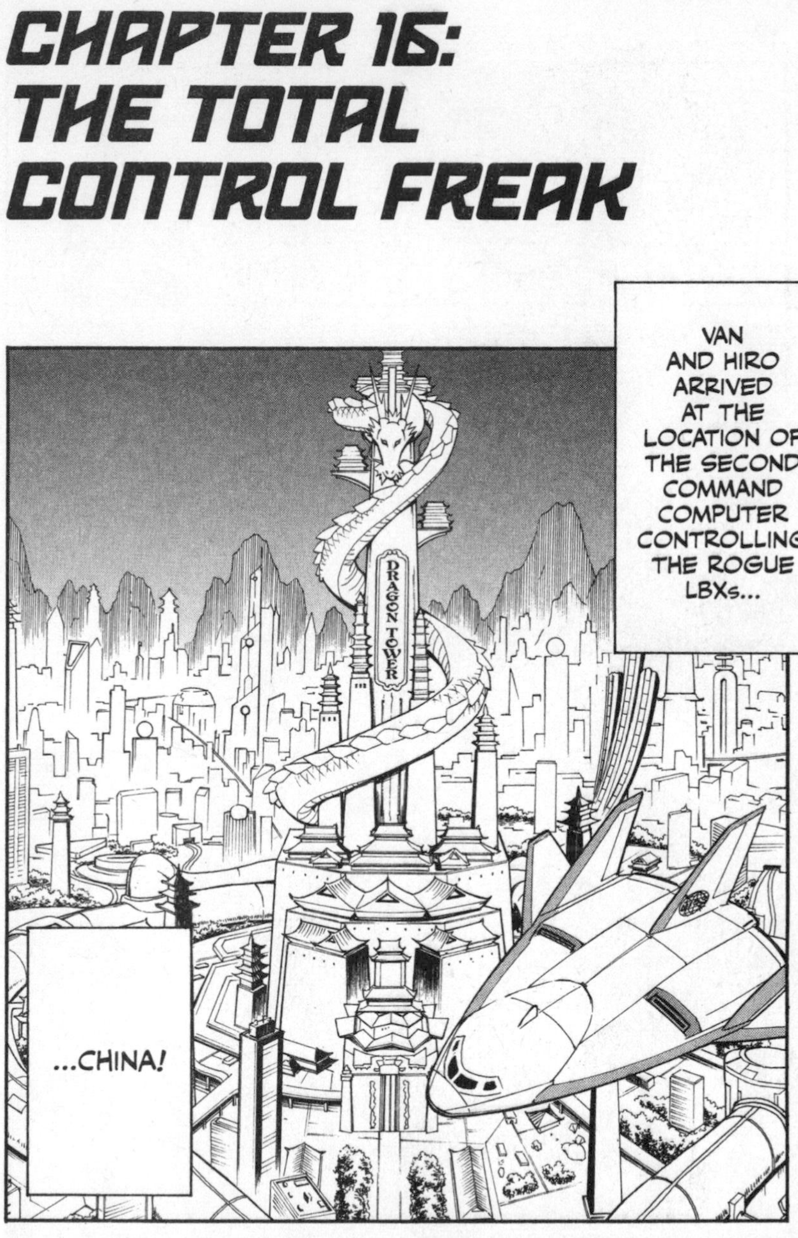
VAN AND HIRO ARRIVED AT THE LOCATION OF THE SECOND COMMAND COMPUTER CONTROLLING THE ROGUE LBXs...
DRAGON TOWER
...CHINA!

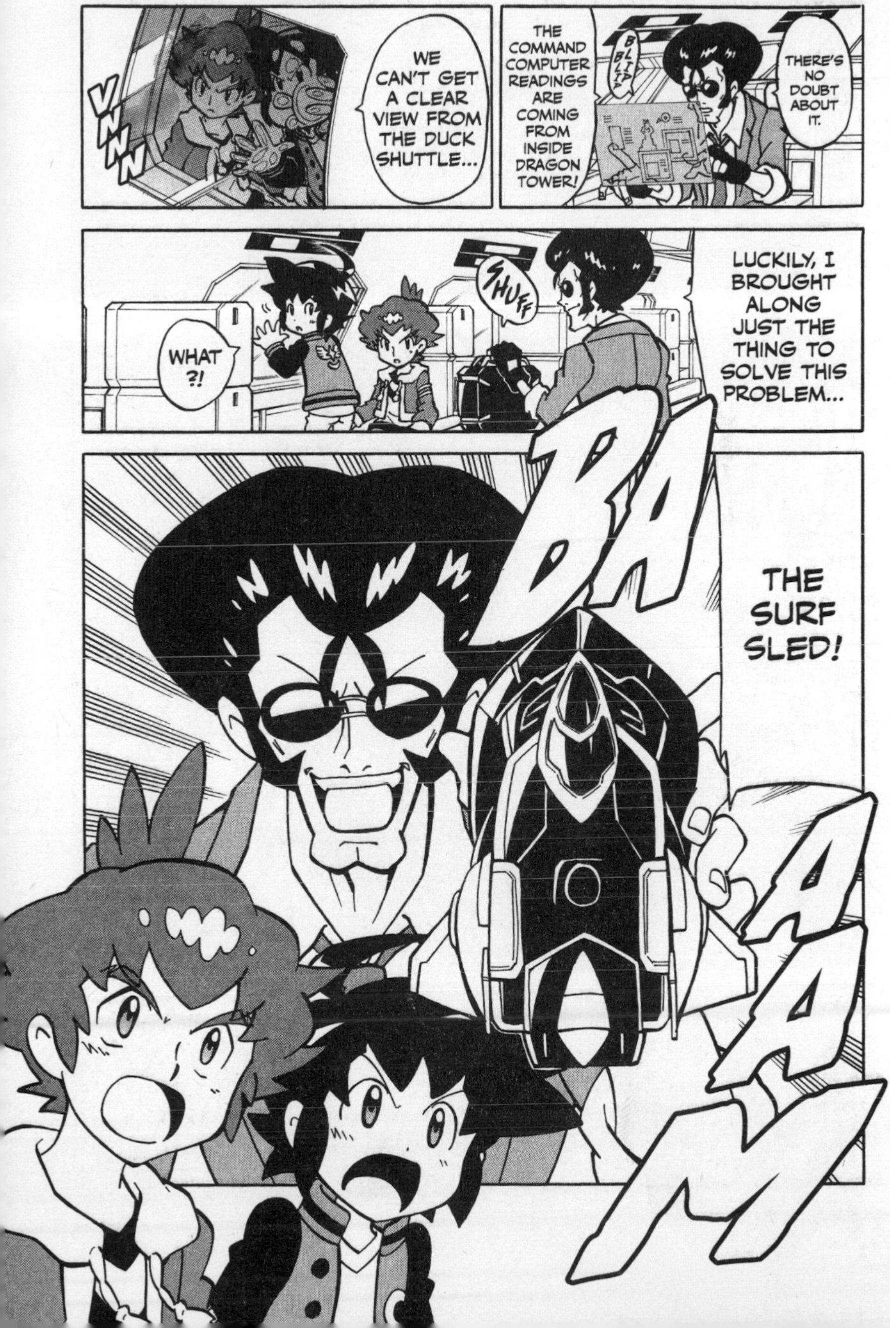
THERE'S NO DOUBT ABOUT IT.
BLIP BLIP
THE COMMAND COMPUTER READINGS ARE COMING FROM INSIDE DRAGON TOWER!
WE CAN'T GET A CLEAR VIEW FROM THE DUCK SHUTTLE...
VNNN
LUCKILY, I BROUGHT ALONG JUST THE THING TO SOLVE THIS PROBLEM...
SHUFF
WHAT ?!
THE SURF SLED!
BAAAM

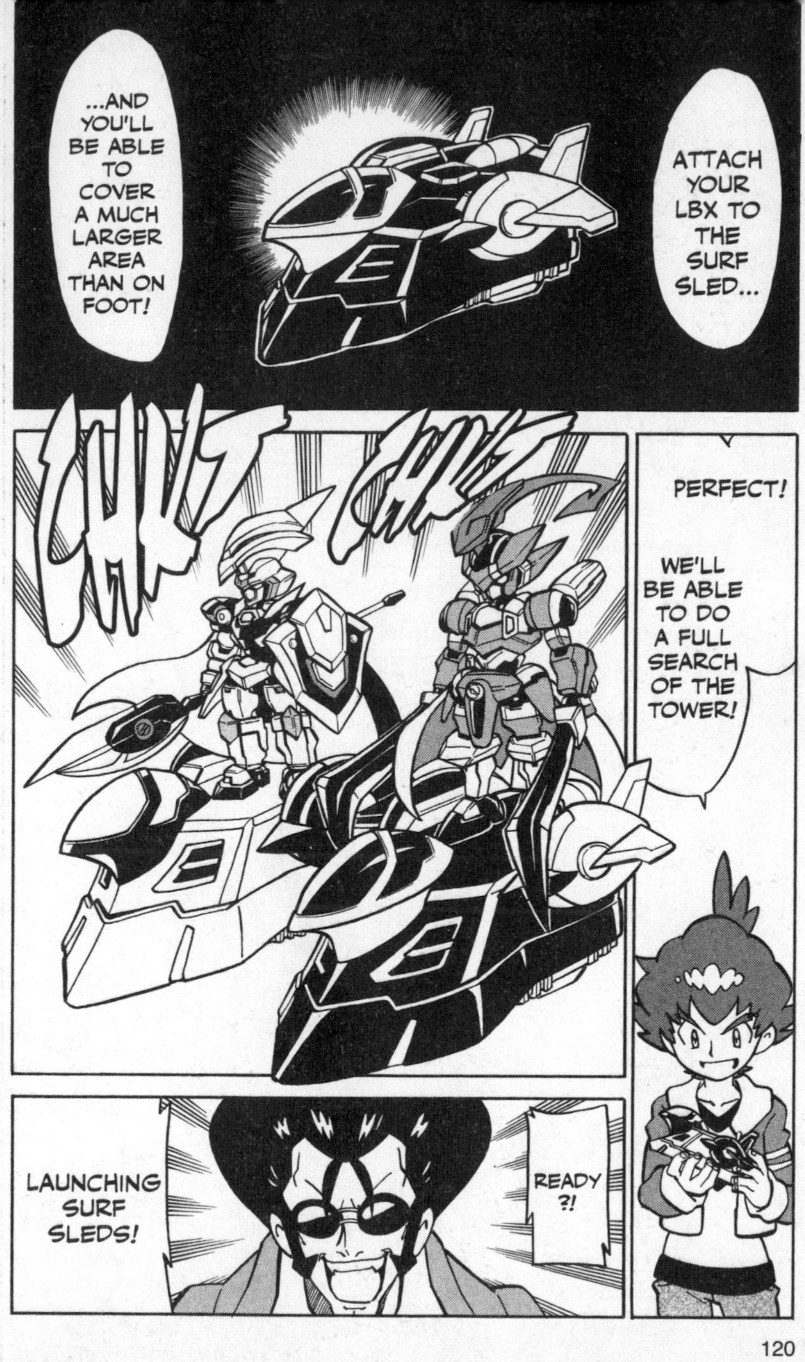
ATTACH YOUR LBX TO THE SURF SLED...
...AND YOU'LL BE ABLE TO COVER A MUCH LARGER AREA THAN ON FOOT!
PERFECT!
WE'LL BE ABLE TO DO A FULL SEARCH OF THE TOWER!
READY?!
LAUNCHING SURF SLEDS!

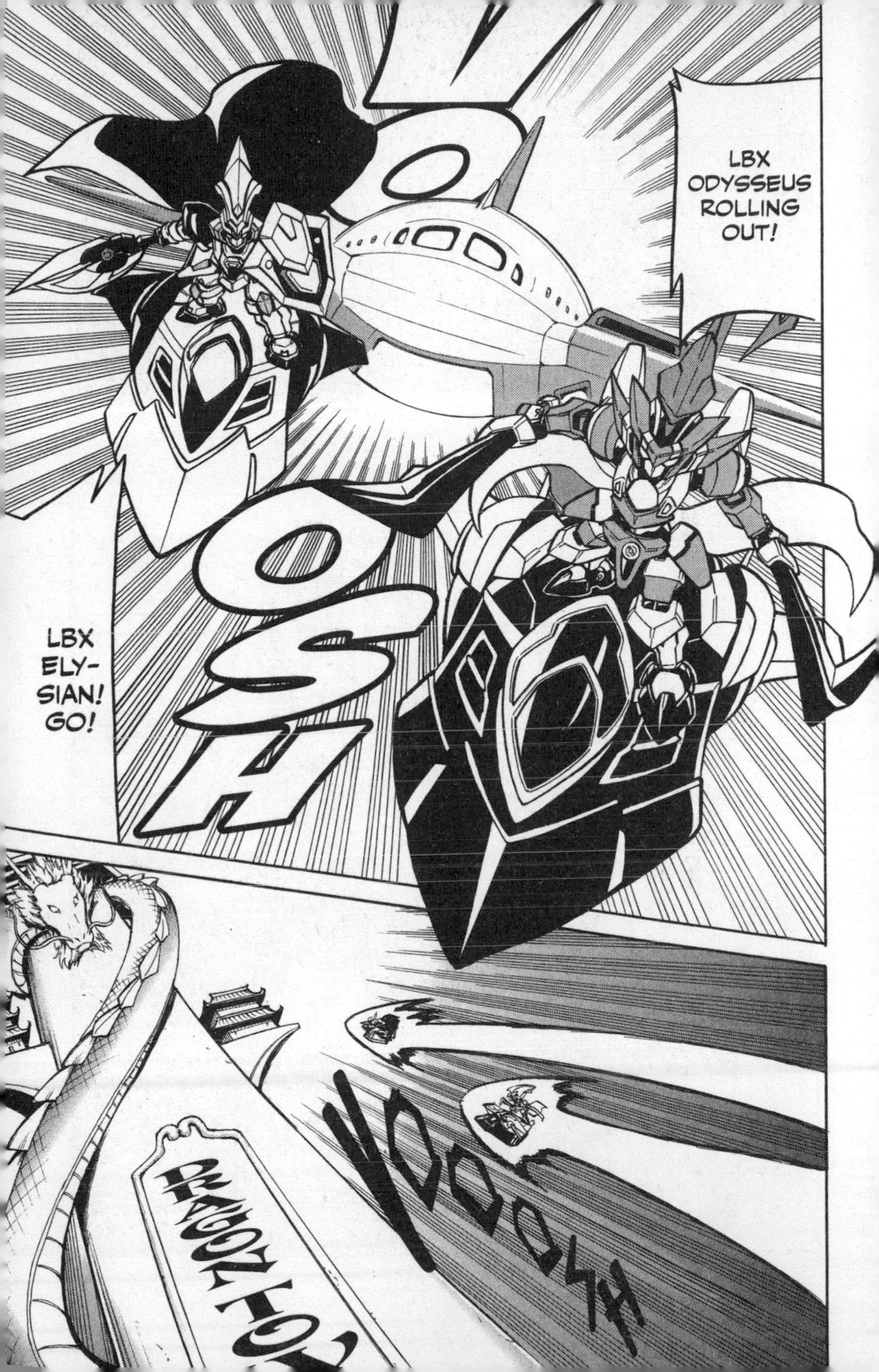
LBX ODYSSEUS ROLLING OUT!
LBX ELY-SIAN! GO!

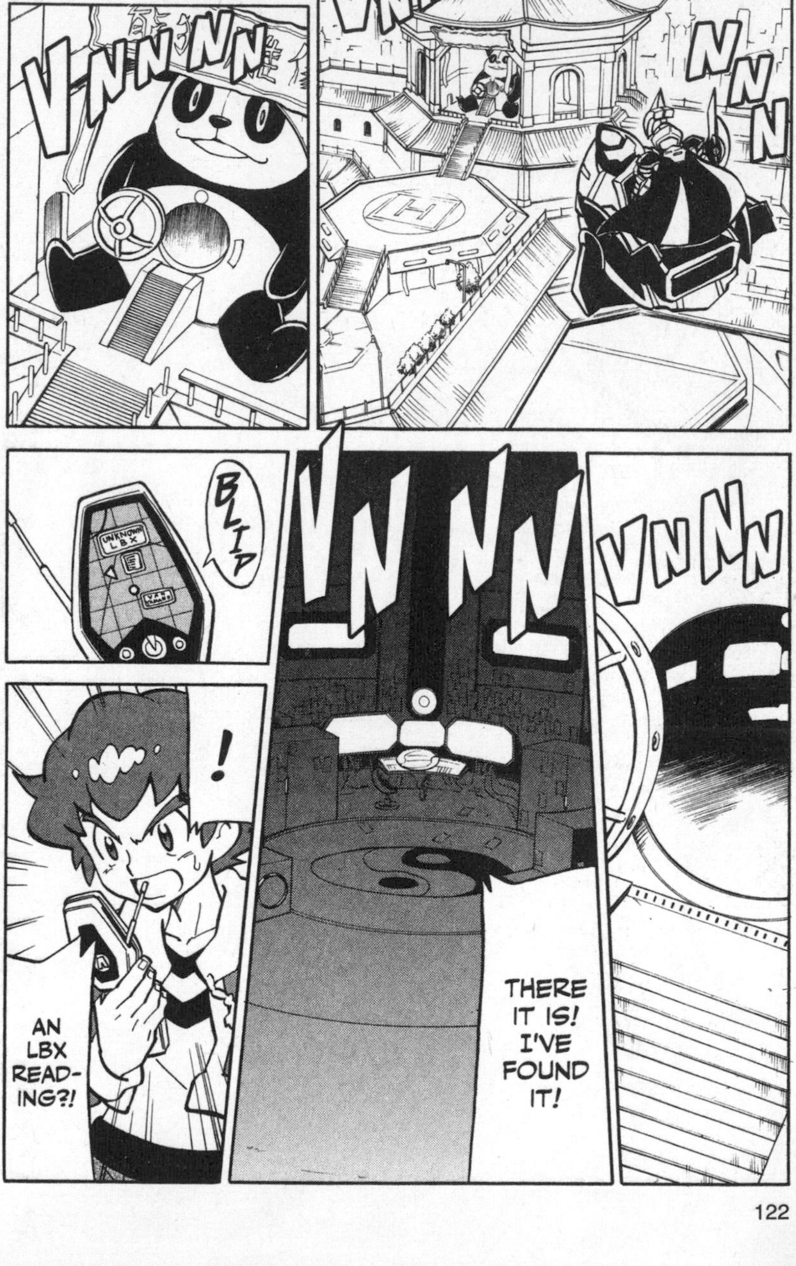
VNNNN
NNN
VNNNNN
VNNNN
VNNN
THERE IT IS! I'VE FOUND IT!
BLIP
UNKNOWN LBX
!
AN LBX READING?!

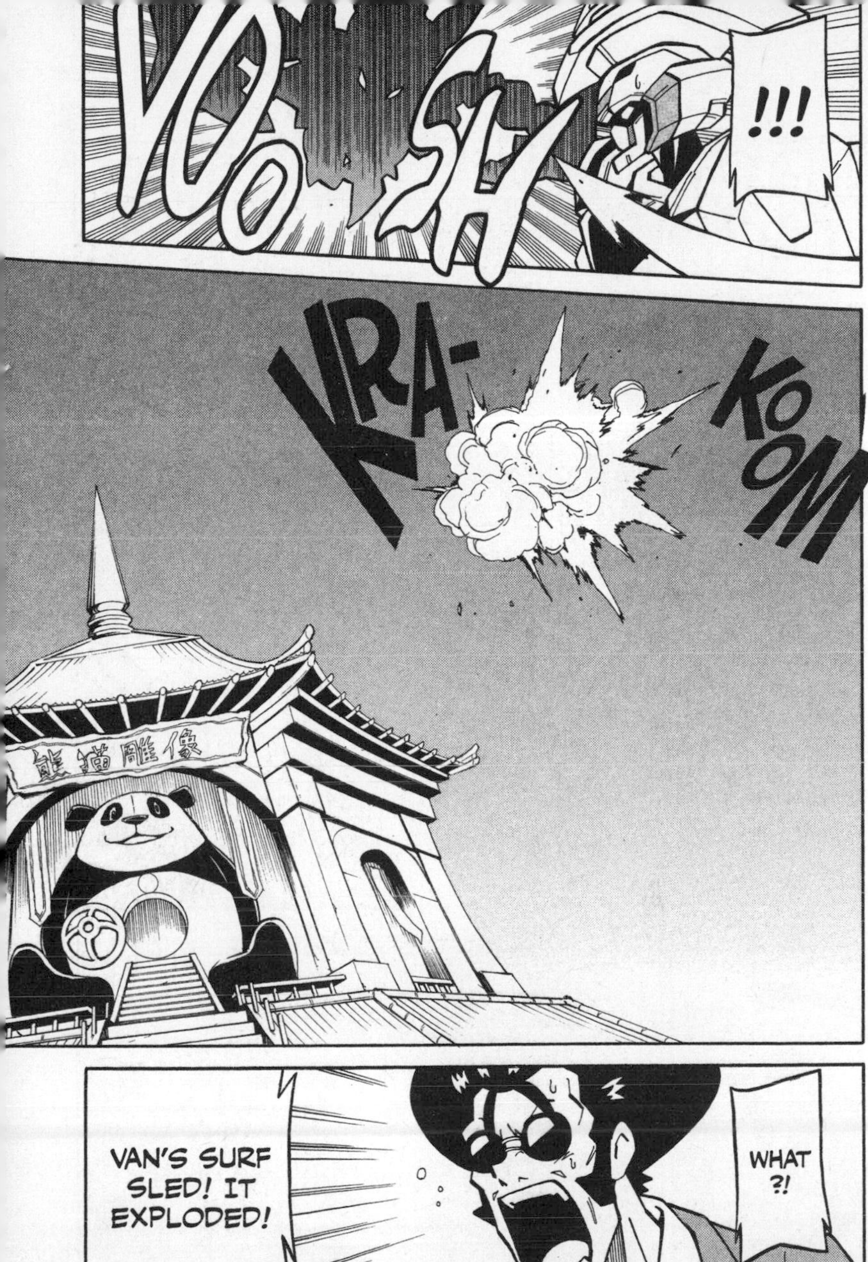
!!!
VOOSH
KRA-KOOM
熊貓雕像
WHAT?!
VAN'S SURF SLED! IT EXPLODED!

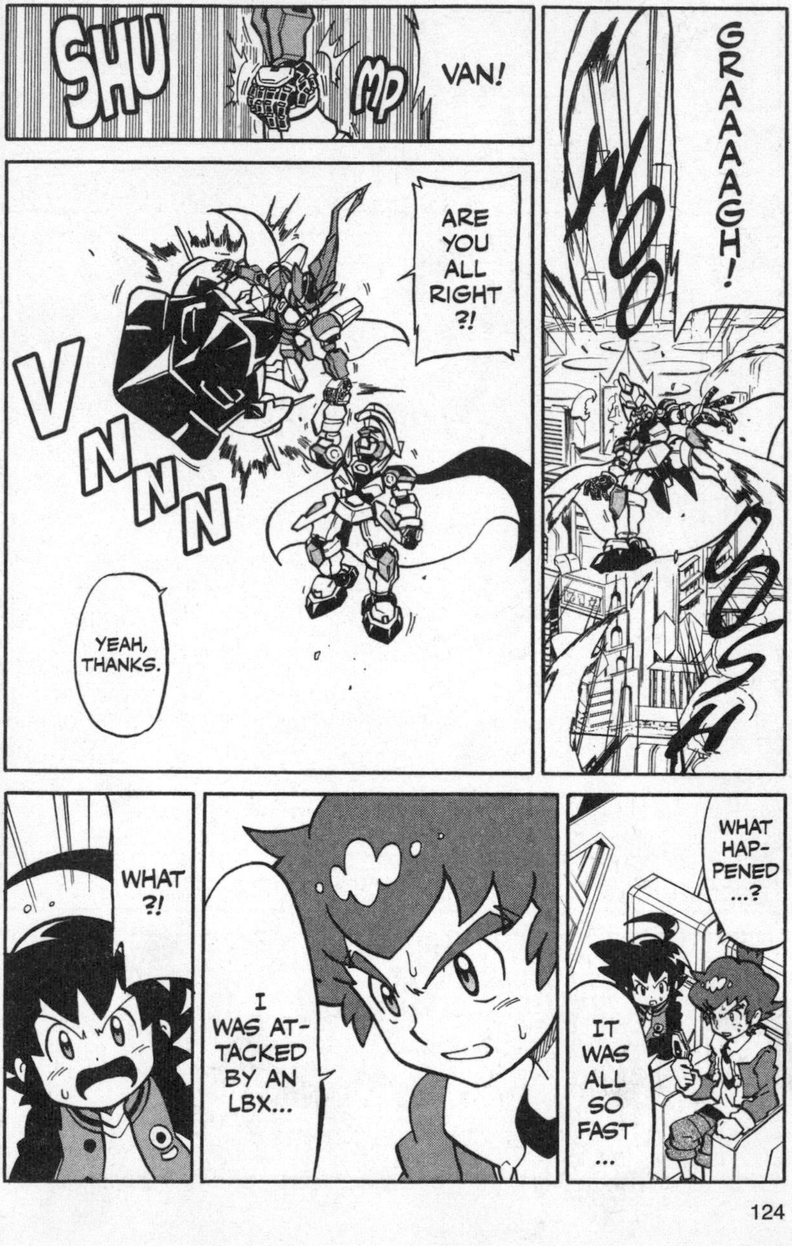
GRAAAAGH!
WOOOOSH
SHU
MP
VAN!
ARE YOU ALL RIGHT ?!
VNNNN
YEAH, THANKS.
WHAT HAP-PENED ...?
IT WAS ALL SO FAST ...
I WAS AT-TACKED BY AN LBX...
WHAT ?!

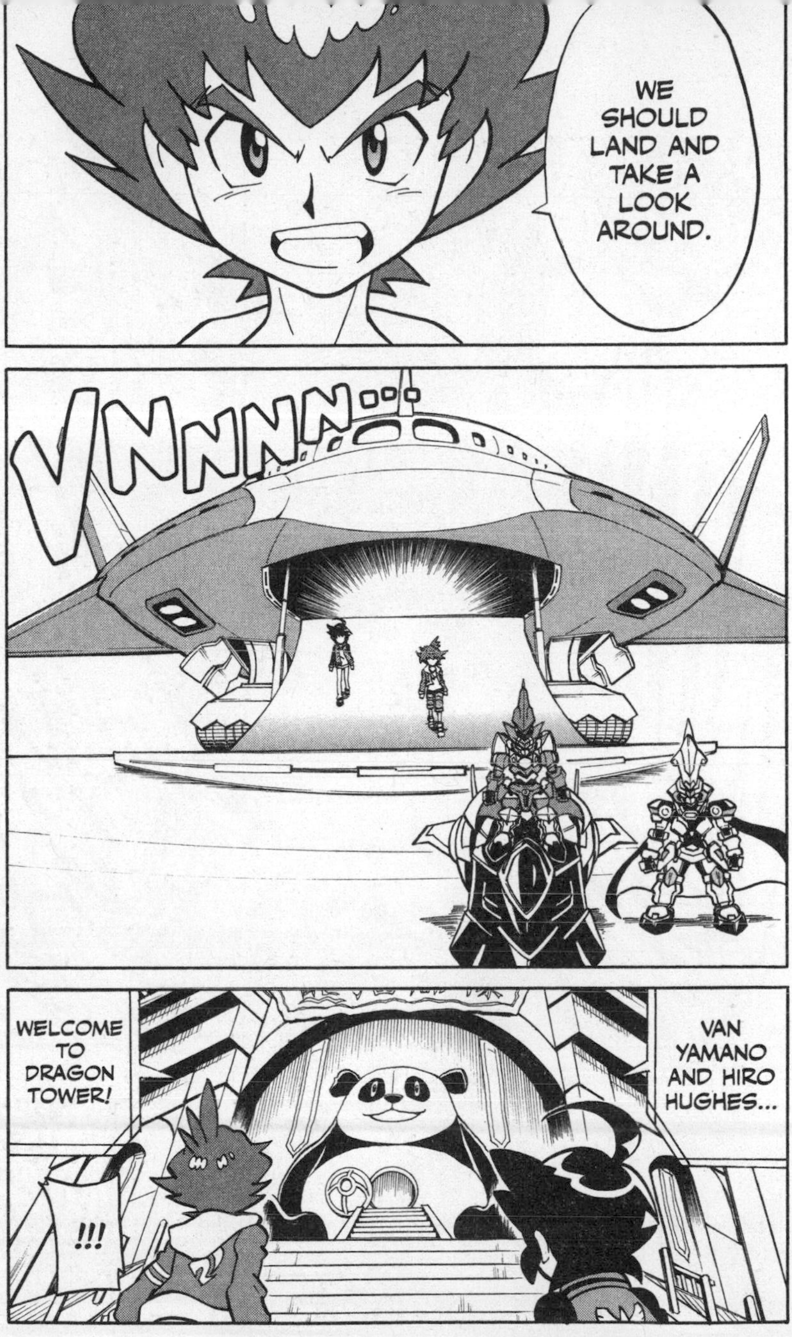
WE SHOULD LAND AND TAKE A LOOK AROUND.
VNNNN...
VAN YAMANO AND HIRO HUGHES...
WELCOME TO DRAGON TOWER!
!!!

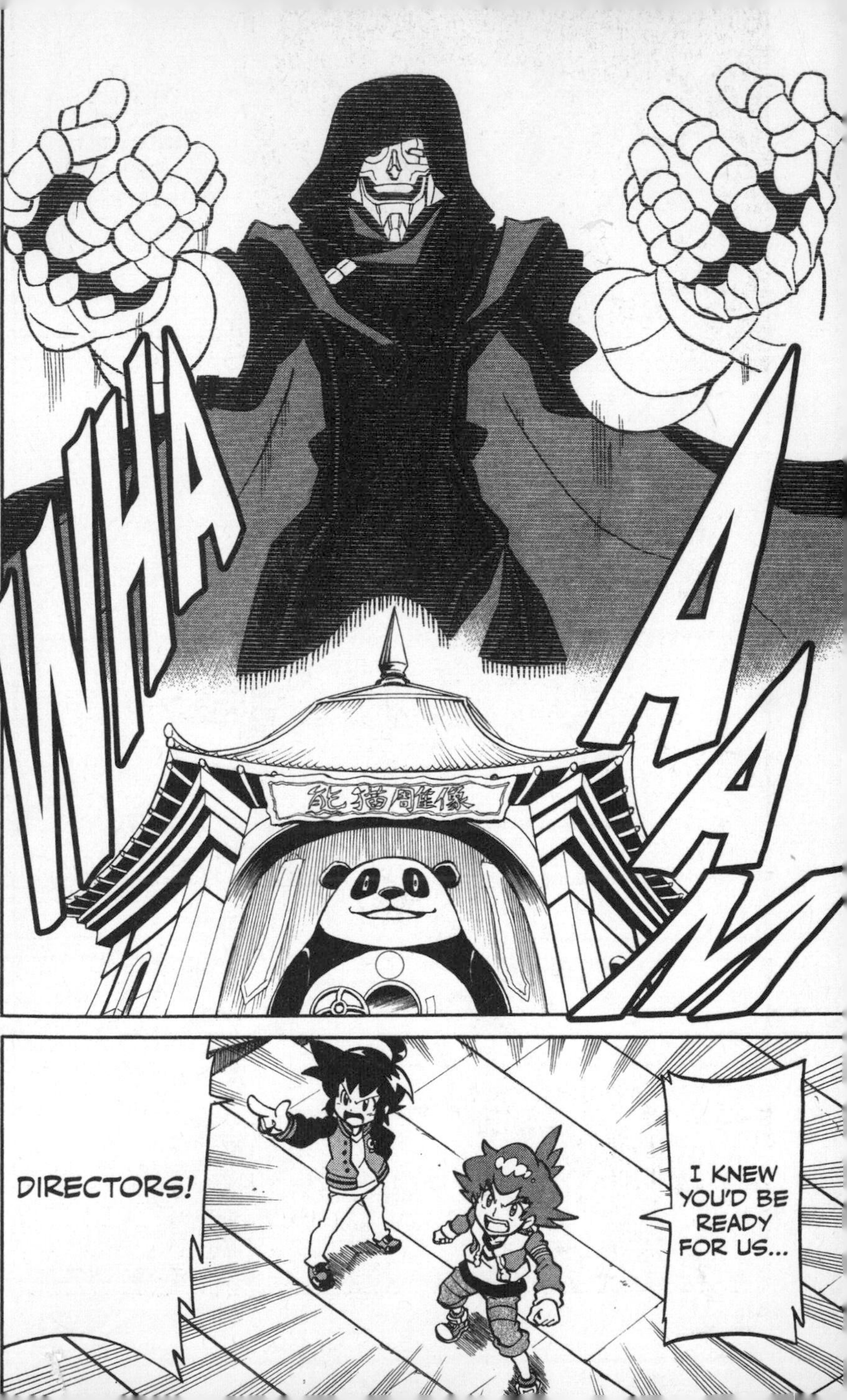
WHAAAM
I KNEW YOU'D BE READY FOR US...
DIRECTORS!

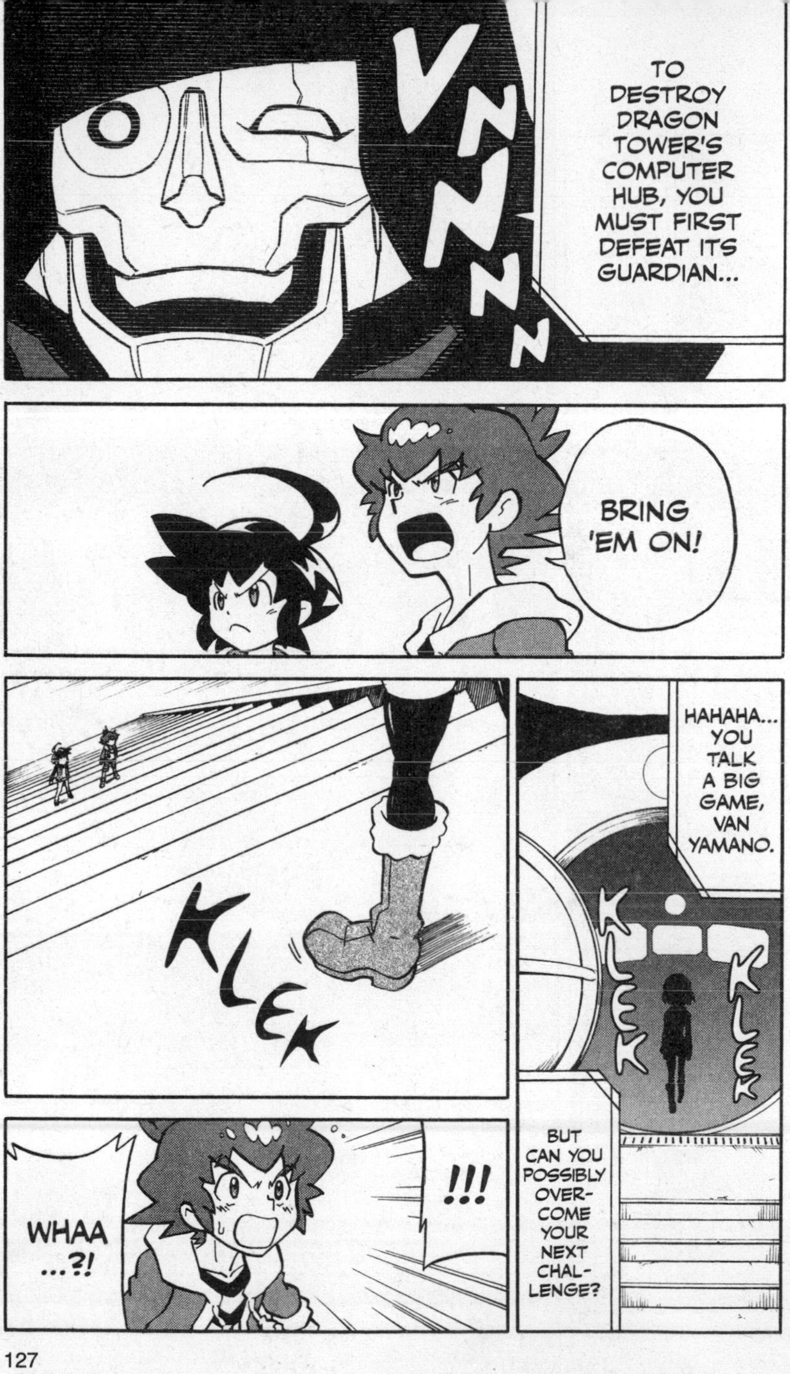
TO DESTROY DRAGON TOWER'S COMPUTER HUB, YOU MUST FIRST DEFEAT ITS GUARDIAN...
VNNNN
BRING 'EM ON!
HAHAHA... YOU TALK A BIG GAME, VAN YAMANO.
KLEK
KLEK
BUT CAN YOU POSSIBLY OVER-COME YOUR NEXT CHAL-LENGE?
KLEK
!!!
WHAA ...?!

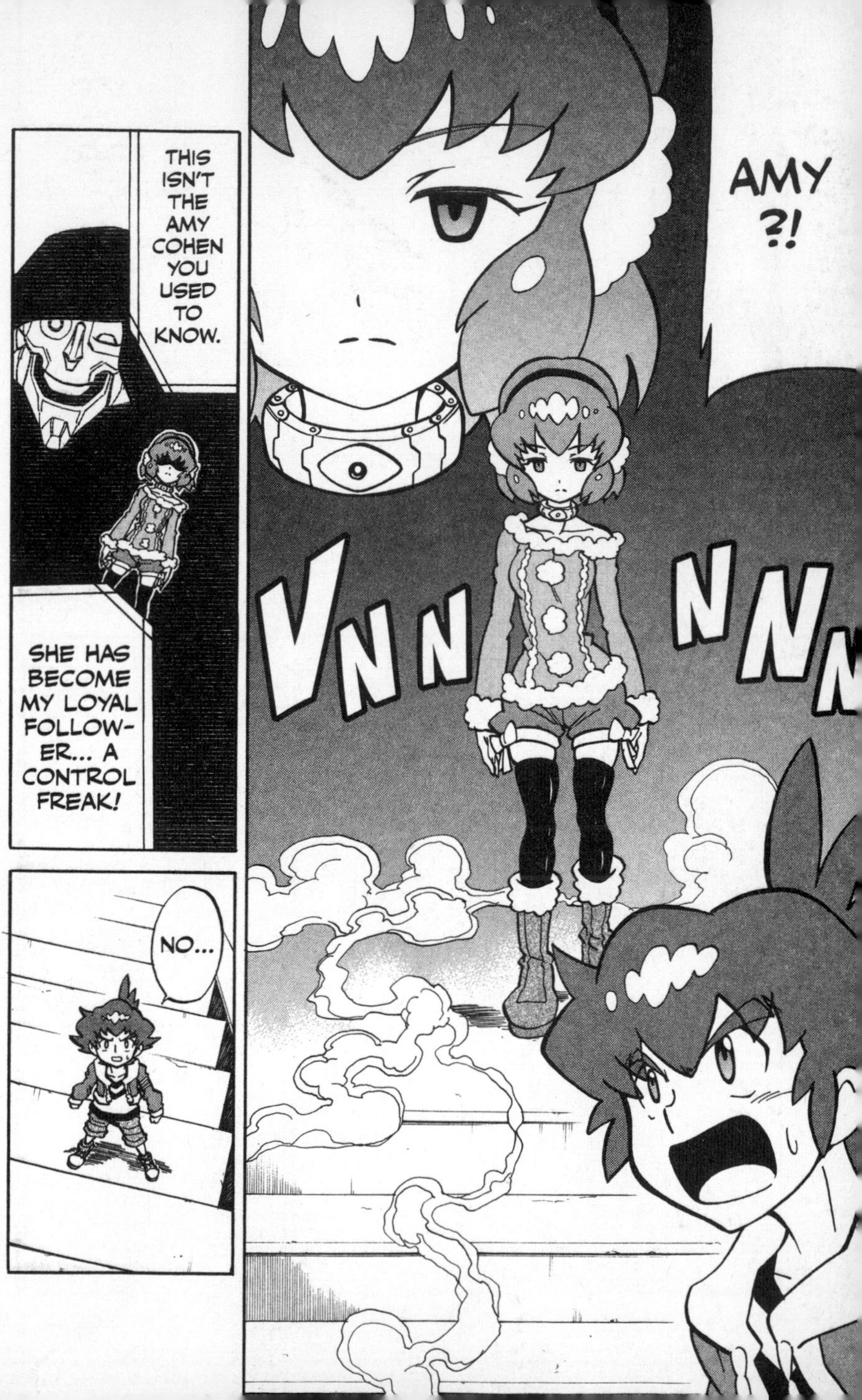
AMY ?!
VNN NNN
THIS ISN'T THE AMY COHEN YOU USED TO KNOW.
SHE HAS BECOME MY LOYAL FOLLOWER... A CONTROL FREAK!
NO...

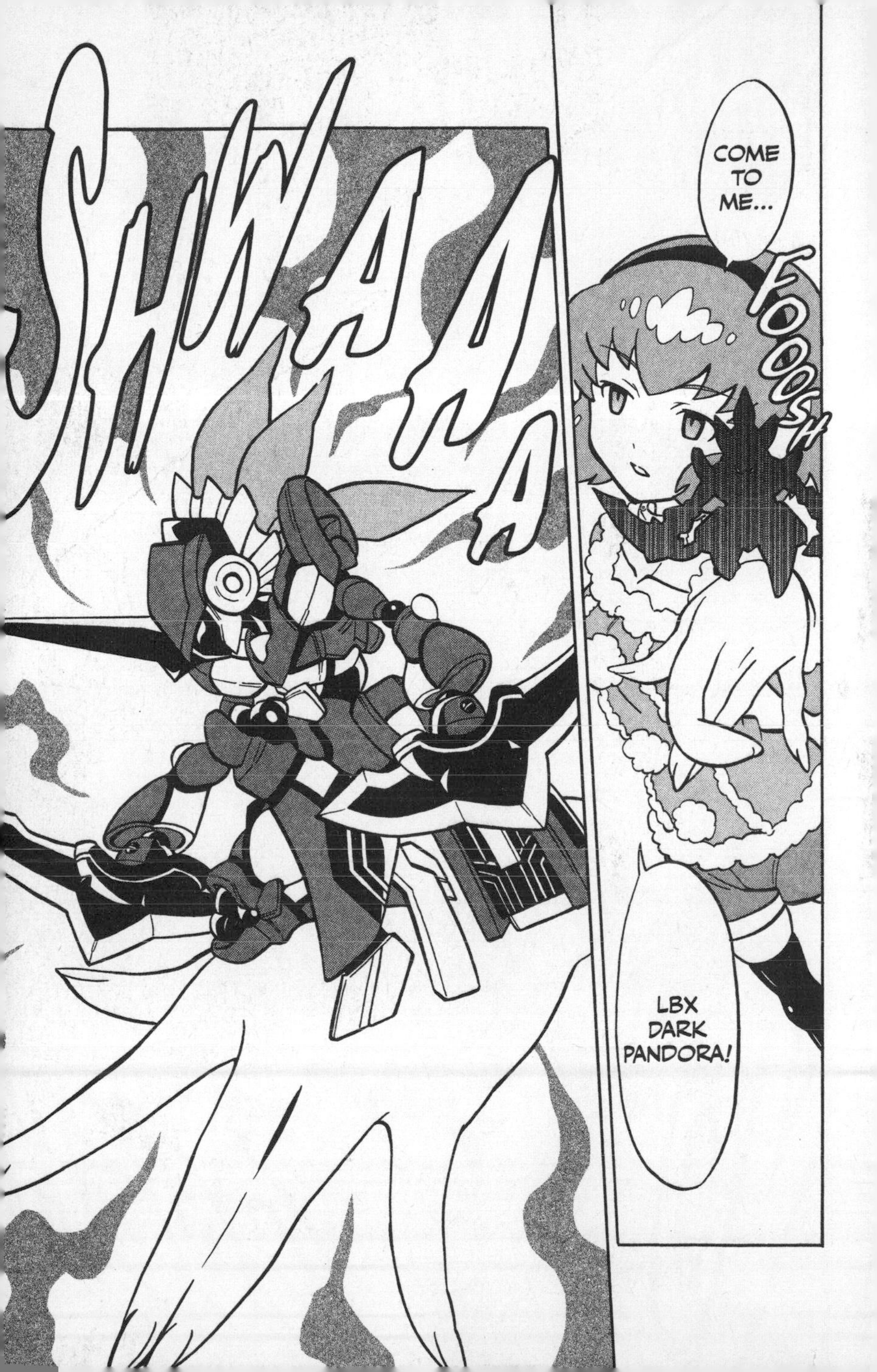
COME TO ME...
FOOOSH
LBX DARK PANDORA!
SHWAAAA

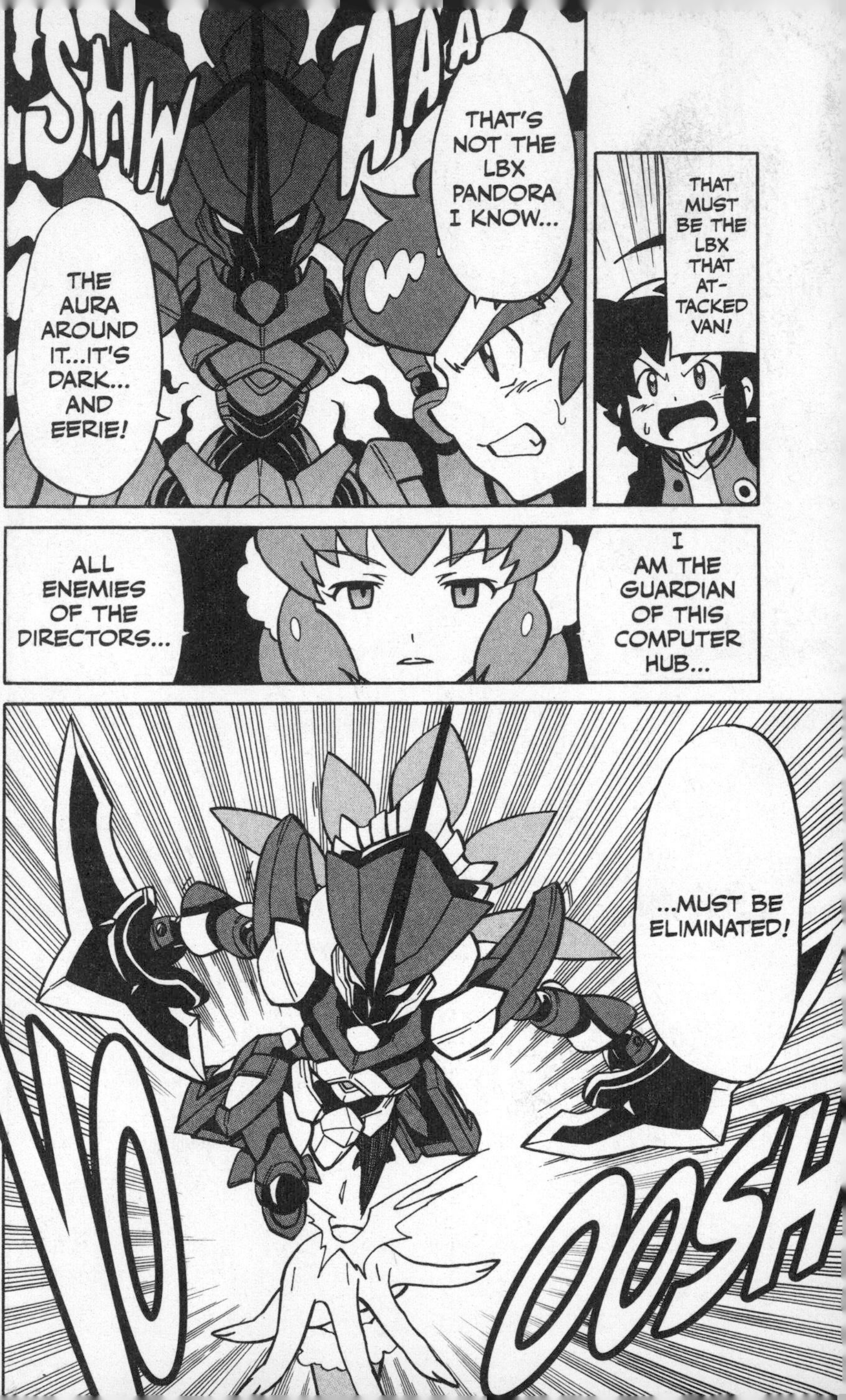
THAT MUST BE THE LBX THAT AT-TACKED VAN!
SHW
AAA
THAT'S NOT THE LBX PANDORA I KNOW...
THE AURA AROUND IT...IT'S DARK... AND EERIE!
I AM THE GUARDIAN OF THIS COMPUTER HUB...
ALL ENEMIES OF THE DIRECTORS...
...MUST BE ELIMINATED!
VOOOSH

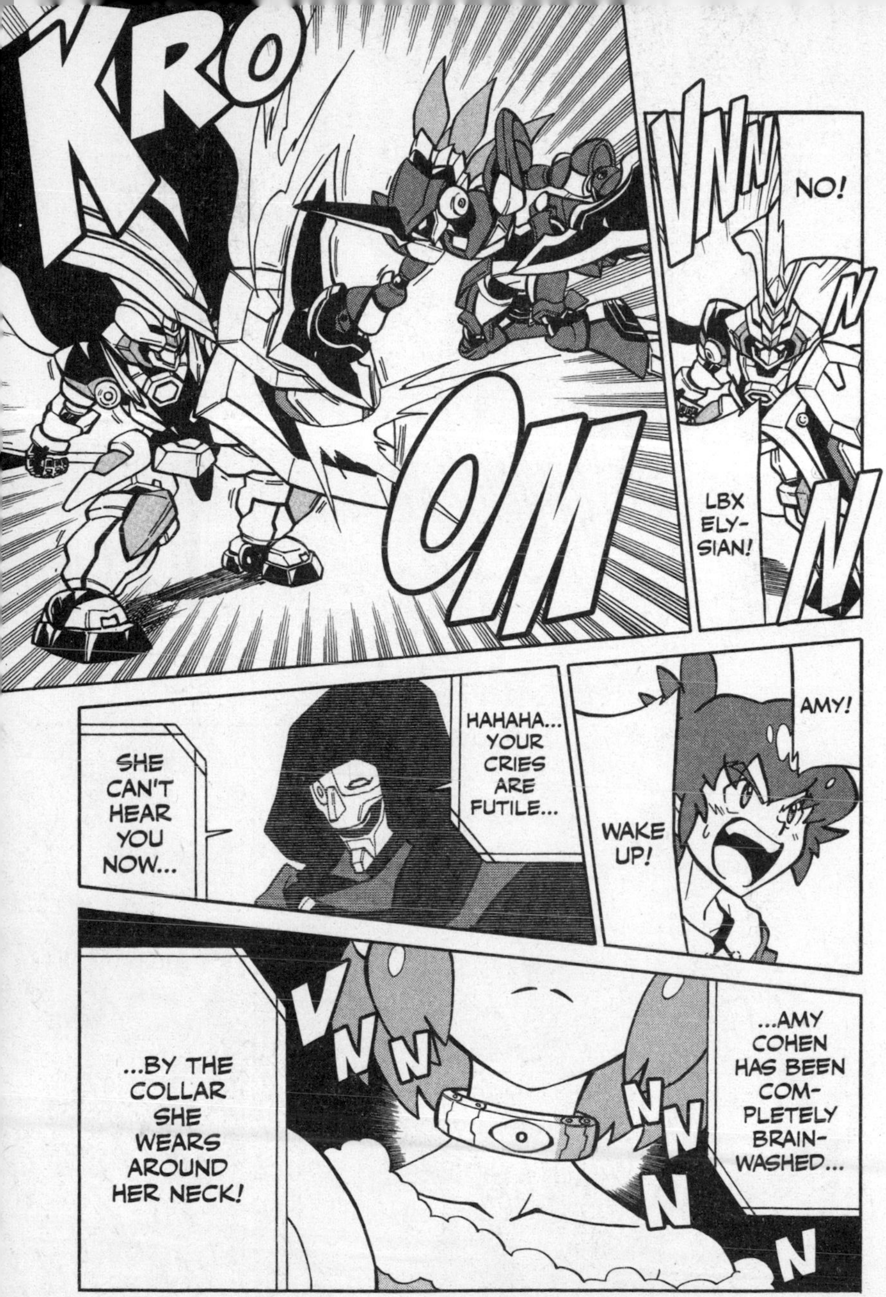
VNNNNN
NO!
LBX ELY-SIAN!
KRO
OM
AMY!
WAKE UP!
HAHAHA... YOUR CRIES ARE FUTILE...
SHE CAN'T HEAR YOU NOW...
...AMY COHEN HAS BEEN COM-PLETELY BRAIN-WASHED...
VNNNNNNN
...BY THE COLLAR SHE WEARS AROUND HER NECK!

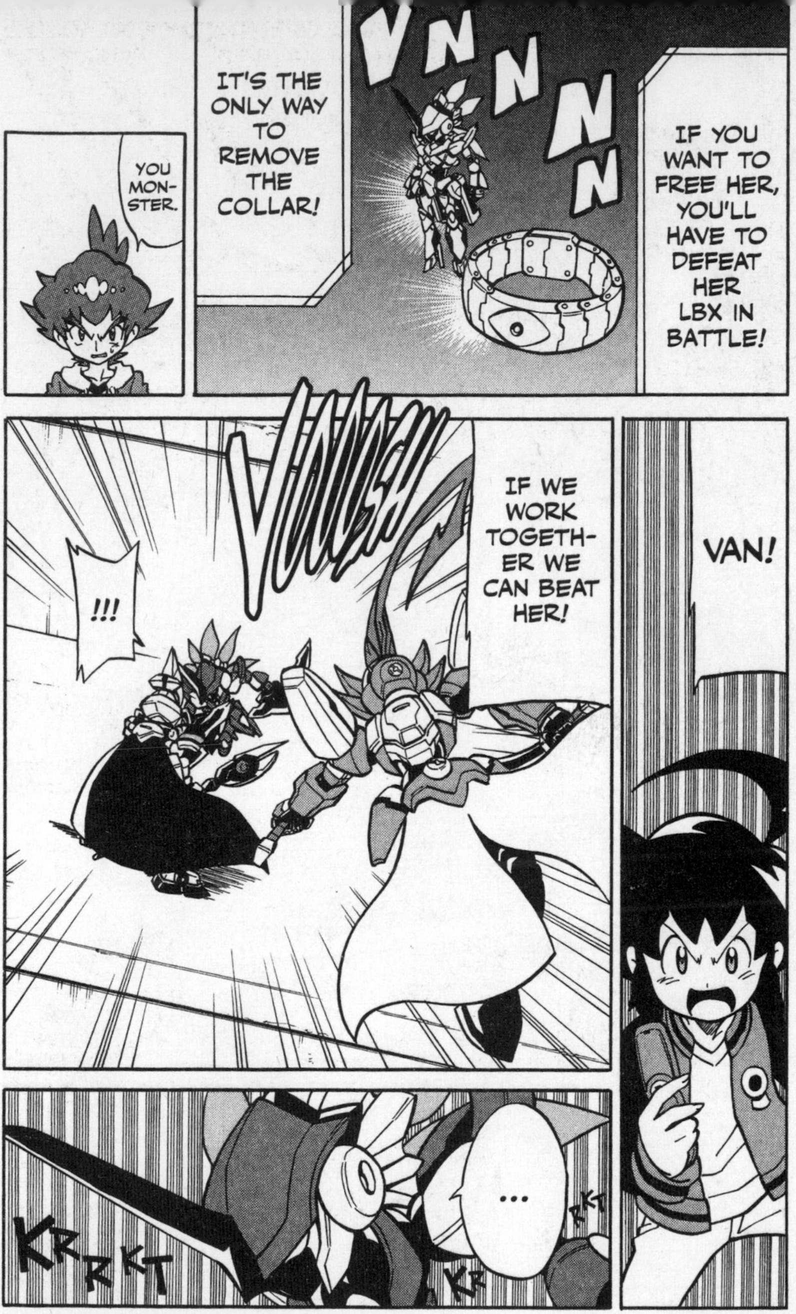
IF YOU WANT TO FREE HER, YOU'LL HAVE TO DEFEAT HER LBX IN BATTLE!
VNNNNN
IT'S THE ONLY WAY TO REMOVE THE COLLAR!
YOU MON-STER.
VAN!
IF WE WORK TOGETH-ER WE CAN BEAT HER!
VWOOSH
!!!
...
RKT
KR
KRRKT

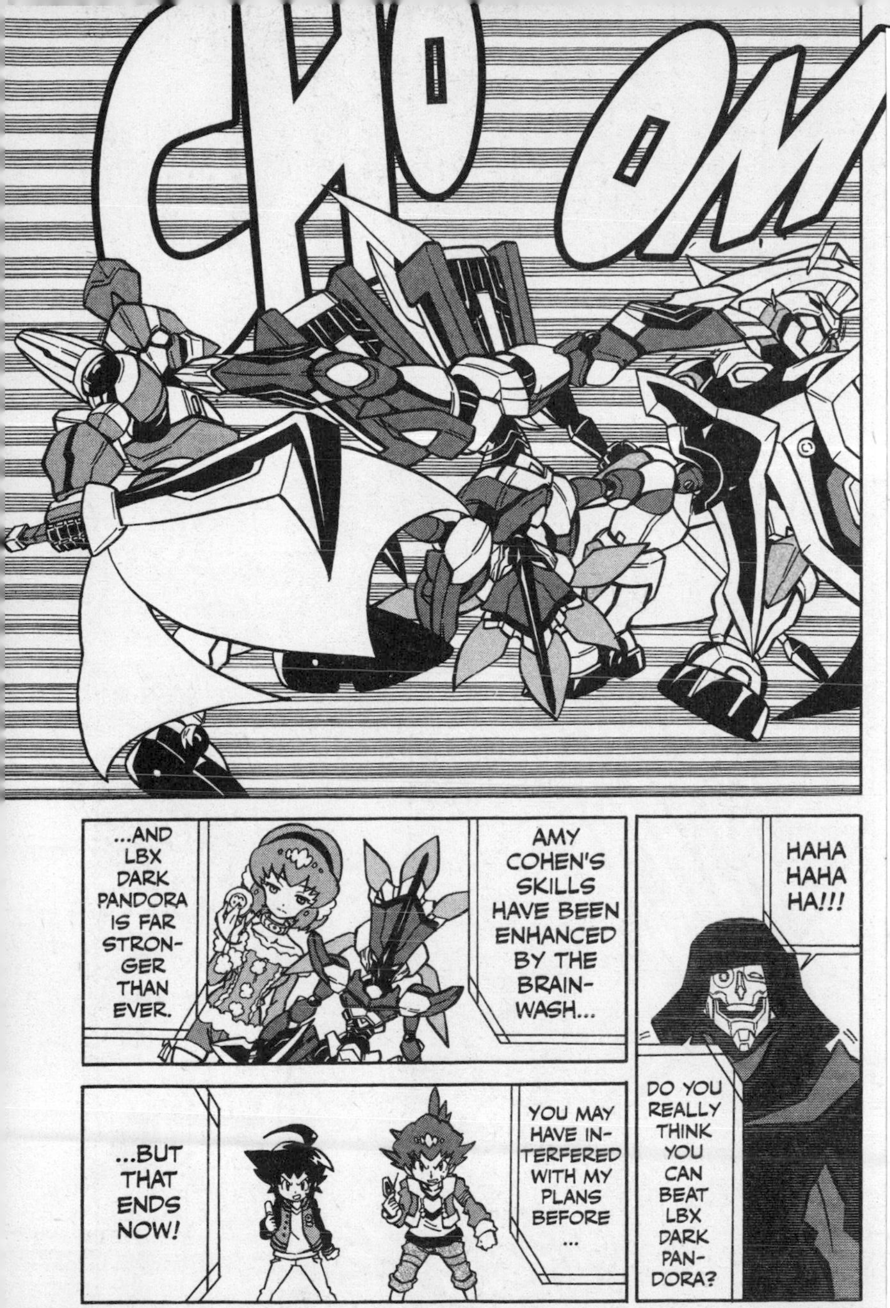
HAHA HAHA HA!!!
DO YOU REALLY THINK YOU CAN BEAT LBX DARK PAN-DORA?
AMY COHEN'S SKILLS HAVE BEEN ENHANCED BY THE BRAIN-WASH...
...AND LBX DARK PANDORA IS FAR STRON-GER THAN EVER.
YOU MAY HAVE IN-TERFERED WITH MY PLANS BEFORE ...
...BUT THAT ENDS NOW!

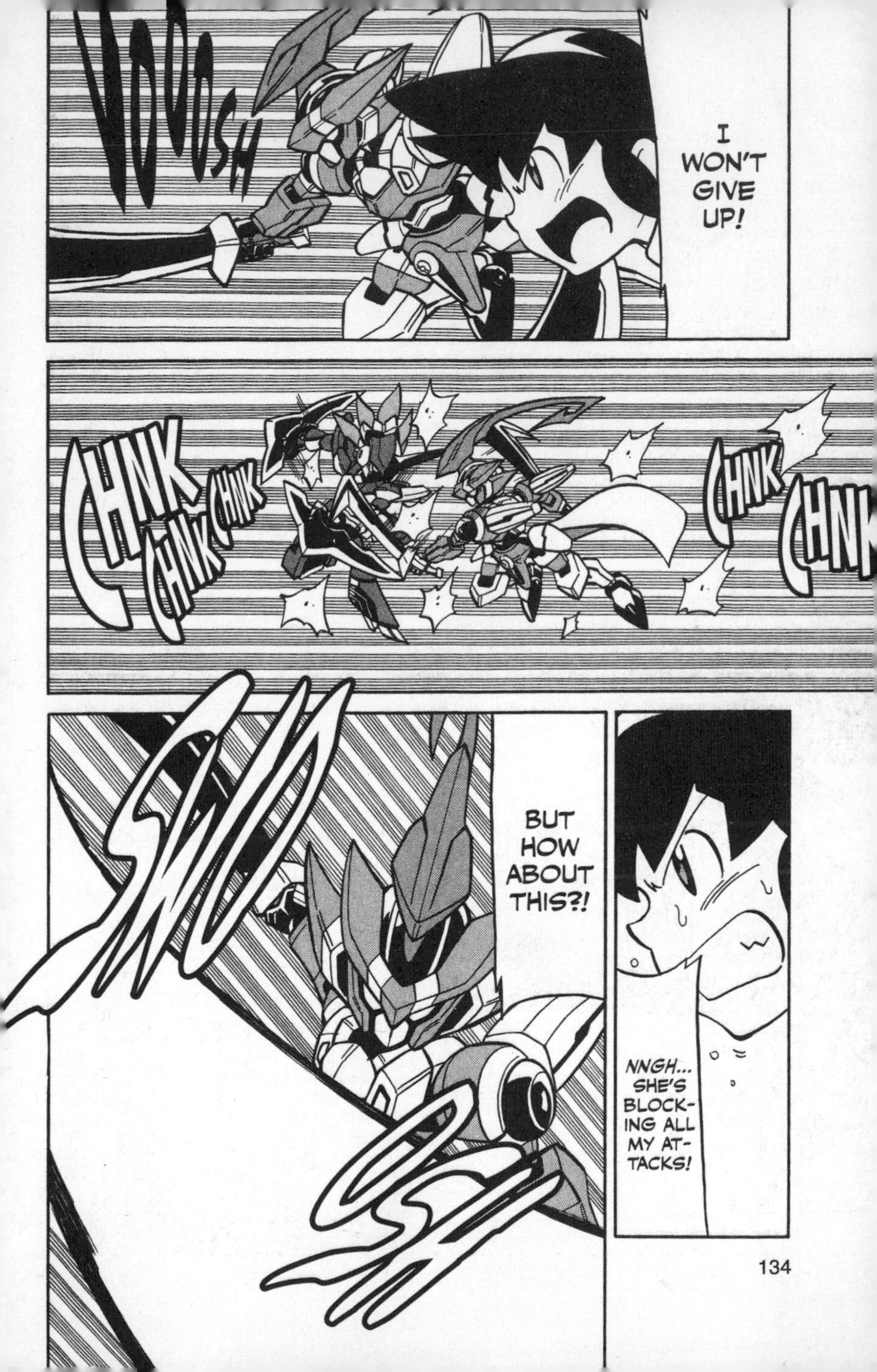
I WON'T GIVE UP!
VOOOSH
CHNK CHNK
CHNK CHNK CHNK
NNGH... SHE'S BLOCK-ING ALL MY AT-TACKS!
BUT HOW ABOUT THIS?!
SWOOSH

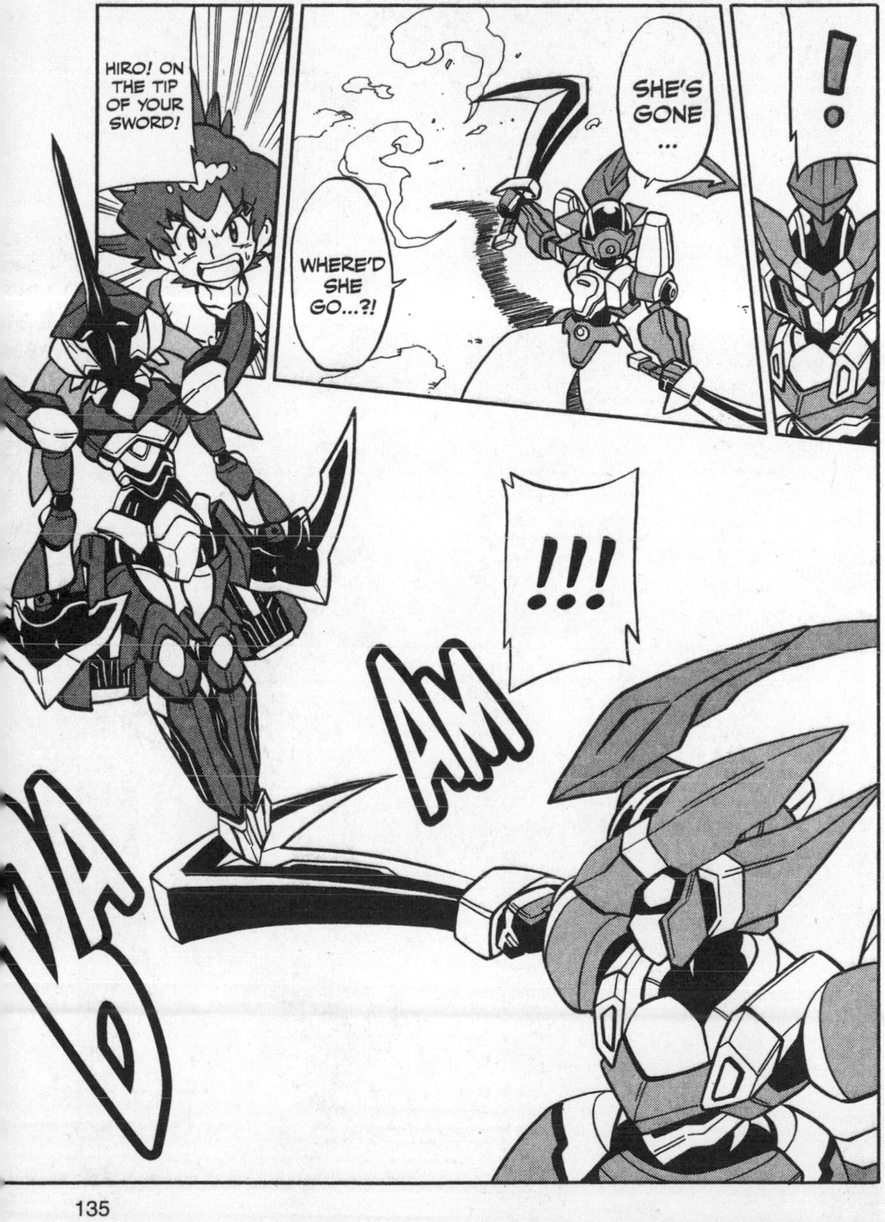
!
SHE'S GONE ...
WHERE'D SHE GO...?!
HIRO! ON THE TIP OF YOUR SWORD!
!!!
BAAM

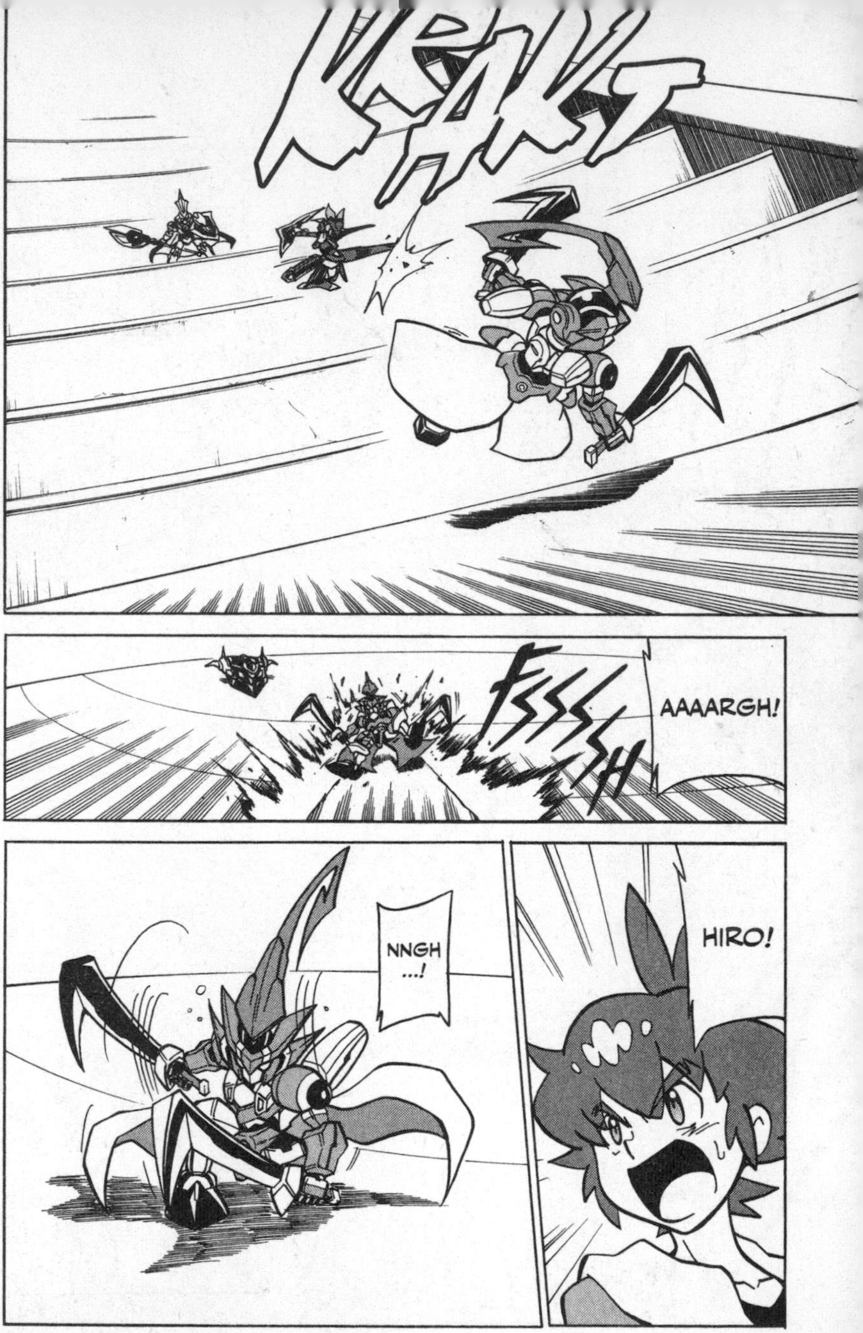
KRAKT
AAAARGH!
FSSSSH
HIRO!
NNGH
...!

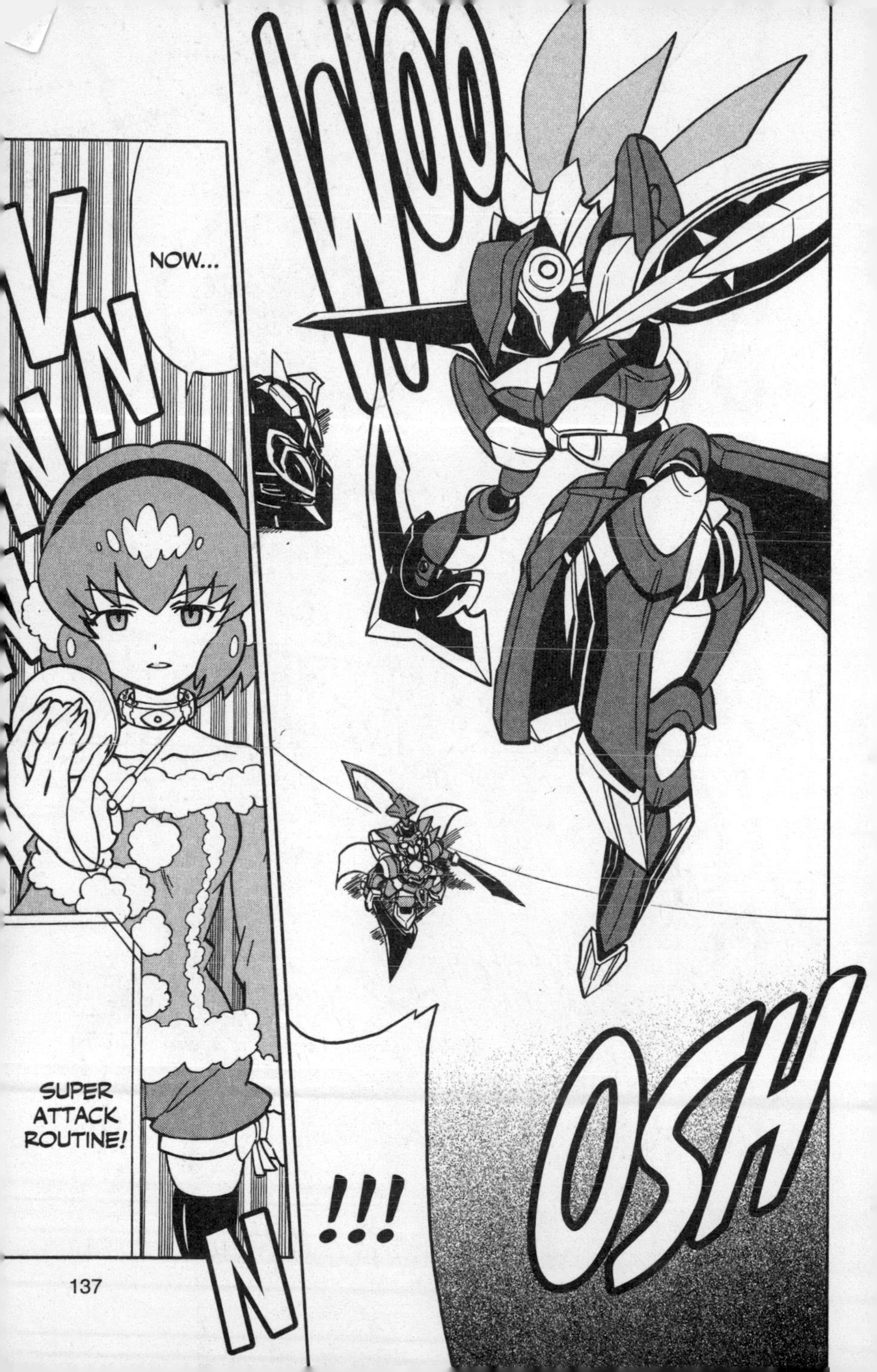
OSH
N!!!
NOW...
SUPER ATTACK ROUTINE!

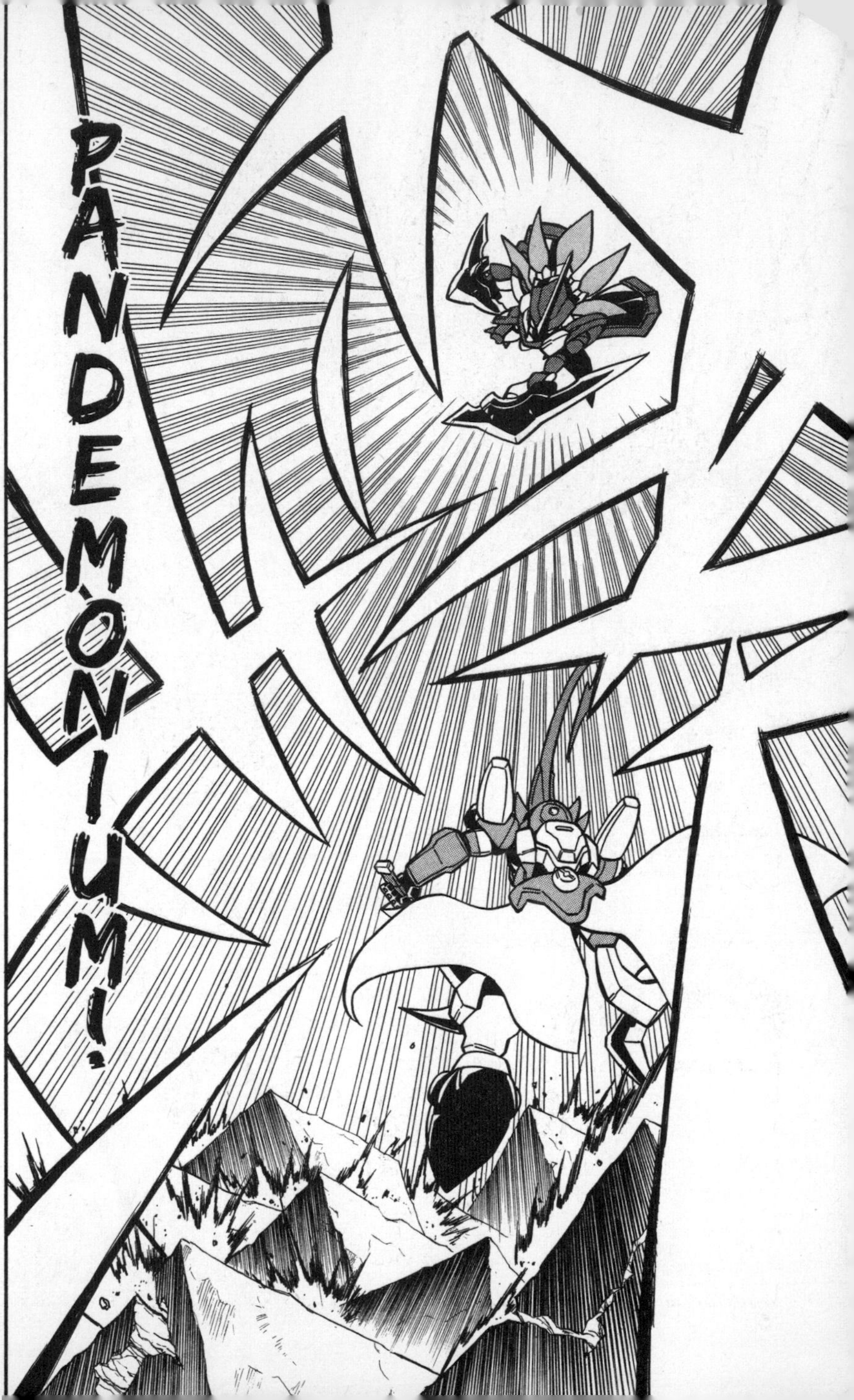
PANDEMONIUM!

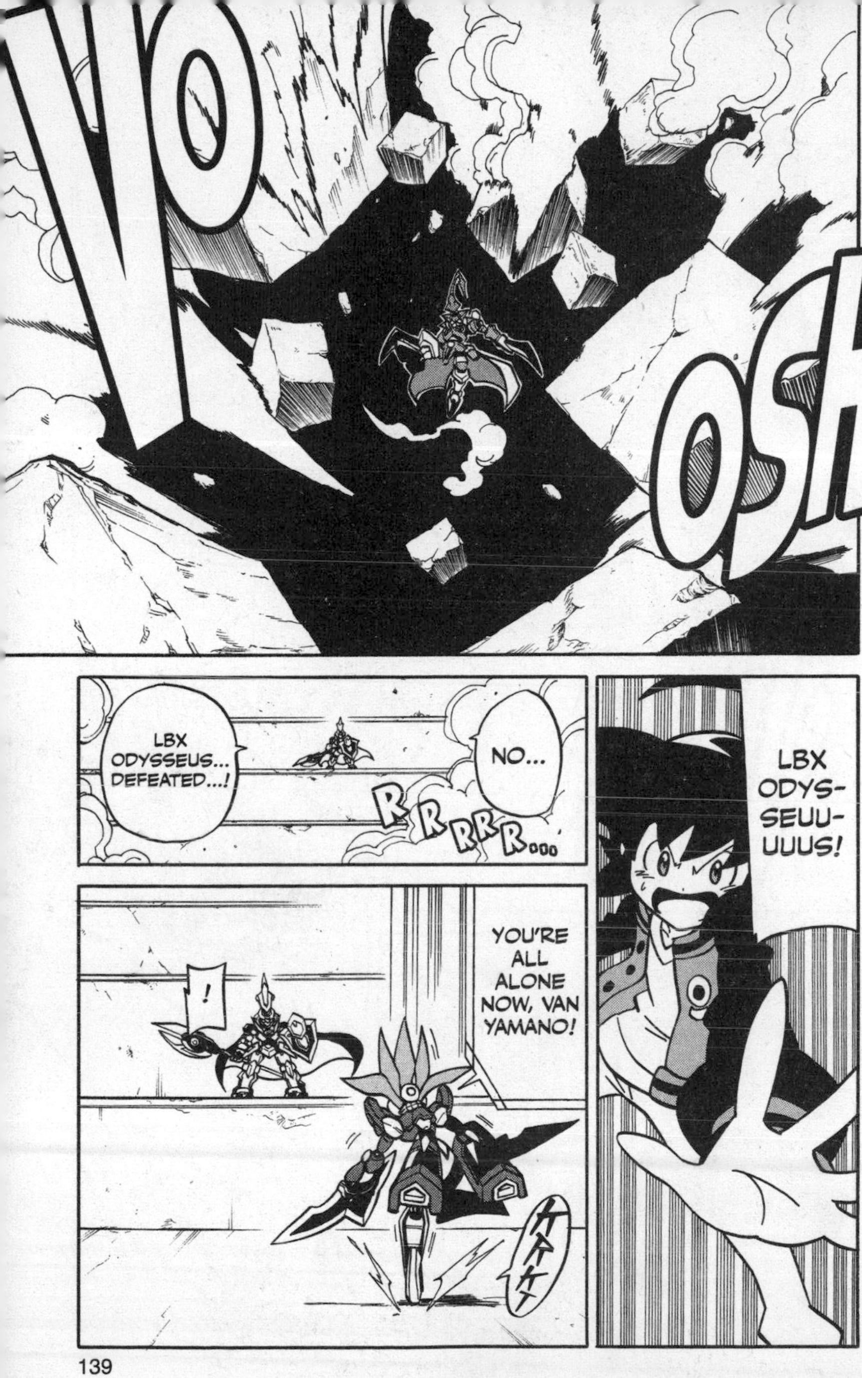
VOOSH
LBX ODYS- SEUU- UUUS!
NO...
RRRRR...
LBX ODYSSEUS... DEFEATED...!
YOU'RE ALL ALONE NOW, VAN YAMANO!
!

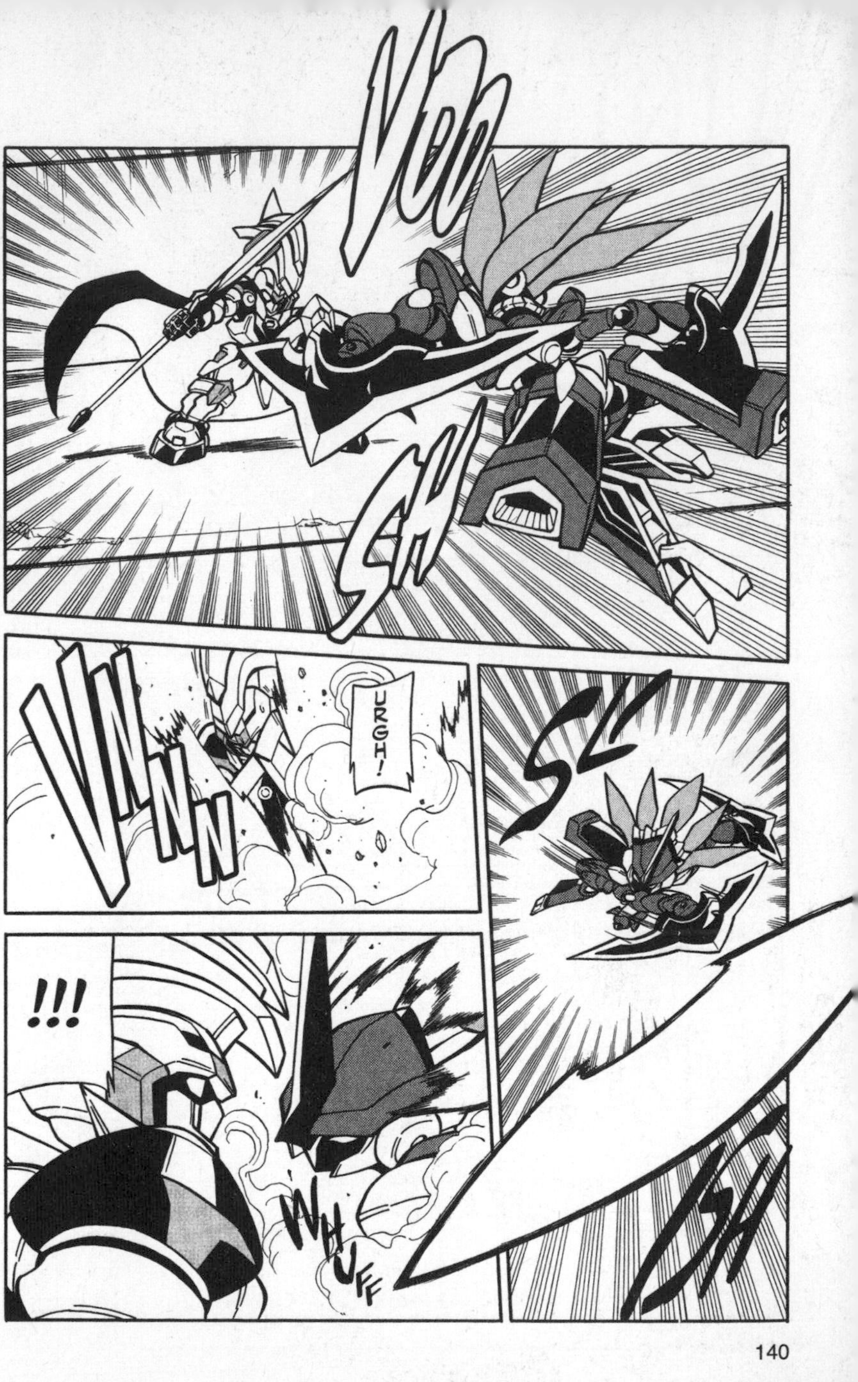
SH
SL
URGH!
VINNNN
!!!
WHUFF

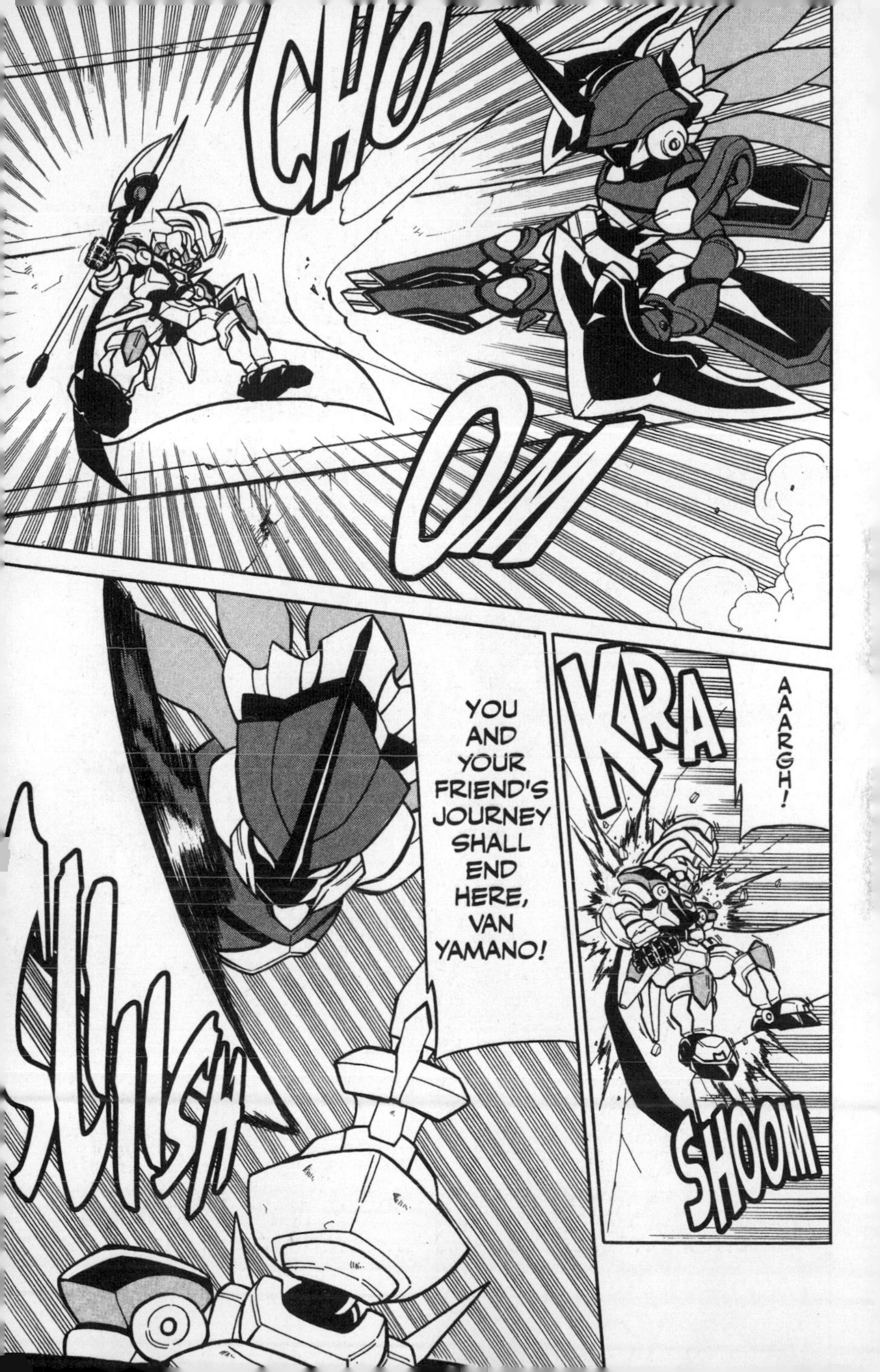
CHO
OW
KRA
AAARGH!
SHOOM
YOU AND YOUR FRIEND'S JOURNEY SHALL END HERE, VAN YAMANO!

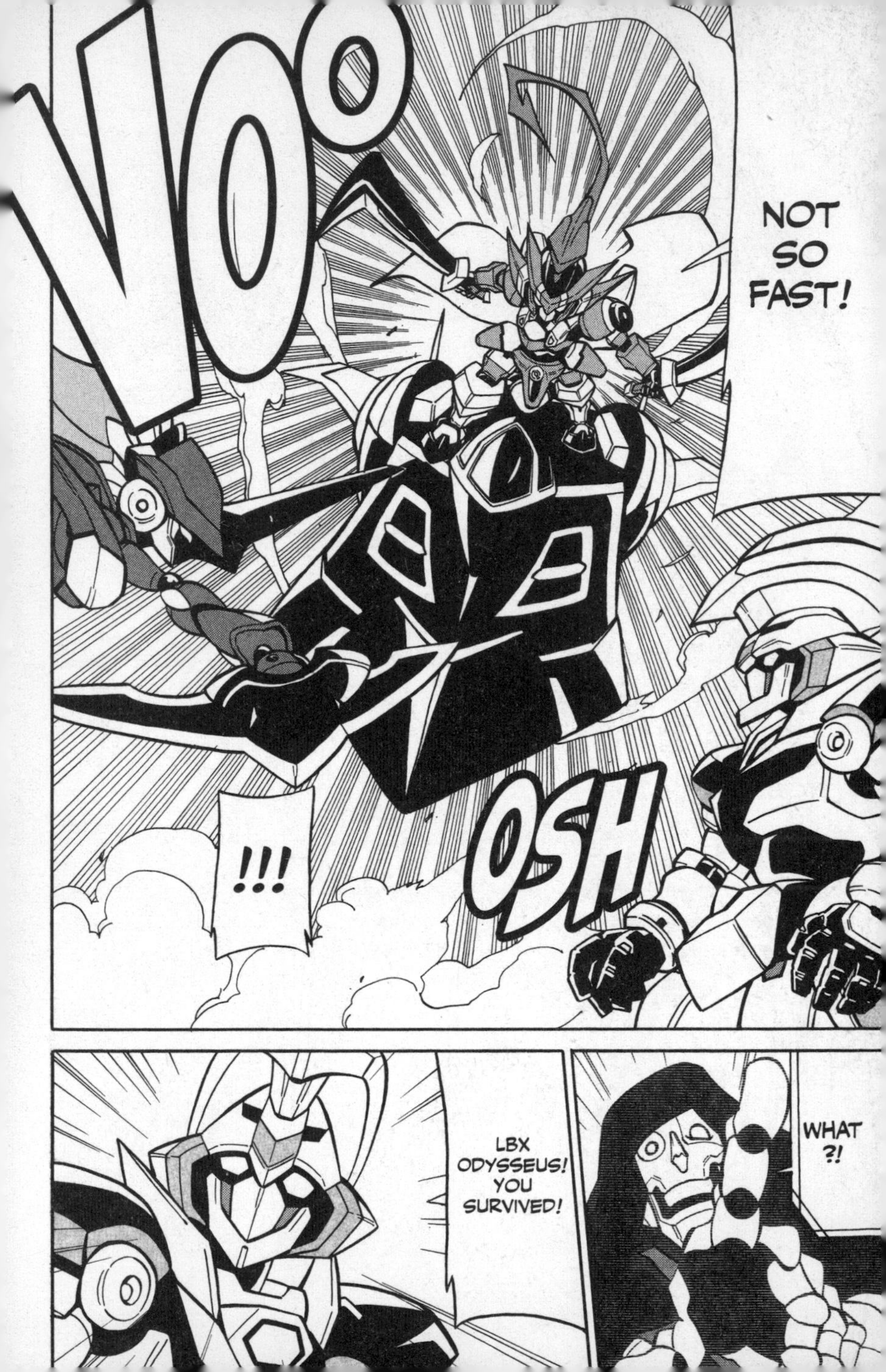NOT SO FAST!
VOO
OSH
!!!
WHAT ?!
LBX ODYSSEUS! YOU SURVIVED!

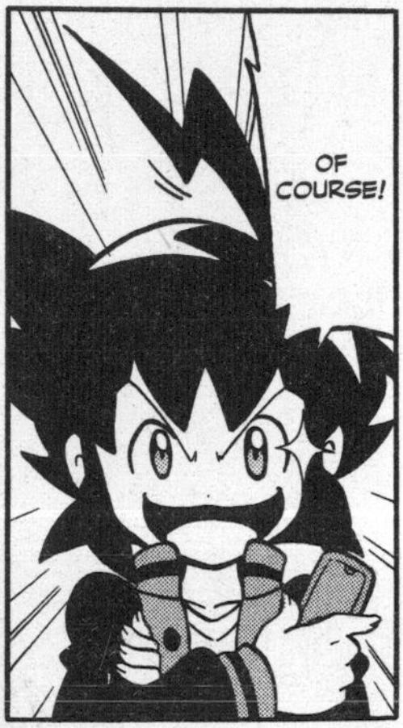
OF COURSE!

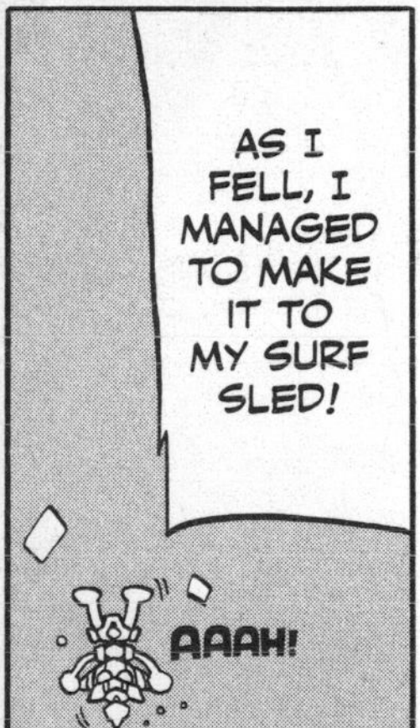
AS I FELL, I MANAGED TO MAKE IT TO MY SURF SLED!
AAAH!
IEEE
CH KT

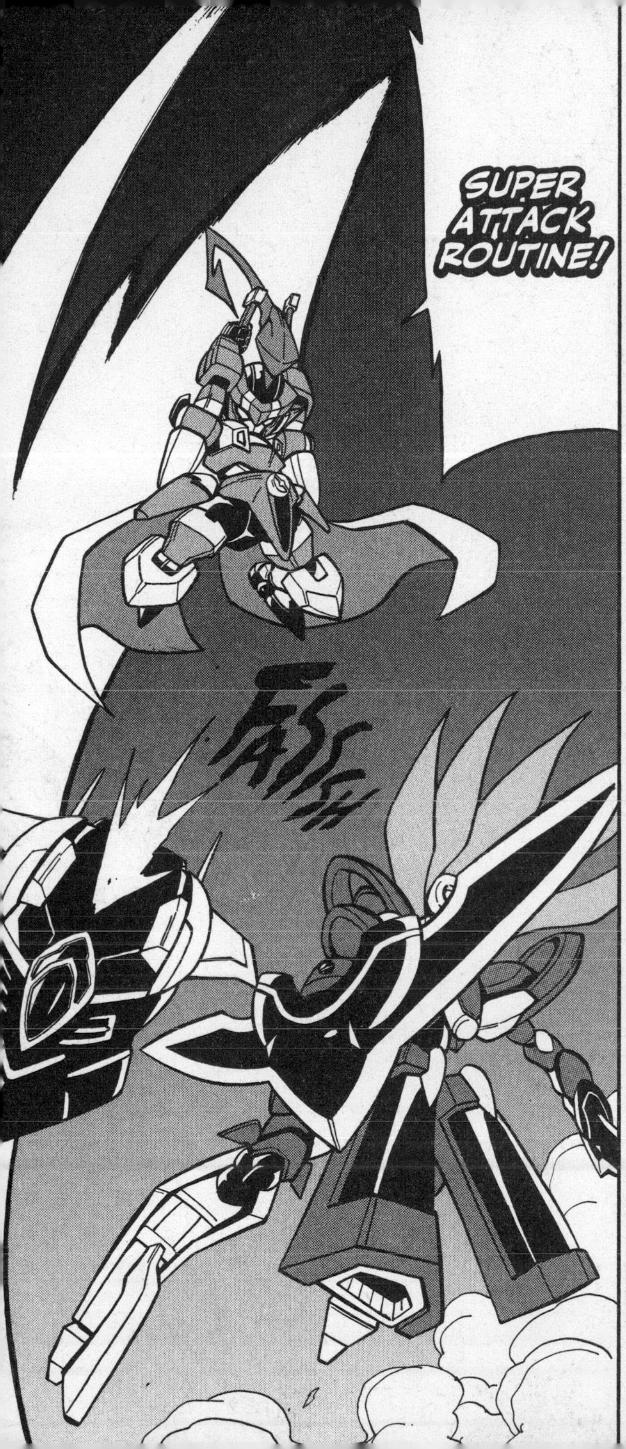
SUPER ATTACK ROUTINE!
FASSH

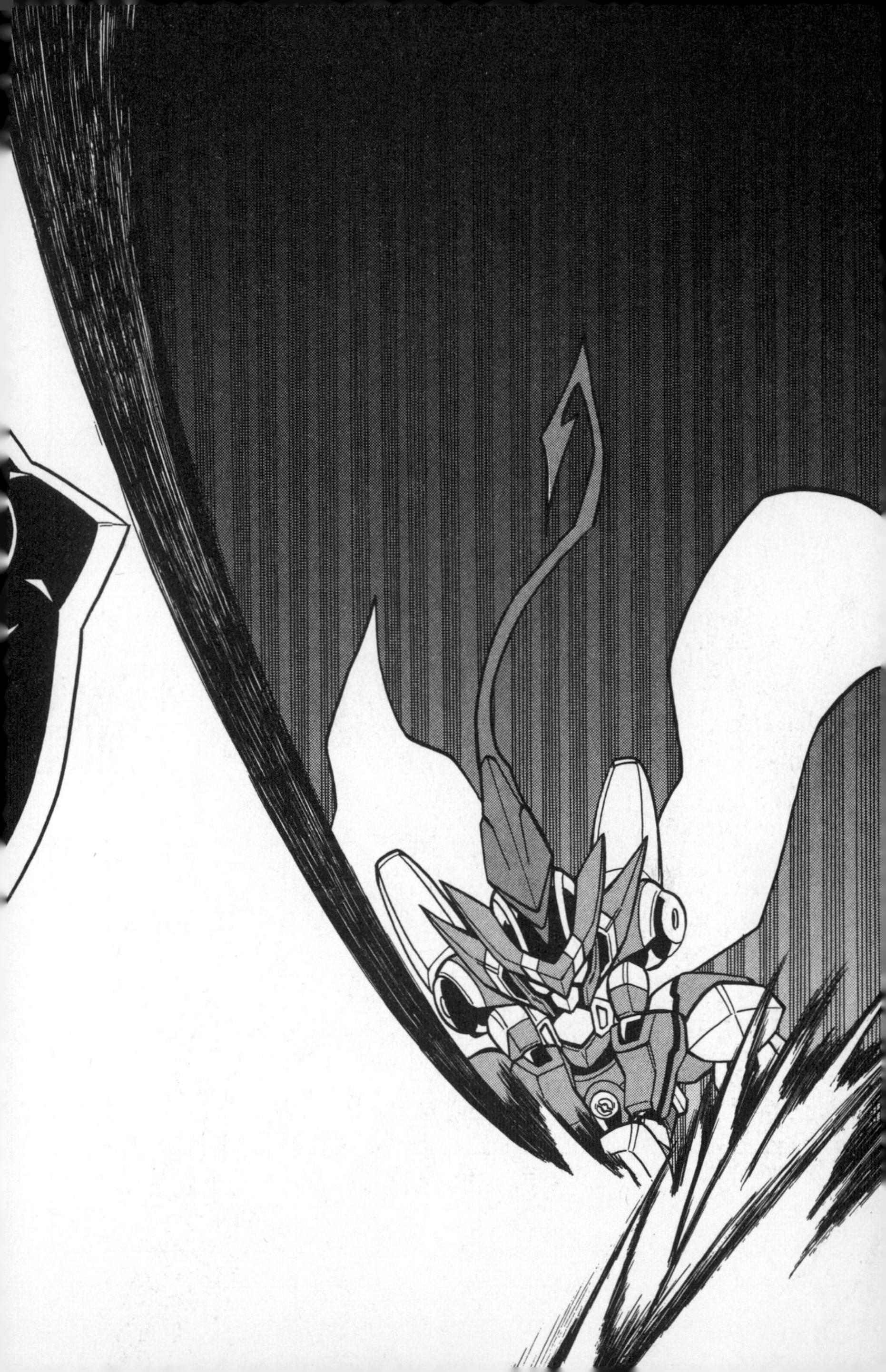

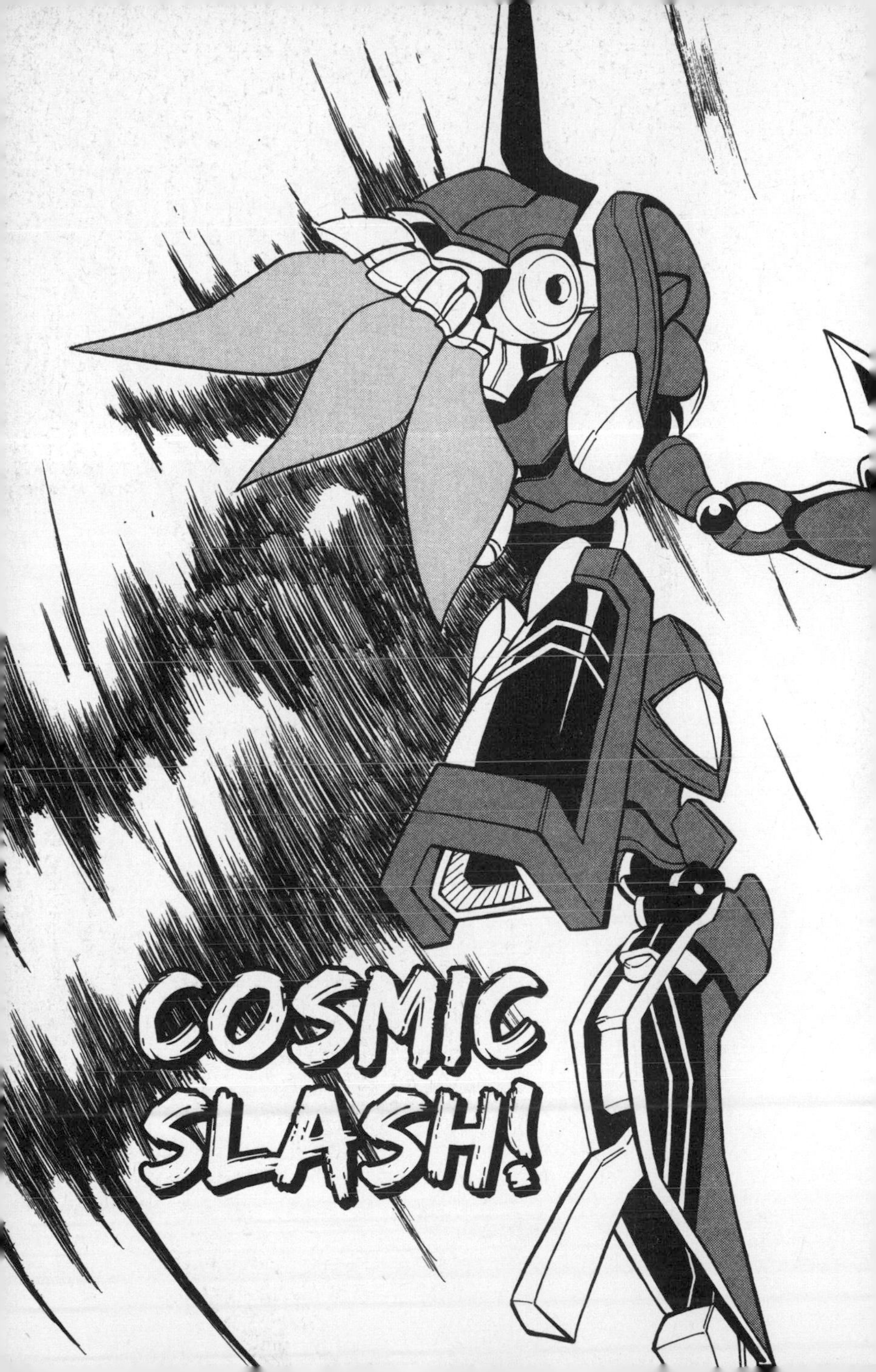

COSMIC SLASH!

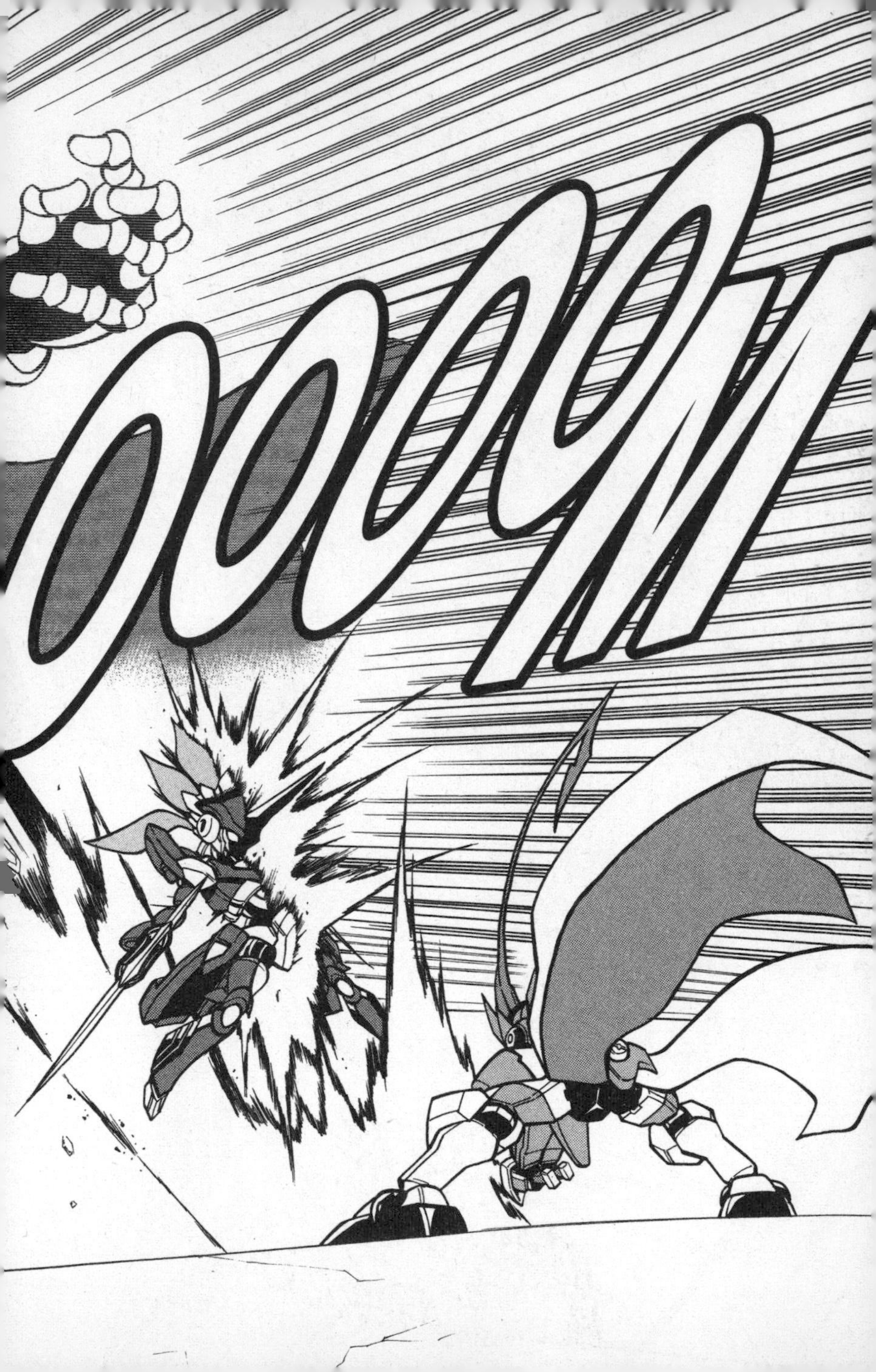

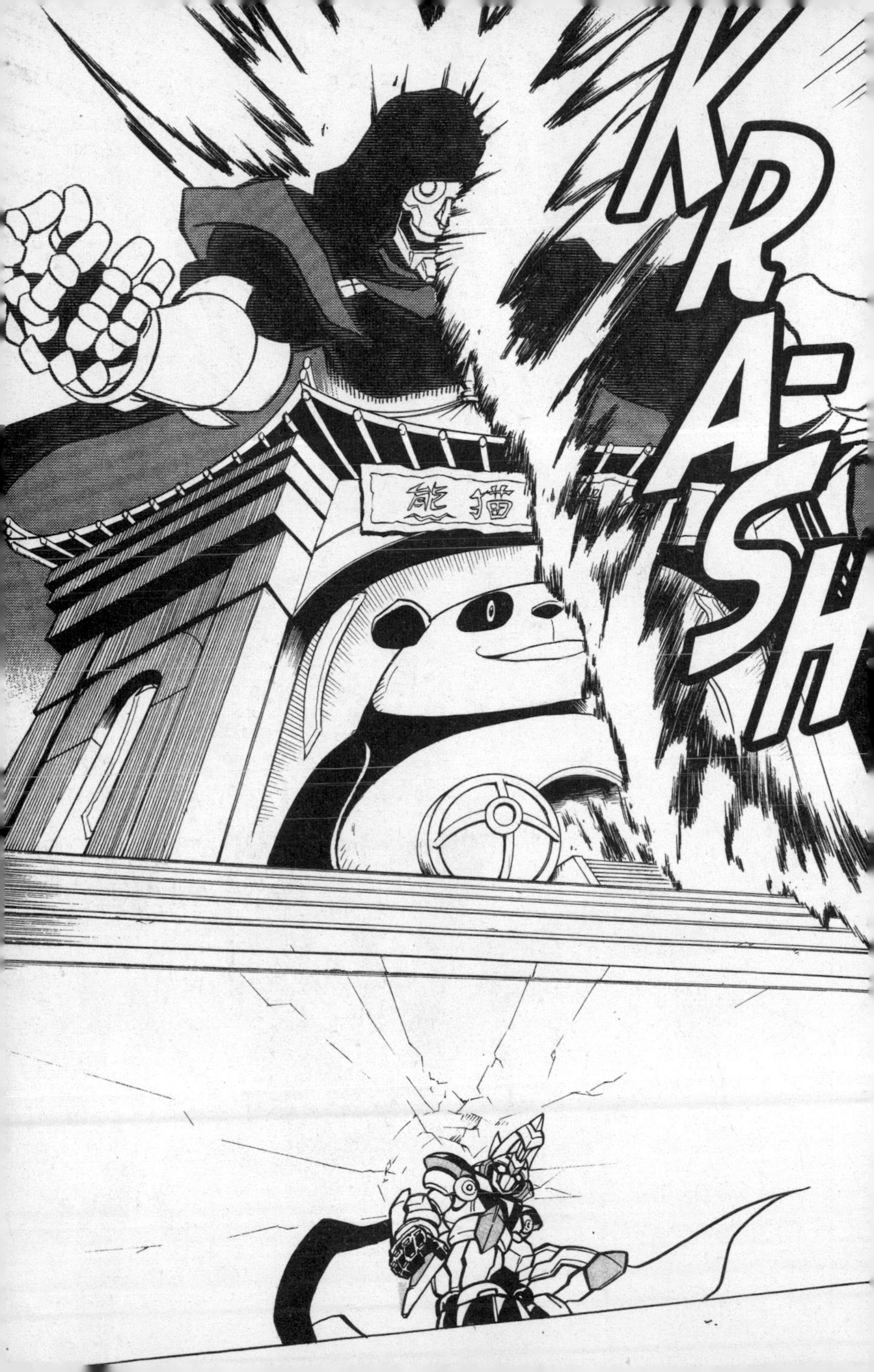
熊猫
KRASH

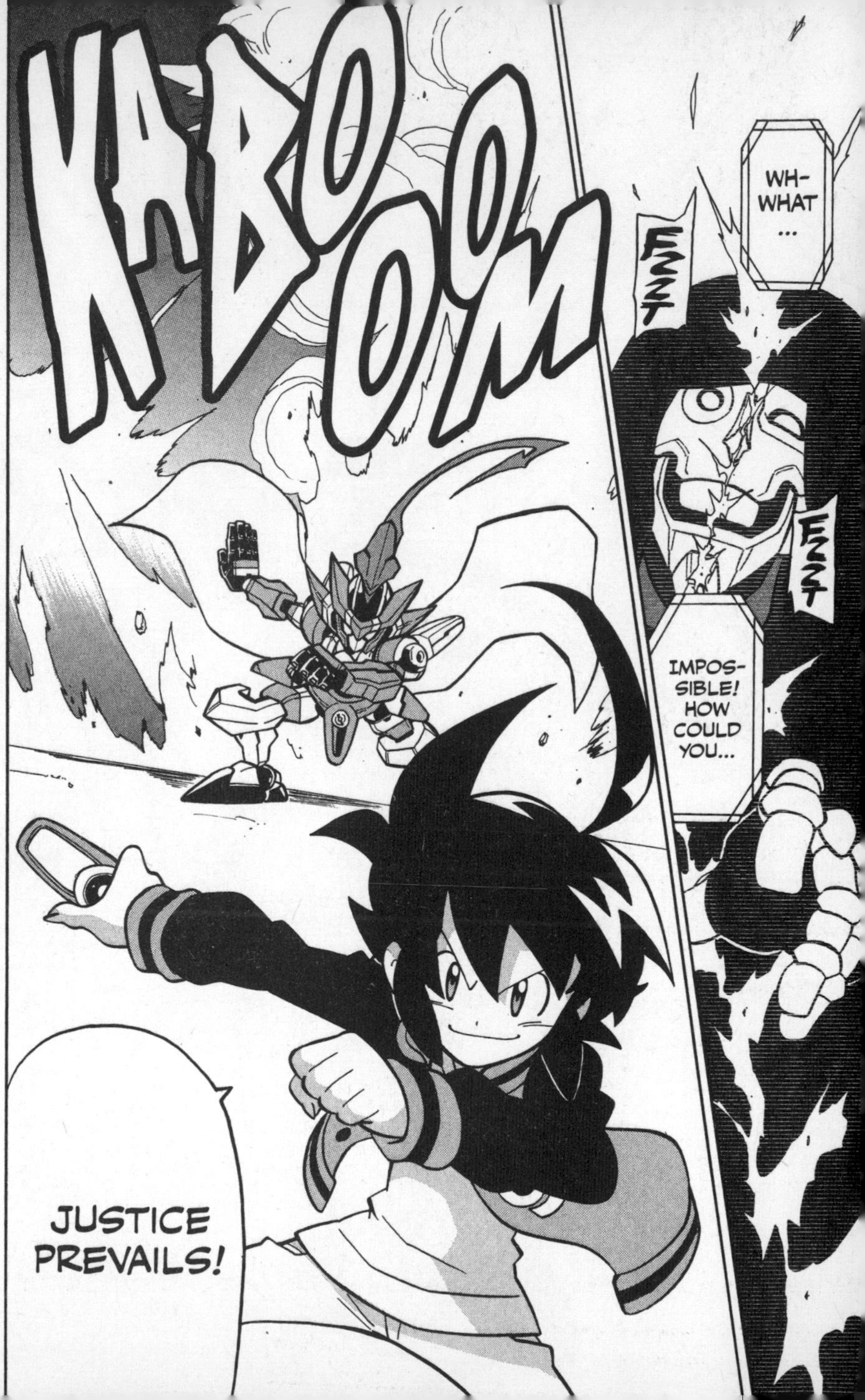
WH- WHAT ...
FZZT
FZZT
IMPOSSIBLE! HOW COULD YOU...
KABOOOM
JUSTICE PREVAILS!

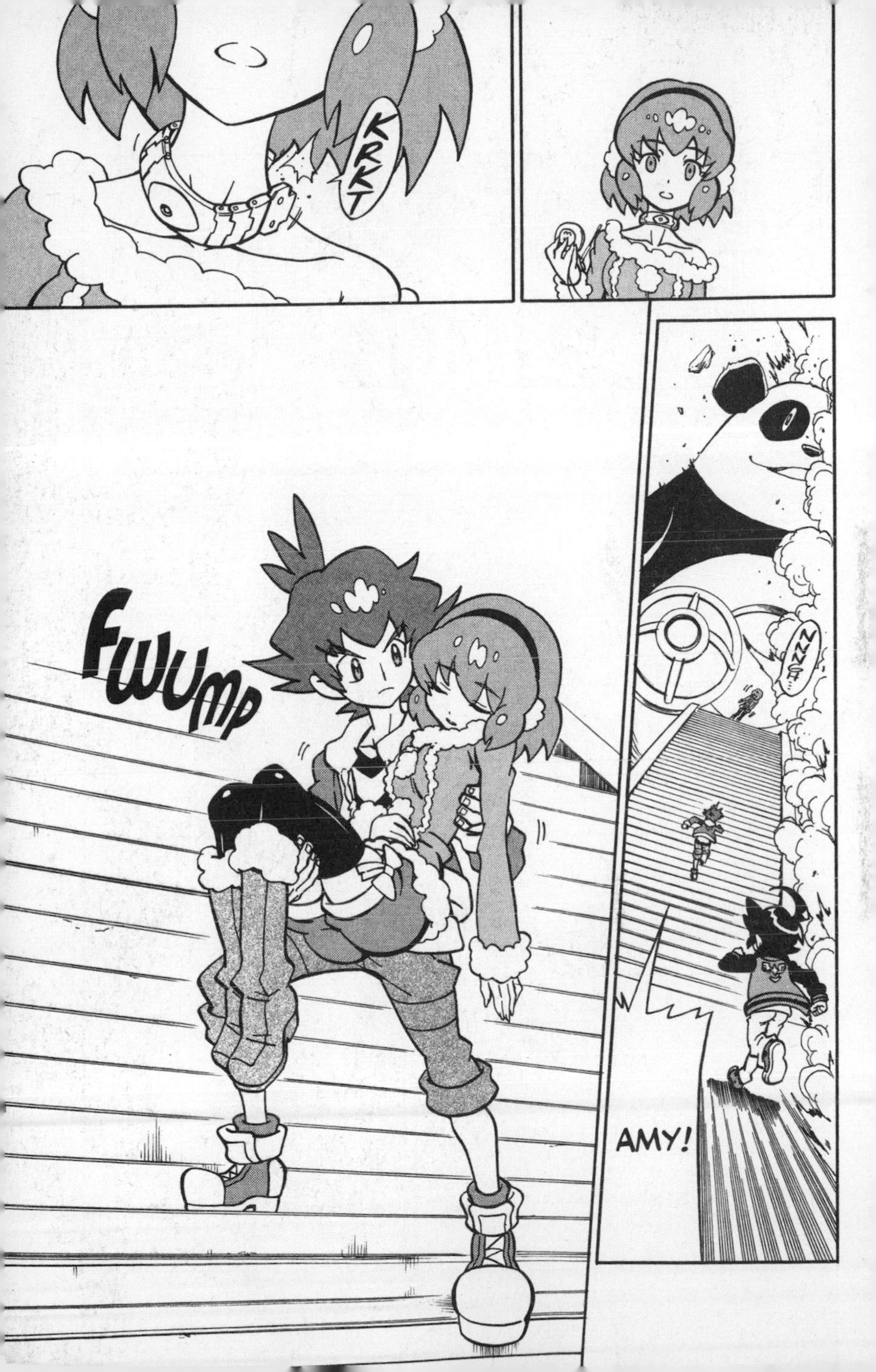
KRRKT
NNNGH...
AMY!
FWUMP

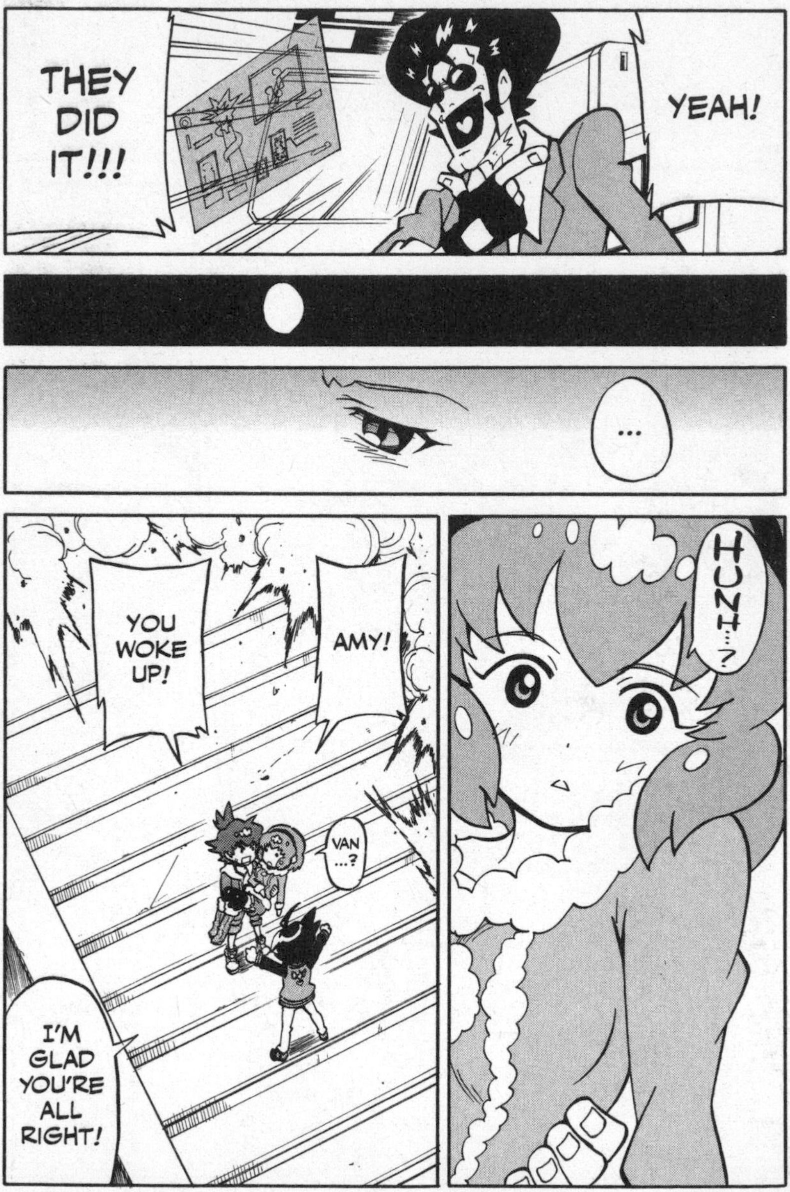
YEAH!
THEY DID IT!!!
...
HUNH...?
AMY!
YOU WOKE UP!
VAN ...?
I'M GLAD YOU'RE ALL RIGHT!

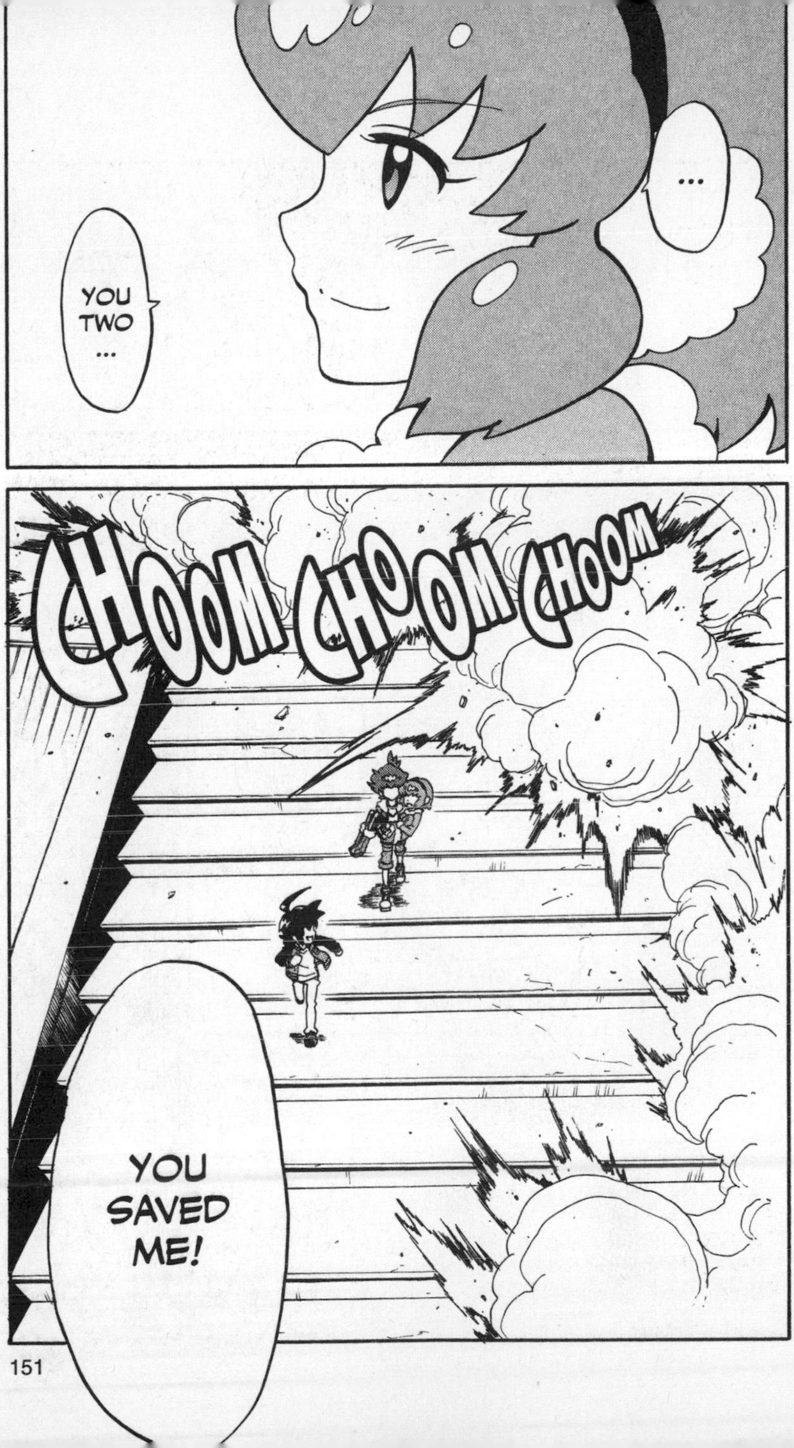
...
YOU TWO ...
CHOOM CHOOM CHOOM
YOU SAVED ME!

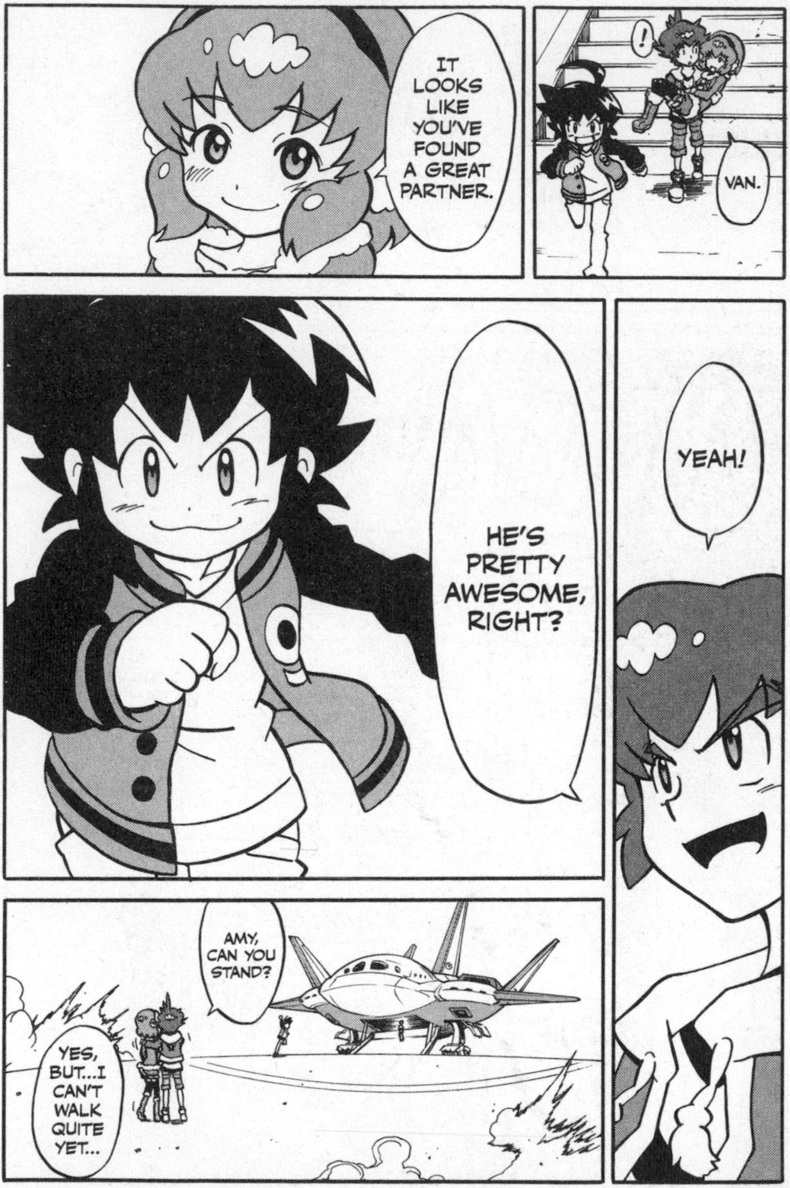
!
VAN.
IT LOOKS LIKE YOU'VE FOUND A GREAT PARTNER.
YEAH!
HE'S PRETTY AWESOME, RIGHT?
AMY, CAN YOU STAND?
YES, BUT...I CAN'T WALK QUITE YET...

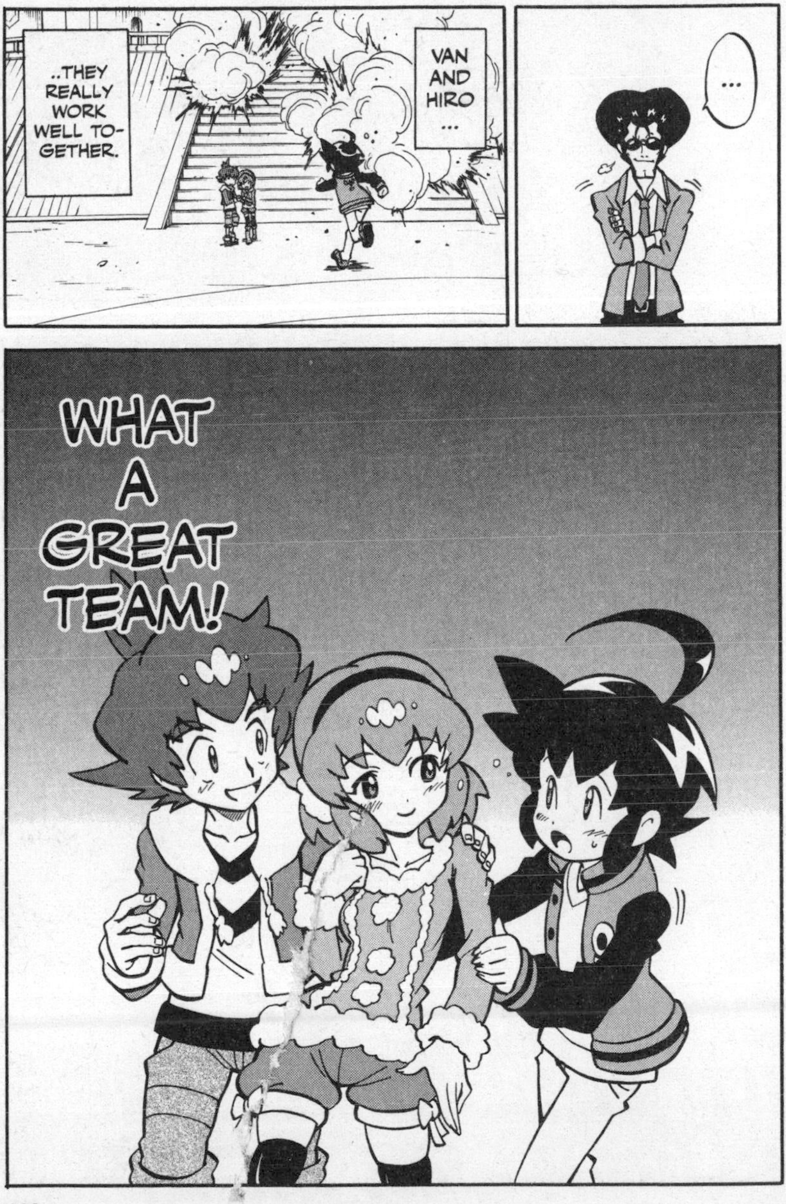
...
VAN AND HIRO ...
..THEY REALLY WORK WELL TO-GETHER.
WHAT A GREAT TEAM!

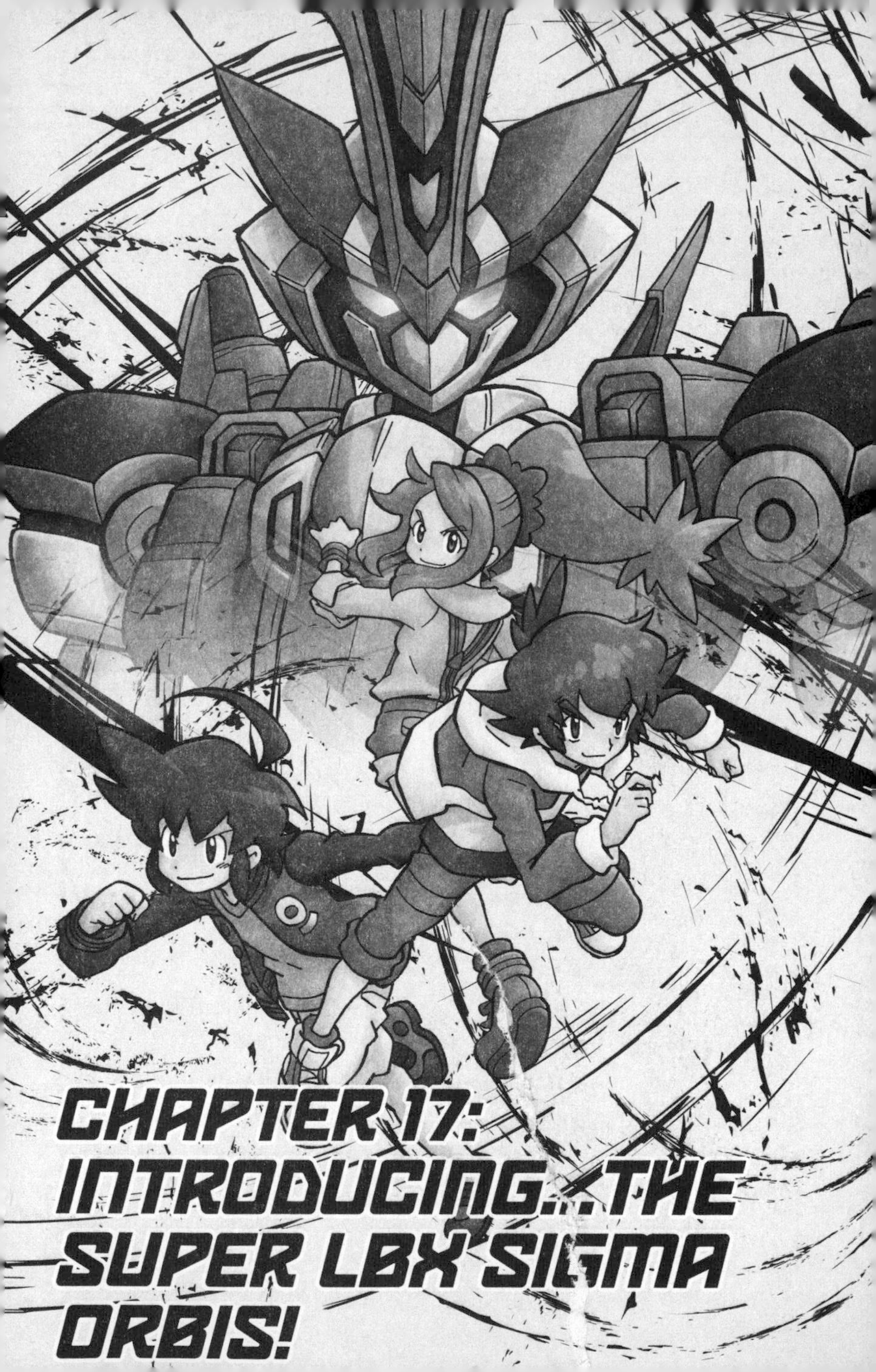
CHAPTER 17:
INTRODUCING...THE SUPER LBX SIGMA ORBIS!

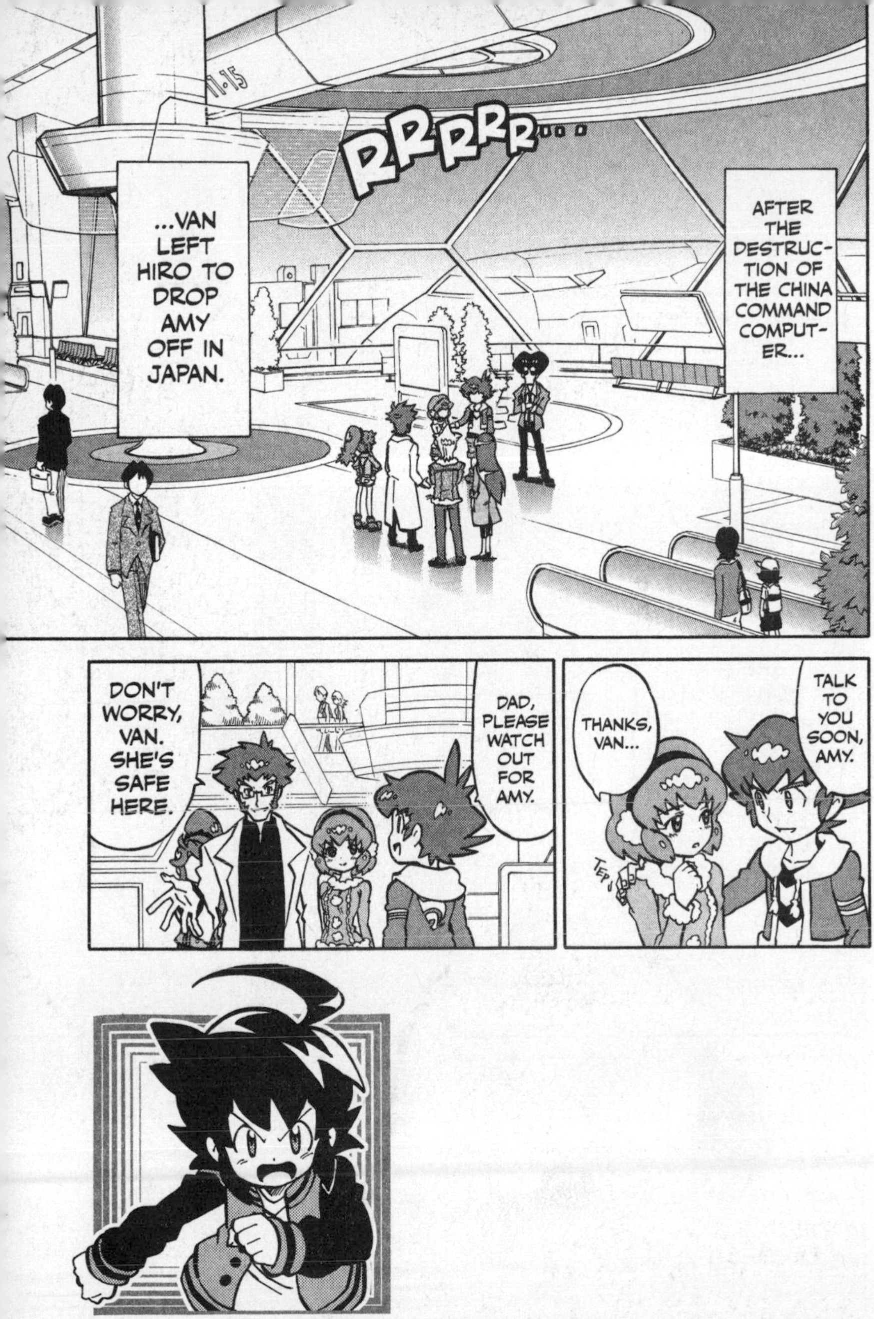
AFTER THE DESTRUCTION OF THE CHINA COMMAND COMPUTER...
RRRRR...
...VAN LEFT HIRO TO DROP AMY OFF IN JAPAN.
TALK TO YOU SOON, AMY.
THANKS, VAN...
DAD, PLEASE WATCH OUT FOR AMY.
DON'T WORRY, VAN. SHE'S SAFE HERE.

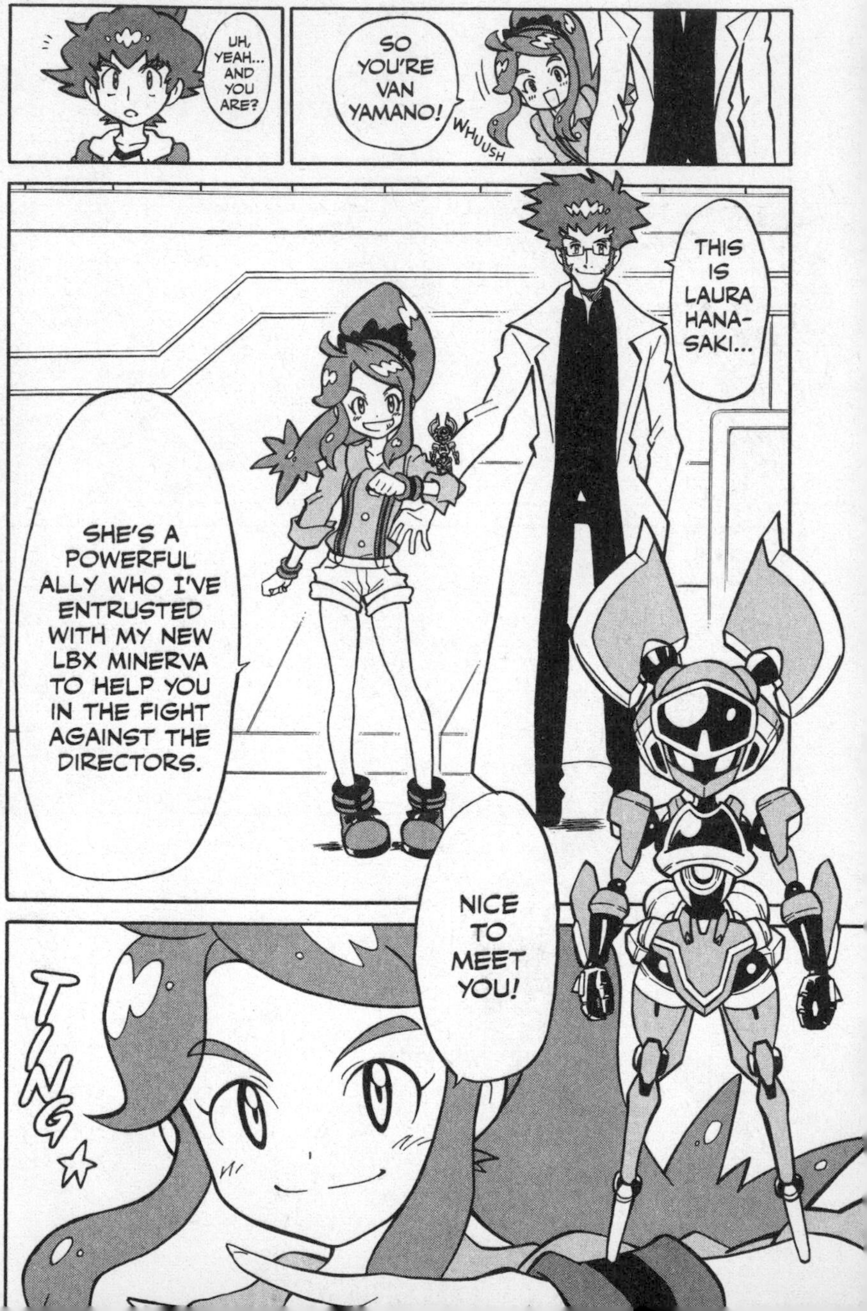
SO YOU'RE VAN YAMANO!
WHUUSH
UH, YEAH... AND YOU ARE?
THIS IS LAURA HANA-SAKI...
SHE'S A POWERFUL ALLY WHO I'VE ENTRUSTED WITH MY NEW LBX MINERVA TO HELP YOU IN THE FIGHT AGAINST THE DIRECTORS.
NICE TO MEET YOU!
TING☆

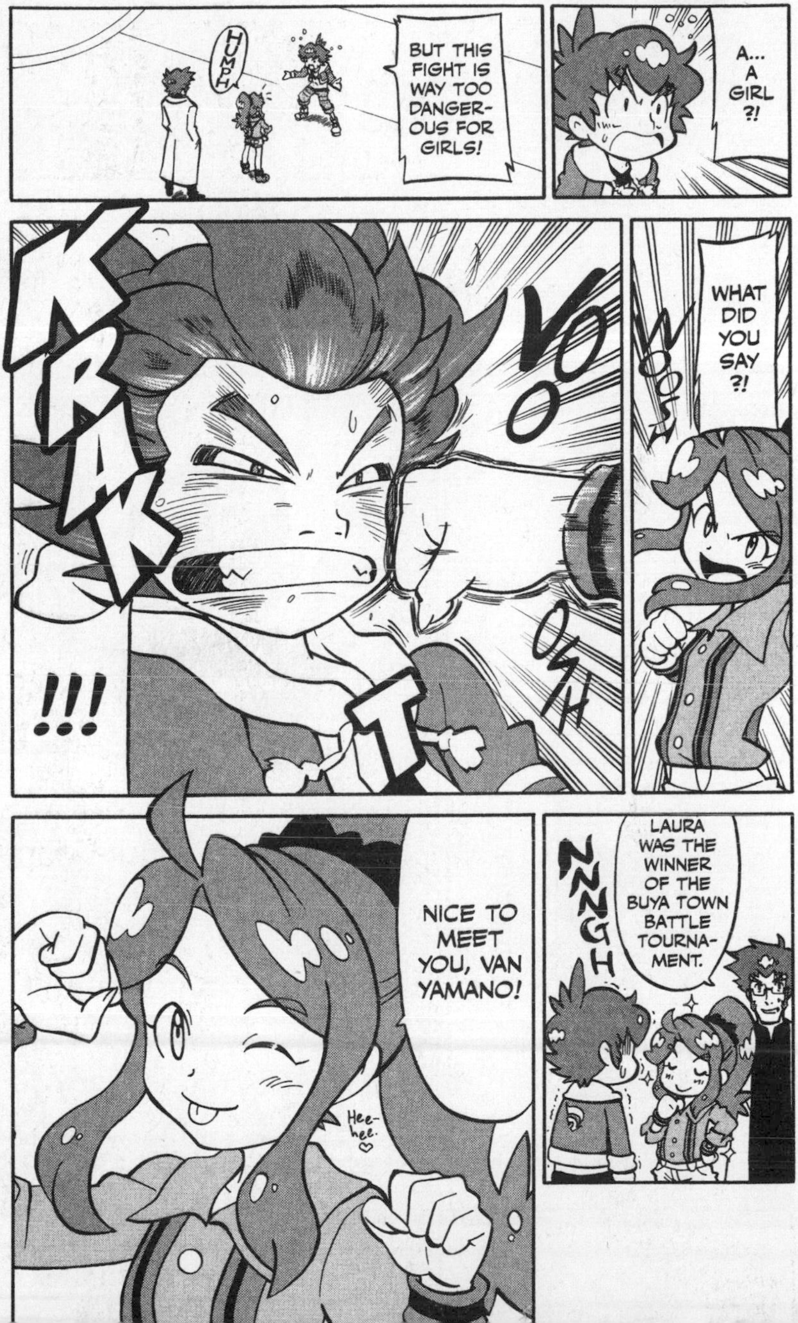
A... A GIRL ?!
BUT THIS FIGHT IS WAY TOO DANGER-OUS FOR GIRLS!
HUMPH
WHAT DID YOU SAY ?!
KRAK
!!!
LAURA WAS THE WINNER OF THE BUYA TOWN BATTLE TOURNA-MENT.
NNNGH
NICE TO MEET YOU, VAN YAMANO!
Hee-hee. ♡

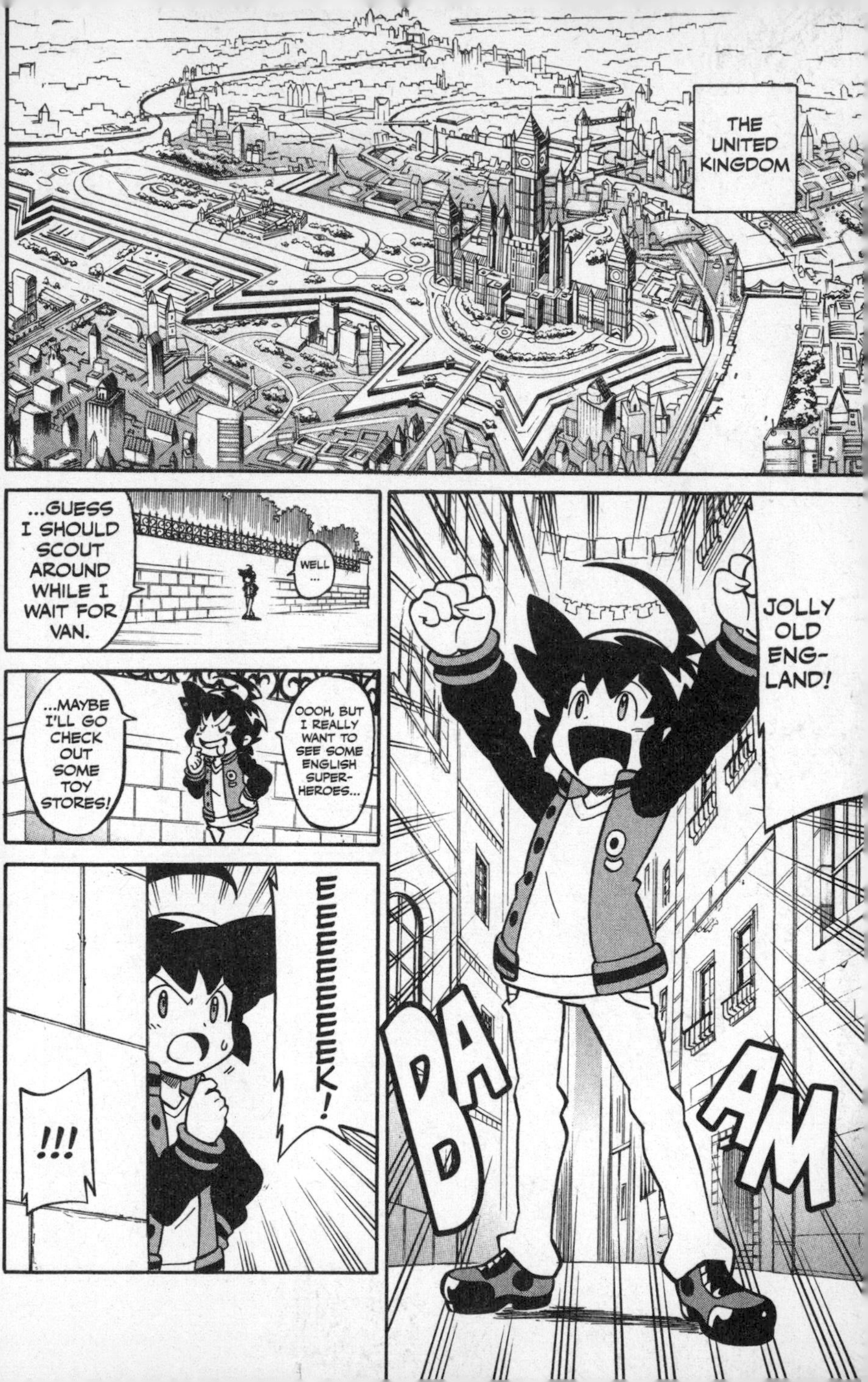
THE UNITED KINGDOM
JOLLY OLD ENG-LAND!
BADAM
WELL...
...GUESS I SHOULD SCOUT AROUND WHILE I WAIT FOR VAN.
OOOH, BUT I REALLY WANT TO SEE SOME ENGLISH SUPER-HEROES...
...MAYBE I'LL GO CHECK OUT SOME TOY STORES!
EEEEEEEEEEK!
!!!

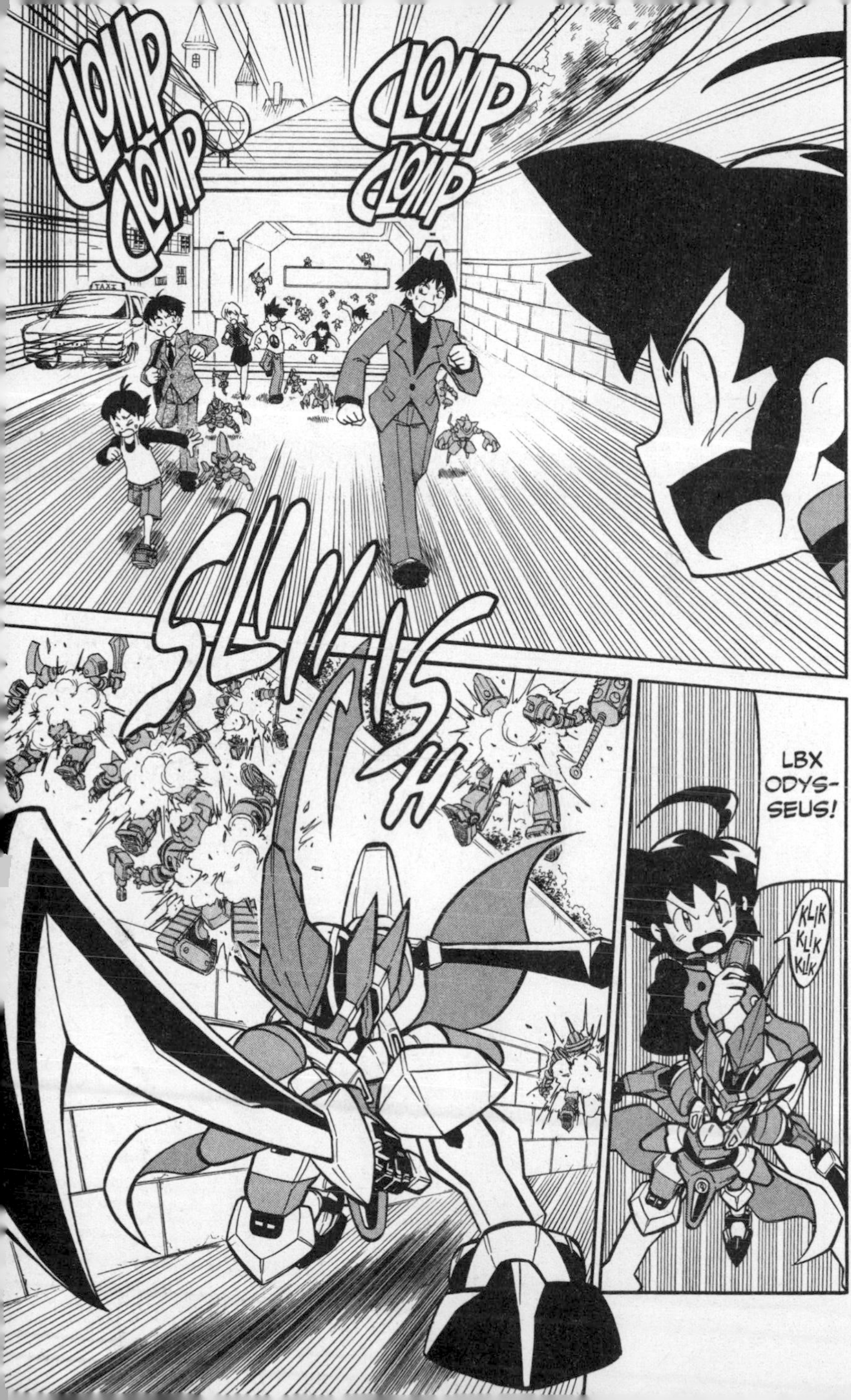
CLOMP CLOMP
CLOMP CLOMP
LBX ODYS-SEUS!
KLIK KLIK KLIK
SLIIISH

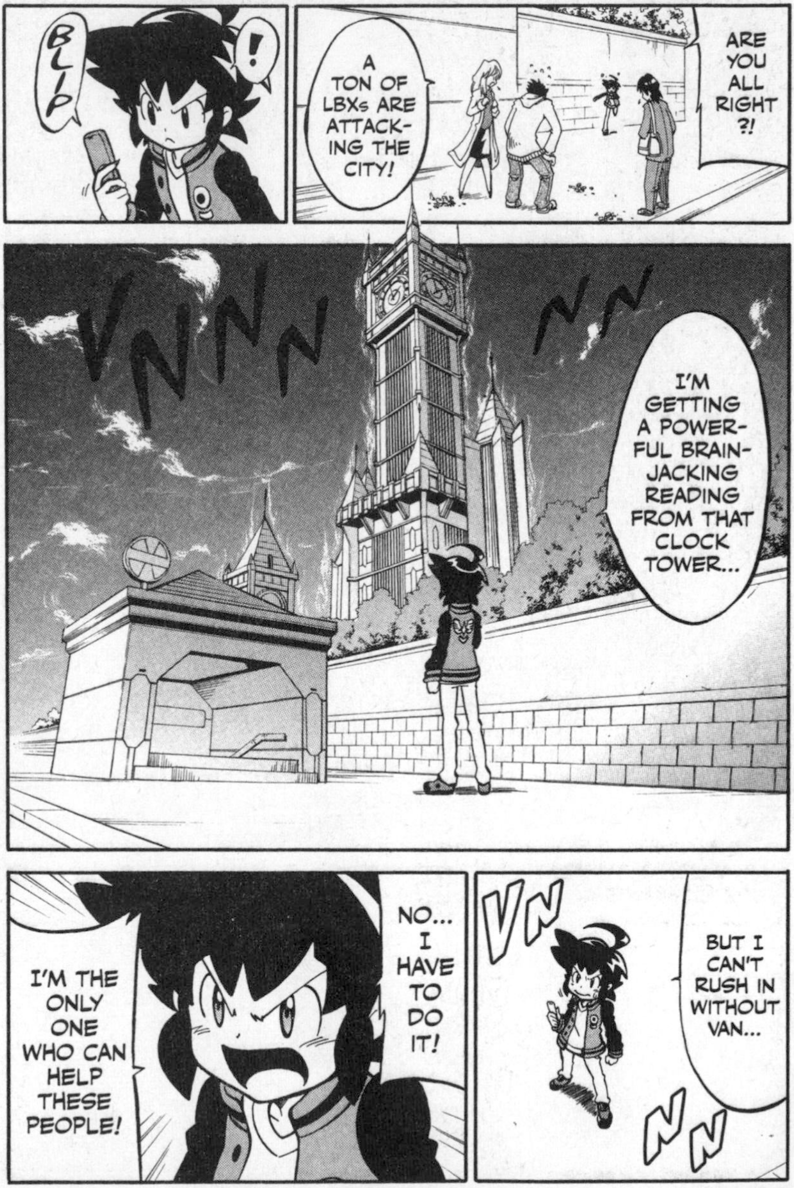
ARE YOU ALL RIGHT?!
A TON OF LBXs ARE ATTACKING THE CITY!
!
BLIP
VNNN
NN
I'M GETTING A POWERFUL BRAINJACKING READING FROM THAT CLOCK TOWER...
BUT I CAN'T RUSH IN WITHOUT VAN...
VN
NN
NO... I HAVE TO DO IT!
I'M THE ONLY ONE WHO CAN HELP THESE PEOPLE!

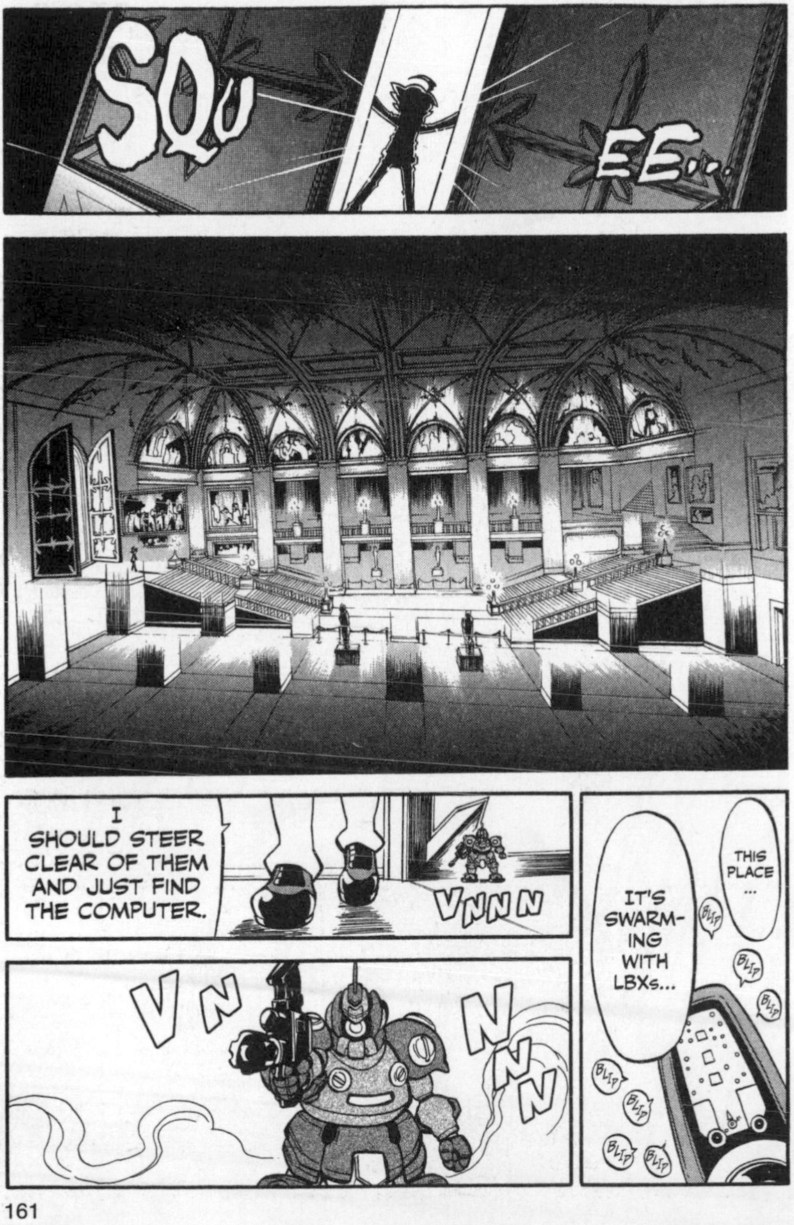
SQU
EE...
THIS PLACE ...
IT'S SWARMING WITH LBXs...
BLIP
BLIP
BLIP
BLIP
BLIP
BLIP
BLIP
I SHOULD STEER CLEAR OF THEM AND JUST FIND THE COMPUTER.
VNNN
VN
NNN

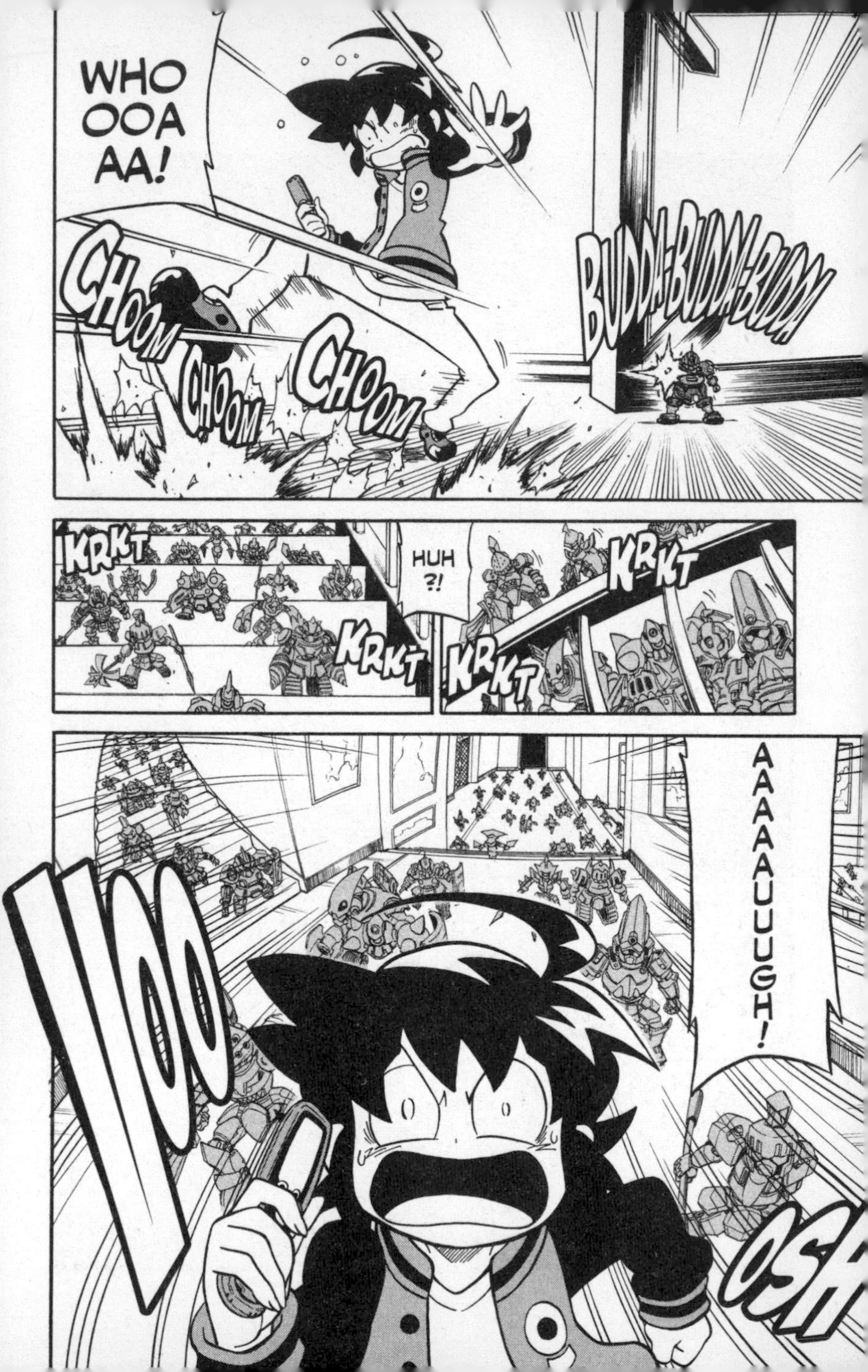

WHOOOAAA!
BUDDA-BUDDA-BUDDA
CHOOM
CHOOM
CHOOM
KRKT
KRKT
HUH?!
KRKT
KRKT
AAAAAUUUGH!
WOO
OSH

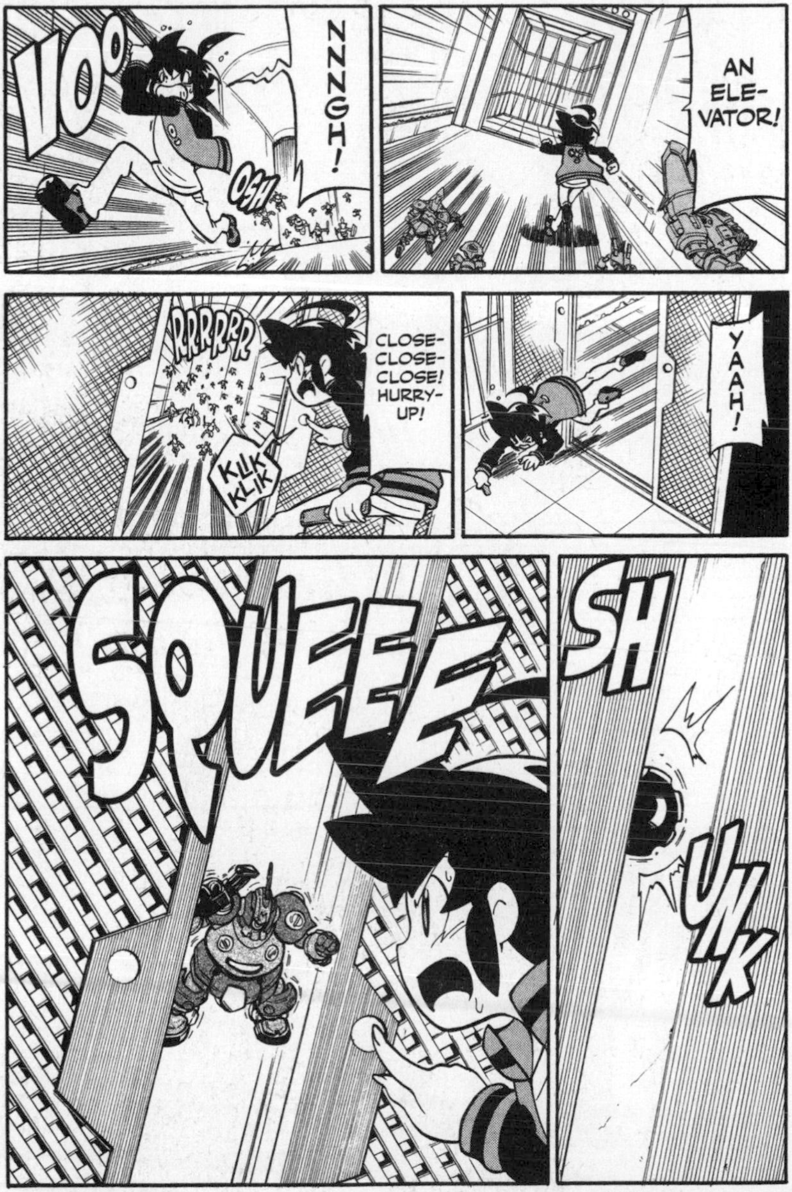
AN ELE-VATOR!
NNNGH!
VOO
OSH
YAAAH!
CLOSE-CLOSE-CLOSE! HURRY-UP!
RRRRRR
KLIK KLIK
SH
UNK
SQUEEZE

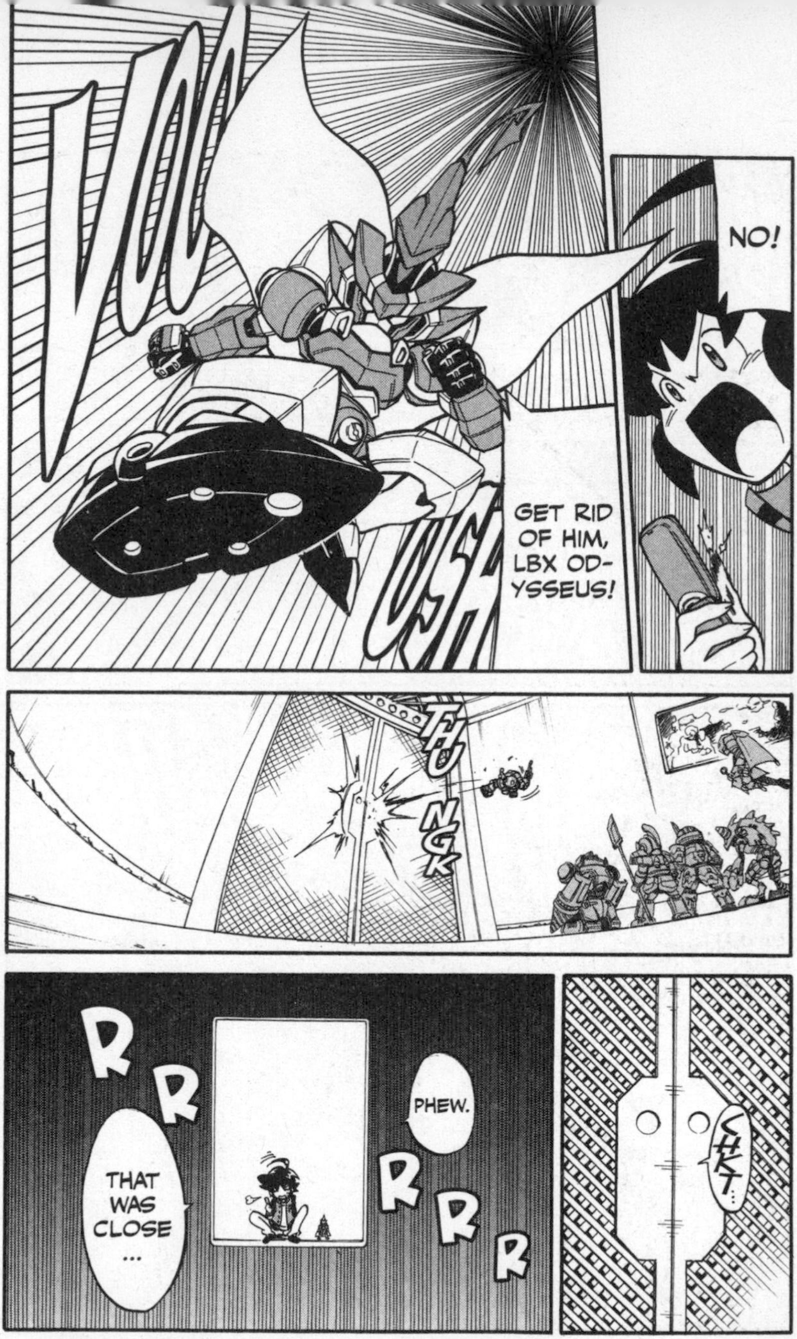
NO!
GET RID OF HIM, LBX ODYSSEUS!
THUNGK
CHKT...
PHEW.
THAT WAS CLOSE ...
RRRRRR

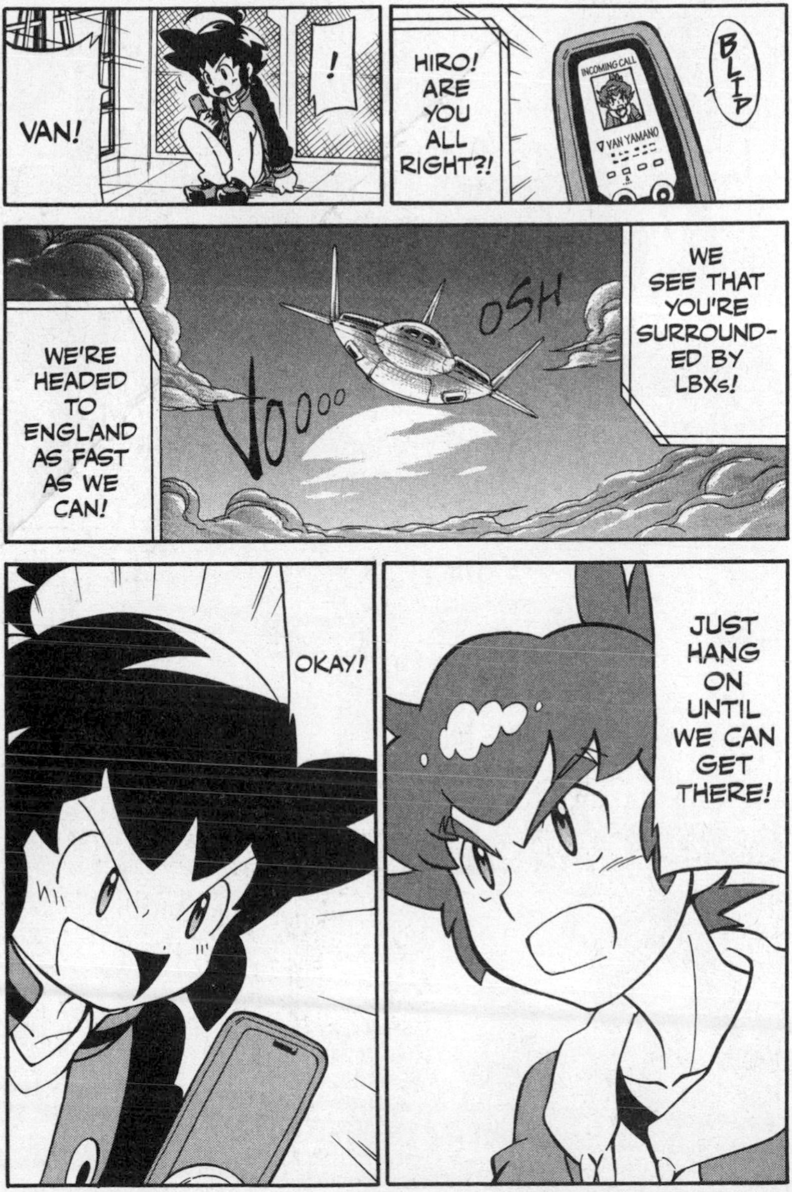
BLIP
INCOMING CALL
VAN YAMANO
HIRO! ARE YOU ALL RIGHT?!
!
VAN!
WE SEE THAT YOU'RE SURROUND-ED BY LBXs!
OSH
VOooo
WE'RE HEADED TO ENGLAND AS FAST AS WE CAN!
JUST HANG ON UNTIL WE CAN GET THERE!
OKAY!

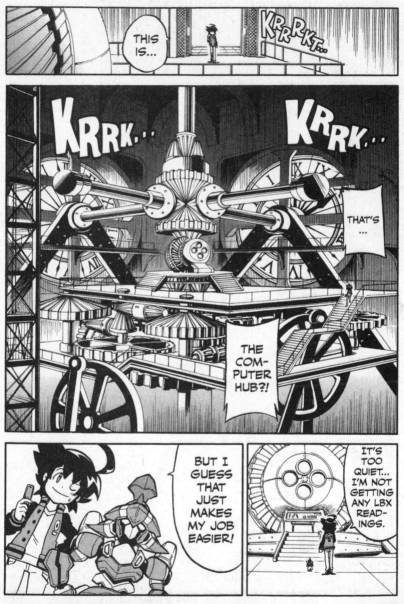

KRRRKT...
THIS IS...
KRRK...
KRRK...
THAT'S ...
THE COMPUTER HUB?!
IT'S TOO QUIET... I'M NOT GETTING ANY LBX READINGS.
BUT I GUESS THAT JUST MAKES MY JOB EASIER!

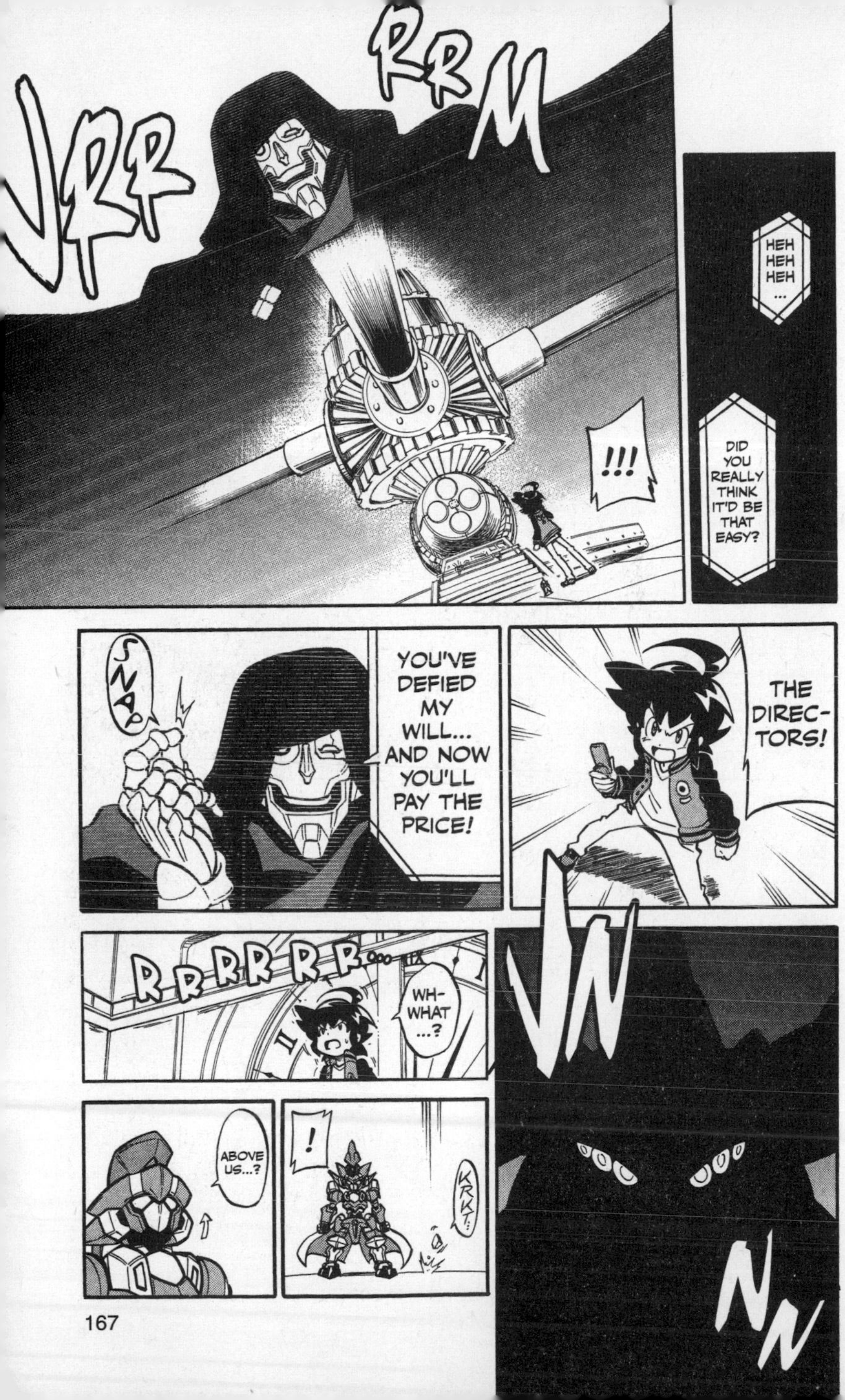

HEH HEH HEH...
DID YOU REALLY THINK IT'D BE THAT EASY?
RRM
!!!
VRR
THE DIRECTORS!
YOU'VE DEFIED MY WILL... AND NOW YOU'LL PAY THE PRICE!
SNAP
VN
NN
RRRRRR
WH-WHAT...?
!
KRKT!
ABOVE US...?

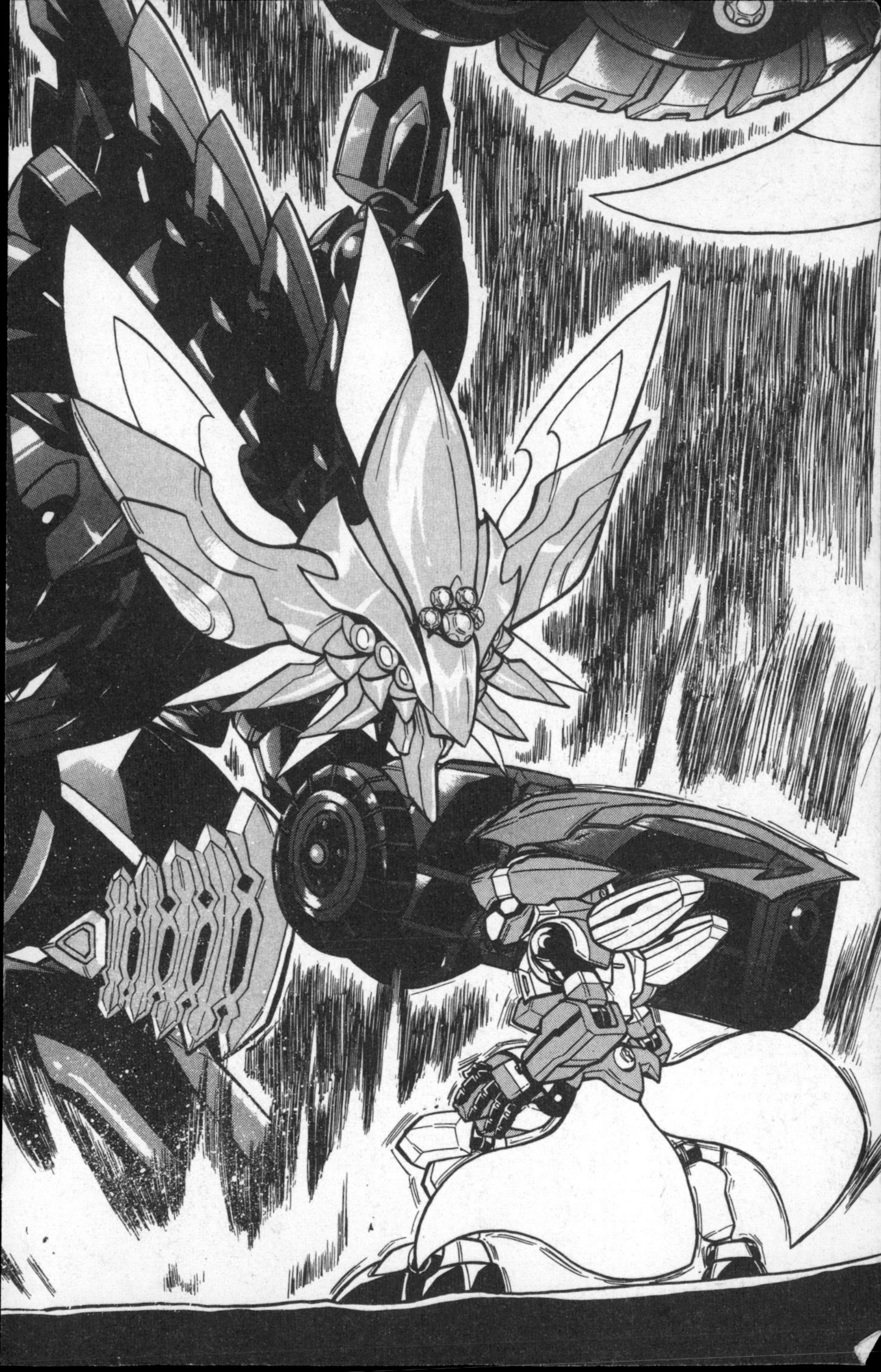

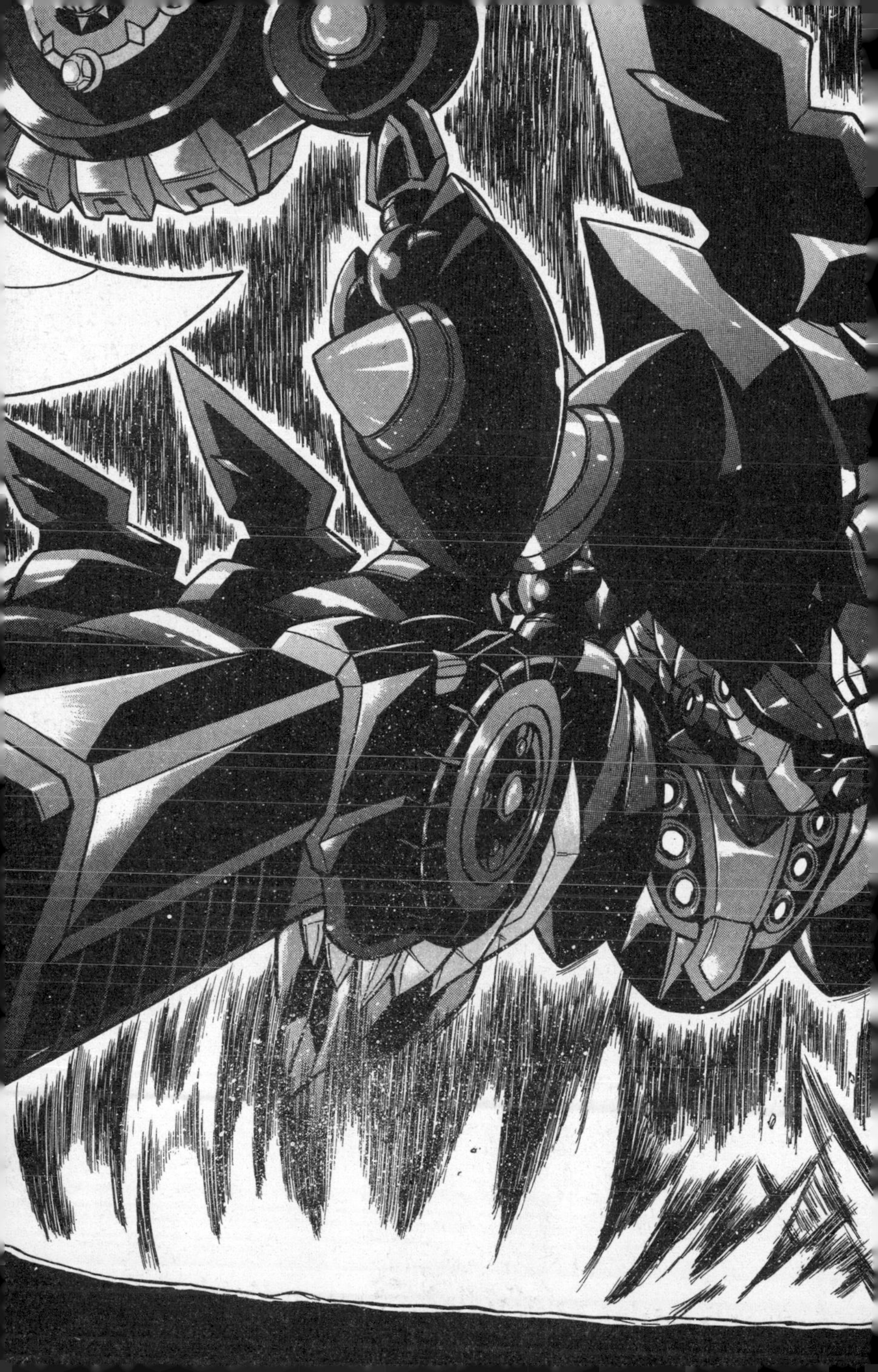

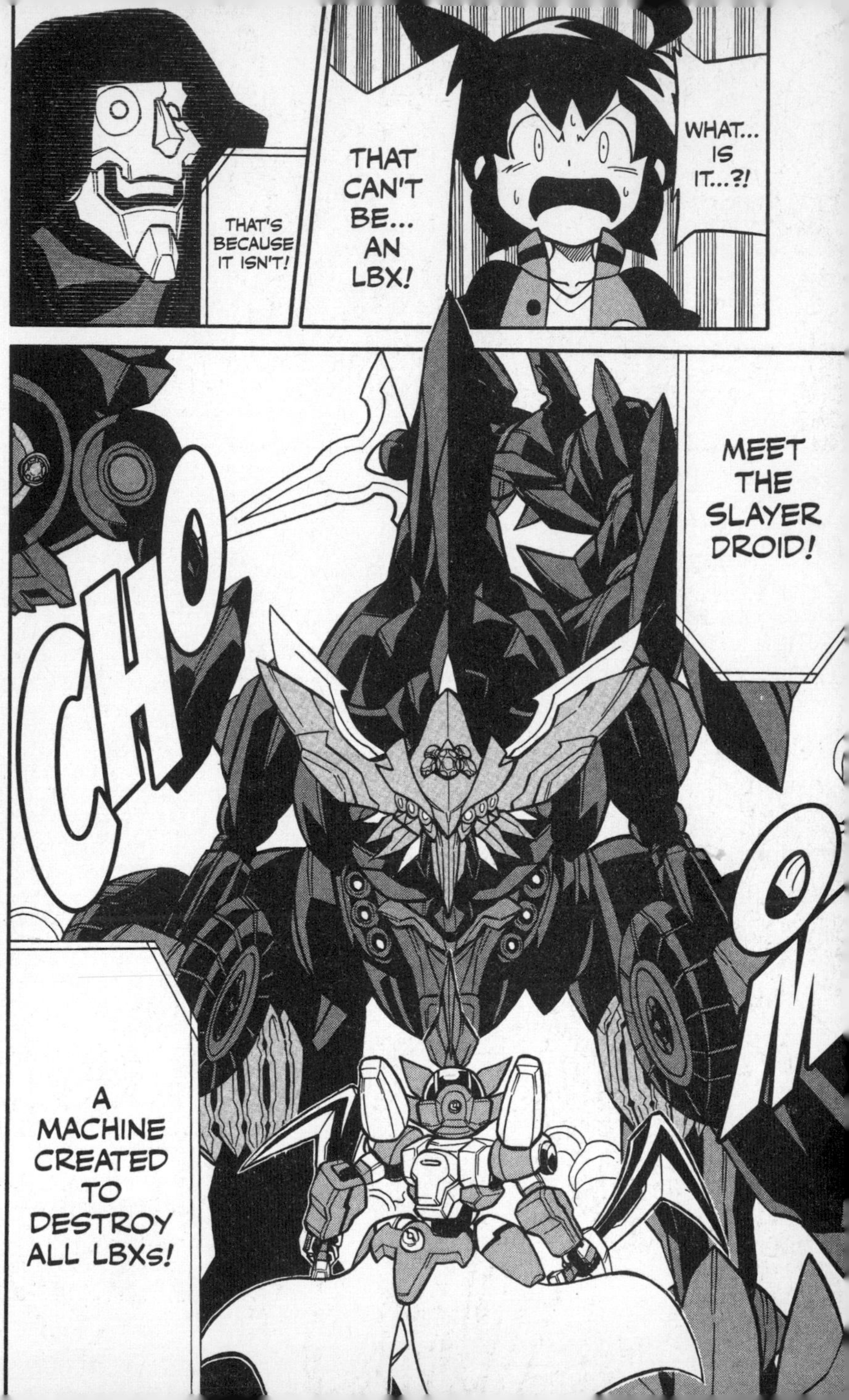
WHAT... IS IT...?!
THAT CAN'T BE... AN LBX!
THAT'S BECAUSE IT ISN'T!
MEET THE SLAYER DROID!
CHO
A MACHINE CREATED TO DESTROY ALL LBXs!

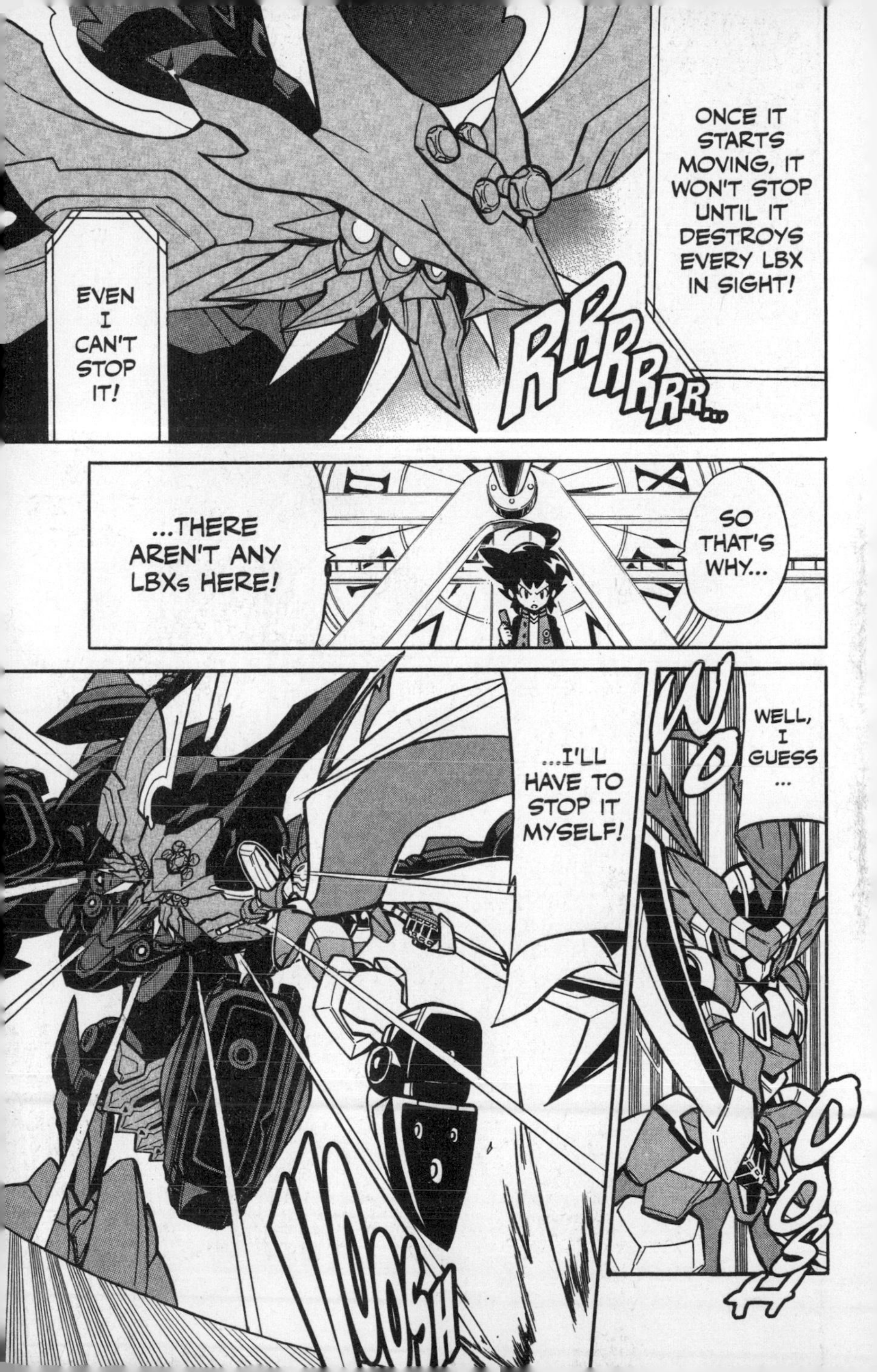
ONCE IT STARTS MOVING, IT WON'T STOP UNTIL IT DESTROYS EVERY LBX IN SIGHT!
EVEN I CAN'T STOP IT!
RRRRRR...
SO THAT'S WHY...
...THERE AREN'T ANY LBXs HERE!
WELL, I GUESS ...
...I'LL HAVE TO STOP IT MYSELF!
WOOOSH
WOOSH

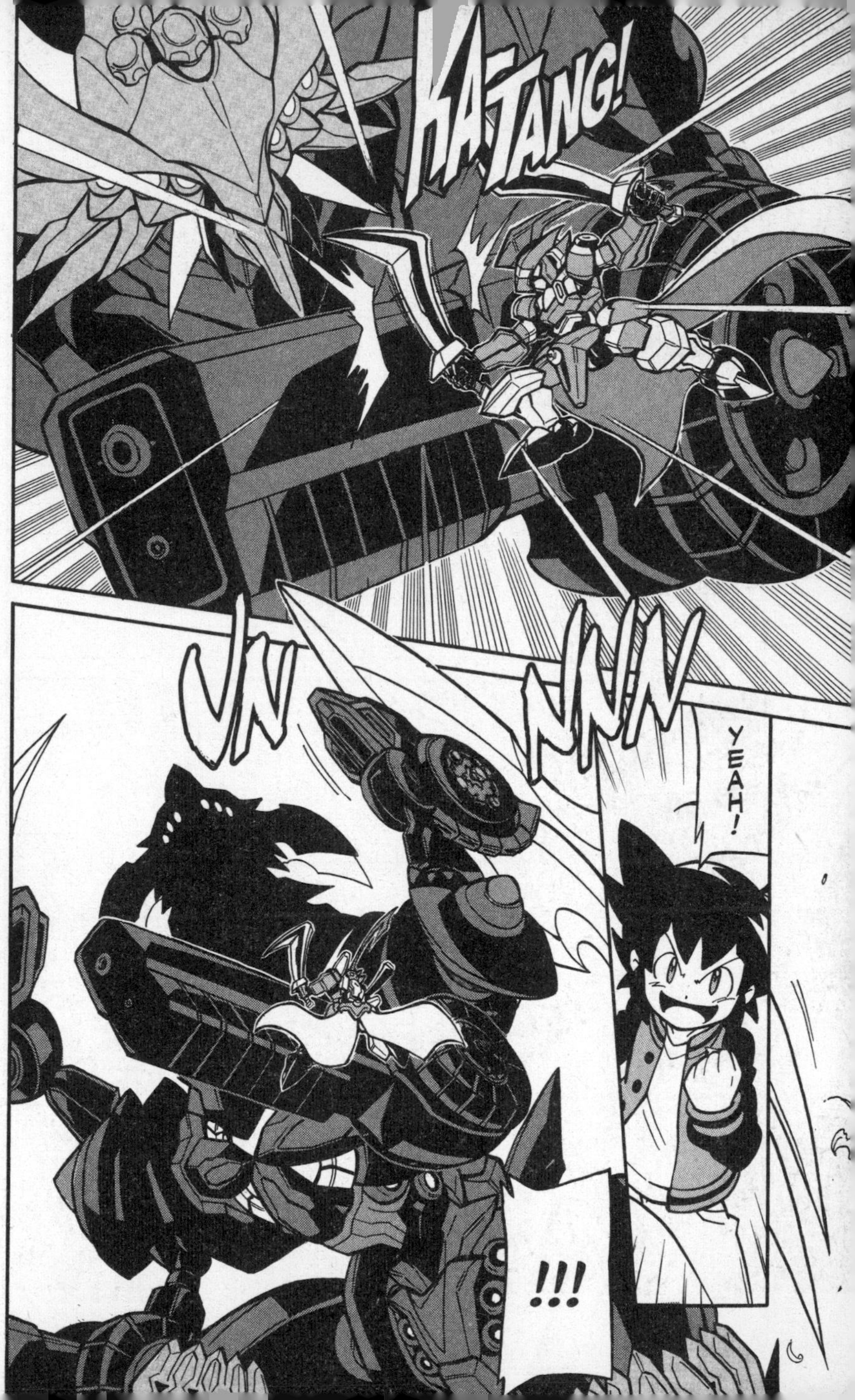
KA-TANG!
JIN
NNN
YEAH!
!!!

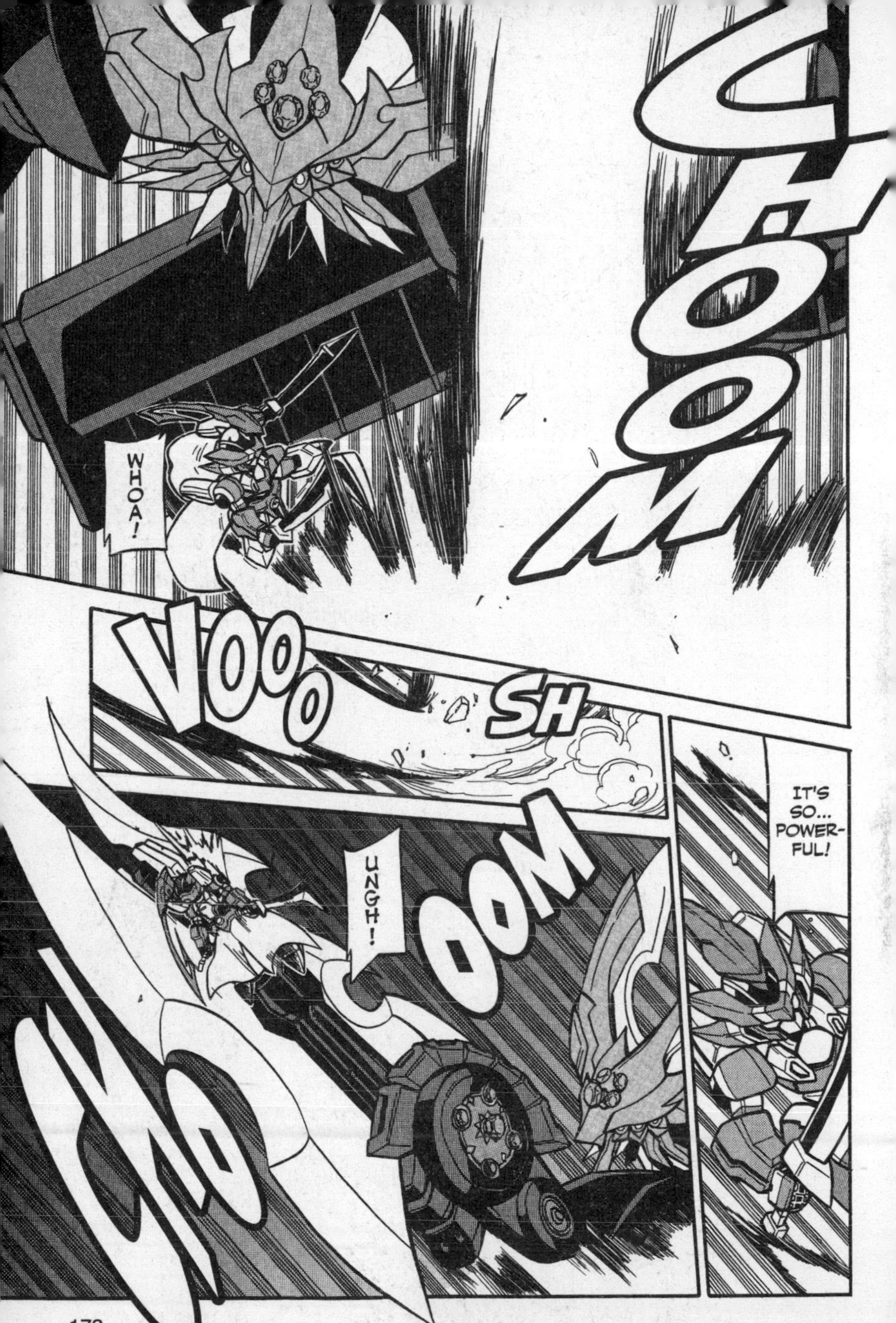
CHOOM
WHOA!
VOOOSH
IT'S SO... POWERFUL!
UNGH!
COOM

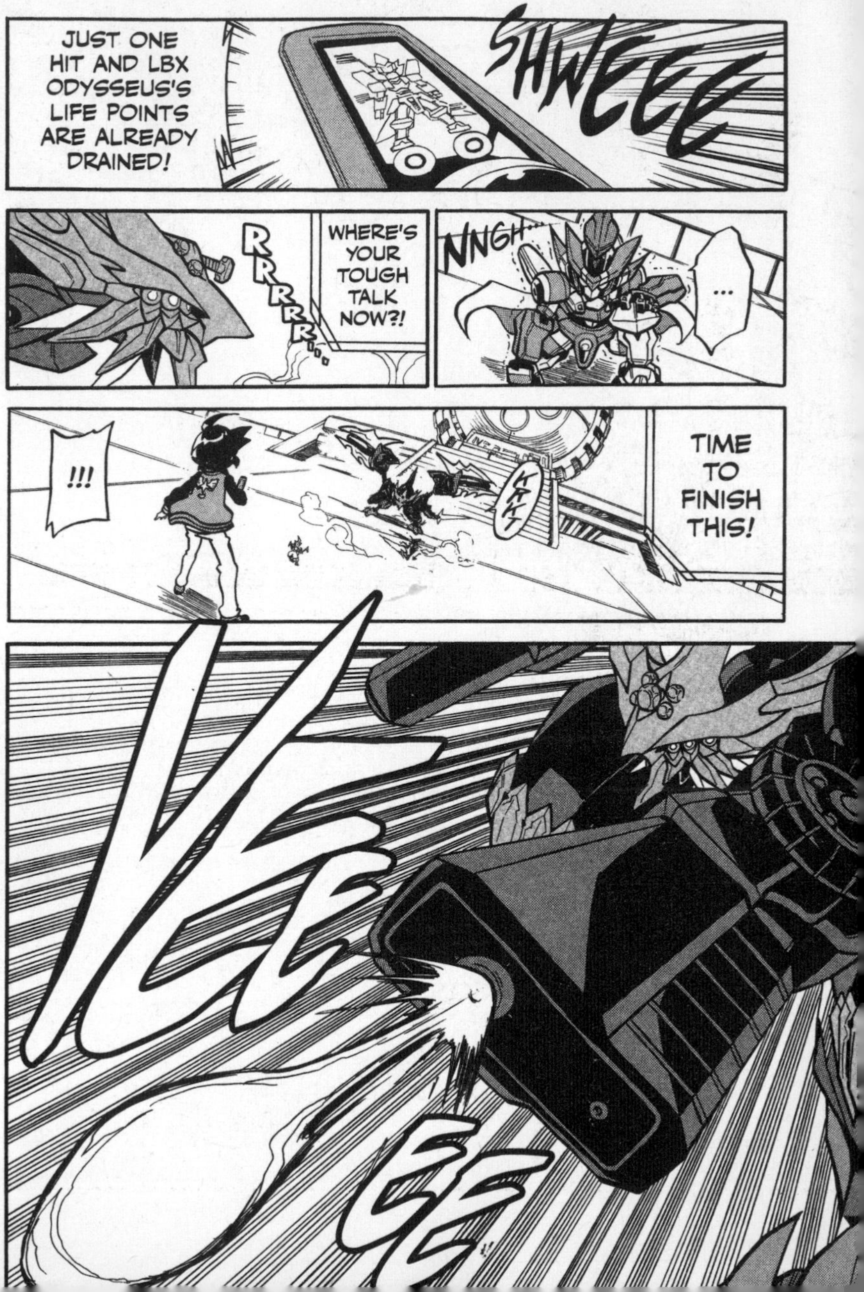
SHWEEE
JUST ONE HIT AND LBX ODYSSEUS'S LIFE POINTS ARE ALREADY DRAINED!
NNGH...
...
WHERE'S YOUR TOUGH TALK NOW?!
RRRRR...
TIME TO FINISH THIS!
KRKT
!!!
VEE
GEE

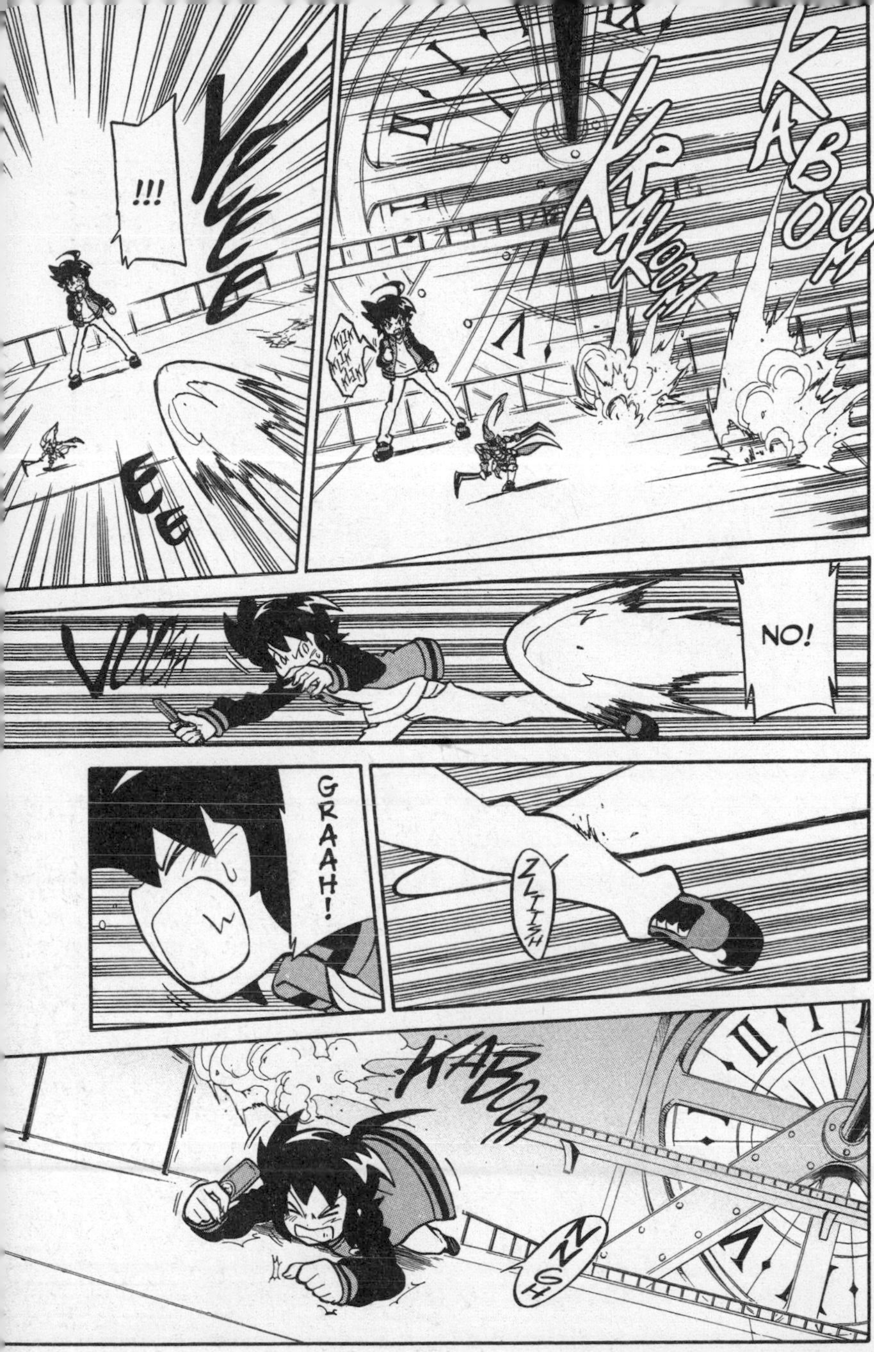
KABOOM
KLIK KLIK KLIK
!!!
NO!
GRAAAH!
KABOOM

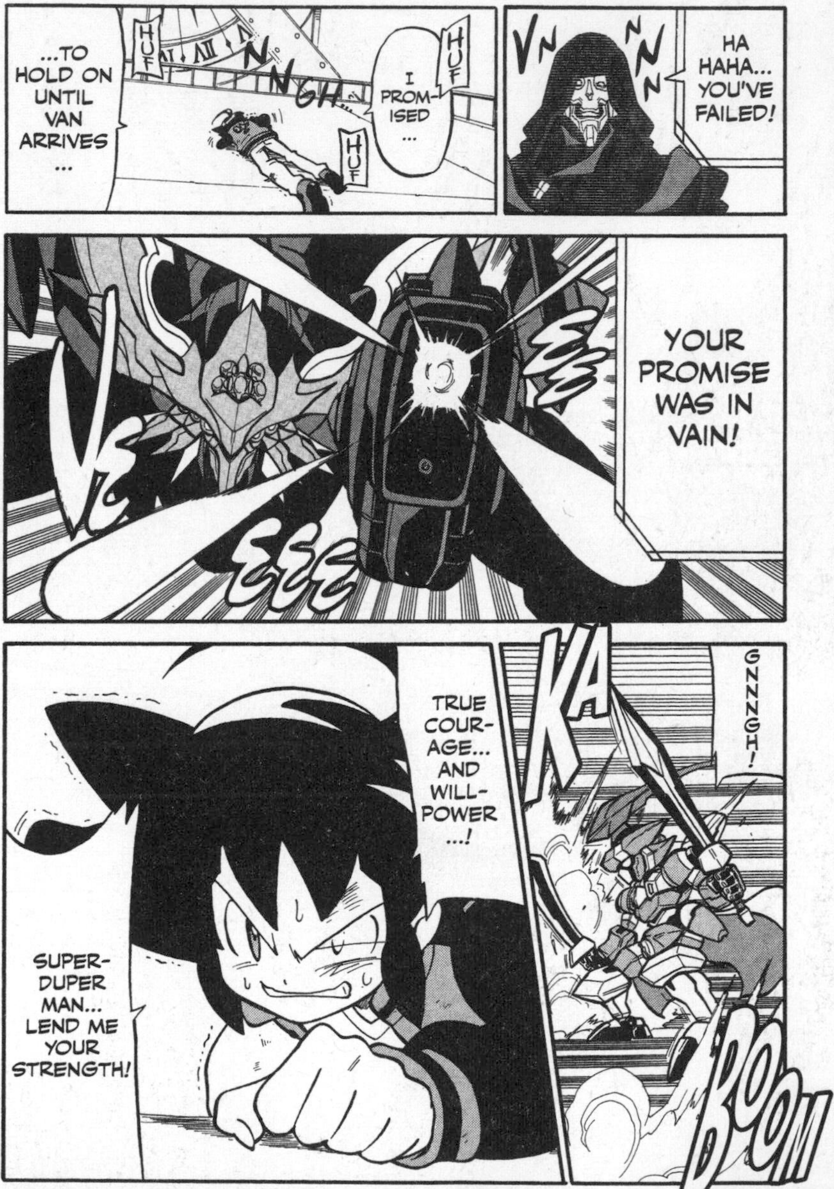
VNNNN
HA HAHA... YOU'VE FAILED!
HUF
HUF
I PROMISED...
NNGH...
HUF
...TO HOLD ON UNTIL VAN ARRIVES...
YOUR PROMISE WAS IN VAIN!
GNNNGH!
KA
BOOM
TRUE COURAGE... AND WILLPOWER...!
SUPER-DUPER MAN... LEND ME YOUR STRENGTH!

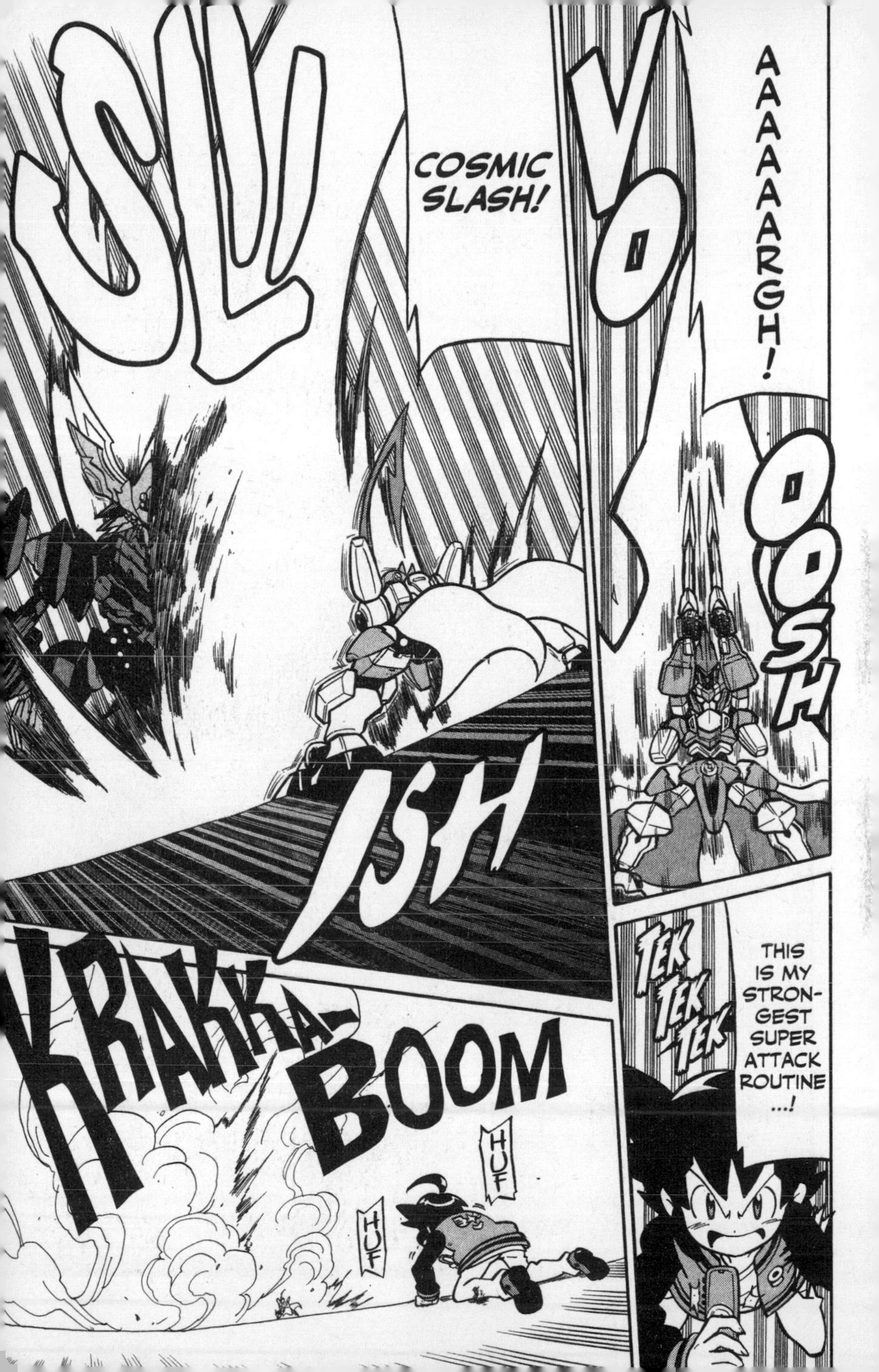
AAAAAARGH!
VOOOOOSH
THIS IS MY STRONGEST SUPER ATTACK ROUTINE ...!
TEK TEK TEK
COSMIC SLASH!
ISH
KRAKKA-BOOM
HUF HUF

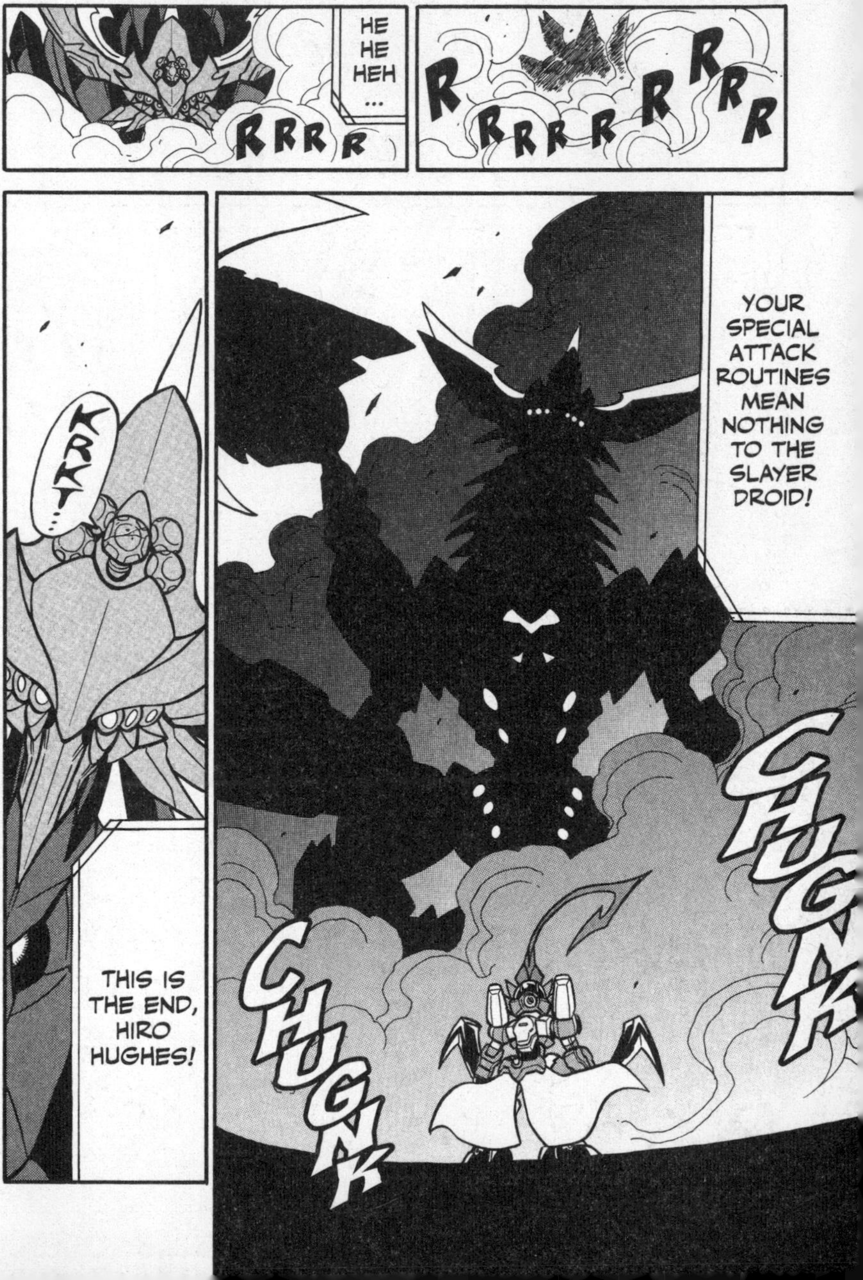
RRRRRRRRR
HE HE HEH ...
RRRR
YOUR SPECIAL ATTACK ROUTINES MEAN NOTHING TO THE SLAYER DROID!
CHUGNK
CHUGNK
KRKT...
THIS IS THE END, HIRO HUGHES!

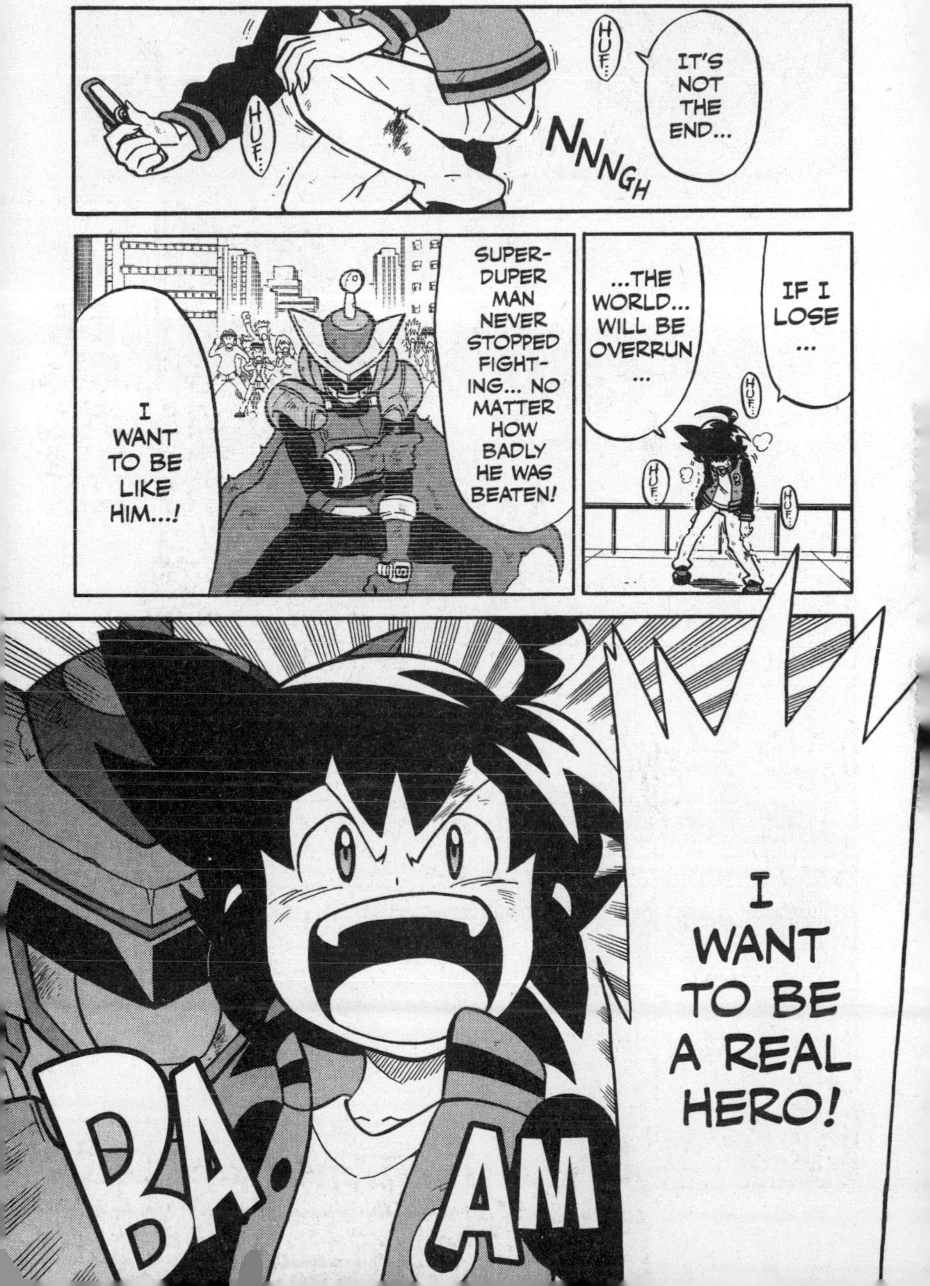
IT'S NOT THE END...
HUF...
NNNGH
HUF...
IF I LOSE ...
HUF...
...THE WORLD... WILL BE OVERRUN ...
HUF...
HUF...
SUPER-DUPER MAN NEVER STOPPED FIGHTING... NO MATTER HOW BADLY HE WAS BEATEN!
I WANT TO BE LIKE HIM...!
I WANT TO BE A REAL HERO!
BA..AM

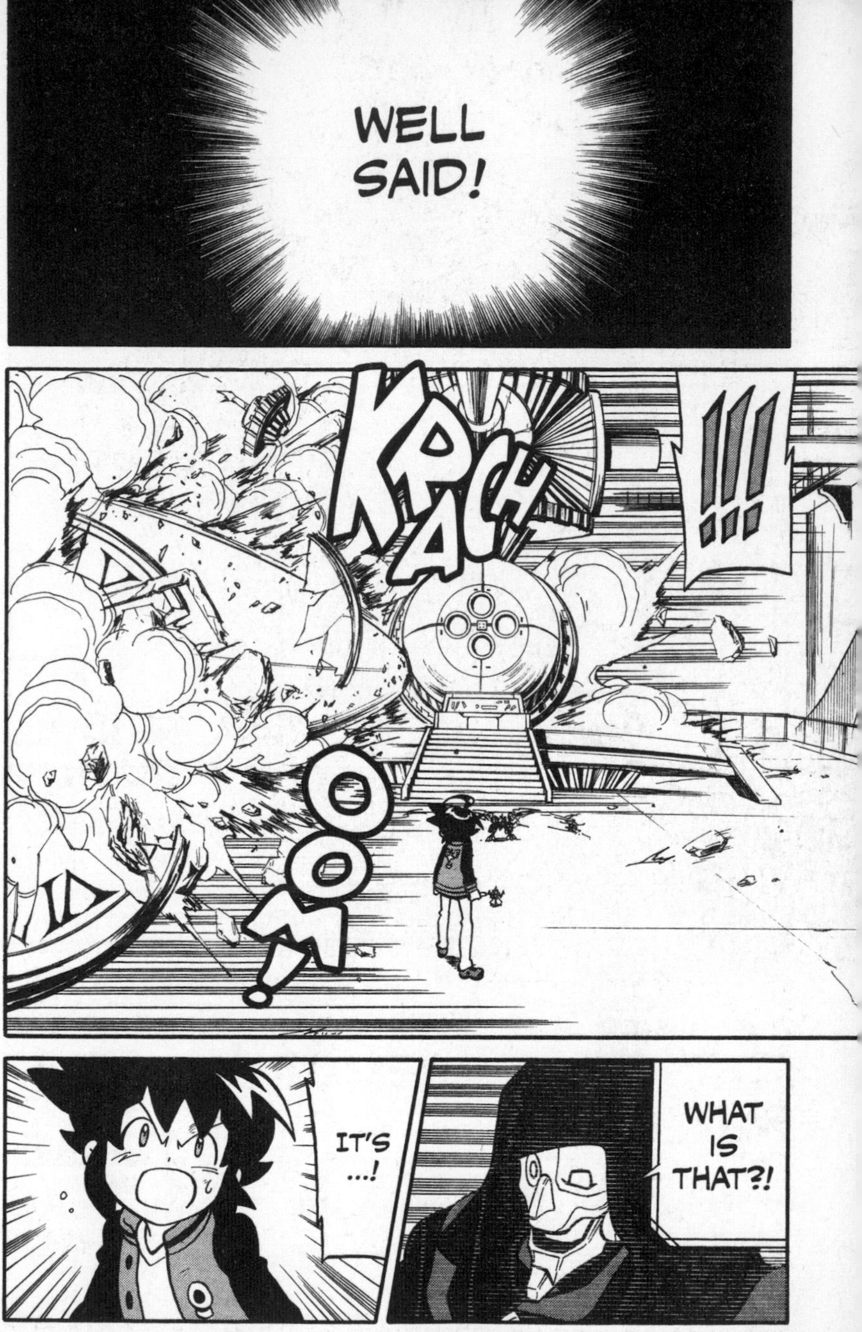
WELL SAID!
!!!
KRACH
WHAT IS THAT?!
IT'S ...!

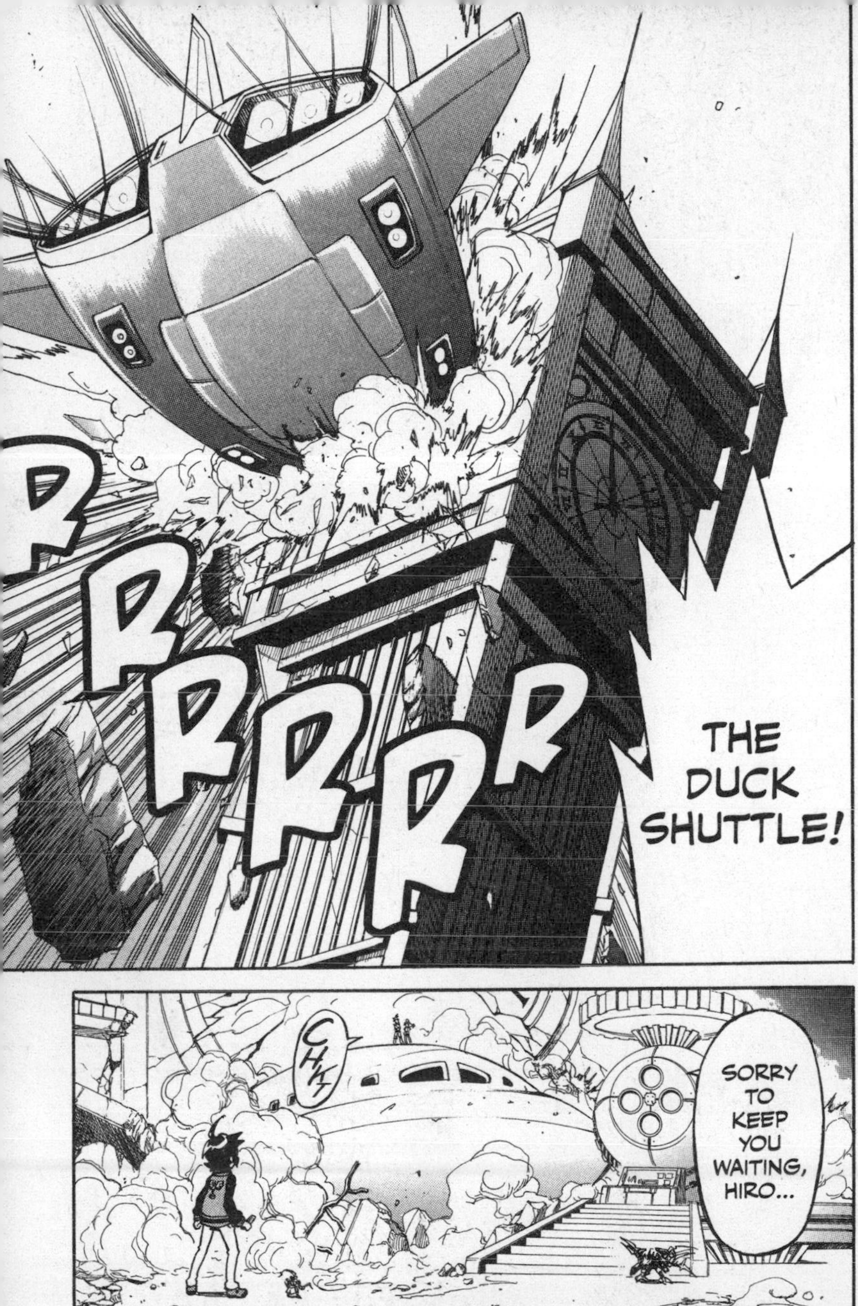
THE DUCK SHUTTLE!
RRRRRR
SORRY TO KEEP YOU WAITING, HIRO...
CHKT

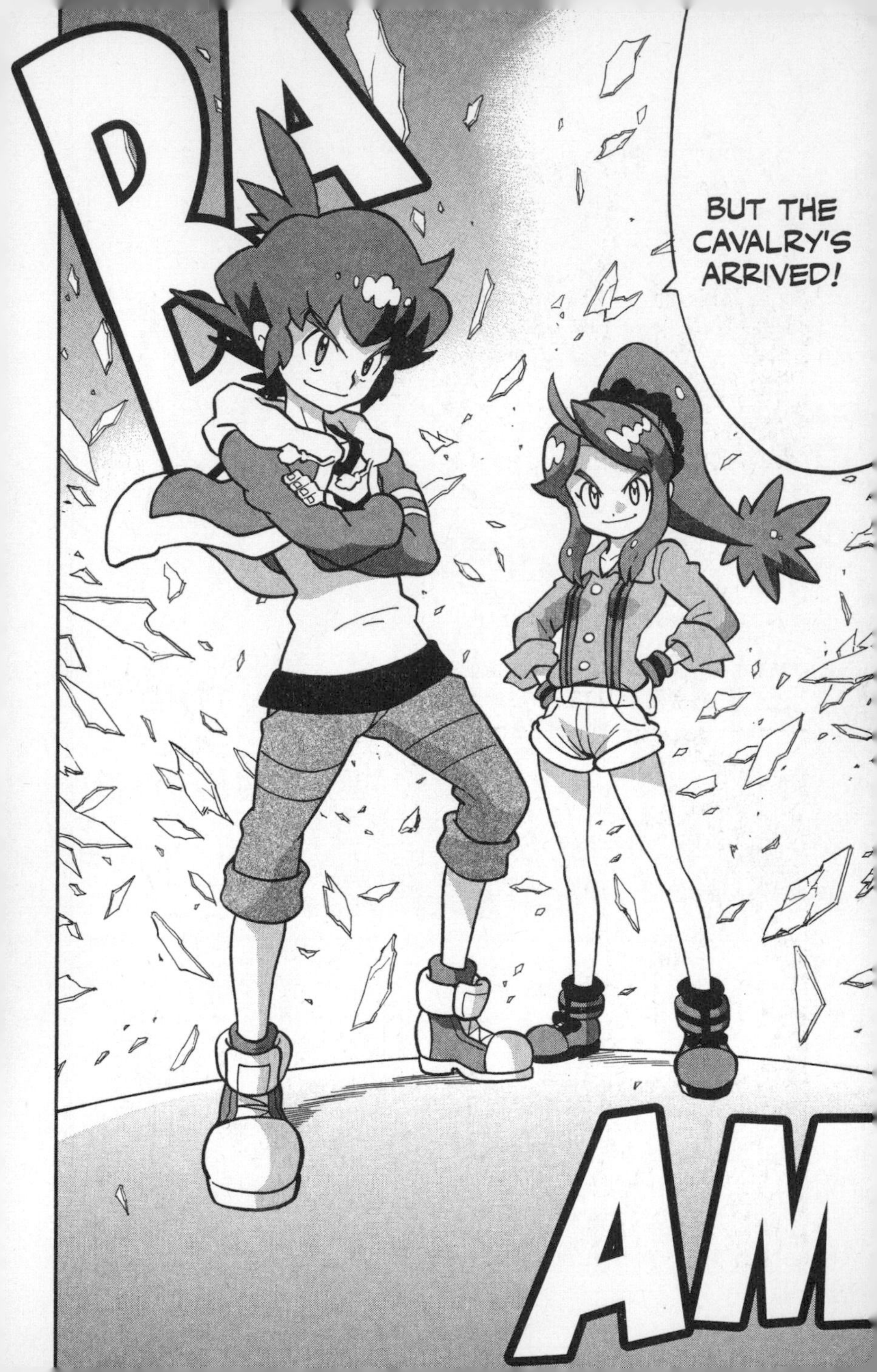
BUT THE CAVALRY'S ARRIVED!
DA
AM

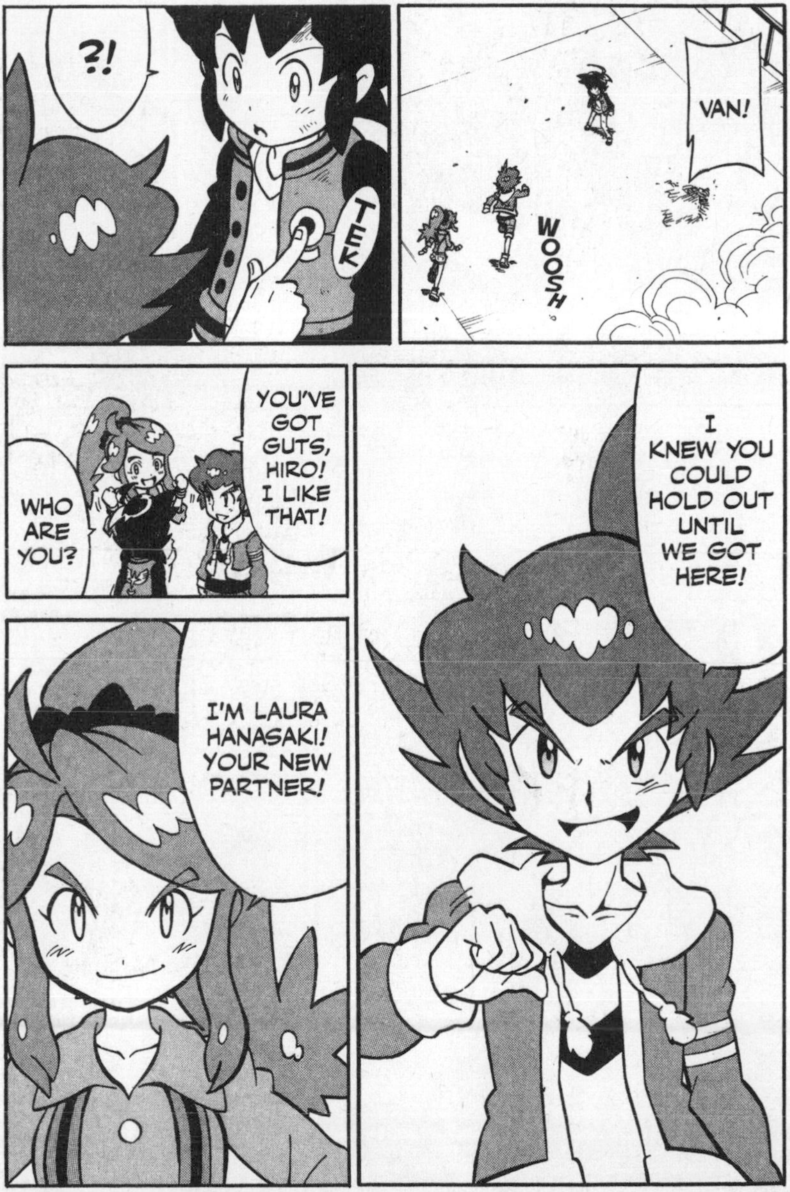
VAN!
WOOSH
?!
TEK
I KNEW YOU COULD HOLD OUT UNTIL WE GOT HERE!
YOU'VE GOT GUTS, HIRO! I LIKE THAT!
WHO ARE YOU?
I'M LAURA HANASAKI! YOUR NEW PARTNER!

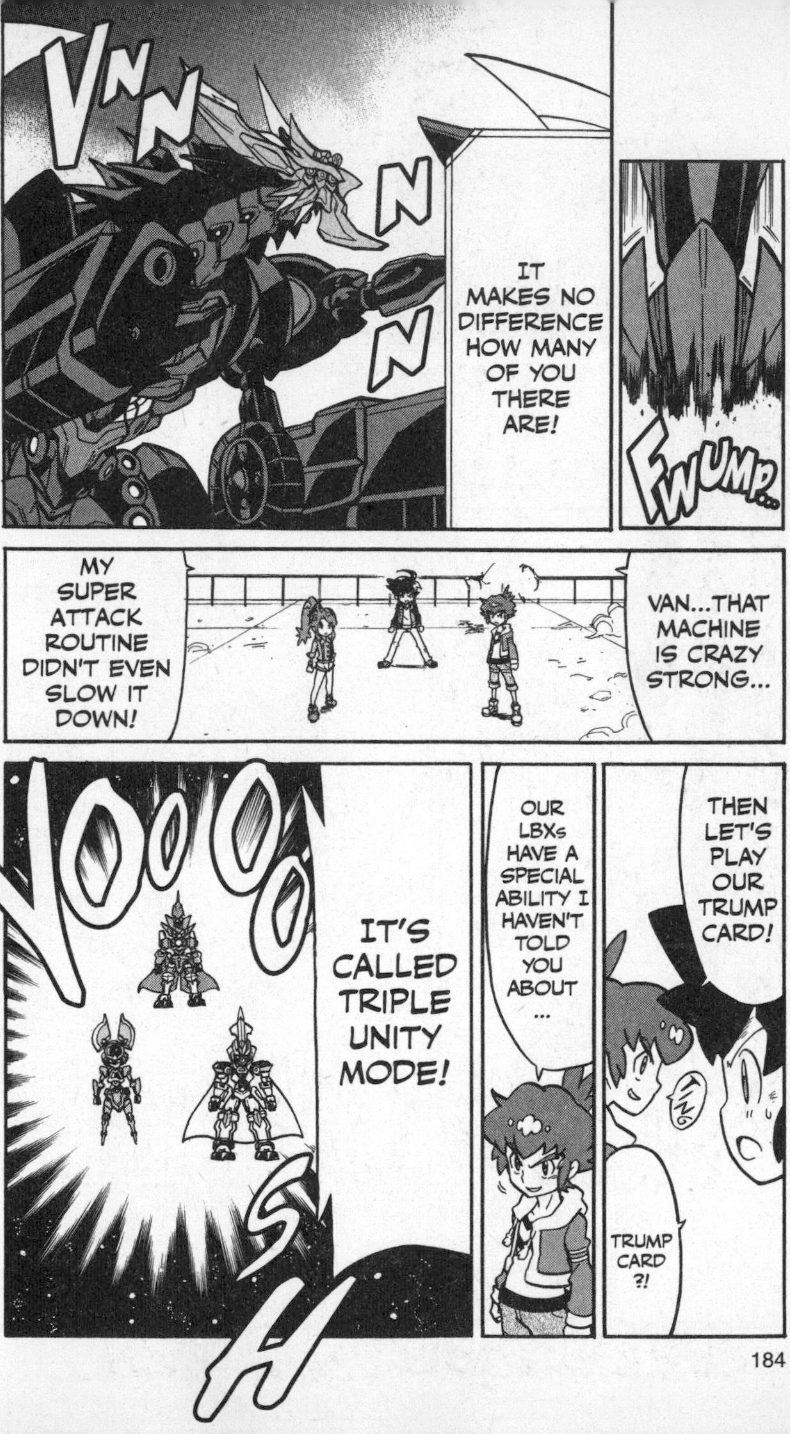
FWUMP...
VNNNN
IT MAKES NO DIFFERENCE HOW MANY OF YOU THERE ARE!
VAN...THAT MACHINE IS CRAZY STRONG...
MY SUPER ATTACK ROUTINE DIDN'T EVEN SLOW IT DOWN!
THEN LET'S PLAY OUR TRUMP CARD!
TING
TRUMP CARD ?!
OUR LBXs HAVE A SPECIAL ABILITY I HAVEN'T TOLD YOU ABOUT ...
IT'S CALLED TRIPLE UNITY MODE!
YOOOOSH

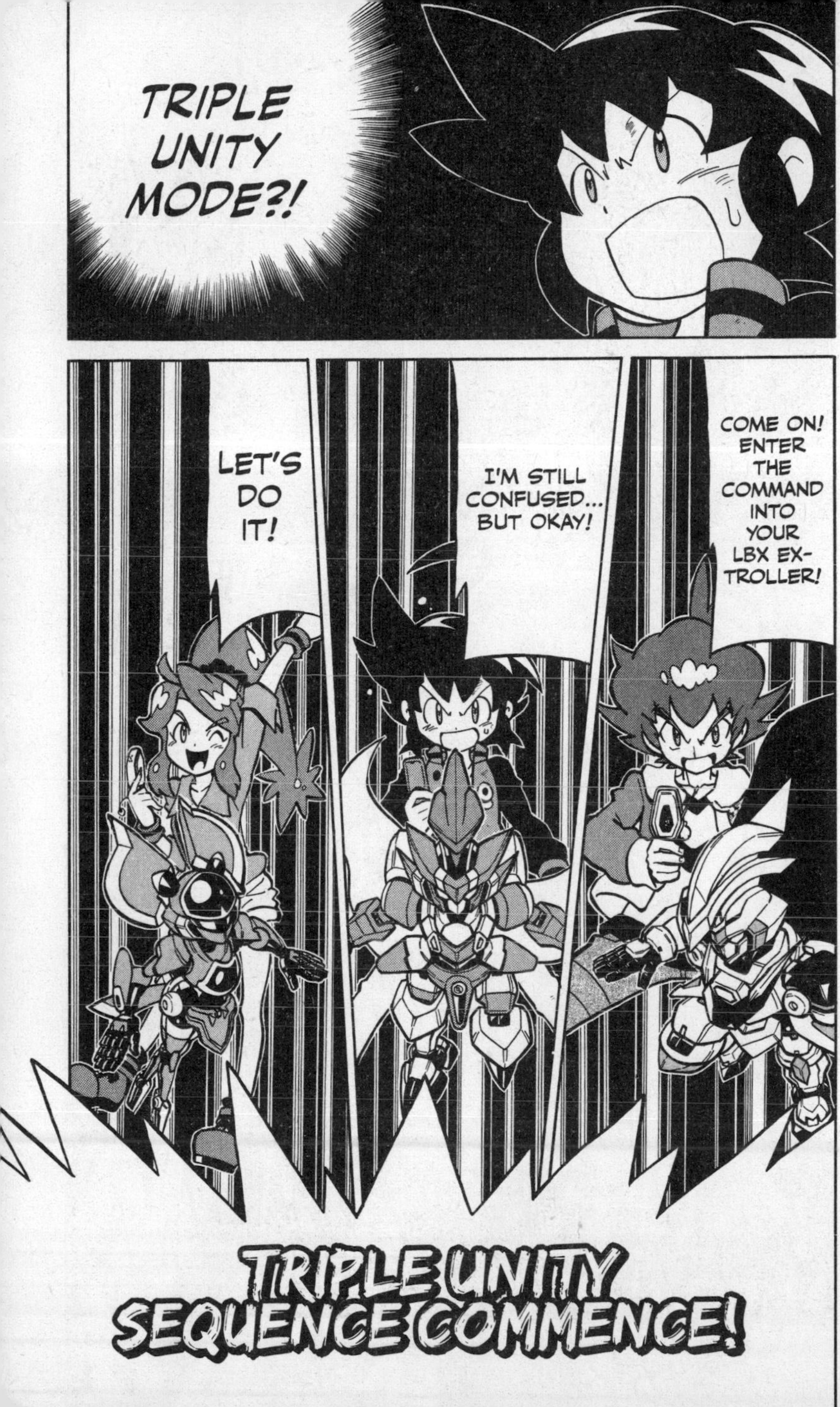
TRIPLE UNITY MODE?!
COME ON! ENTER THE COMMAND INTO YOUR LBX EX-TROLLER!
I'M STILL CONFUSED... BUT OKAY!
LET'S DO IT!
TRIPLE UNITY SEQUENCE COMMENCE!

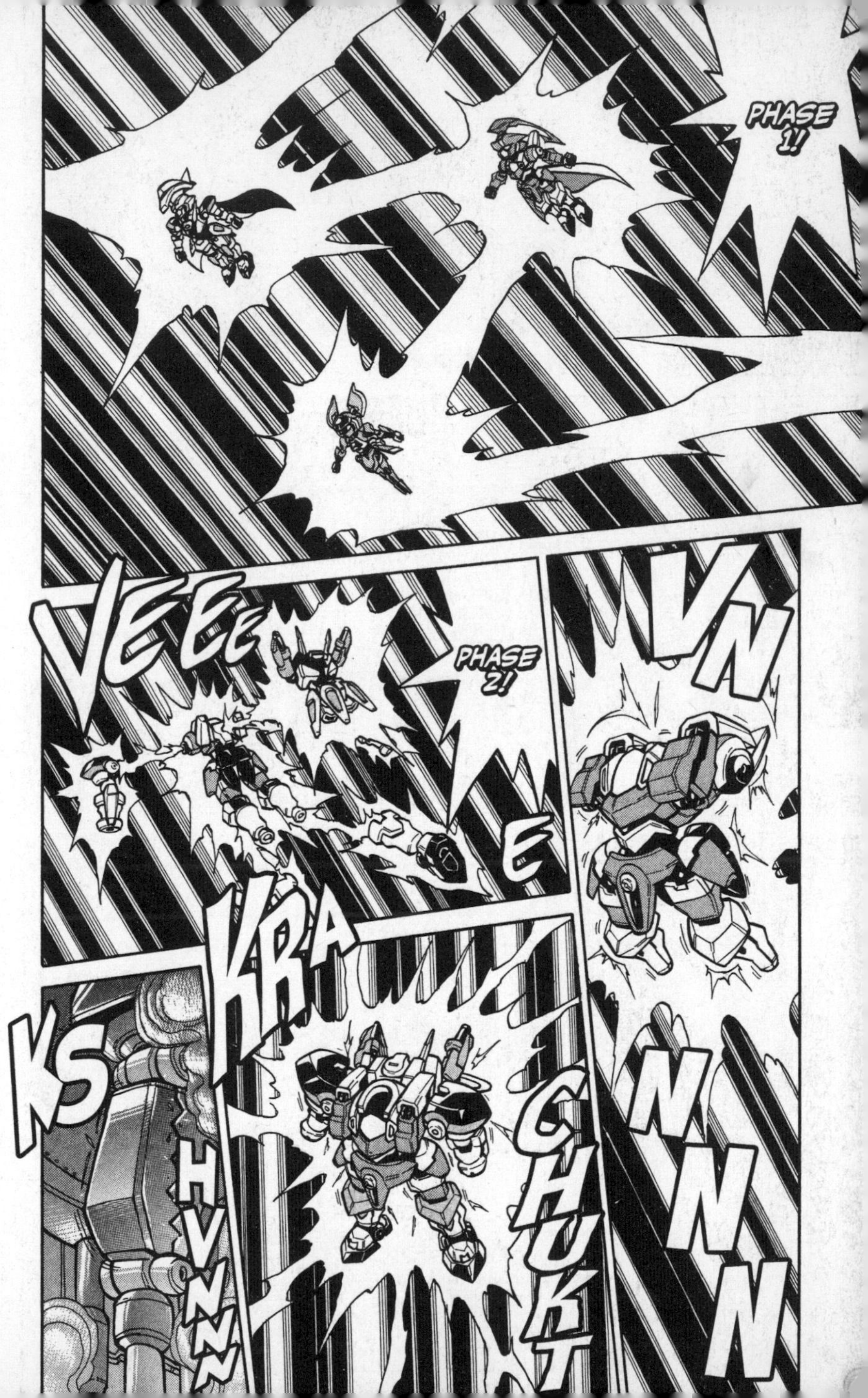

PHASE 1!
VN
NNN
VEEE
PHASE 2!
E
KRA
CHUKT
KS
HVNNN

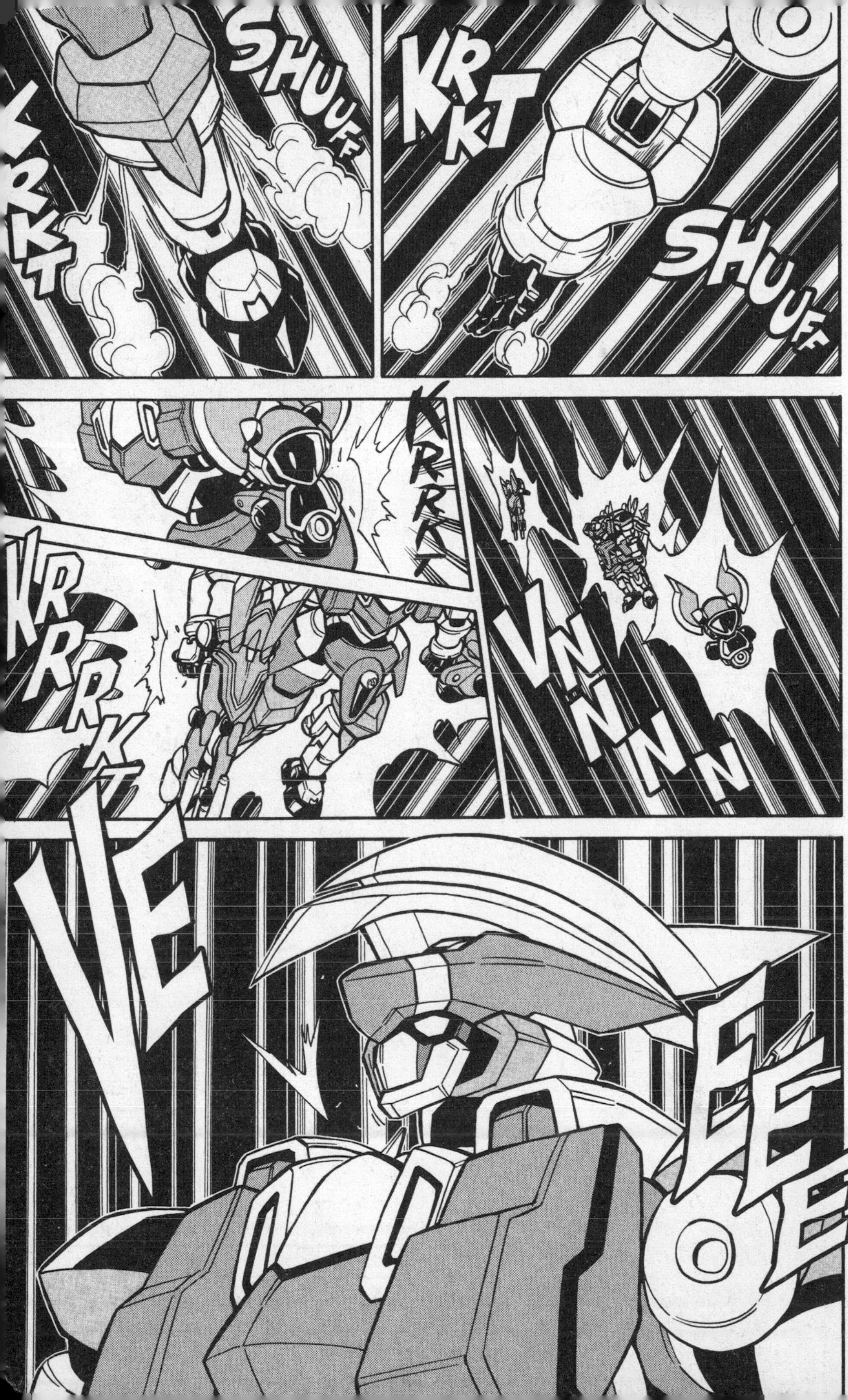
KRKT
SHUUFF
SHUUFF
KRKT
VNNNNN
KRRRKT
KRRRKT
VE
EEE

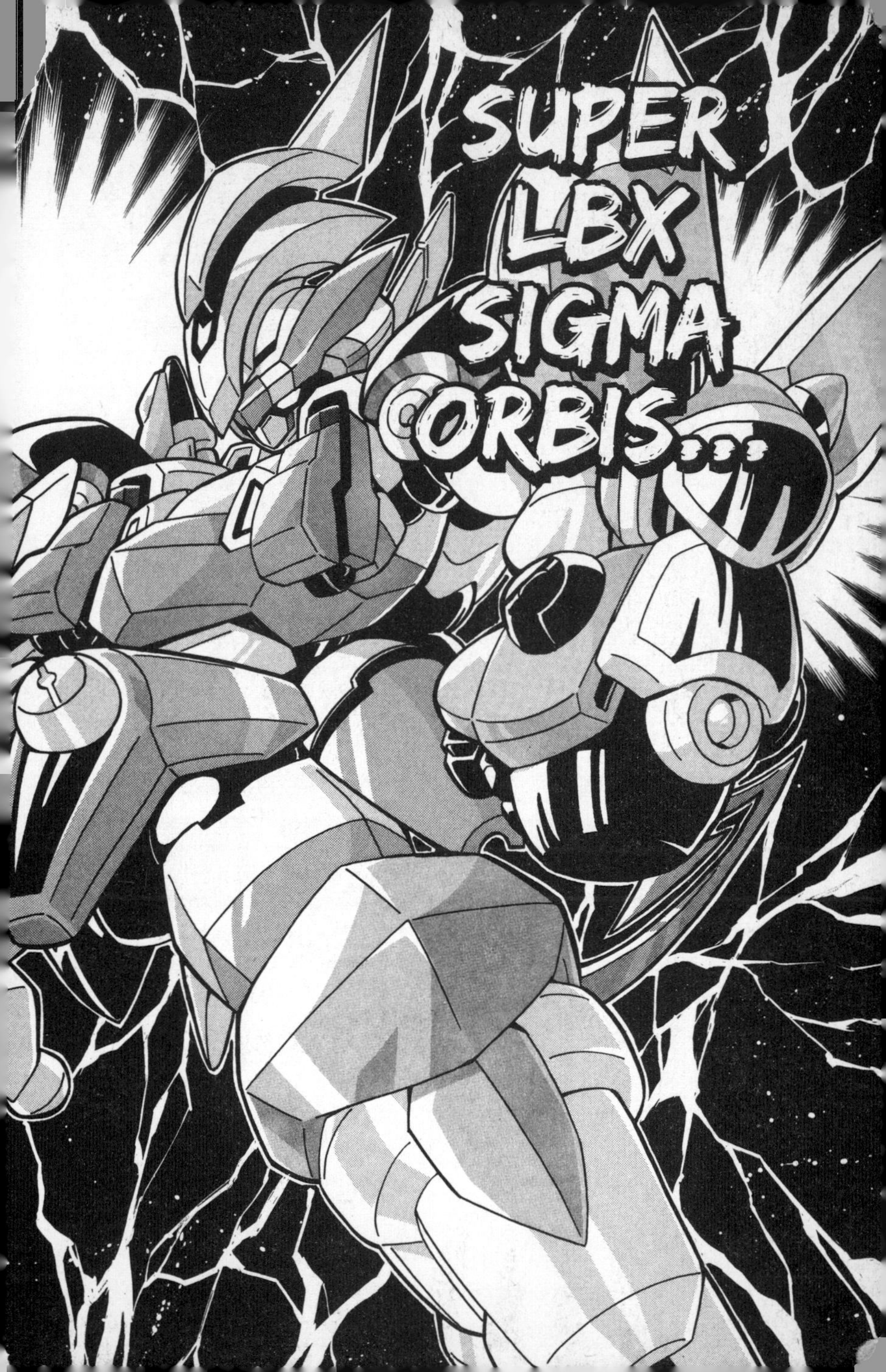
SUPER LBX SIGMA ORBIS...

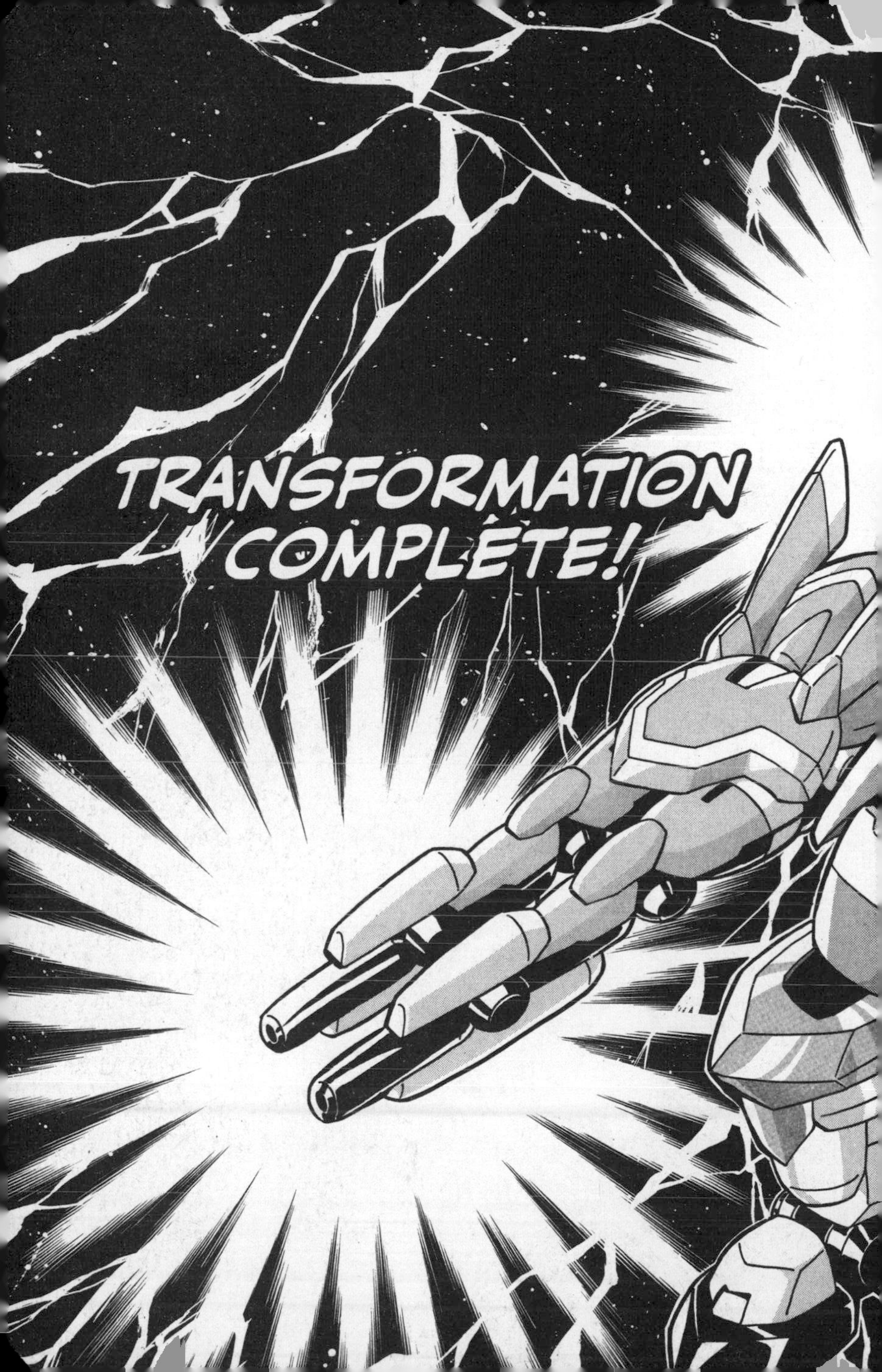
TRANSFORMATION COMPLÉTE!

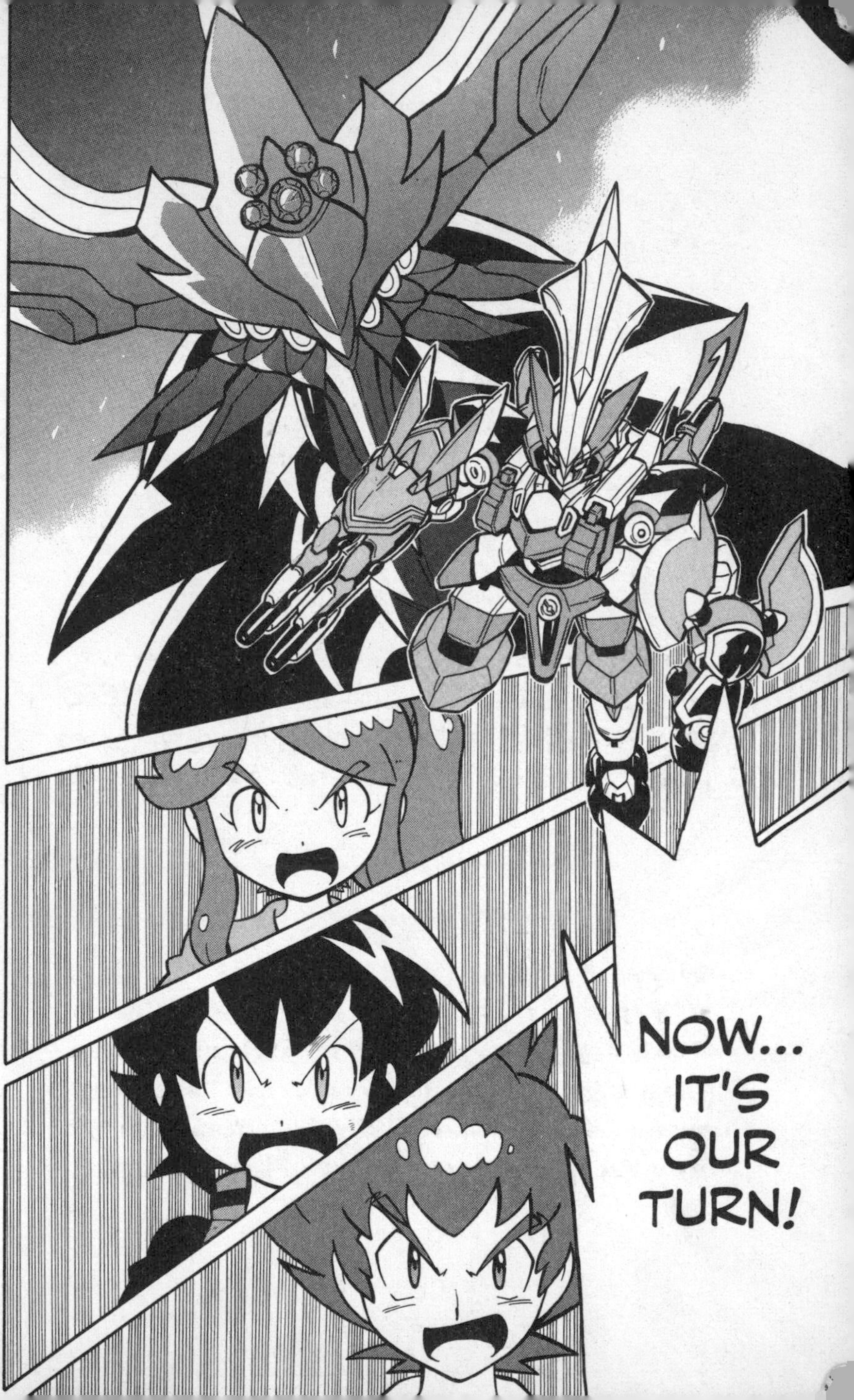
NOW... IT'S OUR TURN!

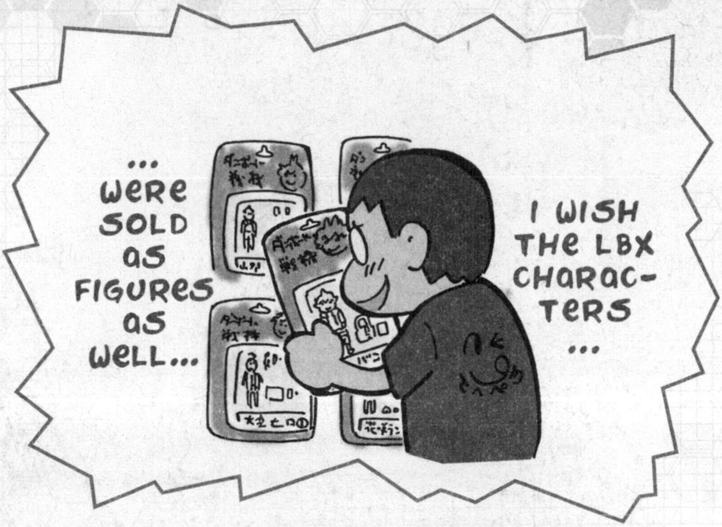
I WISH THE LBX CHARAC-TERS ...
... WERE SOLD AS FIGURES AS WELL...

HIRO HUGHES IS A GUY STRIVING TO BECOME A HERO! VAN YAMANO IS THE GUY WHO SAVED THE WORLD! THE POWER OF THESE TWO WILL NOW BE COMBINED TO FACE OFF AGAINST AN EVIL ORGANIZATION!! NOW! BATTLE START!!!

Hideaki Fujii

Hideaki Fujii was born on December 12, 1977, in Miyazaki Prefecture. He made his debut in 2000 with *Shin Megami Tensei: Devil Children* (*Monthly Comic BomBom*). His signature works include *Battle Spirits: Breakthrough Boy Bashin* and many others. Blood type A.

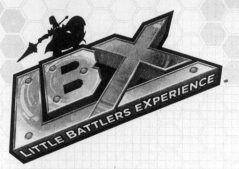

LBX Volume 4
THE SUPER LBX
Perfect Square Edition

Story and Art by Hideaki FUJII
Original Story and Supervision by LEVEL-5

Translation/Tetsuichiro Miyaki
English Adaptation/Aubrey Sitterson
Lettering/Annaliese Christman
Design/Izumi Evers
Editor/Joel Enos

DANBALL SENKI Vol.4
by Hideaki FUJII

Original Japanese edition published by SHOGAKUKAN.
English translation rights in the United States of America, Canada, the United Kingdom, Ireland, Australia and New Zealand arranged with SHOGAKUKAN.

Printed in the U.S.A.

Published by VIZ Media, LLC
P.O. Box 77010
San Francisco, CA 94107

10 9 8 7 6 5 4 3 2 1
First printing, March 2015

www.perfectsquare.com
www.viz.com

PARENTAL ADVISORY
LBX is rated A and is suitable for readers of all ages.
RATED A FOR ALL AGES
ratings.viz.com